ODESSA SEA

TITLES BY CLIVE CUSSLER

DIRK PITT® ADVENTURES

Havana Storm (with Dirk Cussler)
Poseidon's Arrow (with Dirk Cussler)
Crescent Dawn (with Dirk Cussler)
Arctic Drift (with Dirk Cussler)
Treasure of Khan (with Dirk Cussler)
Black Wind (with Dirk Cussler)
Trojan Odyssey
Valhalla Rising
Atlantis Found
Flood Tide
Shock Wave
Inca Gold
Sahara
Dragon
Treasure
Cyclops
Deep Six
Pacific Vortex!
Night Probe!
Vixen 03
Raise the Titanic!
Iceberg
The Mediterranean Caper

SAM AND REMI FARGO ADVENTURES

Pirate (with Robin Burcell)
The Solomon Curse (with Russell Blake)
The Eye of Heaven (with Russell Blake)
The Mayan Secrets (with Thomas Perry)
The Tombs (with Thomas Perry)
The Kingdom (with Grant Blackwood)
Lost Empire (with Grant Blackwood)
Spartan Gold (with Grant Blackwood)

ISAAC BELL ADVENTURES

The Gangster (with Justin Scott)
The Assassin (with Justin Scott)
The Bootlegger (with Justin Scott)
The Striker (with Justin Scott)
The Thief (with Justin Scott)
The Race (with Justin Scott)
The Spy (with Justin Scott)
The Wrecker (with Justin Scott)
The Chase

ODESSA SEA

A DIRK PITT ADVENTURE

Clive Cussler
and Dirk Cussler

G. P. PUTNAM'S SONS   NEW YORK

PUTNAM

G. P. PUTNAM'S SONS
Publishers Since 1838
An imprint of Penguin Random House LLC
375 Hudson Street
New York, New York 10014

Library of Congress Cataloging-in-Publication Data

Names: Cussler, Clive, author. | Cussler, Dirk, author.
Title: Odessa sea / Clive Cussler and Dirk Cussler.
Description: New York: G. P. Putnam's Sons, [2016] | Series: Dirk Pitt adventure
Identifiers: LCCN 2016035295 | ISBN 9780399575518 (hardback) |
ISBN 9780735211995 (export)
Subjects: LCSH: Pitt, Dirk (Fictitious character)—Fiction. | BISAC: FICTION /
Action & Adventure. | FICTION / Suspense. | FICTION / Thrillers. |
GSAFD: Adventure fiction. | Suspense fiction.
Classification: LCC PS3553.U75 O34 2016 | DDC 813/.54—dc23
LC record available at https://lccn.loc.gov/2016035295

Printed in the United States of America
1   3   5   7   9   10   8   6   4   2

Book design by Lauren Kolm

Endpaper and interior illustrations by Roland Dahlquist

ODESSA SEA CHARACTERS

1917

Vadim Rostov   Captain of Russian destroyer *Kerch*

Sir Leigh Hunt   British Special Envoy and former Consul General
to British Embassy in St. Petersburg

1955

Dimitri Sarkhov   Pilot of Russian Tupolev Tu-4 bomber

Ivan Medov   Copilot of Russian Tupolev Tu-4 bomber

Alexander Krayevski   Airman, Russian Tupolev Tu-4 bomber

2017

NUMA Team

Dirk Pitt   Director of the National Underwater and Marine Agency

Al Giordino   Director of Underwater Technology, NUMA

Bill Stenseth   Captain of NUMA research ship *Macedonia*

Hiram Yaeger   Computer Resources Director, NUMA

Rudi Gunn   Deputy Director of the National Underwater and
Marine Agency

Summer Pitt Special Projects Director, NUMA, and daughter of
Dirk Pitt

Dirk Pitt, Jr. Special Projects Director, NUMA, and son of
Dirk Pitt

Jack Dahlgren Underwater Technology Specialist, NUMA

James Sandecker Vice President of the United States and former
Director of the National Underwater and Marine Agency

Officials, Operatives, and Military Officers

Ana Belova Special Investigator, European Police Agency
(Europol)

Petar Ralin Lieutenant, Organized Crime Directorate, Bulgarian
National Police

Maxim Federov Foreign Intelligence Field Director, Russia Main
Intelligence Directorate (GRU)

Viktor Mansfield Field Agent, GRU

Arseny Markovich Commander of Ukraine 24th Territorial
Battalion

Martina Field Agent, GRU

Vladimir Popov Commander of Russian missile frigate *Ladny*

Deborah Kenfield Executive Officer of Aegis destroyer
USS *Truxton*

Wayne Valero Commander of USS *Constellation* volunteer sailors

Alexander Vodokov Ministry of Foreign Affairs, Russian
Embassy, Madrid

Historians, Experts, and Medical Professionals

Georgi Dimitov Archeologist for the Bulgarian Ministry of Culture

Dr. Anton Kromer Chief Archivist, Russia State Historical Museum

Dr. Steven Miller Orthopedic surgeon, Muncie, Indiana

St. Julien Perlmutter Nautical historian and longtime friend of Pitt

Dr. Charles Trehorne Professor of Nautical Archeology, Oxford

Cecil Hawker Major, regimental historian, Royal Gibraltar Regiment

Others

Martin Hendriks Dutch industrialist, owner of Peregrine Surveillance Corporation

Valentin Mankedo Owner of Thracia Salvage

Ilya Vasko Partner in Thracia Salvage, cousin of Valentin Mankedo

Brian Kennedy Chesapeake Bay oysterman and owner of skipjack *Lorraine*

PROLOGUE

DREAD SILENCE
REPOSES

The Kerch near the Bosphorus

FEBRUARY 1917

THE BLACK SEA

White lights danced on the horizon like beacons of death. Captain Vadim Rostov of the Imperial Russian Navy counted five orbs, each from a separate Ottoman warship standing picket at the entrance to the Bosphorus Strait. His orders on this crisp, cold night were simple. He was to engage the enemy with his destroyer and disrupt the picket line. The task, he knew, was akin to crawling through a den of hungry lions with a slaughtered lamb tied to his back.

He bit tighter on the dry stump of a Turkish cigar between his crooked teeth. The dark, hardened eyes, set in a weather-beaten face, had seen the effects of ill-conceived battle plans before—during the Russo-Japanese War of 1904, and again in the Black Sea campaign of the past four years. Rostov was nudging thirty years of service in the Imperial Russian Navy, but all he had known and trusted in those decades was now dissolving. Perhaps it was not so inglorious to end his career in a suicide mission.

He ordered a young lieutenant to find him a signalman, then turned to the living shadow beside him. The guest was a towering soldier, standing proud in the uniform of a Leib, or Imperial Guard, of the elite Preobrazhensky Regiment.

"The designs of fate will soon be revealed and the futility of our mission confirmed," Rostov said.

"There will be no deviation of the directive," the soldier replied.

Rostov had to admire the man. He had stood like a pillar beside him, rifle firm in his grip, since boarding the destroyer with the ship's orders in Odessa. Orders, the captain noted, that had been personally signed by no less than Admiral Kolchak, the commander of the Imperial Navy. The soldier, Rostov thought, had surely witnessed the upper echelons of power, but he was ignorant of the world at hand. Imperial Russia would soon be nothing more than a memory, vanquished by the forces of revolution. The guard's place in the universe was about to vanish. Word on the docks of Odessa was that the Bolsheviks had already signed a peace treaty with the Central Powers, including Turkey. Rostov chuckled to himself. Perhaps the Ottoman ships ahead would let them pass—and shower them with wine and figs in the process.

Such notions were dispelled by a faint whistling overhead as a five-inch naval shell proceeded to crash into the sea behind them.

"The Turkish gunners are not as proficient as the Germans," Rostov said, "but they will find their mark soon enough."

"The enemy is inferior, and you are an expert tactician," the soldier said.

Rostov smiled. "An expert tactician would flee overwhelming odds to fight another day."

The ship's signalman appeared, a raw draftee in an ill-fitting uniform. "Sir?" he said.

"Signal our companion. Tell them to proceed on their mission while we try to draw the enemy off to the west. And wish them luck."

"Yes, sir." The sailor exited the bridge.

Rostov turned to the guardsman. "Perhaps somebody will wish us luck as well?"

The guard gave the captain a steely look but said nothing.

Rostov stepped to the bridge wing and watched the signalman flash a message to a low-lying vessel off the port flank. As the blinking reply came from the other vessel, the specter of death raced through his mind. It was all madness. Perhaps he should turn the destroyer hard over and ram the neighboring boat. Just sink it himself, knowing what it carried. How many more must die for the vanity of the Tsar?

He cursed his own foolish honor. The truth was, no loyalty remained in the Navy's ranks. The mutiny on the *Potemkin* proved as much. And that was a decade before the current revolution. Many of the fleet's ships had already pledged allegiance to the Bolsheviks. The loyalty of his own crew was in question, but at least they hadn't shown any signs of mutiny—yet. They knew as well as he that the Imperial Navy was all but finished. Rostov shook his head. He should have walked off the ship in Odessa and disappeared into the Carpathian Mountains, as some wiser officers had done.

Another shell whistled overhead. Duty took reign in the face of the enemy fire, and he marched stiffly back onto the bridge. *Duty,* he thought. Another word for *death*.

The bridge crew stood at their posts, looking at him with anticipation.

"Give me maximum speed," he told the junior officer. "Helm, set a course bearing two-four-zero degrees."

"Gun batteries report at the ready, sir." The lieutenant rang a brass handle on the bridge telegraph, relaying the change in speed to the engine room.

"Inform all batteries to target the last ship in line to the east," Rostov ordered.

The Russian destroyer's funnel belched black plumes of smoke. The *Kerch,* as she was named, shuddered under the strain as its steam turbines spun at their maximum revolutions.

The change in course and speed threw off the enemy guns, and their shells fell harmlessly behind the destroyer. Rostov gazed at the lights of the Turkish vessels, which now appeared off the port wing as the ship steamed west. Five-to-one, he thought. The odds had been less intimidating two days earlier when they left Odessa in the company of the *Gnevny,* another light destroyer. But the *Gnevny* had developed shaft problems and turned back. Rostov had no such luck. He would have to face the enemy force alone.

The captain waited to open fire until an incoming shell hit the water ten meters off his beam, showering the deck with seawater. All four of the destroyer's four-inch guns fired simultaneously in return, spitting flames into the night sky.

Through skill and good luck, one of the Russian shells struck its target, piercing the vessel's magazine. Rostov raised his binoculars as a fireball erupted from the trailing Ottoman ship.

"Concentrate fire on the next vessel to the west," he told the lieutenant. It had been an extremely lucky hit. His strategy—and prayer—was to disable or damage the two ships guarding the eastern approach, then attack the remaining vessels in pursuit. It was the only hope for the mission to succeed.

The night became alight with fire and thunder. The remaining Ottoman ships opened up with broadside after broadside, countered by the full punch of the destroyer. The Russian ship was surprisingly fast and kept a healthy cushion ahead of the Turkish gunners. But the gap narrowed as two of the Ottoman ships turned to close with the *Kerch*.

"A hit! On the second vessel," the lieutenant cried.

Rostov nodded. He had the most experienced gun crew in the Black Sea Fleet and it was showing. He turned to the Leib Guard, who was peering at the distant inferno. "Your royal odyssey may have a chance after all."

The guard smiled slightly, the first indication of humanity he had shown in two days. Then he vanished in an exploding veil of black smoke.

A Turkish shell had struck the lip of the port deck. The occupants of the bridge were knocked from their feet as a shower of flame shot skyward.

"Helm! Set heading to three-six-zero degrees," Rostov shouted before he staggered back to his feet. To his left, the guard lay facedown on the deck, a twisted piece of shrapnel protruding from his back.

The helmsman acknowledged his order, pulled himself upright by the ship's wheel, and spun it hard to the right. But the evasive move came too late. The Turks had finally found their mark, and another volley rained down. A leading shell blew off the destroyer's prow, while another struck amidships and ripped open the hull. The vessel shook as water poured into the forward compartments, lifting the stern and its spinning propellers out of the water.

Rostov found a megaphone and shouted for the crew to abandon ship. The lieutenant scrambled to launch a lifeboat on the starboard deck. Returning to the bridge, Rostov found the helmsman standing fixed at the wheel, his knuckles white against the wooden spokes.

"Sasha, find a life jacket and get off the ship," Rostov said gently. He stepped over and swung a backhand against the boy's cheek.

Broken from his fear, the helmsman staggered off the bridge, muttering, "Yes, Captain. Yes, Captain."

Rostov stood alone on the bridge now as a loud bang near the stern rattled the ship. A fuel tank had ruptured and ignited. Rostov stumbled to keep his balance, groping along the deck for his binoculars. Raising them to his smoke-burnt eyes, he gazed aft past the wall of flames to a point in the distant sea.

He saw it, just for an instant. A single mast that seemed to protrude directly from the water was cutting a thin white wake toward the Bosphorus. A whistling overhead grew loud as the captain nodded at the vanishing apparition. "Duty served," he muttered.

A second later, the twin shells struck, obliterating the bridge and sending the warship's shattered hulk to the seafloor.

Ice blue lightning flashed before Dimitri Sarkhov's weary eyes. The pilot blinked away the spots that pranced before his retinas and refocused on an expansive panel of gauges and dials. The altimeter fluctuated around the twenty-six-hundred-meter mark. A sudden external buffeting pulled at the yoke, and, in less than a heartbeat, the big plane dropped thirty meters.

"Wretched storm." The copilot, a moonfaced man named Medev, wiped a spilled mug of coffee from his leg.

Sarkhov shook his head. "The weather office calls this a light, low-pressure front." Thick raindrops pelted the windscreen, rendering the night sky around them impenetrable.

"They don't know a thunderstorm from spit. They're real geniuses at wing command, sending us on a training mission through this weather. Especially given what we're carrying."

"I'll take us down five hundred meters and see if the air is more stable." Sarkhov fought the yoke controls.

They lumbered through the storm in a Tupolev Tu-4, a massive, four-engine bomber with a wingspan as long as a tall building. Over the roar of the engines, the airframe creaked and groaned. A sudden burst of turbulence jolted the craft, prompting a flashing red light on the instrument panel.

"Bomb bay door," Sarkhov said. "Probably jarred the sensor."

"Or our usual faulty electronics." Medev called the bombardier to investigate but got no response. "Vasily is probably asleep again. I'll go back and take a look. If the bomb bay door is open, maybe I'll kick him out."

Sarkhov gave a tight grin. "Just don't drop anything else."

Medev climbed from his seat and snaked his way back through the fuselage. He returned to the cockpit a few minutes later. "The doors are sealed and appear fine, the payload secure. And Vasily was indeed asleep. Now he has a print from my boot on his backside."

The plane suddenly pitched and plunged. A loud bang sounded from the rear of the craft, while Medev was flung into an overhead instrument cluster. The copilot crumpled into his seat, his legs jamming against the starboard engines' throttle controls.

"Ivan?" Sarkhov called. There was a trickle of blood on Medev's forehead. He reached over and tried to pull back on the throttle controls. But fighting against the bulk of the unconscious copilot and his tightly wedged legs, he had only limited success.

Sarkhov's entire world seemed to explode. The instrument panel ignited with flashing lights and alarms, and his headset burst with cries from the flight crew. The bomber had entered the worst of the storm and was being pummeled from all sides. As he fought the flight controls, Sarkhov detected an acrid odor.

The cacophony of voices in his headset settled into one panicked voice.

"Captain, this is the navigator. We have a fire. I repeat, we have a fire in the auxiliary flight generator. Navigation and communication stations are—"

"Navigator, are you there? Vasily? Fodorsky?"

No reply.

Smoke began billowing into the cockpit, burning Sarkhov's eyes. Through the haze, he noticed a new array of warning lights. The high-revving starboard engines were dangerously overheating, aided by a ruptured oil line.

The pilot shoved the nose down as he pulled the starboard throttles hard against Medev's limp legs. Keeping one eye on the altimeter, he watched as the bomber descended. He intended to level off at a thousand meters and order the crew to bail out. But a bright flash out the side window dictated otherwise. Overheated and starved of oil, the inside starboard engine erupted in a mass of flames.

Sarkhov throttled back the port engines, but it mattered little. As he descended, the turbulence only got worse. He called for the flight crew to bail out but had no idea if anyone could hear. At the thousand-meter mark, the cabin filled with black smoke. At five hundred meters, he could feel the heat of the flames behind the cockpit.

Sweat dripped from his brow, not from the heat but from the stress of trying to control the massive plane in its rapid descent. There was no thought of bailing out himself, not with the wall of flames he'd have to cross and the need to leave Medev behind. His only thought was to will the plane down, fearing the rudder and aileron controls would vanish under the lick of the flames. He pushed the yoke harder, trying to get beneath the storm and find a place to ditch.

At one hundred meters, he turned on the landing lights, but the heavy rain still obscured his vision. Were they over land? He thought he glimpsed a black, featureless plain.

The flames entered the cabin, igniting the flight plans dangling from a clipboard. Taking a deep breath, Sarkhov cut the power to the three remaining engines and felt the plane surge lower.

From afar, the bomber appeared to be a glowing comet, a fury of flames spitting from its midsection. The fireball descended through the black, wet night until it plunged into the sea, vanishing as if it had never existed.

PART I

THE MISTS OF THE DEEP

NUMA Submersible and Grapple

1

JULY 2017
THE BLACK SEA

A dull glow blanketed the southern horizon in a cottony glaze. Although Istanbul was more than fifty miles away, the electric blaze from its fourteen million inhabitants lit the night sky like a sea of lanterns. Churning slowly toward the light, a weathered black freighter rolled in a choppy sea. The ship rode low, catching the sporadic rogue wave that sent a spray of seawater surging across its deck.

On the wide bridge, the helmsman nudged the wheel to port, fighting a stiff breeze.

"Speed?"

The question came from a bearded man hunched over a chart table. His gray eyes were glassy and bloodshot, and his voice offered a trace of a slur. His sweat-stained clothes hinted at priorities other than hygiene. As the crew expected, in the two days since the ship had left port the freighter's captain had ventured well into his third bottle of vodka.

"Eight knots, sir," the helmsman said.

The captain grunted, estimating the time it would take them to clear the Bosphorus Strait.

A bridge wing door opened and an armed man in brown fatigues entered. He approached the glassy-eyed captain with a mix of concern and disdain. "The sea is getting rough. There is water washing over the decks."

The captain looked at the man and snickered. "You sure it is not just your vomit that is soiling my decks?"

Green at the gills, the armed man found no humor in the comment. "I am responsible for the cargo. Perhaps we should get closer to shore."

The captain shook his head. He'd had an uneasy feeling when the ship's owner phoned him minutes before they were to depart Sevastopol, instructing him to wait for a last-minute delivery. The small gang of armed men that arrived in a battered panel van only contributed to his suspicions as he watched them unload a large metal crate. He'd protested when they'd insisted on placing it in the engine room but muffled his complaints when he was handed a bag of uncirculated rubles. Now he glared at one of the two armed men who had accompanied the secret cargo.

"Get off my bridge, you stupid fool. These seas are for children. The *Crimean Star* can slice through waves five times larger and still deliver your precious cargo intact."

The armed man steadied himself against a roll and leaned into the captain. "The shipment will go through as scheduled— or I will see that you will be scraping barnacles off an icebreaker in Murmansk." The man moved off to the side bridge wing. He stood in defiance, the fresh breeze helping quell his seasickness.

The captain ignored him, studying his charts and tracking the ship's progress.

The freighter rolled along quietly for another twenty minutes before the helmsman called out. "Sir, there's a vessel approaching off our flank that appears to be mirroring our track."

The captain raised himself from the table and stepped to the helm. He glanced at the radarscope, which showed the green blip of a vessel approaching from the stern. A faint smaller blip appeared briefly about a mile ahead of the ship. "Come right, steer a course two-three-zero."

"Right rudder, to two-three-zero degrees." The helmsman rotated the ship's wheel.

The freighter eased onto the new heading. A few minutes later, the shadowing vessel was seen to follow.

The captain scowled. "Probably an inexperienced commander looking for a guide to lead them through the strait. Hold your course."

A moment later, a deep thump sounded across the waves, followed by a slight vibration that shook the decks.

"What was that?" the gunman asked.

The captain stared out the bridge window, trying to focus on the source of the noise.

"Sir, it's an explosion in the water." The helmsman pointed off the bow. "Directly ahead of us."

The captain found his focus and spotted the falling remnants of a large water spire a hundred meters ahead of the ship.

"Engine ahead one-third." He reached for a pair of binoculars.

There was little to focus on, aside from a frothy boil of water

17

in their path. He glanced out the rear bridge window and noticed the lights of the accompanying vessel had drawn closer.

An acrid odor enveloped the bridge, subtle, initially, then overpowering. The armed man near the doorway felt the effects first, choking and coughing, then dropping his weapon and falling to his knees. The helmsman followed, gagging and crumpling to the deck.

His senses numbed by alcohol, the captain was slower to feel the invisible assault. As his two companions on the bridge turned silent and stiff, his mind grasped to understand what was happening. Somewhere nearby he heard a gunshot, then he felt his throat constrict. His pulse raced as he struggled to breathe. Staggering to the helm, he grabbed the radio transmitter and rasped into it, "Mayday! Mayday! This is the *Crimean Star*. We are under attack. Please help us."

Confusion and fear were consumed by an overpowering pain. He swayed for a second as the transmitter slipped from his hand and then he collapsed to the deck, dead.

2

"Sir, there's no response on the emergency channel." The youthful third officer looked up from the communications station and gazed at a lean man studying the ship's radarscope.

Dirk Pitt nodded in acknowledgment while keeping his eyes glued to the radar screen. "All right, Chavez. Let them know we're on our way. Then you best go rouse the captain."

Pitt straightened his tall frame and turned toward the helmsman. "We're well clear of the Bosphorus, so you can open her up. The *Crimean Star* looks to be about thirteen miles ahead of us. Steer a course of zero-five-five degrees and give me everything she's got."

As the helmsman acknowledged the order, Pitt called the engine room and had the chief engineer apply all available power to the vessel's twin screws. A low whine reverberated through the fifty-meter oceanographic research ship as its twin diesels wound to maximum revolutions. A few minutes later, the ship's captain, a large, sandy-haired man named Bill Stenseth, stepped onto the bridge. He was followed by Third Officer Chavez, who resumed his place at the communications station.

Stenseth suppressed a yawn. "We've got a Mayday?"

"A single distress call from a vessel named *Crimean Star*," Pitt said. "Listed as a Romanian-flagged bulk freighter. She appears to be on a direct inbound course about a dozen miles ahead of us."

Stenseth gazed at the radar screen, then noted his own ship's accelerating speed. "Do we know the nature of their emergency?"

"All we picked up was a single distress call. Chavez hailed them repeatedly, but there was no response." Pitt tapped a finger on the radar screen. "We look to be the closest ship in the area."

"The Turkish Coast Guard Command might have some fast-responding resources nearby." He turned to the third officer. "Let's give them a call, Chavez."

Pitt grabbed a handheld radio from a charging stand and stepped toward a bridge wing door. "Chavez, when you're done there, can you ring Al Giordino and have him meet me on the aft deck in ten minutes? I'll prep a Zodiac in case we're needed aboard. Call me when we're clear to launch."

"Will do," Chavez said.

As Pitt started to leave, Stenseth squinted at a bulkhead-mounted chronometer. It read two in the morning. "By the way, what were you doing on the bridge at this hour?"

"A loose davit was banging against my cabin bulkhead and woke me up. After securing it, I wandered up to see where we were."

"Sixth sense, I'd say."

Pitt smiled as he left the bridge. Over the years, he did seem to have a knack for finding trouble around him. Or perhaps it found him.

The Director of the National Underwater and Marine Agency climbed down two levels, then moved aft along the main deck of the oceanographic research ship. A roar from the engine room revealed that the *Macedonia* was pressing her rated top speed of seventeen knots, kicking up white foam along her turquoise sides. She was one of several dozen research vessels in the NUMA fleet tasked with studying the world's oceans.

On the *Macedonia*'s fantail, Pitt released the lines of a Zodiac, secured to a cradle, and pulled back its oilskin cover. He checked the fuel tank, then attached a lift cable. Satisfied as to its readiness, he stepped to the ship's rail and peered ahead for the distant lights of the *Crimean Star.*

He shouldn't even be here, Pitt thought. He had joined the *Macedonia* in Istanbul just the day before, after traveling from his headquarters office in Washington, D.C. A last-minute plea for assistance from the Bulgarian Ministry of Culture to help locate a lost Ottoman shipwreck had lured him halfway across the globe.

Twenty minutes later, the NUMA research ship pulled alongside the black freighter, which drifted silently like an illuminated ghost ship. On the *Macedonia*'s bridge, Captain Stenseth scanned the merchant ship through night vision binoculars.

"Still no response from the vessel," Chavez said. "Turkish authorities report a cutter is en route, and a rescue helicopter is being scrambled from Istanbul, with an estimated arrival time of twenty-six minutes."

Stenseth nodded as he held the binoculars firm to his brow.

There was no sign of life aboard the ship. He glanced at the radar-scope. A small image a half mile distant was moving away from the freighter. Retraining the binoculars, he detected the faint outline of a vessel with no running lights. He picked up a handheld radio. "Bridge to Pitt."

"Pitt here."

"The freighter is still silent and adrift. I see no signs of a list or physical damage. Turkish Coast Guard resources are on the way, if you want to sit tight."

"Negative. There could be lives at risk. Al and I will attempt to board. Pitt out."

Pitt turned to a short, sleepy-eyed man standing next to the Zodiac. He had a broad, muscular frame that looked like it had been carved out of a block of granite.

"Let's get over the side," Pitt said.

Al Giordino yawned. "This better be a real distress. I was cozy in my bunk, dreaming I was in a Turkish harem and the veils were about to come off."

Pitt smiled. "The girls in the harem will thank me."

They lowered the Zodiac over the side, climbed down, and released its lift cable. Pitt started the outboard and spun the throttle, shooting the inflatable boat across the choppy water to the freighter's side. Running down the ship's length, he spotted a lowered accommodations ladder near the stern and ran toward it.

"Nice of them to leave the welcome mat out." Giordino hopped onto the base of the ladder and tied off the Zodiac. He sniffed the air and frowned. "Smells like the Easter Bunny left us a basket of rotten eggs."

"Something in her cargo, perhaps," Pitt said. But the smell didn't seem to originate from the ship.

The two ran up the steps and boarded the ship, finding the foul odor gradually diminished. Under the stark illumination of the deck lights, the passageways appeared empty as they moved forward toward the accommodations block. The deck hatches were secured and the ship appeared undamaged, just as Stenseth had reported.

Approaching a companionway to the bridge, they hesitated. A body blocked the doorway, that of a young man in dark fatigues whose hair was sheared in a short buzz cut. In its frozen state of death, his face expressed a mixture of confusion and agony, his open blue eyes searching for reason. His stiff hands cradled an AK-47.

"He was fighting off somebody." Pitt toed the deck near a handful of spent shell casings.

Giordino played a flashlight on the body. "No visible cause of death."

They stepped over the body and into the companionway, which they climbed to the bridge on the fifth level. There they found another macabre scene. An armed man in fatigues sprawled beside a crewman near the helm. An older, bearded man, likely the captain, had collapsed near a chart table. Giordino checked for signs of life, but bulging eyes, blue skin, and contorted mouths signified a quick but painful end.

"No external wounds, just like the guy downstairs," Giordino said.

Pitt noticed a smell of sulfur and opened a bridge window. "Possible gas leak. Why don't you check the crew's quarters for survivors? I'll let the *Macedonia* know what we've found, then see about getting this floating coffin under way."

Giordino moved down to the companionway to the living quarters beneath the bridge. Pitt relayed a report to Stenseth, then engaged the freighter's engines and turned on a course toward Istanbul, accompanied by the *Macedonia*.

The freighter slowly gathered speed, plowing through an endless line of high swells as it angled south. Pitt was checking for approaching traffic when a small explosion reverberated from the stern. He turned to see a fountain of white water erupt outboard of the port flank. The freighter shuddered as red lights flashed on the helm console.

"What was that?" Giordino's voice crackled over the handheld radio.

"Explosion on the stern."

"Somebody trying to scuttle her?"

"Could be."

Pitt studied a navigation monitor. The nearest land was eight miles. He altered course, hopeful he might run the ship aground if necessary. Additional red lights on the console told him they wouldn't make it. Some papers slid off a corner workstation, confirming the growing list he felt beneath his feet.

"The ship is flooding," he radioed to Giordino. "How are you making out?"

"Two crewmen dead in their bunks. I think there's another suite of cabins to check in the deck below."

Pitt detected something out of the corner of his eye. To his side, a closed-circuit video monitor displayed live feeds from the bow, stern, and engine room. He had seen some sort of movement in the engine room. Looking closer, he could just distinguish a prone figure at the rear of the image.

"Al, finish up and meet me on deck in five minutes. I'm going to check the engine room."

The helm console was ablaze with flashing lights as the flooding crept through the freighter's lower recesses. The bow had already begun rising toward the sky as the stern sank lower. Pitt glanced at the distant lights onshore, then ran from the bridge. He reached the main deck and descended a companionway to the engine room.

Pitt found the floor of the engine bay awash, but the power plants continued to churn with a deafening roar. Through flickering lights, he spotted a figure stretched out on a gray case behind a generator. Pitt waded over to find a young crewman in oil-stained coveralls, his feet dangling in the rising water. His face had a bluish tint as he stared at Pitt through listless eyes, then blinked.

"Hang on," Pitt said. "I'll get you out of here."

He hooked an arm around the stricken man, raised him to his feet, and muscled him up the steps. Pitt glanced around for additional survivors, but the bay was empty. He struggled up the steps with his load, a journey made harder by the ship's list. They reached a hatch door, which Pitt kicked open as a generator below them sizzled to a halt from the rising waters.

Giordino stood near the rail and rushed over to help. "This baby's about to go under. The *Macedonia* is ordering us to evacuate right away."

They were briefly blinded by a powerful searchlight from the NUMA ship that swept over the angled deck. Pitt glanced aft.

Waves were washing over the stern rail. Metallic creaks and groans filled the air, along with sporadic crashes from shifting cargo. The freighter had only seconds left afloat.

Pitt and Giordino dragged the crewman across to the accommodations ladder. The freighter's steep list had raised the stairway to a nearly horizontal angle. Giordino descended first, supporting the engineer over his shoulder as Pitt lowered the injured man by the collar. Alongside them, the freighter shuddered as it fought to stay afloat.

"We've got a problem," Giordino said.

Pitt stared at the Zodiac. Partially submerged, the inflatable was standing on end in the water. As the ship settled, the lower section of the accommodations ladder had dropped underwater. The attached bow line had pulled the Zodiac down with it, leaving it bobbing upright like a cork in the water.

The freighter lurched again, its bow shooting skyward as its stern began sliding into the sea. They could simply wait a few seconds and step off into the water, but they would face the risk of being pulled under by the suction from the sinking ship. Even if they managed to swim free, there was a good chance the semi-conscious engineer would drown.

"Take him and grab hold of the Zodiac," Pitt yelled. Then he stepped off the ladder and dove into the sea.

Pitt struck the surface alongside the upright mass of the Zodiac, the cold water prickling his skin. As he kicked downward, he felt along the inflatable's fiberglass hull. The Zodiac suddenly jerked away from him as the freighter began its final plunge. Pitt kicked hard to keep up, pulling himself along the inflatable's surface wherever he could find a grip. In the dark water, he reached out and felt its pointed prow. Grabbing hold, he pulled himself forward while groping with his other hand for the bow line.

The rope was tightly secured in the Zodiac's interior, so his only chance for a quick release was to free it from the ship's ladder. He pulled himself hand over hand against the rush of water, a flurry of bubbles obscuring the minimal visibility. The growing water pressure squeezed his ears and lungs as he willed himself down the line. His outstretched hand finally banged against the platform and he grasped the cleat that held the line. The rope was pulled taut by the pressure, but he found the end and began working it loose. With a hard tug, the line broke free.

The accommodations ladder smacked his side as the Zodiac began to shoot toward the surface. Pitt nearly lost his breath but clung tightly to the line. With the freighter continuing to slide past him, he had no sense of ascending until his ears popped. A second later, he was flung above the waves by the momentum of the surfacing inflatable. He regained his bearings and swam to the side of the Zodiac. A waterlogged Al Giordino reached over the side and helped hoist him aboard. He grinned at Pitt. "I'm glad you didn't wait to hit bottom before releasing the line."

Pitt forced an exhausted smile. "I wanted to give you your money's worth. How's our friend?"

"If you understand Russian, he can tell you himself. He swallowed a bit of seawater during our thrill ride but actually seems better for it after a bit of retching."

The crewman sat on the floor of the Zodiac, clinging to a bench seat. Though his skin was pale, his eyes appeared steady, and he breathed easily. He glanced up at Pitt and nodded.

Around them, a collection of flotsam coated the water. A

motor sounded nearby and a second Zodiac from the *Macedonia* raced over and towed the battered inflatable back to the research ship. The freighter's crewman was rushed to sick bay while Pitt and Giordino climbed to the bridge.

Captain Stenseth greeted them with mugs of hot coffee. "You boys cut your exit a little close there."

Giordino savored the warm brew. "It being a nice night for a midnight swim, we opted for a dip."

"Only one survivor?"

"Afraid so," Pitt said. "The other crewmen showed no signs of injury. Looks to be a possible chemical or gas leak."

"Something to do with that blast?"

"I'm not sure," Pitt said. "It occurred well aft of the cargo holds."

"She didn't look old enough to be a candidate for an insurance policy scuttling," Giordino said. "That leaves an accident or an aborted hijacking."

They were interrupted by a call from an approaching Turkish Coast Guard helicopter.

Stenseth turned to Chavez. "Tell them the *Crimean Star* has gone down and that we're at the site of the sinking. We'll welcome their assistance in searching for survivors."

The thumping drone of the search and rescue chopper sounded a moment later. Pitt and Giordino stepped to the bridge wing as it surveyed the freighter's small field of floating debris. Its bright searchlight narrowed on a pair of drifting bodies.

Giordino shook his head. "All of her crew gone but one."

Staring at the roiling sea, Pitt nodded. "A death ship that took her secrets with her. At least for now."

3

"Do you want the last *banitsa*?"

Ana Belova looked at the grease-stained bag thrust in her direction and shook her head. "No thanks. Even if I wanted a midnight snack, I prefer to keep my arteries unblocked."

Her partner, an easygoing man named Petar Ralin, slipped a hand into the bag on the car seat between them, fished out the apple-filled pastry, and stuffed it into his mouth. The Bulgarian lawman never seemed to travel without a bag of bread or sweets, Ana thought, yet kept a lean figure despite it.

He brushed a crumb from his shirt. "Looks like the directorate's informant is a bust. There hasn't been a truck through this crossing in two hours."

Ana peered out the windshield of their gray Škoda sedan at the Malko Tarnovo border station. The smallest of a handful of crossing points between Turkey and Bulgaria, the station catered to light car and tourist traffic traveling near the Black Sea coastline. The rugged woodlands of Strandzha Nature Park dominated the Bulgarian side of the border, while a sparse rural landscape spread across the Turkish territory.

Parked on Turkish soil less than fifty meters from the border, Ana watched as a young man on a motorcycle approached the checkpoint. As he cleared the crossing, she could see he carried a small pig in a crate attached to the rear fender.

"Late-night barbecue fix?" Ralin asked.

"You mean early-morning." Ana suppressed a yawn. "I guess we've wasted enough time and downed enough *banitsas* to call it a night."

"Hold on. There's another vehicle coming."

A dim spray of yellow light bounced across a hillside, morphing into a pair of headlight beams as it drew closer. The vehicle pulled to a stop at the checkpoint. It was a battered stake-bed truck with a canvas top over its cargo area. A muddy black-on-white license plate revealed its Turkish registry.

"Why don't you make sure the border guard is awake while I check the plate number," Ana said.

Ralin stuffed the last bite of pastry into his mouth then ambled toward the idling truck. Ana aimed binoculars at the truck and jotted down its license number. She traded the binoculars for a laptop computer and was typing in the number when she heard a sharp yell.

The truck was pulling forward, its engine revving. The border guard was stepping back into his office, having failed to examine the truck or even hold it up for Ralin's inspection, as they had agreed. Ana was too far away to see the fold of currency that bulged in the guard's shirt pocket.

Ralin had yelled, commanding the vehicle to stop. With his left arm outstretched like a traffic cop, he fumbled for his service weapon. Instead of stopping, the truck's driver accelerated toward Ralin. The police agent had to dive out of the way to avoid getting flattened. The truck's fender clipped his legs, sending him sprawling.

Ana clambered into the driver's seat of the Škoda and cranked the ignition. Jamming the stick shift into first, she hit the gas, cursing as the truck rumbled past before she could block it. She hesitated a moment, looking to Ralin. The agent was clutching his ankle, but he turned and waved at her to proceed without him.

The Škoda's tires squealed as she turned the wheel and floored the gas. The truck hadn't traveled far, and she caught up to it in seconds. Watching the cargo cover ripple, she prayed the truck bed wasn't filled with armed thugs. Instead, as the truck passed a streetlamp, she glimpsed a mound of watermelons under the cover. But the man behind the wheel was driving like no farmer.

The truck barreled down a winding hill and into the center of Malko Tarnovo, a dusty Bulgarian farm town twenty-five miles inland from the Black Sea. Beyond lay an expanse of dark, rolling hills that stretched for a dozen miles to the next village. The open terrain was not the place Ana would want to apprehend the truck's occupants single-handedly. Pressing the accelerator, she tried to pull alongside. The truck's driver caught the move and jerked to the side, closing the gap. Ana had to jam the brakes to avoid a parked car as the truck held to the center line. There was no way she could pass.

Ana pictured the town's layout, recalling a main street that ran through the center of Malko Tarnovo and two parallel paved roads that stretched for about eight blocks. Initially approaching a side street, Ana braked again and turned the car left. She sped to the next block and turned right, running parallel to the main road. She gunned the engine and shifted hard, racing down the street and sending the sedan airborne with every bump.

The Škoda quickly ate up five blocks as Ana fumbled to click her seat belt as she drove. She veered right at the last side street, sending the tail of the car into a pair of trash cans as she slid through the corner. Sleepy residents peered out their windows at the streaking gray car whose engine sounded ready to explode.

As Ana approached the main street, the lights of the truck merged from her right. She was slightly ahead, but not far enough to allow a safe turn in front of it. Gauging the distance, Ana held down the gas a second more, then stomped on the brakes. As the car bucked under the antilock brakes, she nudged the steering wheel to the left.

The car pivoted slightly before making contact, the right side of its bumper slamming into the truck's left front wheel well. The bang rattled windows up and down the street. The Škoda's hood vanished under the mass of the truck, which skidded to the curb after its front wheel was decapitated. Under the force of the truck's momentum, both vehicles slid forward until hopping a curb and striking a lamppost.

Acrid smoke filled the truck's cabin as its driver tried to shake off the impact. "Josef?" he called to his partner, who lay motionless across the dashboard, unconscious or dead. The driver didn't bother to check. He wedged his crumpled door open and fell to the street, intending to flee. He glanced at the shattered Škoda. A flattened air bag lay across the steering wheel, but no sign of a driver. He turned—and stepped into the barrel of a SIG Sauer P228 automatic pistol.

With air bag bruises on her face and breathing rapidly, Ana stood with her arms outstretched, pressing the gun into the driver's cheek.

"On your knees. Hands on your head," she said in a deep voice, trying to mask her own state of shock. The stunned driver readily obeyed.

Less than a minute later, Ralin and a border agent roared up in a state vehicle. Ralin hopped out of the car with a limp while drawing his gun on the truck driver. "You all right?"

Ana nodded and watched as Ralin handcuffed the driver and threw him in the back of the car.

The border agent checked on the truck's passenger and returned shaking his head. "The other one's dead."

Ralin put his arm around Ana as she sagged and holstered her weapon.

"After he hit you, I just reacted." She shook her head. "I didn't want him to get away."

"You succeeded." Ralin glanced at the demolished Škoda and smiled. "But I'm not sure the department head will appreciate your sacrificing a new agency sedan for a load of watermelons."

"Watermelons," Ana muttered. She climbed into the back of the truck and began tossing the melons aside. Her arms were aching by the time she burrowed to the bottom of the truck bed and uncovered a trio of long wooden crates.

Ralin helped drag one of them onto the street. He found a tire jack and used it to pry open the crate. Inside was a neatly stacked row of Albanian-made AK-47 assault rifles bound for the black market. "Just as advertised," Ralin said. "Score one for our paid informant."

"I guess his payment will be a reduced jail term," she said. "Not our biggest arms bust, but, hopefully, we saved a few innocent lives somewhere."

"And gained the department enough positive publicity to replace our car."

Within the hour, a contingent of local and state police arrived to arrest the smuggler and seize the evidence. Ana rested in the border agent's vehicle, fighting to stay awake after the rush of the chase had passed. At dawn, tow trucks arrived to remove the wrecked vehicles.

Ralin stuck his head into the open car window. "Ana, I just received a call from headquarters in Sofia. Looks like we're wanted in Istanbul this afternoon."

"Can't it wait? I could use some sleep."

"Apparently, it's a high-priority assignment based on some information out of Ukraine."

"Another arms shipment?"

"I don't think so. Seems to be something more important."

She forced a smile. "Then I guess they'll have to give us a new car."

"I'm not so sure a car will help us on this assignment."

"Why's that? Is it an air shipment? Or a rail transfer?"

"Neither," he said, shaking his head. "It's a shipwreck."

4

A brief drizzle dampened an otherwise temperate afternoon at Istinye Harbor, just north of Istanbul. Walking slowly across the compact marina, Ana and Ralin
spotted their quarry, a bright turquoise-hulled oceanographic
research ship tied at the largest berth.

A short, burly man hoisting aboard a crate watched as they
drew near.

"Is this the *Macedonia*?" Ana asked in English.

Al Giordino regarded the stranger. Her long, dark hair was
pulled back in a bun, exposing a delicate face. She had high Slavic
cheekbones, softened by a small nose and mouth. But her radiant
blue eyes drew his attention. Giordino could see she possessed a
mix of determination and vulnerability.

"You've come to the right place," Giordino said.

"I'm Ana Belova, special investigator with Europol, and this
is Lieutenant Petar Ralin from the Bulgarian Organized Crime

Directorate. We are investigating the sinking of the *Crimean Star*."

Giordino introduced himself. "Europol. Is that an offshoot of Interpol?"

"No, the European Police Office is a law enforcement agency of the European Union. Our primary focus is organized crime and counterterrorism."

"Come on aboard. I'll let you talk to the boss." Giordino guided them to the *Macedonia*'s wardroom, where Pitt and Captain Stenseth were seated, examining a chart. Giordino made the introductions, and coffee was brought for the investigators before they all sat around a table.

"How can we be of assistance?" Pitt asked. "We already gave a full report to the Turkish Coast Guard."

Ana felt his deep green eyes look right through her. She was surprised to feel her pulse quicken as she listened to the tall, rugged man. "Our respective agencies have concerns over the loss of the *Crimean Star*. What can you tell us about her sinking?"

Pitt described the events of the previous night, concluding with the rescue of the assistant engineer.

"Do you think the explosion at the stern was intentional?" Ralin asked.

"I suspect so, but I have no evidence to prove it." Pitt gazed at the investigators. "Do you mind telling us about your interest in the sinking?"

"The answer is threefold," Ana said. "First, we've learned the *Crimean Star* was under charter to a Russian firm called Nemco Holdings. Nemco has suspected ties to the Russian Mafia. It's believed to be involved with smuggling arms to Africa and the Middle East. You didn't happen to examine the ship's holds?"

"No, our aboard time was short. Have you obtained the ship's manifest?"

"Electronic records indicate she was carrying agricultural equipment bound for Alexandria, Egypt."

"Any chemicals or fertilizers as part of that?" Pitt asked.

"None that were listed. But I can't say we put full faith in the manifest, given that the ship originated from Sevastopol. Why do you ask?"

"We suspect a chemical leak may have killed the crew."

"We've just come from a visit to Memorial Şişli Hospital, where the engineer was admitted," Ralin said. "The pathologist said tests on the deceased crewmen indicated that death was caused by a concentrated exposure to hydrogen sulfide gas. He suspects a natural gas leak."

"We detected the odor when we boarded the vessel," Giordino said, "but we didn't identify its origin. Natural gas seems a likely source, but the *Crimean Star* is a bulk freighter, not a liquefied natural gas carrier."

"Yes, that is correct," Ana said. "Our primary concern relates to another fact—the assistant engineer who survived."

"How's the young man holding up?" Pitt asked.

"Quite well. His exposure to the hydrogen sulfide was limited, presumably because he was working in the engine room. He is expected to make a full recovery. But the doctors discovered a second condition that is more disconcerting. It seems the engineer tested positive for trace levels of radioactivity."

"Radioactivity?" Giordino asked. "Perhaps he worked on a nuclear-powered ship before crewing aboard the *Crimean Star*."

"We explored that possibility, and a few others, but he has no history of working around radioactive materials or near nuclear power facilities."

"You think it was something on the ship?" Pitt asked.

"That is our fear," Ralin said. "We have information that the *Crimean Star* may have been used to smuggle radioactive materials for sale on the black market."

Ana turned to Pitt. "Petar and I are part of a task force assigned to prevent the trafficking of weapons and nuclear materials in the Black Sea region."

"There's still unaccounted nuclear materials out there?" Giordino asked.

"Regrettably so," Ana said. "The collapse of the Soviet Union in 1991 brought about a free-for-all in nuclear material smuggling for many years. Stronger controls today have reduced that considerably, but there is still an alarming black market demand—much of it related to materials that were stolen years ago. You may be surprised to learn there are still over a dozen arrests each year in the Black Sea region related to nuclear smuggling. The spread of nuclear materials remains a very dangerous risk, especially with the rise of extremism in the Middle East."

"I suspect war-torn Ukraine hasn't helped matters any," Pitt said.

"You are correct. That's what has us concerned about the *Crimean Star*. Europol has been searching for a container of highly enriched uranium that disappeared from the Sevastopol Institute of Nuclear Energy during the Russian invasion of

Crimea. Intelligence believes it is being transported to Syria, and we suspect the *Crimean Star* was the carrier."

Pitt nodded. "Which explains the assistant engineer's radiation exposure."

"Remote as it may be, it is a possibility we must explore. If the uranium was stored in the engine room or near his cabin, it might account for his trace readings."

"What's the significance of this uranium being highly enriched?" Giordino asked.

"HEU, as it is called, is uranium that has undergone isotope separation to increase its content of U-235. It is the form of uranium used in the most powerful nuclear devices, be it power plants or missiles and bombs."

"So the question," Pitt said, "is whether the *Crimean Star* was intentionally sunk for someone to acquire the HEU?"

"We've obviously strolled down a path of multiple assumptions," Ralin said, "but the circumstantial evidence is compelling."

"I think you've got plenty of reasons to be concerned."

"Mr. Pitt," Ana said, "can you tell us the purpose of your visit to the region?"

"NUMA was invited by the Bulgarian Ministry of Culture to participate in the search for a late-Ottoman-era shipwreck that sank off the Bulgarian coast in the eighteenth century."

Ana glanced at Ralin, then turned to Pitt. "Would you consider delaying the start of your project for a day or so to lend us some assistance?"

"What did you have in mind?"

"I'd like you to find out if there is highly enriched uranium on the *Crimean Star.*"

"If it was ever on the ship," Pitt said, "it may have already been removed by those who sank her."

"A distinct possibility," Ralin said. "We'd like to believe your arrival disrupted those plans."

"Why not use local resources?" Pitt asked. "The Turkish Navy surely has the capability."

"The Turkish Navy can indeed help, but not for another week," Ana said. "Turkey is not a part of the European Union, so our authority here is less respected. If the HEU is still aboard, it won't be for long. There are search and rescue teams still on-site, but their efforts will be called off at dusk. We'd like the ship examined as soon as possible." Her blue eyes met Pitt's. "Could you return to the site and survey the vessel for us?"

Pitt turned to Giordino and Stenseth. "We're already a day late. The *Crimean Star* site is almost on our way. And our Ottoman wreck isn't going anywhere. I think we can delay our historical hunt a bit longer." He turned to Ana. "Besides, we could always use a friend at Europol."

A relieved look crossed the faces of Ana and Ralin. She reached across the table and clasped Pitt's hand.

"You now have one."

5

The unmanned aerial vehicle banked in a lazy arc, its long, slender wings buoyed by a stiff easterly breeze. Dual high-resolution video cameras on the fuselage scanned the earth a full mile wide along its flight path. In seconds, the onboard computers registered a small airfield dead ahead, surrounded by a patchwork of green alfalfa fields.

The drone's operator watched the video feed on a large monitor. The cameras focused on a handful of military transport planes parked near a hangar, then zeroed in on a large black automobile. With the flick of a command, the image was magnified, revealing a Russian-made ZiL limousine, with two uniformed occupants in the backseat.

The operator activated a target sensor, superimposing a flashing red circle with crosshairs over the image of the car. A heavyset man in a blue suit standing beside the operator studied the monitor, then commanded, "Fire."

The crosshairs turned green and a buzzing sounded from the computer.

The man in the suit turned from the operator and shouted toward the ZiL, parked a few yards away. "General, I regret to inform you that both you and the major were just vaporized by an air-launched missile." The man's voice held a clear note of satisfaction.

The Russian Air Force general, an older, sallow man named Zakharin, climbed out of the car and began scanning the gray overcast skies. He saw and heard nothing.

"It's to the south, General."

The Russian spun on his heels and squinted southward. A few seconds later, the slate-colored drone came into view, swooping to a landing on the runway and rolling to a stop alongside the limo. Fractionally longer than the car, the drone featured a sleek, twin-fuselage design that faintly resembled a catamaran with wings.

"It is nearly silent," Zakharin remarked, stepping over to take a closer look.

"That was one of the design drivers for the Peregrine," Martin Hendriks said. A plump-faced Dutchman with dark red hair and a crisp, authoritarian voice, Hendriks gazed at his creation with pride and resignation. His Armani suit and erect posture advertised his success, but his deep blue eyes betrayed a sad intelligence. Eyes that had once known mirth now were vacantly sober.

"The Americans' Predator and Reaper drones are larger and more heavily armed," Hendriks said, "but they are relatively loud and easily visible with radar. That's fine for fighting guerrilla fighters on horseback in Afghanistan, but not so effective against a technologically advanced opponent." He pointed to the drone's sharply angled wings and fuselage. "Please notice the Peregrine's profile. Its shape is designed to deflect radar signals, while its surface is coated with RF-absorbent materials. That enables her to fly nearly invisible to both ground observers and radar."

Zakharin placed his hand on the drone's surface, finding it rubbery. "Not unlike the surface material on our new fighter jet," he said. "How did you make it so quiet?"

Hendriks pointed to the twin fuselage nacelles, which had large oval scoops at either end. "The Peregrine is powered by dual electric-pulse jet turbofans, which act as mini jet engines. They produce sound vibration at takeoff, but once the craft has reached operating altitude, they are virtually silent. The electric motors and onboard electronics are powered by hydrogen fuel cells, supplemented by solar panels in the wings. Once airborne, the Peregrine can stay aloft for two weeks—even longer under sunny conditions. That compares to half a day for the American drones." Hendriks smiled. "And that's only what we've achieved with this prototype. We expect further advances in energy storage and avionics to expand that range."

The general nodded. "There is no substitute for stealth and endurance. Tell me about the armament."

"Peregrine has a flexible weapons rack, capable of multiple air-to-surface missiles or even conventional ordnance. It was designed with NATO weaponry in mind, but is easily capable of modification. Name your desired weapon, General, and we'll make it operational."

"I see. Come, Martin, let us escape the wind and discuss it over a drink."

Zakharin led Hendriks into a borrowed office in the hangar, where a bottle of Stolichnaya was waiting with two glasses. The Russian filled each glass, then toasted his guest.

Hendriks fired down half a glass and took a seat in a frayed leather chair. "So, what is your opinion of the Peregrine?" Hendriks asked, knowing the general had poorly concealed his interest.

Zakharin drained his vodka like he was drinking water and refilled both glasses. "It could be a useful tool in the aggravated regions near our border. Perhaps even Ukraine. I could foresee the Air Force fielding a small squadron. But I must caution you that our own research services are close to completing a Russian drone."

"Your Altius drone is a fat, inferior copycat of the Americans' Reaper vehicle." Hendriks cracked a rare smile. "It failed its initial flight testing and is months behind schedule."

Zakharin raised an eyebrow. "It seems you are well informed," he said, knowing he had just lost any negotiating leverage. "Your Peregrine might indeed fill a temporary void in our reconnaissance needs. But I am aware of a business concern."

Hendriks forced a startled look. "What could that be?"

"It is my understanding that you have recently sold your avionics company. At a price of several billion dollars, if the press is accurate."

Hendriks stared at the linoleum floor and nodded. "Yes, I recently sold my avionics company, and I also divested my other business interests." He unconsciously dipped a hand into his side jacket pocket, his fingers probing for a small metallic object.

"Starting a new chapter in life?"

Hendriks said nothing. Hidden in his coat pocket, his fingers pressed against the sharp metal until they trembled.

"Though you appear a bit young for retirement," the general said, "I believe one should enjoy the spoils of their work while they can. I offer my congratulations. But my point is this. My government has procured avionics equipment from you for many years. I would not feel comfortable purchasing the Peregrine from new owners. And, of course, there is the question of the legality of obtaining this technology."

"I own the Peregrine design personally, with royalty rights for the next three years," Hendriks said. "A retirement gift from the company, you might say. So you would still be doing business with me."

"And your government? The European Union will not allow the export of such an item to Russia at this time."

"Not in this form," Hendriks admitted. "But it is easy enough to circumvent. We piecemeal the parts to you from sources in different countries, and the final assembly can happen here. I'll even send a team to do it for you."

Zakharin considered the response and nodded. "Yes, that may be feasible. But I am curious to know why you are not selling the Peregrine to the NATO countries."

Hendriks's fingers again went to work on the object in his pocket. "Simple economics. The Americans' product will limit my sales to NATO. I believe that I can sell more to you."

"I can make no guarantees."

"I am not here to ask for any. But there is one other item I hope you may consider. I would be able to offer you a personal commission of five percent on every Peregrine sold to the Russian government."

Hendriks knew Zakharin had achieved his rank by cronyism, not skill. In the Russian hierarchy, the higher up the chain of command one traveled, the more corruption blossomed. With no surprise, he saw Zakharin's eyes widen in anticipation.

"What is the selling price?" Zakharin asked.

"The first lot will be twelve million euros each. Less with a quantity purchase. Your commission would be payable in your choice of currency and banking locale."

"I will discuss it with the Procurement Directorate at once. I am positive we will be able to arrange at least a minimum purchase." Zakharin eyed the vodka bottle for a celebratory shot.

"Excellent," Hendriks said with little emotion. "I have an additional request, if I might. It would be a great honor to arrange for the president a demonstration similar to today's."

"President Vashenko?" Zakharin gazed at the ceiling. "It would be very difficult to arrange. But he does appreciate modern technology and might enjoy a viewing. Still, my influence is limited, as I am just a lowly military man."

"I understand. Nevertheless, I would enjoy showing him the Peregrine's capabilities." He winked. "It might increase the quantity purchased."

"Yes, I can see the wisdom in such a demonstration. I will do what I can." The general looked at his watch. "Well, Martin, I hope that we have the chance to continue our friendship. I was just a captain when you began selling digital aeronautical instruments to Aeroflot many years ago. Since that time, we have had a mutually beneficial relationship."

"Agreed," Hendriks said, recalling that Zakharin's vacation dacha near Sochi was at least partially funded by bribes from his company. "You know, General, I am aware of an external business opportunity that might be of interest to you." He paused to let the Russian take the bait.

"Yes, please tell me more," Zakharin said, before downing his third glass of vodka.

"I was recently in Paris and ran into some old colleagues. One has recently brokered a deal for the acquisition of a pair of French attack helicopters in Senegal for the president's security force. But they were unable to acquire armament for the craft and are seeking to purchase a dozen light air-to-surface missiles. I was told your Vikhr laser-guided missiles would fit the bill quite nicely."

"Are they willing to pay a commission?"

"Around six figures, I believe."

The general placed his empty glass on the desk. "I'm sure I could locate a dozen missiles in inventory that could be assigned to field exercises. But transport would be of concern."

"I'm told that if you can make delivery in Ukraine, they will handle the transport to Africa. Could one of their representatives contact you discreetly?"

"Yes, yes, of course." Zakharin rose to his feet, his eyes blurry. "I will let you know about the Peregrine."

"Thank you, General."

Zakharin returned to his limo and was driven off the airfield.

Hendriks approached his technical assistant, who was packing up the Peregrine's portable control station.

"Are you going to leave the Peregrine here with the Russians?" he asked Hendriks.

"So they can copy us blind? No. They've seen all I want them to see. Have it broken down, placed in the truck, and returned to the factory at once."

"Yes, sir. I will take care of it."

Hendriks stepped across the tarmac to a waiting private jet.

The jet's pilot greeted him as he climbed aboard. "We're cleared for takeoff to Amsterdam at your convenience, sir."

Hendriks dropped into a leather seat. "Proceed with our flight plan to Amsterdam. But once we clear Russian airspace, divert us to Kiev. I need to make a stop there before we return home."

Minutes later, the jet roared into the damp sky, leaving the Russian airfield near Moscow hidden beneath dark clouds. Hendriks stared out the window with a dull sense of relief. It was the first glimmer of satisfaction he had known in more than three years.

6

The *Macedonia* cleared the Bosphorus Strait ahead of a gray dawn and retraced its path toward the site of the freighter's sinking. A passing Turkish Coast Guard frigate reported the search and rescue efforts had been abandoned the prior evening and no additional survivors had been found.

The lights of another vessel appeared before them, stationary in their path.

"Somebody's still on the site," Captain Stenseth said, reaching for his binoculars.

Ana and Ralin stood with Pitt on the bridge. They all gazed at the twinkling lights that cut the morning gloom.

"Another Coast Guard vessel?" Ana asked.

Stenseth deferred judgment until they drew close enough to see it was some sort of work ship or salvage vessel that teemed with cranes. A tattered white, green, and red flag of Bulgaria fluttered from the bridge mast. The transom conspicuously lacked a ship's name.

"Could they be an insurance investigator?" Ana asked.

"Possible," Pitt said, "though it's not likely they would be here already."

"Then they have no authority to be here," Ralin said. "May I borrow your ship's radio?"

Stenseth handed him the transmitter, and the police agent hailed the unidentified ship. "This is Inspector Petar Ralin of the Bulgarian National Police aboard the NUMA ship *Macedonia*. Please identify yourself and state your business at this location."

A minute later, a grumbly voice blared through the bridge speaker. "This is a private salvage vessel. We are engaged in excavations on the shipwreck *Kerch*. Please stand clear."

"You are near the coordinates of a shipwreck under police authority," Ralin said. "Identify yourself and move off-site."

This time, there was no response.

Pitt glanced at a nautical chart. "He's right, on one score. There is a wreck marked less than a quarter mile from where the *Crimean Star* sank." On the helm's navigation screen, the freighter's position was marked by a red X. Pitt turned to Stenseth. "We're still a bit short of the mark."

"Are they on the *Crimean Star*'s coordinates?" Ana asked.

"Near to it," Stenseth said. "Looks like they are a bit to the west . . . and moving off in that direction."

In the faint early light, Pitt could make out numerous large cranes on the ship as it eased away. The salvage vessel slowed and held its position several hundred meters away, exactly over the position of the marked wreck.

Pitt sat at a side computer terminal and typed in the wreck's name, *Kerch*. "She was a destroyer of the Russian Imperial Navy, built in 1916." He pulled up a photo of the ship. "It says she sank during an engagement with Ottoman naval forces off the Bosphorus Strait in February 1917."

"Do you think they are actually working on that wreck and not the *Crimean Star*?" Ralin asked.

"Not likely, but there's one way to find out," Pitt said. "Who's up for a dive in a submersible?"

Ralin's face went blank, while Ana produced a faint smile.

"The lady it is," Pitt said. "Come, follow me, Ms. Belova, for a guided trip to the deep."

"You'll bring her back?" Ralin asked, only half joking.

Pitt winked. "I haven't lost a paying customer yet."

ANA'S HEART WAS POUNDING forty minutes later when a rush of seawater washed over the acrylic bubble viewport of the NUMA three-man submersible. Seated in the rear, she looked over the shoulders of Pitt and Giordino at a rush of bubbles that dissipated into a wall of turbid green water. A slight claustrophobia crept over her when she realized visibility was only a few feet. "Is that as clear as the water gets?" she asked.

"The scenery will get much better shortly," Pitt said. "The deeper waters of the Black Sea are actually anoxic, or oxygen-depleted, which makes for crystal clear viewing. We're not going very deep, but we should still get a taste of that."

Giordino tracked a depth monitor. "We should hit the mud at about three hundred feet."

Pitt's words soon rang true. Like a veil being pulled away from the viewport, the visibility suddenly expanded to nearly fifty feet, aided by the bright LED lights on the submersible's exterior.

Ana felt her pulse slow with the improved visibility and the obvious calmness of the men at the controls. "My parents used to take me swimming in the Black Sea off Romania as a child, but I was always afraid of sea creatures."

"There's not much to worry about in the Black Sea, except maybe jellyfish," Pitt said. "You were born in Romania?"

"Yes. I grew up in Bucharest. My father was a history teacher and my mother a seamstress. We would spend summer vacation at Constanța, where my father loved to swim and snorkel in the sea every day."

"Sounds like my kind of guy," Pitt said. "How'd you end up carrying a gun and a badge?"

"My brother was killed by a drug smuggler when I was in high school." The pain was still evident in her voice. "I found myself in law enforcement academy a few years later, perhaps as a subconscious means of avenging his death. I soon found I actually enjoyed the challenge of the work. After a few years with the Romanian police, I took an assignment with Europol and never left. It's been a satisfying adventure." She waved a hand toward the viewport. "I never know where the job might take me."

A faint, distant light appeared beyond her fingertips.

"What's that?" she asked.

"Must be an ROV or submersible from the salvage ship," Giordino said. "Maybe they are playing on the other shipwreck."

The light faded as they neared the bottom. To their right, the dark image of the *Crimean Star* materialized a short distance away. Pitt adjusted the submersible's ballast until they hovered a few meters above the sandy seafloor, then engaged the thrusters. A few seconds later, they approached the slab-sided hull of the ship near its bow.

The freighter sat upright on the bottom, appearing mostly unscathed. The ship's stern had struck the seabed and augered in, as evidenced by the rising slope of the bow. Absent any algae, encrustations, or entangled fishing nets typical of most wrecks, the ship had an alien appearance.

Pitt approached the freighter's stern and headed to its port flank to investigate the explosion.

"You sure it was this side of the ship?" Giordino asked.

Pitt nodded, nudging the submersible alongside the hull. "The main damage must be concealed in the sand." He squinted out the viewport. "Take a close look at those plates."

He pivoted the submersible so its exterior lights shone across the side of the hull. A slight gap was barely visible along a horizontal hull plate just above the seafloor.

"You're right, they're buckled," Giordino said. "There must be much more damage hidden by sand, given how fast the ship sank."

"Is there any way to tell if she was sunk intentionally?" Ana asked.

"Not without a bit of excavation," Pitt said. "The ship's insurer might find it worth the effort, if they have a chance of dodging a payout."

Giordino nodded. "Truth suddenly becomes important when a buck's involved."

Pitt engaged the thrusters and brought the submersible up to the freighter's main deck. As the sub glided over the side rail, he brought it to a hover beneath the accommodations block. Looking across the forward deck, they saw the freighter's four large holds fully exposed. Each hold cover was lying to the side, extending over the starboard rail.

"Were those removed or jarred loose when she sank?" Ana asked.

"They look too orderly to have been knocked off by chance," Giordino said.

Pitt propelled the submersible to the nearest steel cover and examined its painted surface. Fresh gouge marks were clearly visible on one edge.

"By the look of those marks," Giordino said, "somebody's scraped those pretty recently."

"The salvage ship would have the means to do so," Pitt said. "Let's see if they left anything behind."

He cruised to the first hold. The opening was more than double the size of the submersible, and Pitt easily dropped the vessel into the hold. At its bottom was a yellow tractor lashed to the deck, surrounded by miscellaneous farm equipment.

Giordino smiled. "Looks like Old MacDonald's barn is still there."

"The contents appear fully intact," Pitt said. He elevated the submersible and hopscotched over and into the next three holds. Each looked identical, containing a tractor and related agricultural equipment. All of the holds appeared undisturbed.

Giordino turned to Ana. "I guess your ship's manifest was legit."

"Yes," she said, "but it would appear that the salvors were interested in something else."

"If the HEU was carried aboard," Pitt asked, "what size container would it require?"

"Not large, depending on the quantity. If precautionary measures were used, it would be stored in a protective canister, which would then be enclosed in a small, secure crate. The engineer's radioactivity exposure may indicate it was lightly protected—possibly disguised as ordinary goods."

"Then the engine room it is," Pitt said.

He turned the submersible around and traveled aft, cutting around the accommodations block to reach the squat rear deck. Unlike the forward area, the stern was a disrupted, mangled mass of twisted steel. A gaping hole was carved along a lower companionway, exposing the aft section of the engine room.

Ana turned pale. "They've cut into the engine room," she said in a low voice.

"In a big way," Giordino said. "Doesn't look like they used explosives, though."

"Maybe a grapple device," Pitt said.

Giordino grunted. "They sure caused a lot of destruction. If it was just the HEU they were after, some divers could have carried it out."

Pitt maneuvered the submersible to the jagged edge of the opening and tilted it forward. The craft's lights flashed across the deck of the engine room, revealing a clean and unmolested bay. The sight triggered his memory. "The crate. I should have remembered it. There was a gray crate in the engine room. The assistant engineer was sprawled across it when I found him."

They scanned the compartment, but Pitt's gray box was nowhere to be seen.

"That must have been what they were after," Giordino said. "Your uranium story might have some teeth to it after all."

"I was hoping otherwise," she said.

Pitt ascended the submersible and hovered for a moment over the *Crimean Star*'s fantail. He eyed a digital compass and then propelled the craft on a westerly heading.

"Are we surfacing?" Ana asked.

"A slight detour on the way up," he said.

Giordino was already scanning the terrain ahead. After they traversed a thousand meters, he motioned to Pitt. "Possible target ahead on the left."

Pitt saw a dark smudge in the distance and angled toward it. A short time later, the corroded remains of the *Kerch* materialized. It looked nothing like the proud warship he had examined in the photo. The ship sat keeled over against a large sand dune that partially covered her stern. The bow was crumpled from colliding with the bottom, while the central part of the ship was a brown mass of concretion-encrusted, rusting steel.

Pitt brought the submersible amidships, where more damage was visible on the remains of the superstructure. He noted an obvious difference in the mangled steel that was twisted open along the side of the bridge, where numerous raw gouges were evident. "Recent handiwork here as well," he said. "Certainly not from 1917."

He followed the damage to the rear of the superstructure, where an even larger hole had been carved out of a lower-level bulkhead.

Giordino pointed to a black object sitting on the deck beneath the gap. "Take a look at that."

Pitt dropped the submersible to the deck level and faced the object. Its perfectly square shape was disrupted on one side by a protruding dial and handle.

"It's a safe," Ana said.

"Probably for the ship's payroll," Pitt said. "The salvors must have recovered it from the captain's cabin."

"It still looks locked and sealed," Giordino said. "I wonder why they left it here."

Like an asteroid from the heavens, a faint light approached from above, gradually growing brighter. The glow morphed into a half dozen xenon lights that radiated from the top of a massive lifting claw. The giant grapple drew to a stop midway between the safe and the submersible, dangling a few meters above the deck. Ever so slowly, the device extended its titanium-tipped fingers like a cat extending its claws.

Ana watched, mesmerized. "It's big enough to hoist a car."

"Or rip open the deck of a ship," Pitt said.

As if it had a mind of its own, the claw eased over the safe, using a bank of side thrusters. It hesitated, then reversed course and accelerated toward the submersible. Pitt had eyed the heavy thrusters mounted on the claw's frame and reacted instantly. Hovering the submersible against the back of the *Kerch*'s superstructure, he drove the craft sideways across the deck.

"What's it doing?" Ana asked.

"Trying to shake hands." Pitt applied full power to his own thrusters.

The streamlined claw was quick to move laterally and pursue the submersible, guided by its multiple video cameras.

As they approached the rusting remains of the side rail,

Pitt had no choice but to ascend. The action scrubbed off just enough speed for the claw to close the gap. As both machines slipped over the rail, the claw retracted its fingers to grab the submersible.

A metallic scraping reverberated through the interior as the claw grasped at the submersible's topside. Pitt jammed the thruster controls forward and tried to descend. The grating abated for a moment, then they heard a secondary clang. The submersible nosed forward and jolted to a halt. Ana shrieked.

Pitt turned the thrusters and tried to pull away, but the heavier grapple countered with its own propulsion. The lifting claw rotated, throwing the submersible against the hull of the *Kerch*. The submersible struck hard by the bow and skittered.

Immediately, the claw spun in the other direction.

Pitt countered the move with his own power, but it wasn't enough. The submersible was whipped around and thrown stern first against the wreck. A clatter churned the water as the main thruster broke free and was smashed to bits.

Giordino reached back and pulled Ana's safety belt as tight as he could. "Hang on, sister, we're in for a ride."

Powerless to counter the salvage grapple, Pitt, Giordino, and Ana clung to their seats as the vessel was pummeled from side to side. The submersible was repeatedly slammed against the old ship until its exterior resembled a dented soup can. Only when the vessel's lights flickered out and a stream of bubbles sprayed toward the surface did the hydraulic claw cease its thrashing and release its grip.

The salvage grapple returned to the *Kerch*'s deck and clasped its fingers around the ship's safe. With its prize secure, the claw reeled upward toward the surface. As it rose from the bottom, its video cameras caught a final glimpse of the NUMA submersible. Lying inverted and still, the battered craft was left to the silence of the blackened depths beside the long-dead warship.

7

All Pitt could see was red.

It wasn't blood but a tiny emergency light that pulsed near his face. He blinked away a shooting pain in his head and shoulder, then called into the darkened interior. "Everybody okay?"

"I'm good," Ana said with a frightened voice.

Giordino grunted. "I guess we survived the tumble dry setting." Like Pitt, he had been pitched forward from his seat when the submersible flipped over and he lay prone on its ceiling. He rose to his knees, splashing water around him.

"I don't like the sound of that." Pitt noticed his own wet feet.

Both men had water up to their ankles as they awkwardly stood. Around them were sounds of hissing and crackling mixed with an acrid, burning odor.

Pitt found a small flashlight and scanned the interior as Giordino helped release Ana from her seat.

"Pressure seems to be holding," Pitt said. "Must be a hairline crack or a viewport seal."

"Good thing we're not a thousand feet deeper," Giordino said. He knew that a similar breach at those depths could flood the submersible in an instant.

Though Pitt and Giordino discussed the situation with casual calmness, Ana could tell things were dire. "How bad is it?"

"No need to don our swim trunks just yet." Pitt gave a reassuring smile. "We have limited power at our disposal, but it is currently restricted to just a few applications. Al will do some rewiring to keep our oxygen scrubbers operating."

"Can't we call the *Macedonia*?"

"At the moment, we don't have power to our communication systems. Plus, there's our inverted position. Our communications transponder is located on the submersible's topside, which is now buried beneath us. We might not have much of a signal to transmit. But, no matter, as the *Macedonia* will come hunting for us soon enough."

"Can't we surface on our own?"

"Normally, we could, by thrusters or ballast. But our thrusters were knocked off, and the hissing you hear is a rupture to our ballast tank."

"That still leaves our emergency drop weights," Giordino said.

Pitt pointed up. "They're atop us now. We can't release them upside down."

A cold shudder ran through Ana. "How long can we stay down here?"

"If we can keep our scrubbers running, we're good for at least twenty-four hours."

Giordino cleared his throat. "We've got a recycle interruption."

"Manageable?" Pitt asked.

"The O_2 tanks were separated from the frame." He spoke the words casually for Ana's benefit, disguising the severity. The submersible's supply of oxygen had been ripped away during the assault and now lay unavailable on the seabed. "Power's down on the scrubbers, but I'm checking a work-around."

In the darkness, Pitt saw Giordino give him a faint shake of the head. There was no hope for repair.

The gears in Pitt's head started turning. The severed lines meant they had no access to fresh oxygen. Absent the operation of the carbon dioxide scrubbers, the air in the submersible would grow deadly. He didn't need a calculator to compute the time. With three people packed into its tight confines, it wouldn't take long.

Pitt had no doubt the *Macedonia* would find them. The depth was shallow enough that divers could attach a lift cable and pull them to the surface. But time was now the enemy. The *Macedonia*'s crew would think they were still on the freighter's wreck site. If their emergency beacon was muffled, it would take hours, maybe a day, to be found and rescued. More time than they had.

"How about another thought," he said. "We roll her upright. Or, at least, half over. Far enough to jettison our emergency weights."

Giordino shined his flashlight out the viewport, highlighting a rusty, growth-covered hull plate. They were positioned alongside the *Kerch* on an uneven, sandy surface.

"We can only move laterally," he said, "away from the wreck."

Pitt rapped a knuckle on the steel above his head. "We've got twin ballast tanks. If we can flood the port tank ahead of the starboard tank, the weight might pull us over."

"Worth a shot . . . if the pumps are operational. I'll see if I can get them some juice."

He wrenched open a side fuse panel and attacked the myriad wires that were housed inside. After a few minutes, he called to Pitt. "Give it a try."

Pitt reached around the pilot's seat and toggled the controls to flood the port ballast tank. A whirring could be heard overhead, followed by gurgling water.

"Nice work, Sparky," Pitt said.

As the ballast tank filled, they could feel the submersible shift slightly. But when the tank reached full and the pumps shut off, it still held to its inverted position. The three tried to help with the weight transfer by all standing on the port side. Giordino even jumped up and down a few times, but the submersible held firm.

Ana let out a low sigh. "We're still stuck." The initial sense of claustrophobia crept back into her thoughts, magnified by the stuffy air that was beginning to make her feel light-headed.

"I think we're close," Pitt said.

Giordino retrieved a toolbox and some dive gear and stacked it on the weighted side. "I'm afraid we don't have much else that isn't nailed down to give us an extra push."

Pitt regarded his comment. "Actually, we don't need any more weight, we just need another hand. An extended one, that is."

Giordino looked at him a moment, then grinned. "Of course. We can try pushing ourselves over." He brushed past Pitt to the fuse box and began tracking the wires.

"What do you mean?" Ana asked.

"The submersible has a robotic arm mounted to its base," Pitt said. "If Al can find it some power, we can shove against the *Kerch* and push ourselves over."

The interior of the submersible had grown cold and the air noticeably stale when Giordino pronounced electrical success a few minutes later. "We drained a good piece of our emergency reserves with the ballast pumps," he said. "You might not have much to work with."

"One push is all we need," Pitt said. He leaned against the inverted pilot's seat, reached up to a joystick on the console, and activated the controls. Pitt extended the manipulator from beneath the submersible's prow and extended it laterally until its articulated grip scraped against the *Kerch*'s hull. Ana and Giordino took up positions on the port side and held their breath.

Applying full power to the robotic arm, Pitt did the same. A faint murmur sounded from the hydraulics as the red interior light dimmed from the increased electrical draw. Then a creak came from somewhere on the submersible's frame and the vessel began to tilt. Pitt continued to push with the manipulator, and the submersible leaned to the side until momentum took command. In a slow, easy roll, the submersible tipped onto its side as the occupants scrambled to regain their footing. Sloshing water splashed over the console, and the manipulator controls fell dead.

"I guess that does it for power," Pitt said. "Perhaps it's time we surface."

He opened a floor panel, reached inside, and twisted a pair of T bolts. On the base of the submersible, two lead ballast weights dropped from their cradles and tumbled to the seabed.

Despite its partial flooding, the NUMA submersible tilted off the sand and began to ascend. Ana smiled as Pitt shined his flashlight out the viewport and they watched the *Kerch* fall away beneath them. The black water surrounding them soon gained color, and Ana was relieved to see the return of the murky green soup that at first had frightened her.

The submersible broke the surface minutes later in a rocky sea doused by steady rain. Craning out the viewport, Ana spotted the *Macedonia* rising on the swells a half mile away. Giordino didn't attempt to rewire the radio, seeing the ship turn in their direction and churn the water behind it in full acceleration.

Petar Ralin was pacing the aft deck when the submersible was hooked and lifted aboard. His face melted with relief as Ana climbed out of the hatch, followed by Pitt and Giordino.

Stenseth helped them to the deck. "A longer dive than scheduled," the captain said. He motioned toward the submersible's dented frame and mangled thruster mounts. "You run into a sea monster down there?"

"Well, something that did have some sharp claws." Pitt scanned the gray clouds. "Our salvage friends took a personal interest in our submersible. Are they still about?"

"They steamed off an hour ago."

Ralin stepped up and gave Ana a hug. "We were so worried about you." He noticed a fresh bruise on her head. "What happened?"

"They grabbed us with their salvage claw, banged us against the *Kerch*, then flipped us over. I thought we were trapped, but cooler heads prevailed," she said, nodding at Pitt and Giordino. "Petar, we need to find that salvage ship before they reach port."

"Do they have the HEU?"

She looked at Pitt and he responded for her. "It would seem a pretty good reason to try and kill us." He ran a hand across the dented submersible.

Ana turned to Stenseth. "Can we catch them? Or at least track where they went?"

"They've got a healthy jump on us, but we'll certainly try. Unfortunately, this weather gives us no visibility, and lousy radar coverage."

The group hustled up to the bridge, where Stenseth ordered the helm to bring the ship to top speed. He joined Pitt at the radarscope. "She moved off to the southwest when she left the site."

Pitt adjusted the radar's range to maximum and studied the screen. Large white blotches covered much of it, representing heavy rainfall. At the far edge of the screen, a faint dot pulsed sporadically.

"Could be them," Pitt said, "on a heading of two-four-zero degrees."

"Running for the Bosphorus." Stenseth relayed a course adjustment to the helm.

"Ms. Belova? Mr. Ralin?" Pitt said. "Perhaps you could persuade the Turkish Coast Guard to make a temporary shutdown of the straits?"

"It's *Ana* and *Petar*," she said with a smile. "And, yes, we can do that. Thank you."

Ralin made the call and relayed his success a few minutes later. "The Coast Guard has a vessel standing by near the Yavuz Sultan Selim Bridge, monitoring all southbound traffic. They'll pull her aside when she appears."

"We'll do our best to track her," Stenseth said.

They were able to follow the radar target to the approach of the Bosphorus but lost it amid all the traffic entering and exiting the strait. Continuing heavy rainfall added to the confusion, as the many targets filling the radar screen vanished and reappeared amid the white fuzz of weather distortion. The NUMA crew eventually tracked two southbound targets entering the strait and tried to draw close.

The rain lightened as the vessels reduced speed in the strait, expanding the range of visibility. As the *Macedonia* pushed the imposed speed limit of ten knots, the first target came into view, a Russian-flagged bulk carrier. The *Macedonia* slipped past the slower ship to try to catch a glimpse of the second vessel.

The modern Yavuz Sultan Selim suspension bridge poked through the drizzle ahead as an aged freighter began slipping beneath it.

"Was that the second target?" Ana asked.

"Afraid so," Pitt said.

A radio call to the Coast Guard picket confirmed their disappointment. The salvage ship had not appeared.

"Where could they have gone?" Ana asked.

"They must have turned near the mouth of the Bosphorus," Pitt said, "perhaps for the very purpose of getting lost in the traffic and foul weather. No telling where they might have gone."

"We can take it from here," Ralin said. "We'll issue alerts to all of the friendly seaports on the Black Sea. We have a rough description. There can't be too many vessels that fit her profile. She'll turn up somewhere."

"I think you're right about that," Pitt said.

"We're almost back to Istanbul, so we can drop you there, if you like," Stenseth said.

"That would be fine." Ana turned to Pitt. "We can't thank you enough for your help. I'm confident we'll locate the ship in short order."

"You'll do me a personal favor by putting them out of business," Pitt said. "Especially after what they did to my submersible."

Ana grinned. "The submersible ride was more excitement than I bargained for, but I think I've acquired a taste for the sea."

"Then I guess we can call our foray into the deep a success. Next time you need a ride downstairs, you know where to come."

"I'll remember. Good-bye."

Ana and Ralin climbed to the lower deck and waited for the *Macedonia* to nudge against the Istanbul commercial dock. Jumping ashore, she silently swore to herself never to set foot on a boat again.

Nearly a century earlier, the ten-passenger water taxi had carried diplomats from the Golden Horn of Istanbul to their summer mansions on the upper stretches of the Bosphorus Strait. Its fine mahogany hull was now covered in a thick coat of aged black paint, while its glass-enclosed passenger canopy had been reconfigured with dark-tinted windows. What little brightwork that survived was dull and oxidized. The only opulence that remained from the Italian-built beauty was hidden in the engine bay. The original twin in-line, eight-cylinder engines gleamed with loving care and still snarled as they did when new.

The antique boat charged across the outer harbor of Burgas as dusk began to settle over the Bulgarian city. Its target, the salvage vessel *Besso*, sat moored a half mile from shore. As the boat slowed and pulled alongside, a pair of long-haired crewmen accepted her lines and tied her fast. A stepladder was lowered to accommodate the lone passenger who stepped from the cabin.

Valentin Mankedo boarded the salvage ship with the steady sea legs of a man who had spent the better part of his days on the water. His trim but hardened frame matched the tautness in his bearded face. Stepping purposefully aboard, he ignored the tending crewmen and marched straight to the wheelhouse. He entered an open door to find a muscular, bald man scanning the harbor with binoculars. His scalp, neck, and arms were covered with tattoos.

He glanced at the intruder and set down the binoculars. "I would have come to see you in the morning."

"We are playing with fire, Ilya Vasko," Mankedo said, giving him a cold stare. "There can be no room for error in this operation. Now, tell me what has happened."

"The *Crimean Star* was attacked successfully, as planned. All went well, except that the bridge was able to issue a brief call for help. There was nothing we could have done to prevent it." The bald man rubbed his neck, stroking the head of an octopus tattoo that climbed up from his shoulder. "It was just a single distress call, but it was answered by an American research ship, the *Macedonia*, which happened to be nearby. We tracked her on the radar as she responded. We boarded the freighter but could not locate the crate. It was not on the bridge, as we had been led to believe. In no time, it seemed, the research ship appeared."

"Our port informant in Sevastopol has not always been reliable," Mankedo said. "Why didn't you radio the Americans from the freighter and tell them it was a false emergency?"

"The research ship contacted the Turkish Coast Guard, and we knew they would soon arrive and investigate thoroughly."

Mankedo stared at him through dark eyes that burned with intensity, but he said nothing.

"I took the assault crew off the freighter, affixed an external explosive to the stern, and stood off," Vasko said. "The *Macedonia* sent a few men aboard and tried to make for Istanbul. The explosive charge ended the attempt. The boarders actually did us a favor, as they brought the ship into shallow waters before she sank."

"Did they find and remove the container?"

Vasko shook his head. "They wouldn't have known to look, nor did they have the time to remove it. They had to evacuate after the explosives detonated, as the ship sank quickly."

"So you just monitored the site?"

"We stood off about ten miles while the search and rescue vessels arrived and scoured the area at daylight. We moved back in and stood over the *Kerch* site for some practice drills until it got dark and the rescue ships abandoned the area."

"The *Kerch*?"

"You remember. We worked her about ten years ago. Pulled up an anchor and a steam condenser, if I recall. She's a Russian destroyer. Sank in World War I. She's sitting less than a kilometer from the *Crimean Star*. I've got something to show you from her, down in the machine shop."

"I don't care about that," Mankedo said. "What about the uranium?"

"We wasted a lot of time searching the holds before one of our divers found it in the engine room. He was due to surface, so we had to send down two more men. In the meantime, we picked up a radar contact headed toward the site. I didn't want to leave empty-handed again, so I dropped the claw and opened up the stern deck. The divers bounced in and dragged it within range and we grabbed it with the claw."

"You got it?"

"We had to move fast. We barely got the divers up when we realized the approaching vessel was the same American ship, the *Macedonia*. They radioed us and said the Bulgarian police were aboard. We short-hoisted the claw, still holding the crate, and moved off to the *Kerch* site and waited. They dropped a submersible on the freighter, then went snooping around the site. We pulled in the crate, then roughed up the submersible."

"What do you mean?"

"We dropped the claw back on the *Kerch*, and their submersible was there, poking around. They must have seen the damage to the stern of the *Crimean Star* and realized we'd taken something. I decided we needed to buy more time, so we destroyed the submersible and left the site. The weather was poor, so we feigned toward the strait before turning north. Radar showed that nobody tracked us to Burgas."

Mankedo bit his lower lip. "They can identify the *Besso*."

"They will be too busy recovering the submersible and its dead occupants. We'll be rid of the package before they can possibly locate us and then it will be too late. What will they have? No proof of anything. We were there working the *Kerch*. And I brought back something for you that proves it."

Mankedo brushed the comment aside. "We don't need any-one tracking the *Besso*, now or in the future. I have a lot of money invested in this ship. I can't afford to put it into hiding or move it to Georgia for months on end."

"You'll be able to buy three new ships after we make the de-livery," Vasko said.

"Show me the uranium."

"I can't, at the moment." Vasko pointed at the deck. "Once we moored, I took the claw and dropped the crate onto the sea-floor beneath the moon pool. If someone searches the ship, it's perfectly safe. Once we're ready to make the delivery, we can hoist it quickly and be on our way."

"You confirmed it was the highly enriched uranium?"

"We didn't open the interior container, but it was sealed in a silver case, as described, and the exterior crate was marked with radioactive warnings." He lowered his voice. "Have you made contact with the Iranians?"

Mankedo slowly nodded. "You can be thankful that the transfer will take place on the open seas and not in port some-where." He pulled a slip of paper from his pocket and handed it to Vasko. "Here are the coordinates, thirty miles off of Sinop. The transfer will occur in about three days. I will advise you of the exact time when it is confirmed."

"And we will be taking on a shipment of Fateh-110 surface-to-surface missiles in exchange?"

"Twelve of them. They will be hidden in a barge, which you will take charge of. Then you will head to Ukrainian waters near Sevastopol and await further instructions."

"Back to where the uranium came from, eh?"

"Yes, but to a different side of the fence."

"I will be looking forward to the payday."

Mankedo nodded, his lips hinting at a smile. "The reward will be generous for us all." He stepped to the bridge window and gazed at the first twinkling lights of the city shoreline. "It is too dangerous here. Move up the coast before daybreak and hold station out at sea. I want you out of sight until the deal is done."

"Yes, Valentin, as you say. But first, come. There is something from the *Kerch* I must show you before you leave."

He led Mankedo from the bridge to a cluttered work bay off the stern deck. Centered near some acetylene tanks was the *Kerch*'s concretion-covered safe. "The sands have shifted dramatically around the wreck since we worked her back in '03," Vasko said. "The forecastle is now almost fully exposed. We did some grappling while waiting for the search and rescue teams to go away and we found the captain's safe. The boys think it's still watertight, though I have my doubts. I had one of the men cut away the lock but waited to open it until you got here."

He picked up a crowbar and handed it to Mankedo, who eyed the safe. Scouring the Black Sea's depths for scrap and treasure had been Mankedo's passion for most of his life. It began while fishing off the Burgas coast as a teen when his line had snagged on the bottom. Jumping over the side with a leaky dive mask, he traced his hook to the rail of a sunken trawler. After a dozen more free dives, nearly drowning in the process, he dislodged the vessel's small brass bell and pulled it to the surface. The prize stirred his soul and sent him scouring the local waters from dawn to dusk.

He made a decent living at first, hiring his cousin Vasko and learning to dive, while befriending the local fishermen, who knew where all the good wrecks were. But salvage values waned with the flood of cheap steel from China. With the collapse of the Soviet Union, smuggling soon became much more lucrative, and he had the knowledge and resources to carve out a profitable niche along the western Black Sea. Small arms and drugs were his bread and butter, but recent contacts with a Middle East broker and a wealthy Dutch client involved in the Ukrainian conflict had elevated his business.

Mankedo's salvage company remained operational, mostly as a cover for his smuggling, but also as his ingrained love. Like all good salvors, if there was money to be made at the bottom of the sea, he was first in line to grab it. No matter the value, a relic from the sea always stirred his soul.

He approached the safe with a gleam in his eye. Noting the seam where the welder had cut through the lock mechanism, he wedged in the tip of the crowbar and heaved. The safe door resisted, then opened with a rusty creak.

Both men crowded forward to peer inside. To their surprise, the interior was in pristine condition, the safe having remained watertight for a century. Their excitement dimmed when they saw that the safe was empty save for a thin folder. Mankedo opened it, finding a military report written in Russian.

"No payroll, I'm afraid." Mankedo shook his head. "Not even a few emergency rubles for the captain."

Vasko failed to hide his disappointment. "Nothing but sailing orders, I suppose." He cursed. "I am sorry, Valentin. I had hoped a chest full of gold was waiting for us."

Mankedo tossed aside the crowbar. "Life's riches usually do not come so easily. Let us remain focused on the payoff within our grasp. Keep yourself invisible, Ilya, until the deal is done. We will obtain our riches soon enough."

HE DEPARTED THE SALVAGE SHIP, motoring out of the harbor under the cover of darkness. As he watched the lights of Burgas slip by, he opened the sailing orders from the *Kerch*. The contents startled him and he studied them again carefully to make sure of their details. He pulled out his cell phone and dialed a number.

"Yes?" answered a sleepy voice.

"It's Valentin. I need you to get me everything you have on First World War Russian submarines in the Black Sea Fleet, along with a destroyer named *Kerch*. I mean, everything." He hung up without waiting for a response.

Perhaps, he thought, Vasko had in fact delivered much, much more than a chest of gold.

9

Ralin's head had barely hit the pillow when his cell phone chirped. He didn't have to look at the number to know who was calling. "Good evening, Ana."

"Petar, how soon can you be ready to drive to Burgas?"

"About five minutes."

"I'll be there in three."

Ralin dragged himself to his feet, dressed quickly, and exited his apartment. Ana was waiting on the street out front. Ralin smiled as he climbed into a gray Škoda sedan identical to the one she had crashed two nights earlier. "You mean to tell me that the directorate chief has already entrusted you with another state vehicle?"

"My first stop when we got back to Sofia."

"And he actually said yes?"

"Not exactly," Ana said, shrugging. "But I agreed to let the motor pool administrator take me to lunch next week in exchange for the car."

"Extortion at its finest." He laughed. "So what's this late-night excursion all about?"

"Our salvage ship may have reappeared. The harbormaster in Burgas sighted a vessel moored in the harbor that matches our description. He thinks it arrived just a few hours ago."

"They might have already offloaded the HEU—if they ever had it in the first place."

"It's a possibility. I'm hoping the fact that they didn't bring the ship to dock means it's still aboard."

"What's our plan? Do we have clearance to board her?"

"The Burgas police have the ship under surveillance. I just woke up some people in legal and have requested a search warrant. I propose going aboard at dawn and searching her from top to bottom."

"You're banking on miracles, my dear."

"You don't think there's a chance the HEU is still there?"

"No, not that." He shook his head. "Obtaining a warrant from the Bulgarian judiciary before dawn. The salvage ship could sail to Antarctica and back before that's likely to happen."

"Petar, when did you turn into such a pessimist?"

He smiled. "When I joined the police force."

Leaving Sofia, Ana drove fast through the night, arriving at the port city of Burgas three hours later. They threaded their way through the empty streets, reached the waterfront, and drove to the commercial port terminal. At the complex's security office, a sleepy guard directed them to a small patrol boat docked nearby. Two uniformed city police officers sat in the wheelhouse, monitoring a distant ship with binoculars.

"I am Lieutenant Dukova," the older one said. He dismissed his underling, who scurried off the boat.

"Where is the salvage ship moored?" Ana asked.

Dukova handed her the binoculars. "She's the large vessel in the middle of the bay." He pointed to the lights of a ship a half mile away.

Ana could just make out a myriad of deck cranes under the ship's lights. She nodded at Ralin. "That appears to be her. How long has she been there?"

"Port security said she was identified around six this evening. She was already at anchor, so we are unsure as to her exact arrival. We've had her under surveillance since seven-thirty." He stifled a yawn. "The harbormaster thinks she's a local vessel named *Besso*."

"Any external activity?" Ralin asked.

"A small black crew boat tied up alongside for about an hour at dusk."

"Was anything transferred from the ship?" Ana asked.

"Not that we could see. A lone man boarded and later left by himself. There didn't appear to be any transfer of goods."

"Did you track the crew boat?"

"No. It left the harbor. I didn't have the resources to follow it." Feeling Ana's eyes bore into him, he waved a hand toward a bench seat beneath a wide window. "Why don't you sit down and get comfortable? There's coffee in the galley."

Ana and Ralin sat and took turns watching the *Besso* while loading up on Dukova's coffee.

At half past three, Ralin cleared his throat. "I see some black smoke from the funnel. I think they've started their engines."

Ana pursed her lips and pulled out a cell phone. After a quick call, she shook her head at Ralin. "Still no word on the warrant."

Ralin studied the ship with the field glasses. "I see a crewman on deck. It had been deserted until now. I think she's preparing to leave port."

Dukova nodded. "She could be relocating her mooring, but I doubt it. A half hour to warm the engines and she'll be on her way."

"Where's the rest of your assault team?" Ana asked Dukova.

He looked at his watch. "My team was to assemble at the security shack at four-thirty."

"Can you get them here now?"

Dukova gave her a doubtful look. "I can try."

Ralin kept scanning the salvage ship. "Perhaps we can just track her until we get the warrant."

"I don't have much range with this," Dukova said, patting the boat's wheel. "It could get difficult on the open sea, particularly in poor weather."

"There seems to be some activity in the wheelhouse," Ralin said.

"We can't let them leave." Ana stared at Dukova. "Take us to her."

"We can't board without a warrant," he said. "We're too few for an assault anyway."

"I'll take responsibility. Just get us aboard—unseen, if possible."

Dukova looked to Ralin, but the Bulgarian agent saw the determined look in Ana's eyes and merely nodded.

Dukova cast off the lines and motored the patrol boat from the dock. With its running lights extinguished, he guided the boat in a broad arc around the harbor to approach the salvage ship from her stern. A hundred meters from the ship, he cut speed to a bare idle.

No one was visible on the *Besso*'s stern as they approached at a cat's crawl. Dukova brought the small boat alongside with an expert touch, allowing Ralin to leap aboard from the pilothouse roof. Ana tossed him a line and he tied the boat to a stanchion. The Europol agent climbed aboard with her gun drawn, Dukova following a few seconds later.

They moved forward a few steps and stopped in the shadow of a large generator. Ana jumped when the device suddenly churned to life with a puff of black smoke. Ahead of them, a circle of lights flashed on, illuminating a round moon pool in the center stern deck. Above the pool, the huge grappling claw dangled by a thick cable that wound through a crane. On the far deck, a bulky bald man sat in a glass-sided control booth that managed the crane and claw.

"Let's hold up a minute and see what they're up to," Ralin whispered.

The three law officers clung to the shadows as an array of lights flickered on and the grapple mechanism was lowered into the moon pool.

"Is that the device that wrestled with you in the submersible?" Ralin asked.

Ana nodded as she watched it disappear into the water.

"Nasty-looking thing," he said.

They waited as the bald man manipulated the claw's controls with the aid of a bank of video monitors. Two crewmen in foul-weather jackets appeared and stood by the moon pool. After several minutes, the crane's cable drum reversed direction and began reeling in the line. The claw appeared a short time later and rose out of the water. Clutched in its grip was a gray box the size of a small coffee table.

Ralin nudged Ana's arm. "That has to be it," he whispered.

Ana nodded as a cold chill surged through her. Her intuition was on the mark. Not only had the *Besso* taken the HEU, they had concealed it where a shipboard search wouldn't find it. Now it was right in front of her. She watched as the grapple set the crate on the deck and the two crewmen approached it. "Let's take it," Ana said.

She stepped from the shadows with her gun drawn, Ralin marching alongside. Dukova followed a few steps behind, calling the harbor security office on a portable radio for backup.

The agents stepped to the near edge of the moon pool before they were spotted by a crewman on the far side.

Ana yelled out, *"Politsiya!"*

The crewman dove behind the crate, calling out a warning as he hit the deck. His partner spun around, producing a short-barreled Uzi from beneath his coat, and opened fire.

The law enforcement agents, not expecting the crewmen to be armed, were slow to react. Ralin squeezed off two snap shots, then dove at Ana. He flew into her side as she returned fire, jarring her aim as they both fell.

Dukova was left standing, fumbling with his radio, and paid the price for it. The shooter paused, adjusted his aim, and fired a second burst. The Bulgarian policeman caught the full spray to his torso. He staggered backward a few steps, then fell over dead.

Ana and Ralin were lying in the open on the deck as they returned fire, driving the crewman to lunge behind a stanchion. Ralin eyed a hefty tool bin yards to their right. He nudged Ana and pointed to it. "Go when I fire," he yelled over the renewed whir of the grapple crane.

Ralin rose to a crouch and emptied his clip at the armed crewman, who danced behind the stanchion for cover and immediately fired back. Ralin's aim was better, and he tagged the man in the neck with his last two rounds. Spurting blood from his throat, the dying crewman held his trigger depressed and sprayed the last of his clip toward Ralin as he collapsed. His aim was low, but a bullet ricocheted off a deck grating and struck Ralin in the leg.

Ana was halfway to the tool bin when she saw her partner rise and stagger. "Petar!" she screamed, paying no heed to a dark blur to her side.

Ralin threw up a hand to halt her as he buckled forward. "No!" His eyes screamed in protest. The cry wasn't for his wounds but to stop Ana. He tried to wave her back, but his leg collapsed and he fell forward into the moon pool.

Ana lunged to try to grab him—as the object in her peripheral vision grew large. Too late, she glanced to her side and saw the grapple claw. Having been swung like a pendulum, the huge mechanism was speeding directly toward her.

She dove to the deck, but not in time. The exterior band of one of the grapple's claws caught her across her head and shoulder. She flew across the ship, her world turning to black before she hit the deck.

10

na's body pulsed with a low vibration, which intensi-
fied the shooting pain in her head. She took a leisurely
journey back to consciousness, eventually raising a
hand to feel a throbbing knot on the back of her head. She had
to use her left hand, as her entire right torso was numb. Slowly,
she pried open one eyelid, then the other. Blurry vision gradually
focused on the heels of a scuffed pair of boots rocking in front
of her.

As her senses aligned, she realized it was her head rocking,
not the person wearing the boots. A gentle sea swell was the
cause, as she detected a mixed odor of saltwater and diesel exhaust. The vibration was from the engines of the *Besso*, rattling
the cold deck plate beneath her. She leaned up on her good elbow,
shaking away the dizziness, and looked around.

Multiple high windows and the glow of an overhead radarscope told her she was on the salvage ship's bridge. The man in

boots was talking in low tones with another man at the helm. Ana's mind cleared and she thought of Ralin. Was he dead? Images of him falling into the moon pool made her shudder. She reached for her kidney holster.

Empty.

The sea breeze from an open side door ruffled her hair, and she saw it was just a short crawl away. Escape was her best option, her foggy mind told her. Murmuring voices from the helm signaled the crewmen were still busy. Pulling forward on her side, she made for the doorway, moving at a turtle's pace to avoid detection. She nearly reached it. Her hand was crossing the threshold when a deep voice cut the air.

"Going somewhere?"

Ana looked up to see a hefty bald man, the same one who had operated the grappling claw, step toward her. She tried to flee, but he was already there, grabbing the back of her jacket and yanking her to her feet.

A spasm of pain shot through her right arm and shoulder. The ache raced to her head, and she nearly passed out.

He grinned. "Feeling better after your kiss from the claw?"

Ana flinched from his rancid breath. She saw only malice in his dull, dark eyes, framed by a ragged scar that cut across his brow. The tentacles of an octopus tattoo on his back scalp seemed to reach out for her. She resisted the urge to scream. "I am a Europol police officer," she said. "Release me at once."

Vasko slipped a hand around her upper arm and pinched her with an iron grip. "Release you?" He laughed, poisoning the air with his breath. "That's not how we welcome nosey intruders aboard our ship."

Turning from his imposing face, Ana gazed toward the helmsman, an equally tough-looking character who grinned at her with brown teeth. Beside him, her SIG Sauer pistol lay on a console—tantalizingly close.

"Return this vessel to Burgas at once," she ordered, surprising herself by the strength in her voice. Adrenaline overcame her wooziness, and she punctuated the statement by kicking her knee at Vasko's groin while throwing a punch at his throat.

Vasko's quick reflexes thwarted both moves. As she turned on him, he simply gave her a hard shove. Weak and off balance, she crashed hard into a chart table. Grasping its edge for support, she noticed a pair of brass calipers lying there. Before she could collect herself, Vasko grabbed the back of her shirt and yanked her toward him.

She reached back and grabbed the calipers, hiding them at her side as he spun her around.

Holding her from behind, Vasko slipped his left arm around her throat and squeezed while grabbing a fistful of hair and yanking back her head. "What are you doing aboard my ship?" His lips were just inches from her face.

Pain surpassed fear as Ana struggled to breathe. Vasko slowly loosened his grip, allowing her to gasp for air.

She let her nerves settle before answering. "The highly enriched uranium from the *Crimean Star*—we know you have it."

Vasko showed no reaction. "You were aboard the NUMA vessel?"

Ana looked him cold in the eye. "I was aboard the submersible you tried to destroy."

She caught a flicker of his brow.

"You are mistaken. The uranium is not aboard. We searched but did not find it." He stuck out his chin and looked down his blunt nose at her. "You cost the lives of your two companions by coming aboard."

He released his stranglehold and shoved her across the bridge. His brute strength sent her stumbling to the knees of the helmsman. "Lock her up in an empty cabin."

With a wolfish grin, the helmsman grabbed her and dragged her off the bridge. Ana feared the worst, but he simply led her to a barren cabin and locked the door.

The crewman returned to the bridge and retook his position at the helm. He gazed at Vasko. "What are we going to do with her?"

Vasko stared out the bridge window, his face a mask of concentration. "Same thing we'll do with her dead police friend on the rear deck," he said with an indifferent shrug. "We wait till we're thirty kilometers offshore and throw her over the side."

11

He felt like he was plunging down a well wrapped in a straitjacket. His world grew dark and cold. He couldn't breathe, he couldn't even seem to move. Death tapped him on the shoulder, but he shook off the unwelcome specter. Petar Ralin wasn't yet ready to die.

His mind began to function, shaking off the shock of being shot and plunging through the ship's moon pool. He was about to drown and he knew it. He struggled to get his limbs moving. His legs felt like they were made of lead, but his arms responded. Kicking and flailing, he headed toward a faint light that flickered above. The distance closed quickly, but then he stopped.

The light was from the *Besso*'s moon pool. He couldn't surface there or he would be picked off. He turned away, but had to surface quickly. His lungs ached for oxygen. He kicked harder, then collided with the underside of the *Besso*. Despite the new spasm of pain, he kept moving. Ralin scraped along the hull until he finally broke free and stretched to the surface.

Gasping for air as quietly as he could, he heard voices and movement on the deck above but no gunfire. Dukova was surely dead, but what of Ana? He had to help her, but at the moment that was impossible. He didn't have the strength to climb aboard even if he wanted to. No, he must try to get help.

He waited until the deck turned quiet and his pulse stopped racing, then pushed off from the ship and began paddling toward shore. The lights of Burgas were less than half a mile away, but the distance might as well have been a thousand. In seconds, Ralin became light-headed. He barely had the strength to make headway against the light current. A wave of fatigue from his bleeding leg wound swept over him. But he pushed on, resisting the urge to give up and sink.

A yellow object in the water caught his attention and he struggled toward it. He recognized it as a mooring ball, and, for Ralin, it was a lifesaver. He swam to the metal sphere and grasped its float chain. Clinging for life, he waited until a friendly wave rolled past, lifting him higher. He used the momentum to slide his torso onto the top of the large metal ball and lay outstretched on it like a drowned rat.

Through blurry eyes, he raised his head and gazed at the lights of the *Besso* a short distance away, then promptly passed out.

12

Georgi Dimitov paused to wipe the perspiration from his face as he scanned the Varna commercial docks, eyeing the *Macedonia* at a far berth. Walking past some heavy equipment and stacked commercial cargo, the plump Bulgarian archeologist waddled up to the research ship. He clutched a painting under one arm and tugged a beaten-leather satchel with the other.

A NUMA crewman welcomed him aboard and escorted him to the stern deck, where a tall man in a welder's mask was repairing a seam on the damaged submersible.

Pitt extinguished the welding torch and removed the face shield. "Dr. Dimitov?" he asked.

"A pleasure to meet you, Mr. Pitt." He dropped his satchel and shook hands. "It is an honor to have NUMA's support for my research project." The archeologist glanced at the damaged submersible. "Your submersible . . . is it operational?"

Giordino popped out of the craft's hatch, clutching a loom of electrical wiring, and introduced himself. "She's a little dinged up, but the damage isn't as bad as it looks. Once we replace the thrusters and perform some safety tests, she'll be ready to go—in forty-eight hours, tops."

Pitt nodded. "Our sidelined submersible won't have any impact on our ability to survey."

"I'm happy to hear that," Dimitov said, "as I know your time in the Black Sea is limited."

Pitt eyed the man's painting and satchel and pointed amidships. "Georgi, let's get out of the sun, and you can tell us about the *Fethiye*."

The three men reconvened in a nearby lab, where Giordino helped the archeologist set the painting against a bulkhead. "You don't travel light," Giordino said.

Dimitov smiled. "It's the only known image of the *Fethiye*, painted at the time of her launch in 1766. The curator of the Bulgarian National Art Gallery is a friend of mine and he let me borrow it."

Pitt studied the painting, which depicted a three-masted frigate gliding out of the Golden Horn under full sail. A large red banner fluttered from the stern post, identifying the ship as a vessel of the Ottoman fleet. "A fine-looking ship," Pitt said. "What can you tell us about her?"

"She was built as a fast frigate, in support of the larger ships of the line. She apparently spent some time on station in Alexandria before returning to the service of the Sultan."

"How did she end up sinking in the Black Sea?" Giordino asked.

"Early in the Russo-Turkish War, the Russian Army advanced through what is now Ukraine and Moldova, scoring a major victory at the Battle of Kagul. One of Sultan Mehmet III's wives was at the nearby fortress of Izmail, visiting an injured son, when hostilities drew near. The Sultan dispatched the *Fethiye* from Constantinople to retrieve them from danger. The royal entourage boarded the ship and sailed down the Danube in August 1770, never to be seen again."

"Sunk by the Russians?" Pitt asked.

"A few historians believe so, but there is no historical record to substantiate it. Most believe, as do I, that she was lost in a storm somewhere off the Bulgarian coast."

Pitt shook his head. "Sounds like the makings of a pretty large search area."

"You know better than I the difficulties in locating a lost shipwreck," Dimitov said. "The truth of the matter is, the *Fethiye* could be within a fifty-thousand-square-mile area. I could spend the rest of my life chasing her wake. But I recently discovered some additional information that I think will enable a fruitful search." He opened his leather case and retrieved a photocopied page of a handwritten diary entry.

Pitt saw it was written in Turkish and thought he recognized a notation about weather. "A ship's logbook entry?"

"Precisely," Dimitov said. "It's from an Ottoman merchant schooner named *Cejas*. A researcher at the Bulgarian Academy of Sciences came across it in the school's archives and kindly advised me about it."

"What does it reveal?" Giordino asked.

Dimitov translated, line by line: "Moderate breeze from the

southeast, seas weakening. Departed our mooring off Erulska bluff at noon after weather improved, and resumed passage to Galaţi. Lookout reported concentration of debris to leeward one hour on, including a section of mast with a red *tughra* banner."

"Did they mark their position?" Pitt asked.

"I'm afraid not." Dimitov retrieved a chart of the western Black Sea and unrolled it across the table. "The Erulska bluff proved a bit troublesome, as there are no modern references to such a place along the shoreline. It took a bit of geographical snooping, but we finally found it in an ancient reference to a village north of Varna."

"They would likely anchor close to shore if riding out a storm from the southeast," Pitt said.

"We know they departed this point and were headed up the coast toward Romania," Dimitov said, "so we can make a reasonable guess as to their heading."

"However far they traveled in an hour along that line would put us in the ballpark," Pitt said.

"Exactly. But we don't know their speed, which expands the probable area. A merchant schooner of the typical variety would likely average eight to ten knots, so that gives us a good starting place."

"What we don't know is, when the *Fethiye* sank," Pitt said, "or how far her debris field may have drifted before crossing the *Cejas*'s path."

"Another assumption of our model. The entry states the wreckage seen was concentrated, which leads me to believe she foundered not long before that. We know the state of the sea and wind, so I incorporated some amount of drift in the estimate. It is, of course, a gamble." Dimitov smiled. "But I have zeroed in on a hundred-square-mile area I feel has the highest probability of her position."

"Seems reasonable," Giordino said, eyeing the red grid penciled on the chart. "But how certain are you that the wreckage was actually from the *Fethiye*?"

"A good question. The key is the red banner." Dimitov pointed to the painting. "Note the mainmast."

Giordino nodded. "It has a small red pennant with some sort of swirling logo."

"That's called a *tughra*. It's a calligraphic monogram of the Sultan, representing his reign. Only the Sultan's personal ships would fly such a banner. That's why it was noteworthy in the logbook. They specifically mentioned the *tughra*. The mast seen in the water most certainly came from the *Fethiye*."

"Okay, I'll bite," Giordino said. "So where do we start searching?"

"Now you are talking." Dimitov clapped his hands. "I suggest we begin in the northwest corner of the grid, which is only a few miles up the coast."

Pitt looked at the eager archeologist. "It appears we have a workable search plan. Are you prepared to stay with us for the full survey?"

Dimitov opened his suitcase and pointed to a stack of paperback novels. "I am aware of the tedium associated with an underwater search," he said with a grin.

The *Macedonia* slipped her dock lines within the hour and sailed up the Bulgarian coast, arriving at Dimitov's search grid after dusk. The ship eased to a halt as Giordino launched an autonomous underwater vehicle over the side. The AUV contained a battery of electronic sensors packed into a torpedo-shaped housing that could skim above the seabed while running a preprogrammed route. Pitt supplemented the AUV survey by releasing a towed array sonar behind the *Macedonia*. Both underwater units contained a multibeam sonar system that could provide imagery of a shipwreck, or any other object of size, that protruded from the seafloor.

Dimitov joined Pitt and Giordino on the ship's bridge to monitor the real-time results from the towed sonar. After a few hours of watching a drab, undulating sea bottom pass by on a large screen, he stood and retrieved one of his paperbacks. "Good night, gentlemen."

Giordino raised an eyebrow. "Retiring from the fight already?"

"Temporarily, my friend, just temporarily. The *Fethiye* has been resting for over two centuries. I'm sure she will still be there for the hunting tomorrow." The archeologist gave a formal bow, then stepped out the bridge door and into the night.

13

imitov's words proved true, but just barely. Giordino was manning the *Macedonia*'s towed array sonar system at five in the morning when a scraggly, oblong shape scrolled across the monitor. He saved an image of the object and continued the survey until Pitt and Dimitov stepped onto the bridge two hours later.

"Picked up an interesting target on the last survey lane," he said as Pitt handed him a cup of hot coffee.

"Can you show it to us?" Dimitov crowded close to the monitor.

Giordino retrieved the image and magnified it, revealing details of a largely intact shipwreck.

Dimitov's eyes grew wide, then he shook his head. "It appears to be a sailing ship, but it must be more modern. You can see a capstan, the rudder, even a mast lying across the deck. It is in too good a condition to have sunk two hundred and fifty years ago. Still, an intriguing wreck."

"What's the depth of the target?" Pitt asked.

"Just under seventy meters."

"That's in the ballpark for the anoxic zone," Pitt said. "The lower depths of the Black Sea are deprived of oxygen and therefore lack destructive marine organisms. There've been a handful of ancient shipwrecks discovered at that depth in an excellent state of preservation. If this wreck is lying in a low-oxygen state, it could in fact be a nicely preserved *Fethiye*."

"The dimensions look close to the known specs of the *Fethiye*," Giordino said. "It certainly gives the appearance of a three-masted frigate."

"Yes, I can see it," Dimitov said with growing excitement. "It would be too good to be true. Can we investigate further?"

"It certainly warrants some attention," Pitt said. "What are our options, Al?"

"The submersible is dry-docked until we receive some parts from the States. That leaves dropping an ROV over the side or putting down some divers on mixed gas."

"I vote for the latter." Pitt had a gleam in his eye. "You up for joining the party?"

Giordino grinned. "Like a New Year's Eve reveler."

Dimitov looked puzzled. "You mean, you two are going to dive the wreck?"

"Why leave the fun and glory to someone else?" Pitt said.

The *Macedonia* returned to the target site for a few additional passes with the sonar to better mark its position. The crew then retrieved the towed system and dropped a buoy alongside. The ship moved off and took up a stationary safety position a few hundred meters away to await the return of the AUV.

Wearing cold-water dry suits, Pitt and Giordino climbed into a Zodiac, which was lowered over the side. Pitt raced the inflatable to the buoy, where Giordino attached a mooring line. Each pulled on a Dräger Mk25 rebreather system, which kept them from having to carry multiple tanks of mixed-gas air while allowing for extended bottom time.

Giordino rinsed out his dive mask before fitting it over his head. "You think Dimitov got lucky?"

"She looks pretty good on sonar, but the Black Sea is littered with wrecks. We ought to be able to tell soon enough."

"He's pretty excited about it. You sure there's no treasure aboard?"

"None that the history books speak of."

"I'll bet you a beer there's something interesting on that wreck."

Pitt nodded. "Let's go see what it is." He slipped his regulator between his teeth and rolled backward off the Zodiac into the water. Checking that his rebreather unit was working properly, he purged his buoyancy compensator and slid slowly under the waves. Giordino splashed into the water beside him a moment later, and the two men kicked for the bottom.

The water grew cold and dark as they reached the hundred-foot mark, and each clicked on an underwater light. They were immune to the cloistering effect of the black depths, having experienced hundreds of dives in every imaginable condition. Pitt felt a jolt of excitement at the prospect of exploring a shipwreck that had lain undiscovered for over two centuries.

They followed the drop line that tailed from the buoy until reaching the bottom, at slightly over two hundred feet. At that depth, they had less than twenty minutes of bottom time.

Pitt spotted a dark shadow to their side and led the way, hovering a few feet off the muddy, featureless seafloor. His light showed a large pronged object. He swam closer and saw it was an anchor. Still secured by its thick chain, the black iron mass hung from a ruddy-colored hull. The anchor, like the wreck itself, was covered by a heavy layer of brown silt.

Pitt followed the anchor chain up toward the bow rail and turned his light across the deck. Despite the layers of silt, he could see the wreck was an old sailing ship in an excellent state of preservation. Giordino joined him as he kicked his way to a fallen mast and fanned away the sediment. Fragments of rope and sail lay on the deck, partially preserved in the oxygen-deprived water.

Giordino activated a small video camera strapped to his rebreather harness and began filming details of the wreck as they worked their way aft. A pair of intricately carved cabin doors with glass inserts caught his attention on the main deck, while Pitt investigated a swivel gun mounted on the port rail. They were astounded at the condition of the ship, as most wooden shipwrecks disintegrate into a debris-strewn mound after just a few years. Seeing just a few metal fixtures, Pitt was certain the vessel was well over two centuries old.

The two met at the helm on the quarter deck, looking for the jackpot. Even if well-preserved, a wooden shipwreck with few known unique details was a difficult challenge to identify. The dead giveaway was the ship's bell, often engraved with the vessel's name.

They found the helm's large spoked wheel still affixed and upright on its frame, but there was no bell alongside it. Giordino felt Pitt tap his arm and point to the main deck. A cone-shaped item lay on its side near the bulkhead. It had to be the bell, having fallen after the disintegrating mounting collapsed under its heavy weight.

Pitt beat his partner to the object, set it upright, and brushed away the sediment. Giordino had his camera ready as the silt settled and a bronze bell emerged, complete with Turkish lettering across its base. He filmed it from all sides, then turned and gave Pitt a thumbs-up.

Pitt checked his orange-faced Doxa dive watch and saw their bottom time had nearly expired. Motioning toward the surface, he waited for Giordino's acknowledgment, then kicked up from the quarter deck. Shining his light a final time across the wreck, he hesitated at the sight of something on the aft deck. Giordino followed as he turned and swam toward the object, concerned by its human shape.

It was indeed a body, lightly covered with silt. Approaching from the side, Pitt swished his hand above it to remove the thin coating. The probability of finding a human body lying perfectly preserved on the deck of the frigate after two hundred and fifty years seemed astronomical. Still, he couldn't help but expect an eighteenth-century seaman to emerge from the murk, dressed in a loose-sleeved blouse, pantaloons, and buckled shoes.

But as the water cleared, he instead faced the body of a blue-eyed airman, grimacing at him, in a twentieth-century flight suit.

14

The first thing Ana did was vomit.

The fear, tension, and stress, combined with the ship's rolling, had sent her stomach into convulsions. A miniature cabin sink caught the discharge, and she was thankful for some running cold water to rinse her face. Feeling drained but suddenly calm, she took in her surroundings.

The locked, windowless cabin wasn't much larger than a closet. A pair of built-in bunk beds competed with the washbasin for the room's square footage. Her head still pounding, Ana shuffled to the lower bunk, lay on the wafer-thin mattress, and closed her eyes.

Her headache eased marginally, allowing her to weigh her circumstances. The salvage ship most certainly had recovered the highly enriched uranium. Why else would their boarding meet with such a vicious response? She winced as she pictured Ralin plunging into the moon pool. The bald, tattooed thug who ran the ship seemed capable of anything, brushing off the murder of her comrades like they were mosquitoes. If only the Bulgarian SWAT team had arrived. With an adequate team, things would have played out much differently. She knew she was at fault for rushing in without support. Now the port policeman and Ralin were dead. She fought back tears at the thought.

After a moment, she pried open her eyelids and stared at the dusty underside of the top bunk. She knew she was also doomed. As a witness to the others' deaths, she wouldn't be allowed to live. Ana took a few deep breaths, and the throbbing slowly eased from her skull, giving notice to a sharp pain in her backside. She was being jabbed by the points of the calipers she had pocketed on the bridge.

She pulled the device from her pocket, held it before her face, and touched its needle points. It wasn't much as a weapon, but it could serve as a useful tool. She rose from the bunk and studied the cabin door lock. It was a simple dead bolt, keyed on both sides.

She stared at the lock, contemplating her choices. There was no sense in lingering. She had been thrown in the cabin as a temporary reprieve. She might have days to live—or just a few hours. There was no reason to wait and surrender to her fate.

Spreading open the calipers, she jammed one of its points into the keyhole and twisted and prodded. She labored for twenty minutes, realizing the rounded point was a poor candidate to pick a lock. She yanked out the calipers, threw them on the bed, and gave the cabin door a hard kick.

The door rattled with an encouraging sound. She leaned her head against the door and rapped it with the heel of her palm.

There was a tiny echo, matched by a slight vibration on her hand. It was an inexpensive hollow-core door. Ana smiled at her luck.

She sat on the bunk for a moment, mapping her next moves. Her heart raced over the danger involved, but the greater risk was to do nothing. She listened at the door to ensure an empty corridor, backed across the tiny cabin, and took a deep breath. Sprinting forward in the confined space, she leaped up, extended her legs, and thrust her feet against the door.

The door splintered but held loosely together. Ana regained her footing and waited, expecting to hear a cabin door open and close down the corridor, but it was quiet. Then she gave the door another hard stomp near the handle. The door separated from the lock and flew open.

Ana stepped into the corridor, cleaned up the splinters, then refit the door. At a passing glance, it would look intact. She moved aft toward an open side hatch that drew a cool, outside breeze. She swayed with the rolling ship as she approached it and peered out.

Beneath a canopy of low clouds, an empty expanse of the Black Sea spread beyond the ship's rail. A brown ripple of land on the horizon indicated they were either following the coastline or had just recently left Burgas.

She stuck her head through the hatch to survey the deck—and smacked into the chest of a passing crewman. The young deckhand wore the grease-stained coveralls of an engineer and toted a toolbox. He stared at Ana in surprise.

Keyed up for a confrontation, Ana grabbed him by the lapels and lunged to the side. Burdened by the heavy toolbox, the crewman tripped over Ana and fell awkwardly to the deck. Ana sprang up and kicked the man hard on the chin. Dazed, he was unable to defend himself from a flurry of additional kicks that finally laid him out.

Gasping for air, Ana spun around, expecting the short brawl had drawn attention. But the deck was empty. She grabbed the crewman by his feet, dragged him through the hatch, and left him in the corridor.

She knew her time was now even more limited. She rushed onto the deck, moving aft in search of a dinghy or shore boat. The moon pool sloshed to her right. Across it, an inflatable boat lay secured to the roof of an elevated stores bin. There was still no one around, so she sprinted around the moon pool. She made it halfway, then stopped in her tracks.

There it was.

She stared at the gray crate that had been pulled from the *Crimean Star*, presumably containing the HEU. The crew hadn't bothered to move it after their hasty departure from Burgas—or had left it ready to be ditched underwater again if need be. Ana put a hand on the box and gave it a shove, feeling a heavy object inside.

Her heart began to race again. She stepped to the inflatable boat, untied its lashings, then pulled it flat to the deck. She checked the interior, found a full fuel tank, and connected its rubber line to the small outboard motor. Across the deck was a large cable winch, still attached to the crate. It was too conspicuous to use. She found a small deck winch near the rail, likely for use with the boat. Her suspicions were confirmed when she found latches on the nearby rail that allowed a section to be lowered to the deck.

She quickly popped the latches, dropped the rail, and returned to the winch. Locating its power control, she activated the machine and fiddled with its control levers. She discovered the cable take-up and threw it into reverse. Then she stepped around the winch arm, grabbed the unwinding cable hook, and pulled it across the deck. Ana dragged it past the inflatable to the HEU crate, which still had a rope harnessed around it. She unhooked the main winch line, snapped on her own lift hook, and ran back to the controls. She reeled in the loose cable and watched as it dragged the crate across the deck. She pulled it close to the Zodiac, then halted the controls.

She muscled the crate into the inflatable and then reattached the line to a lift cable on the craft. She returned to the crane, hoisted the small boat off the deck, and swung the inflatable over the open rail until it dangled above the water. She was easing out the cable when a cry rang out behind her.

Hailing from across the deck, it was not a friendly call. The crewman who'd earlier wielded the Uzi was pointing at her and yelling. He wasn't armed but gave her a menacing look and began running toward her. Ana pushed the cable release to high speed and stepped to the rail.

She didn't stop to watch the inflatable drop to the sea nor did she hesitate at the rail. She had one chance only to escape and she didn't falter. She stepped to the edge of the deck, grabbed the unspooling cable, and leaped over the side.

It was a fifteen-foot drop, and the inflatable reached the water first. Dropping hard, the Zodiac bounced violently, before jerking backward from the hull of the ship. Ana arrived a second later, catching the boat on the upswing as she struck an inflated side tube. Any later and she would have splashed into the water. Instead, she bounded up and into the bow, losing her grip on the cable as she crashed to the boat's deck.

She tried to stand and re-grab the cable but was knocked to her knees when the inflatable careened against the ship's hull. Despite the unreeling cable, the speed of the ship yanked the inflatable like a drunken water-skier. Ana rose to her knees, grabbed the cable hook, and pulled, but the tension was too tight. She looked up and saw that the crewman had reached the crane controls and reversed the line.

Ana remained patient as the boat was viciously tossed around. The savagery would be her savior. She clung to the hook, riding the bucking boat beneath her. She watched as the inflatable suddenly jerked forward, momentarily easing the cable's tension. Instantly, she released the hook and heaved it skyward.

The inflatable fell back off the ship as the hook rattled against its sides. Ana moved to the stern and primed the outboard motor as she had seen her father do a thousand times, praying it would start. Luckily, with only two heaves on its pulley starter, the motor wheezed to life. She twisted the throttle grip to full and spun the boat toward shore.

She sped fifty meters before daring a glance over her shoulder, only to see the *Besso* gradually turn in her direction.

15

The dark smudge of land grew closer with agonizing slowness. A mile behind Ana, the gray silhouette of the *Besso* plowed after her, foam sputtering off the bow. With every passing second Ana was putting more distance between herself and the salvage ship. Of greater concern was a dark object off the ship's bow that was quickly growing closer. She knew the *Besso* had more than one shore boat, and by the looks of it, the one chasing her was both bigger and faster.

Steering toward the closest apparent landfall, Ana spotted a ship slightly off her port bow. Over her shoulder, the pursuing boat had drawn closer. She could now identify it as a dirty orange Zodiac, appearing to be carrying three men.

The sight made her feel weak again and she momentarily lost her grip on the throttle. Twisting the rubber handle with an aching hand, she looked across the waves and saw a sudden cause for hope. The vessel ahead showed no wake. And then there was its color.

The ship was painted turquoise.

It was too good to be true. She recalled Pitt telling her the NUMA ship would be surveying near Burgas—and there it was.

Her joy was short-lived when the HEU crate in front of her began to disintegrate in a shower of splinters. Startled, then confused, she looked back and saw muzzle flashes from the pursuing Zodiac. The noise from her outboard was muffling the gunfire.

Ana ducked as low as she could, catching a sliver of wood in her cheek. But her attention was focused on a seam of holes appearing in one of the boat's inflatable chambers.

As the deflating section sagged, she felt her speed drop. She was still yards ahead of the pursuing Zodiac, but the gunmen were no longer following directly behind. Instead, their boat was angling to her left. The orange inflatable would easily intercept her before she could reach the turquoise ship.

She looked at the approaching shoreline, but it also loomed out of reach. Then she noticed another boat, a small inflatable like hers, moored to a float. It was bobbing, empty, on the ocean, and had a large motor. If nothing else, at least it was fully inflated.

As another section of her own boat drooped from the gunfire, she nosed the bow toward the mystery boat and held her breath.

16

Pitt broke the surface as a light rain began to pelt the sea. A rising surge of bubbles announced the appearance of Giordino a few seconds later. Having followed their shot line to the surface, they found their inflatable boat tied off a few feet away.

Both men bellied into the boat and had begun removing their dive gear when they noticed a roar of approaching boats, followed by the popping sound of gunfire. Pitt turned to see a faded orange inflatable with three men chasing a smaller black Zodiac piloted by a lone woman with flowing black hair. He tensed, realizing it was Ana.

She was barely a hundred yards away, driving directly for them in a deflating boat that wallowed and was slapping the waves.

Again there came a muzzle flash from the orange inflatable, which was between them and the *Macedonia*.

"Al, cut the mooring line," Pitt said.

As Giordino released the bow line, Pitt started the outboard and gunned the throttle. He turned the boat toward Ana, quickly closing with her. She and Pitt cut their motors as the boats pulled alongside, bow to stern, and Giordino secured them momentarily.

"Need a lift?" Pitt asked.

Ana kicked open the splintered wooden crate and yanked out a heavy metal cylinder, then staggered to the gunnel. Giordino extended his arms and hoisted it into his boat.

"It's the HEU." She jumped off her shattered inflatable and into the NUMA boat.

Pitt gunned the motor again, turning away from the pursuing boat.

"Get down!" Ana said. "They have guns."

As if on cue, a burst of gunfire rippled the water alongside them.

"Is that the salvage ship?" Pitt motioned toward a distant vessel.

"Yes, the *Besso*. Petar and I found her in Burgas and boarded her this morning. Petar is dead." Her eyes welled with tears. "They took me to sea with them, but I escaped. As we suspected, they had the HEU."

"And I think they'd like to have it back," Giordino said as another burst of fire slapped the waves.

Pitt eyed the *Macedonia* a half mile to the south. He turned toward the ship, but the orange inflatable did likewise. He held his course for a moment, gauging the other boat's speed.

"I tried for the *Macedonia*, too," Ana said, "but they drove me away."

Pitt gave her a half smile. "They're not going to let us go home, but I think we can stretch them to shore."

Ana stared at Pitt. He was as calm as a man sipping a beer in a hammock.

He eased the bow to the west, casually watching the pursuing boat follow suit. The boats were now less than a hundred yards apart, but Pitt could see that they were equally matched. The pursuers ceased shooting, conserving their ammunition amid the difficulties of accurate marksmanship on a bouncing boat now pelted by a steady rain.

Aboard the NUMA Zodiac, Giordino began pitching their depleted air tanks over the side to lighten their load and perhaps create an obstacle for the chase boat. Next he uncoupled the lead weights from their dive belts and began flinging them toward the pursuers. The pilot of the chase boat ignored the barrage until one of the weights bounced off his inflatable's bow and struck him on the shoulder. Temporarily losing his grip on the throttle, he swerved to avoid Giordino's final artillery shells, adding a few precious seconds to the chase.

Pitt peered through the falling rain at the green coastline, spotting the amber-colored buildings of a town to the south. It was Balchik, a small tourist village he'd seen on the charts a few miles up the coast from Burgas. Pitt angled toward the town. Within a few minutes at full throttle, they approached the entrance to its harbor.

Giordino spotted renewed muzzle flashes from the pursuing boat. "Incoming."

Pitt crouched low behind the motor, and Ana and Giordino sprawled on the floorboards.

"They don't want us to reach port," Ana said.

Several bullets found their mark. One ricocheted off the engine housing, while four more punctured the side inflatable compartments. Pitt ignored the gunfire and aimed for a freighter tied up at the lone commercial dock.

They raced into the harbor, the gunfire increasing as Pitt approached the freighter. He drove along its length, then cut sharply across its bow. He moved straight to the side of the dock, cutting the motor just before they collided with the wharf. Giordino sprang from the bow as they mashed into a support pole, clambered onto the elevated dock with a bow line in hand, and yanked the boat to a halt.

"Everybody off the bus," he said. He reached down and grabbed Ana's outstretched hand and pulled her brusquely onto the dock.

"Wait," she said, "the uranium."

Pitt lifted up the container and heaved it up to Giordino, who hoisted it onto his shoulder as if it were made of feathers. Pitt scampered onto the dock and surveyed their surroundings. To their right, the Greek-flagged freighter was awaiting a thick stack of shipping containers. To their left, the dock fed onto a busy waterfront street that circled into the town center. At the moment, the entire wharf was empty. Lunch hour had arrived moments before, and the local dockworkers were congregated in a break shack, out of the rain, eating fish stew and beans.

Pitt got a gleam in his eye. The dock's loading derrick was still harnessed to a full container atop the stack.

He pointed to the road. "See if you can find some transport out of here. I'll try and slow them down."

Ana hesitated, but Giordino grabbed her arm and pulled her toward the street. "You heard the man. No time for debate." They took off at a run, Giordino leading Ana toward a dilapidated pickup truck parked near the dock entrance.

Pitt ran to the lift crane's controls and fired up its diesel motor. Deciphering its controls, he hoisted the shipping container and pivoted the crane head toward the ship's hold. But he kept rotating the crane until it dangled over the edge of the dock.

Pitt had no time to spare, as the orange inflatable roared up to the same spot as the NUMA Zodiac. Pitt jammed the cable release and the yellow container crashed to the lip of the dock, then teetered upright and over the side. The blunt end slammed onto the bow of the inflatable, crushing one gunman. The other two were hurled forward as the boat jackknifed under the container's weight. One slammed face-first into the container, falling limp into the water with a broken neck. Vasko was more fortunate. Flung against the dock pylons, he managed to grab a steel ladder midair.

The crashing prompted a group of dockworkers to come investigate. A distressed crane operator ran up to the cab, waving his arms, as Pitt climbed out.

Pitt shrugged. "The controls, they're a little loose," he said.

He turned toward the street but froze when the glass windshield of the crane cab shattered next to him. At the edge of the wharf, a burly, bald, tattooed man was pulling himself onto the dock, holding a smoking pistol aimed at Pitt.

17

Ilya Vasko had recognized the tall, dark-haired man climbing from the crane as the pilot of the inflatable that aided Ana. He knew the shipping container that had dropped on him was no accident. With his assault rifle at the bottom of the harbor, he pulled a pistol from a holster. The best he could do was to fire a snap shot from the ladder before climbing onto the dock and catching his breath. He stood for a moment, shaking off the impact of his ejection from the boat, and glanced at the water. The bodies of his two crewmen floated alongside the punctured inflatable.

Vasko steadied himself against the dock and raised his pistol. A dozen dockworkers scrambled for cover as he scanned the wharf for the tall man with black hair.

Pitt had already jumped away from the crane and was sprinting down the dock. He zigzagged around a forklift and some assorted crates as the pop-pop-pop of gunfire sounded. A pair of bullets whistled past, striking a fence post just in front of him. He searched ahead for Giordino and spotted his partner, waving from the driver's seat of a dilapidated pickup.

It was a Romanian-built Dacia, at least forty years old, used for light duty around the port. The HEU container lay in the truck's open bed, and Ana sat in the passenger seat, urging Pitt on with her eyes. Blue exhaust smoke indicated Giordino had already found the keys and started the old truck.

"Go!" Pitt shouted while still a few yards away.

Giordino threw it into gear and rolled forward as another volley sounded from Vasko's pistol. Pitt caught up to the truck and dove into its bed as a shot tore through the tailgate, followed by another that shattered the cab's rear window.

Pitt called up to the cab as he lay low. "Fastest you could find?"

"Only thing I could find," Giordino called back, "with keys."

The old truck gained speed, and Giordino wheeled it through an open gate at the end of the dock and turned onto the main waterfront drive. Traffic was light, and he was able to accelerate ahead. Police sirens sounded as Vasko ran into the middle of the road after them. A college student on a motorcycle approached from the south and Vasko stood, rock-like, in his path, his gun raised. The startled rider skidded to a stop just a few feet away.

"Off!" Vasko stepped forward and grabbed the handlebars.

The student jumped off and backed away with his hands raised, then turned and ran. Vasko tucked his gun into his waistband and climbed aboard.

A quarter mile ahead, Pitt watched the scene as Giordino drove into the center of town. Like most Bulgarian seaside villages, Balchik was filled with stodgy but colorful buildings and shops that summer tourists found inviting. The truck wheeled around a large traffic circle with a marble statue of the Greek god Dionysus in the center, then sped past a row of cafés and coffee shops.

Pitt moved to sit with his back to the cab. "Gunman's on a bike in pursuit," he told Giordino.

"Where are those police cars?" Giordino asked.

Pitt listened to the wailing sirens in the distance. "Coming from the other side of the dock, I'm afraid."

"Figures."

Pitt glanced at a man lugging a sack of flour down the street, then turned to Giordino. "Pull to a quick stop, then go up a block and circle back around to the traffic circle. We ought to be able to catch the police there."

Giordino stood on the brakes. "Okay, but why the stop?"

When he got no response, he turned back to see that both Pitt and the HEU canister were gone.

Ana spied Pitt jogging down the sidewalk. "He jumped out!"

"Taking the heat off us," Giordino said.

He followed Pitt's instructions, accelerating up to the next block and turning left. They could hear the high-revving motorcycle behind them as it speeded through traffic.

Vasko entered the traffic circle, his eyes on the old pickup turning left up ahead. Bursting past some slower cars, he swept around the circle, then braked hard at a familiar sight. It was Pitt, walking across the circle as if on an afternoon stroll, except for the jaundiced eye he leveled at Vasko. Though his presence was unnerving, his hands were empty and he posed no threat, so Vasko let off the brakes and sped forward.

Giordino pushed the truck through a second left turn before the motorcycle loomed up in his rearview mirror. As the traffic cleared, he swerved the truck back and forth across the road to prevent the rider from pulling alongside.

Vasko slowed behind the pickup, removed his pistol, and awkwardly fired a few shots at the cab with his left hand. The vehicles reached the end of the block, and Giordino turned left once more, heading for the traffic circle, now in view. As he turned, Vasko had a clear shot and pumped two rounds into the engine compartment.

Steam erupted from under the hood, while a thick trail of oil spilled from beneath. Giordino held the accelerator to the floor despite the eruption and the engine's clatter. The spray coated the windshield, forcing Giordino to drive blindly toward the traffic circle. Distracted, he lost track of Vasko, who roared alongside the truck's passenger side. The gunman gazed into the truck bed and saw no HEU canister. He pulled alongside Ana's door and looked inside for the uranium while pointing his pistol at her.

Ana screamed and Giordino snapped the dying truck to the right. Vasko was already on the brakes, saving himself from being sideswiped. The truck rumbled on, its occupants again hearing the whine of the motorcycle. But, this time, the sound grew more distant.

Sailing blind into the traffic circle, Giordino poked his head out the side window just in time to see a sidewalk in front of him. As he applied its worn brakes, the truck bounded up and over the curb and skidded across a patch of grass. Amid a cloud of steam, it smacked into a fountain at the base of Dionysus and ground to a halt.

Giordino turned to Ana. "You okay?" he asked over the wail of approaching sirens.

"Yeah." Ana rubbed her shoulder, which had struck the dashboard. "Is he gone?"

"Yep." He grinned. "Couldn't keep up with Speedy Al."

They climbed out of the truck into the glare of flashing lights from three police cars. Pitt stood in the center of the road and directed the lead cars after the motorcycle, while the third car screeched up alongside the battered truck. As the policemen hopped out with guns drawn, Ana and Giordino threw their hands in the air. Producing her Europol badge, she quickly defused the tension and explained their situation.

Pitt stepped over to check on his friends. "Glad you made it back in one piece."

"Not so sure about the truck." Giordino patted one of the smoking pickup's fenders.

"I thought the police were going to come through here," Pitt said. "I hoped I could organize a welcome party by the time you came back around. Guess my timing was a bit off."

"Close enough to save our skin," Giordino said.

Ana joined them after an animated conversation with the police officers.

"They were alerted by the *Macedonia*," she said, "and the dockworkers sent them after their stolen truck."

Pitt nodded. "Plenty of confusion to go around."

Giordino looked at the puddle of oil next to a front wheel. "I guess we owe the port a new truck."

"NUMA might manage to fund a replacement," Pitt said.

"Glad to hear it," Ana said. "I'm already down a vehicle, with my boss in Sofia." She peered into the back of the truck and turned pale. "The HEU canister! Did he get it?"

"No." Pitt gave a reassuring grin. "I put it someplace he wouldn't be able to reach easily."

Ana looked around at the shops and apartments. "Did you hide it in a house or café?"

"No, I hid it in plain sight." Pitt winked and pointed over his shoulder.

Ana and Giordino followed his finger toward the statue and looked up.

Cradled in the outstretched arms of Dionysus, a dozen feet off the ground, was the canister of deadly uranium.

18

The *Macedonia* eased into Balchik a short time later, arriving amid a glow of flashing police lights along the waterfront. Captain Stenseth found a ship's berth near the main dock, where he watched a police dive team retrieve two bodies from the water. The divers then assisted some agitated dockworkers in lifting a yellow container from the depths in front of a large freighter.

Once his ship was moored, the captain went ashore, taking a quick peek at the saturated bodies that had been hastily covered with a tarp. Relieved to see they bore unfamiliar faces, he turned his attention toward the lights of police vehicles near the town center. Walking the few blocks to the main traffic circle, he jumped aside as a fire department ladder truck roared up onto the sidewalk and stopped beside a tall marble statue. The statue itself was surrounded by a growing throng of policemen.

Stenseth made his way to the opposite side, where a battered pickup truck was mashed against a fountain at the statue's base. Its tailgate was down, and two men in wetsuits were seated on it, speaking to the police.

The *Macedonia*'s captain approached Pitt and Giordino with a relieved smile. "You boys didn't tell me you were planning some sightseeing after your dive."

"We just offered a ride to a local hitchhiker." Giordino pointed toward Ana, who was arguing with several Bulgarian police authorities.

"Ana?" Stenseth said. "I didn't recognize her when the mayhem started. Bad timing on our part, as we were well off your dive site recovering the AUV when you surfaced."

"As I requested," Pitt said, "though I kind of wish you hadn't listened to me."

"We saw the gunfire and tried to give chase, but we couldn't match your speed. I knew things were bad when the salvage ship materialized out of the mist. I take it Ana was aboard the vessel?"

Pitt nodded. "She tracked the *Besso* to the harbor at Burgas— and was abducted during a raid. Ralin apparently wasn't so lucky."

Stenseth shook his head. "We alerted the Coast Guard, who in turn called the local police when you were spotted entering port."

"A good thing, too," Giordino said. "Our beloved chariot here was about to give up the ghost, with us in it, when the police finally appeared."

"I saw at the wharf that you got two of them."

Giordino smiled. "Dirk dropped a load on them."

Stenseth pointed to the bullet holes that peppered the truck. "And the third gunman?"

"Got away on a motorcycle," Pitt said. "Hopefully, the police will catch him." He looked to the dock. "Any trouble from the *Besso*?"

"No. They ran a parallel course to shore with us, then turned back to sea when we got close to Balchik."

Ana extricated herself from the policemen and stepped to the truck. Her body sagged under the weight of the turmoil of the last two days, but her eyes smiled at the sight of the three NUMA men. "It took some conniving, but I talked the police out of arresting the two of you and impounding your ship."

"I guess this means a ticker-tape parade is out of the question?" Giordino asked.

"There is the matter of a stolen pickup truck and a sunken cargo container that has a few of the locals upset. They obviously don't understand what was at stake, and even the police are slightly skeptical. They've asked that you and your ship remain in Balchik until they confirm the contents of the HEU canister."

Pitt frowned. "How long is that likely to take?"

"They've called in an Army bomb disposal unit to transfer the canister to a military installation near Sofia. I suspect we won't have an answer until late tomorrow."

"So be it. You're welcome to bunk aboard the *Macedonia* tonight, if you're going to be detained here yourself," Pitt said.

"Thank you. It appears I will be coordinating enforcement response with the local authorities for a bit longer."

"There's one thing I don't understand," Stenseth said. "If the HEU was aboard the *Besso*, where is the canister now?"

Pitt gave him a crooked smile and pointed at the statue. They all watched as a ladder was extended from a fire truck to the marble Dionysus, a replica of a statue found in the waters off the town centuries earlier. A pudgy fireman climbed the ladder and nervously collected the canister. When he descended, he was surrounded by a circle of policemen, who made him set the canister on the ground as they huddled around. Nearly an hour later, a bomb disposal unit from the Bulgarian Army arrived to collect it. They loaded it into a van, then roared out of town with an armed escort, leaving the townspeople to gawk at the two divers on the pickup truck and contemplate what strange things they had brought to town.

IT WAS EARLY EVENING before Ana and the NUMA men returned to the *Macedonia* under a police escort. They stopped to examine the damaged container now sitting on the dock alongside the two mangled Zodiacs.

Thankful to board ship, they cleaned up for dinner after Ana was shown to a guest cabin. An hour later, she bounded into the wardroom, refreshed from a shower and a short rest. Wearing a borrowed ship's jumpsuit, with her hair hanging freely, she raced to the table where Pitt, Giordino, and Stenseth awaited her.

"You look like a new person," Pitt said.

Her eyes misted with joy. "I received a message from my office with fabulous news. Petar is alive!"

"I knew he was a tough cat," Giordino said.

"He somehow survived his gunshot wound and was rescued in the harbor. He's recovering at a hospital in Burgas."

"That is indeed happy news." Pitt stood and offered her a chair. "We'll run down to Burgas and check on him once we're cleared to leave port. I'm sure he'll be happy to know you are all right."

Georgi Dimitov entered the room and approached the table. "There you two are. Safe from your adventure, I'm glad to see."

As Dimitov took a seat at the table, Pitt introduced him to Ana.

"I've heard all kinds of rumors aboard ship about your chase today," Dimitov said. "Pray tell, what was all the excitement about?"

"Ana got caught up with some smugglers that happened our way," Pitt said. "We helped her to shore and waited for the authorities to arrive."

"Saved my life, would be more accurate," Ana said. "And the lives of many others."

"We were all quite worried aboard ship, I can tell you that."

Pitt and Giordino eyed each other, knowing the archeologist was bursting with curiosity about the shipwreck.

Dimitov broke quickly. "We were wondering, as well, what you discovered on your dive?"

"Hmm, do you recall, Al?"

"Let's see," Giordino said. "I saw a nice lobster, but he eluded me in the debris of that old shipwreck."

"It's an old wreck?" Dimitov asked, his voice rising.

"Yes, easily two hundred years old," Pitt said. "A beautifully preserved three-masted warship of about forty meters. Appeared to have a Turkish inscription on the bell."

"You found the ship's bell!" Dimitov popped out of his seat.

"Al's got video of the whole thing, if we can find his camera in the harbor. Congratulations, Doctor, you've got a nice shipwreck on your hands . . . that is in all probability the *Fethiye*."

Dimitov hopped around the table and shook Pitt's hand, nearly pulling his arm off. As he tried the same with Giordino, Al jokingly crushed his hand in return.

"This is news that was worth waiting for." He couldn't stop smiling. "I trust that you will be able to return to the wreck site for additional dives?"

"Certainly. We're stuck in Balchik for the moment, and awaiting some parts for the submersible, but we should be able to return to the wreck site at full strength soon enough and perform a detailed investigation. Plus, there is a delicate matter associated with the wreck that we'll need to address with the local authorities."

"What's that?"

"A mystery, of sorts." Pitt reached into his pocket and handed Dimitov a set of dog tags he had carefully removed from the submerged airman's body. "On the wreck, we discovered the body of a man in a military flight suit with a parachute. The anoxic waters at that depth have left him quite well preserved. Judging by the suit, I'd say he's been there forty or fifty years."

Dimitov's joviality vanished as he grasped the tags.

Anna shook her head. "I thought you said the shipwreck dated from the eighteenth century."

"It does. Sank in 1770, if we have the right wreck."

"Our flyboy likely bailed out of an airplane and drowned," Giordino said. "As he sank to the depths, he may have been pushed along by a deep current until his parachute snagged on the wreck."

"It's quite macabre," Dimitov said as he carefully studied the metal identification tags. "He's Russian, a sergeant by the name of Alexander Krayevski. His unit is listed as the Fifty-seventh Bomber Division. And his blood type is O positive."

"That info should get him a formal burial," Pitt said.

"I believe so. I know an amateur historian near Burgas who would be very interested in this discovery."

"Perhaps he could tell us about what happened to his airplane," Ana said, "and help make burial arrangements."

"Yes, quite possibly."

Pitt turned to Stenseth. "Well, Captain, I guess our next destination has been determined, once we obtain our walking papers from Balchik."

Stenseth gave an affirming nod. "Burgas it is."

19

The grim faces that greeted Martin Hendriks foretold bad news.

"I wasn't expecting a visit," Valentin Mankedo said, "but it is good of you to come on short notice." He ushered the Dutch industrialist and Vasko into the office of his marine salvage yard thirty miles north of Burgas.

"I was traveling when I received your text and decided a personal visit might be in order," Hendriks said. "Your message was a bit cryptic, but it seemed to indicate the worst. Tell me what happened."

"We have lost the highly enriched uranium," Mankedo said.

Hendriks said nothing, but his ruddy face flushed.

"Europol and the Bulgarian police took an interest in the *Crimean Star* accident, working off an American research ship in the area," Mankedo said. "I believe they had suspicions about her cargo, which may have been leaked by your Ukrainian supplier."

"It is unrealistic to expect fidelity when you are dealing with thieves." Hendriks shook his head. "I understood that you initially recovered the uranium?"

"We did. But the American ship came across our recovery operation shortly before its conclusion. Ilya was able to retrieve the HEU and left the site, but they realized we had recovered it." He felt no need to mention Vasko attacking the *Macedonia*'s submersible.

"So how did they acquire it?"

Mankedo nodded at his cousin to take the rap.

"The American ship followed us," Vasko said, "but we lost them near the Bosphorus. We sailed to Burgas, where we were awaiting instructions on the rendezvous with the Iranians. As we were preparing to leave port, we were boarded by a law enforcement team. We killed two of them, and I lost three of my men. In the engagement, the HEU was spirited off the ship."

"I see. Not only did you lose the HEU, you potentially exposed us all."

An icy silence filled the air. "All has not been compromised," Mankedo said. "Our dead were anonymous contract workers from Ukraine, and the *Besso* escaped custody."

"The authorities surely know her name and appearance. They will find her and track her to you."

"I am making arrangements to remedy that . . . and hope to move the vessel out of the Black Sea shortly. I am confident in our safety, and in your secrecy. There will be less attention in fact since they recovered the stolen HEU."

Hendriks leaned back in his chair and stared at the ground. "I recently had a meeting with Colonel Markovich in Kiev. He has indicated that the Russians are amplifying their presence in eastern Ukraine, while Europe and the United States watch idly. The national Army is demoralized and in disarray. The only effective counterforce has been Colonel Markovich's band of irregulars."

He turned his gaze to Mankedo. "As you know, I have contributed to their cause. In the process, I have paid you considerable sums to smuggle weapons and supplies to Markovich's forces. They are facing a critical turning point. The Iranian missiles would have permitted a strike back at Crimea in a bold fashion that would have raised the cost of Russia's intervention." He scowled. "That opportunity is now lost."

"Is there no way to acquire the missiles in another manner?" Mankedo asked.

"They are not for sale. The HEU was the only barter the Iranians would consider. Believe me, I pursued all avenues."

"The operation was not without its risks," Mankedo said. "It was in fact carried out exactly to plan. We couldn't have foreseen the intrusion by the Americans nor the apparent foreknowledge of Europol, which I am convinced originated in Ukraine."

Hendriks nodded and receded into his thoughts. His right hand unconsciously dipped into his coat pocket and his fingers located the reassuring shard of metal. "It is important that we act," he said in halting words. His eyes regained their sharpness and he gazed out the office door. "I noticed you have in the compound a large number of crates marked 'munitions.'"

"They are mostly ancient mines and artillery shells we recovered a few months ago." Mankedo shook his head. "They came from a Russian World War II munitions ship that sank near Sochi. The brass shell casings have salvage value, when commodity prices are at the proper level."

"How much do you have?"

"About twenty tons," Vasko said.

"Do they still retain their explosive capability?"

"They are still quite dangerous," Mankedo said. "The shells, in particular, show only light corrosion, due to the depth of the shipwreck. But they are of little use as weapons, considering their age and caliber."

"But their explosive content has worth." Hendriks looked at a painting on the wall, an amateurish seascape of gulls gliding above a curled breaker. "Your attack on the *Crimean Star*," he said. "Tell me again how the crew was incapacitated."

"Much of the waters of the Black Sea are devoid of oxygen," Mankedo said. "Near the coastline, this begins at a depth of around fifty meters. Farther from shore, the oxygen-deprived waters occur at one hundred meters and deeper. Eons ago, the Black Sea was like a swamp. The algae consumed all the oxygen in the water, which in turn killed all the living organisms, then the algae itself. Over time, the dead organisms chemically converted to hydrogen sulfide, which remains locked in the depths. It is relatively harmless to swim through but turns into a deadly gas when it reaches the surface."

"So you set off an underwater explosion ahead of the ship and the rising gas killed the crew?"

Mankedo nodded. "We discovered the phenomenon while salvaging a freighter off of Romania. We were blasting the wreck to get at its cargo. One of our dive boats was anchored directly above it. The explosion released a gas bubble that enveloped the boat. The entire dive crew died. I lost four good men, and learned that the Black Sea can be deadlier than we know."

"If you can make a small blast," Hendriks said, "then why not a large one?"

"I suppose there's no limit on the size of the hydrogen sulfide cloud you could create, given a sufficient explosion and the appropriate location. What did you have in mind?"

"I want to annihilate Sevastopol."

It was Mankedo's turn to fall silent. "That would be mass murder," he finally said.

"I'm not interested in striking the city. I'm interested in striking the Russian fleet's port facility."

Mankedo eyed the Dutchman. He had known him less than three years yet had seen a drastic change in his personality. The billionaire had transformed from a buoyant, arrogant man to a brooding and wrathful lost soul.

"I will pay you three times the market value for your munitions, plus five million euros for the attempt."

"That is a generous proposal," Mankedo said, "but it is not such a simple act. For the *Crimean Star*, we dropped a small explosive in her direct path and she sailed into the ensuing cloud. Targeting a fixed point on land is not controllable."

Vasko sat up straight. "I worked the commercial docks there one summer as a youth. The prevailing winds are westerly. Providing there are no unusual weather patterns or heavy rains, you might target an explosion offshore that would drift over the port."

"There is still the difficulty of approach," Mankedo said. "The Russian Navy is not known for its welcoming behavior."

"It depends on the depths and corresponding anoxic level," Vasko said. "We might not need to get that close."

Mankedo considered the payoff. "Let's take a look at the port entrances. I believe I have a nautical chart of Sevastopol in storage."

After he stood and left the room, Hendriks turned to Vasko. "Your accent. You are not Bulgarian. Are you from Ukraine?"

"Yes. I was raised in Petrovske, a town near Luhansk. I hear it was destroyed during the Crimean invasion."

"Your family?"

"My father drank himself to death years ago. My mother and sister fled to Kiev when the artillery shells began to fall. They are living there with cousins, the last I heard."

"How do you feel about Russia today?"

Vasko stared him in the eyes. "I will help you kill as many Russians as you desire."

Mankedo returned with a chart, which he unfurled across the desk. The three men huddled around it, studying the narrow harbor of Sevastopol that cut into the western coast of the Crimean Peninsula.

"The Russian fleet is based here." Vasko pointed to the northern side of the harbor. He dragged his finger due west, past the harbor entrance. "A mile or so out, the depth is about one hundred and twenty meters. Deep enough to reach a strong anoxic zone. The question would be, how much explosive is enough to set it off?"

"Twenty tons ought to be enough to send a message," Hendriks said.

"I am no scientist," Mankedo said, "but from what we've experienced, I would have to believe that would release an extremely powerful cloud of gas." He gave Hendriks a hard look. "An act such as this would draw a great deal of attention."

"You get me a towboat and barge filled with explosives and I will pilot it myself," Hendriks said in a low tone.

"There is no need for such heroics," Mankedo said. "We can set an unmanned boat on a course with either timed or remote charges to make the attack."

Vasko nodded. "We can place a small explosive on the barge that will cause it to sink when it reaches a GPS-coded location, with a second timed charge to detonate the munitions at the designated depth. We will need a tow vessel capable of making the trek—one that would be untraceable to us."

"A Russian-flagged vessel might be best," Hendriks said.

"We might be able to acquire something out of Sochi," Mankedo said.

"That will take too long," Hendriks said. "I wish to strike soon. What about Turkey? Or a foreign ship?"

"A foreign ship, you say?" Vasko gave Mankedo a hard, knowing look. "I think I know just the vessel."

20

It was late the next day when Ana received the word from the Bulgarian authorities that she was waiting to hear. Climbing the steps to the *Macedonia*'s bridge, she found Pitt and Giordino and relayed the news. "Bulgarian Army scientists have confirmed that the canister contains twenty-two kilos of weapons-grade highly enriched uranium."

"So it was the real deal," Pitt said.

"Enough to construct a sophisticated nuclear weapon, I'm told. It matches the material stolen from the Sevastopol Institute of Nuclear Energy in 2014."

"Congratulations on its recovery," Giordino said. "Do you know where the stuff was headed?"

"We suspect it was originally bound for a weapons dealer in Syria. But we're still behind the curve in identifying its more recent owners. It seems our bald friend managed to elude the police yesterday."

"What about his two associates?" Pitt asked.

Ana shook her head. "Neither was carrying any identification. Forensics has come up empty in matching anything in the Bulgarian databases. One was carrying Ukrainian coins in his pocket, so we suspect they were foreign workers operating under the radar."

"That still leaves the *Besso*," Giordino said.

"A more hopeful source," Ana said. "The ship is registered in Malta to a shell company, but the Burgas harbormaster reports she has been a familiar sight in these waters. With some canvassing of the nearby port towns, we should be able to track her down."

Captain Stenseth stepped over and joined the conversation. "If you really want to find her, just stay aboard the *Macedonia* a few more days," he said with a laugh. "We can't seem to avoid her."

"I appreciate your hospitality, but I'm happier with solid ground under my feet. Are you still intending to sail to Burgas?"

"Just as soon as we're cleared to depart."

"I'll pay a visit to the Balchik police chief and make sure that takes place right away."

The NUMA ship was on the move within the hour and reached the port of Burgas just after sundown. Giordino joined Pitt and Ana on the bridge as the *Macedonia* nudged into an open berth and cast its mooring lines.

Giordino frowned. "I'm told our submersible parts won't be delivered until morning."

"Guess that means we have the night off," Pitt said.

"Why don't you two come with me to visit Petar?" Ana said. "He'd be happy to see you."

"He could probably use some cheering up," Pitt said.

The three made their way down the gangway, where they encountered Dimitov exiting the ship.

"Where are you off to, Professor?" Pitt asked.

"I'm going to call on my associate and see what we can find about your mysterious aviator. The ship isn't leaving soon, is it?"

"We'll be here at least until midday tomorrow," Pitt said. "We won't leave without you."

Pitt hailed a taxi to the MBAL Burgas Hospital a mile away, where Ralin had a private room on the third floor. Ana peeked into his room and found him fast asleep. Letting him rest, the trio hiked a short way to a café for dinner, where they dined on grilled Black Sea turbot.

When they returned to his room, Ralin was groggy but awake. At the sight of Ana, his face lit up.

"I heard about Lieutenant Dukova," he said, "but they told me nothing about you."

"I feared the worst about you," Ana said, sitting on the edge of his bed. "How do you feel?"

"Mostly just tired from the medication they keep pumping into me."

Pitt eyed his heavily bandaged left leg. "How soon before you can dance again?"

"The doctors tell me I should make a complete recovery, but I can expect a few weeks of therapy. My femur got nicked up, but I'm bolted back together, with a leg full of titanium."

Ana squeezed his hand. "I am so glad you are all right."

"What happened on the salvage ship after I went for a swim?" he asked.

Ana relayed her escape from the salvage ship with the HEU and her fortunate encounter with the NUMA men.

He looked to Pitt and Giordino. "You two seem to have a nose for rescue."

"Trouble smells us out all too often," Pitt joked.

"Did the ship get away?"

"Unfortunately," Ana said.

"We'll find her sooner or later."

"We're searching," Ana said. "Now, tell us what happened to you after you fell in the moon pool."

"There's not much to tell. I swam to the surface and clung to a mooring ball until a passing fishing boat spotted me. Good thing they found me when they did. The doctors say I wouldn't have lasted much longer."

An overweight nurse with slate gray eyes entered the room holding an intravenous bag and gave the visitors a petulant gaze. "It's a bit late for visitors."

"We'll leave you to your care," Pitt said to Ralin. Then he turned to Ana. "Are you going to return to the ship with us?"

Ana caught a fond look in Ralin's eyes and pointed to a stuffed chair in the corner of the room. "I think I'll stay with Petar tonight. I have to travel to Sofia in the morning to make my reports, so I'll just leave from here."

The NUMA men said their good-byes, promising to check on both agents the next time they were ashore. Exiting the hospital just after midnight, they found no taxis, so opted to walk back to the ship.

"They make a nice couple," Giordino said.

"It would seem they're on the verge of figuring that out."

"I hope they don't become targets for the gang that stole the HEU."

"Someone won't be happy," Pitt said, "but they're probably smart enough not to pick a fight with Europol."

The bustling town had grown silent as they walked its narrow streets. They skipped the temptation to visit one of the smoky pubs still open along their route and hiked to the waterfront.

The commercial dock was dark and quiet as they stepped across its diesel-soaked timbers. Approaching the *Macedonia*'s berth, both men tensed, then stopped in their tracks. In front of them, the black harbor waters lapped gently against an empty dock.

The *Macedonia* was gone.

PART II
THE GLOOM OF
THE GRAVE

The Macedonia Under Attack

21

Heavy raindrops splattered against the window of the high corner office in the headquarters building of the Main Intelligence Directorate. A blanket of gray obscured the normally expansive vista across the Khoroshyovsky District of Moscow.

The GRU's foreign intelligence field director, Maxim Federov, was oblivious to the weather as he sat at his desk, silently studying a crinkled document. The spymaster was equally unmindful of a slight, bespectacled man who sat nervously in front of him. Federov looked up only when a knock rattled against his office door and a third man entered.

Tall, with an athlete's build and a soldier's posture, he crossed the room with an air of confidence. His short blond hair framed a well-tanned face and striking blue eyes. Federov grimaced at the man's beige Yves St. Laurent suit, yellow tie, and Italian loafers.

"Viktor Mansfield, you are ten minutes late," Federov said. "Say hello to Dr. Anton Kromer of the State Historical Museum."

"The unexpected rainfall was a deterrent to traffic." Mansfield fell into a chair alongside Kromer and shook hands with the professor.

"Rain in Moscow in July is hardly unexpected," Federov said.

"I hope this won't take long." Mansfield glanced at his watch. "I have tickets to the Bolshoi."

Federov gave him a cutting stare. Viktor Mansfield, a *nom de guerre*, was one of his best field agents. His cover long established as a wealthy Austrian playboy with a murky royal background, Mansfield had made inroads with Europe's leading industrialists and politicians, along with a few movie starlets. He played the role well, Federov thought. Perhaps too well, judging by his expense reports.

"Dr. Kromer has recently uncovered a historical document that has great importance to the state."

Federov looked to Kromer to continue.

The pale academic cleared his throat. "I am the chief archivist for the State Historical Museum, which houses a sizable collection of artifacts from the Romanov era. We were preparing an exhibit on the works of nineteenth-century Russian artists held in the Imperial Collection and had retrieved some paintings from long-term storage in St. Petersburg. There were twenty-two paintings, some marvelous works. We were cleaning them in preparation for the exhibit when an interesting discovery was made on the back of one."

He opened a thin photo album and showed Mansfield several

shots of a large painting, brushed in vivid colors, of mounted Cossacks.

"Looks like an Ilya Repin," Mansfield said.

Kromer smiled. "Indeed it is. One of just three in the collection."

"What exactly was found with the painting?"

Kromer flipped a page to reveal several photos of the back of the painting. A close-up showed a piece of parchment wedged into one corner. "A sheet of aged paper, inserted facedown, was found affixed to the painting. We thought it would be some artist's notes or perhaps an early sketch of the painting. It turned out to be something quite different."

Federov held up the document. "It's a treaty, of sorts."

"What kind of treaty?" Mansfield asked.

"The Treaty of Petrograd, or so it is labeled. It's an agreement between the Russian Empire and Great Britain." Federov returned the fragile document to his desk. "The heart of the agreement entails a transfer of twenty percent of the oil and mineral rights of lands occupied by the Russian Empire to the British for a period of one hundred years, beginning some months after the treaty's signature date."

"That's mad," Mansfield said. "Who would sign such a document?"

"The Tsar himself."

Kromer nodded. "We have verified the signature of Tsar Nicholas II on the document."

"Why would he have signed away so much wealth?" Mansfield asked.

"To protect his own," Federov said. "It was a reflection of the times. Dr. Kromer can explain."

"The treaty is dated February 20, 1917. It was a desperate time for the Tsar. The Army was demoralized and unraveling after repeated battle losses to the Germans. Riots by factory workers and citizens had erupted in St. Petersburg. The Bolsheviks were beginning to stage violent protests throughout the country in the name of revolution. Sympathy for the cause existed not just among the peasants and factory workers, but also by many in the military. Nicholas knew the empire was slipping from his fingers and he looked for salvation from the Allies."

"The Romanovs had many relatives throughout Europe," Mansfield said.

"They certainly did. Both Nicholas and his wife, Alexandra, were first cousins to Britain's King George V, as well as other European heads of state. And Nicholas had ongoing business dealings with the Allies during the war, especially for arms procurement. So the contacts were in place as the pressure closed in around him. Little did Nicholas and Alexandra know that after abdicating the crown on March fifteenth, they and their four children would be shipped off to the Urals—and assassinated a year later."

"What was the Tsar hoping to gain by passing off a portion of the nation's mineral wealth?"

"Political support," Kromer said, "and, more critically, military assistance to the armed forces still loyal to him, which later evolved into the White Army. That, and security for a substantial sum of his own royal assets."

"I assume you mean gold."

"Aside from controlling the assets of the State, the Romanov family personally owned many of the gold mines in the Urals. It is well known that the State's supply of gold bullion gradually disappeared during the revolutionary years. There has been much documentation about the Romanov gold in foreign hands, but little is known of the whereabouts of the family's personal stock."

"The treaty states," Federov said, "that a to-be-determined sum of royal family assets were to be transferred to the Bank of England for safekeeping until stability was restored to the Imperial Russian Empire, at which time the treaty would be voided."

"That didn't work out so well," Mansfield said. "How much did the Brits end up with?"

Federov gave him a blank look.

"We don't know," Kromer finally said. "I have a team researching the issue. There is evidence that some members of the Leib Guard escorted a shipment from St. Petersburg to Odessa shortly after the treaty date. Official records from that era are quite sporadic due to the chaos at the time. But rumors have persisted in some circles that a substantial sum of the Tsar's gold was shipped out of Moscow banks."

"No records on the British end?"

"The British banking records were heavily scrutinized by the Bolshevik government in the 1920s concerning the gold shipments made during the war for munitions purchases. But no evidence was ever uncovered of a supplemental deposit on behalf of the Romanovs. My own feeling is, the assets never made it into the hands of the British."

"How much are we talking here?"

Kromer shrugged. "Without further clues, it is impossible to say. Given estimates of the Romanovs' wealth and what was known to have ended up in the Bolsheviks' coffers, easily one hundred and twenty-five to one hundred and fifty billion rubles, in today's currency, were never accounted for."

"Two billion U.S.?" Mansfield said, accustomed to spending cash in euros and dollars.

Kromer nodded. "It was presumably intended to be a sizable sum."

"Well, it is a very interesting tale." Mansfield sat up in his chair. "Is the GRU planning to publish a history book on the lost wealth of Imperial Russia?"

Federov stared daggers at Mansfield. "There are just four people who have seen this document." He tapped the treaty with a stiff finger. "The three of us in this room—and the President. I can tell you that the President is extremely concerned about the contents of this treaty. At the very least, its existence represents a potential embarrassment to the Russian Federation, not to mention the possible legal and financial claims against the government."

"Then why not just stuff it beneath Lenin's tomb?" Mansfield said. "Or, better yet, put a match to it?"

"Because it may not be the only copy."

"The treaty was signed by Tsar Nicholas II and British Special Envoy Sir Leigh Hunt," Kromer said. "If one or more copies of the treaty was in Hunt's possession, as seems likely, then for some reason they were never delivered to Whitehall."

"Why's that?"

"Hunt boarded a British cruiser named *Canterbury* in Archangel shortly after the treaty was signed. The vessel was sunk by a German submarine less than a week later, somewhere in the Norwegian Sea. There were no survivors."

"Then the other treaty copies were destroyed," Mansfield said. "End of story."

Federov gazed out the window at the rain falling in ever-larger drops. He continued staring at the rain while responding to Mansfield. "As I indicated, the President has taken a specific interest in the matter. He has directed the agency to find and destroy any evidence or remaining copies of the treaty—and to pursue any links to the Romanov gold that was spirited out of the country and remains unaccounted."

"There is a possibility that the treaty's heavy parchment could survive cold-water immersion in a consular travel bag," Kromer said. "And we don't know what other communications may have been sent by Hunt."

Mansfield got an uneasy feeling. Federov was in an impossible situation, and now the spy chief was sharing the same fate with him. To disappoint the current Russian president would not only be career-limiting, it could also be life-limiting. Federov gave him no chance to bow out of the assignment.

"Viktor," Federov said, "you are an ex–Navy commando trained in underwater demolitions. You also have experience in piloting submersibles, even if lately it has been for the benefit of fat, wealthy Europeans looking at fish in the Mediterranean." He gave him a cold smile. "You are the best-qualified man I've got for this assignment, and you will not fail me."

"I appreciate your continued faith in me," Mansfield said with just a hint of sarcasm.

"You will have the full support of the agency, as well as

Dr. Kromer and his team, who will continue their historical research."

"I understand." Mansfield sighed. "When do I start?"

"The Arctic oceanographic ship *Tavda* is awaiting you in Murmansk. You have twenty-four hours to get aboard."

"And if there is nothing left of the British ship when we find her?"

Federov looked out the window once more, wishing he could trade positions with Mansfield. He looked at the spy and cast a grim smile. "Then you will have enjoyed a nice sea cruise in a place only slightly less hospitable than Moscow."

22

The assault team came from two small boats, deployed from a vessel that remained offshore under cover of darkness. Landing at a remote corner of the Burgas commercial dock, the eight black-clad intruders made their way to their target like a pack of alley cats on the prowl. At the ship's gangway, the team divided into three groups. One held to the dock and manned the mooring lines while the others boarded the *Macedonia*.

Captain Stenseth was up late, computing fuel reserves with the second officer on watch. Two armed men stormed the bridge and leveled compact Uzi assault rifles at the two NUMA officers. But black knit hats and facial greasepaint didn't cover the tattooed octopus tentacle on one of the intruder's necks.

"What's this all about?" Stenseth said.

Vasko leveled his weapon at the captain's head. "We are borrowing your ship. Attempt to interfere and you will die. Now, tell me, how many are aboard?"

The *Macedonia* was carrying a complement of forty, plus the visiting archeologist. But Pitt, Giordino, and Dimitov were ashore. Stenseth was mentally dropping another head or two from the count, hoping someone might escape detection, when the Uzi erupted.

Vasko fired a single shot, which tore through Stenseth's right arm just above the elbow. The sleeve of his white officer's shirt grew red as blood ran down his arm. "I want the answer—now."

The second officer took a step forward and dove at Vasko. But the Bulgarian detected the move and jumped aside. As the officer grabbed at his legs, Vasko fired a stream of bullets across his back, killing him instantly. Stenseth dropped to his knees to try to aid the man, but Vasko kicked him in the shoulder. "The crew count?"

"Thirty-eight," Stenseth said through gritted teeth. The *Macedonia*'s captain was pulled to his feet, shoved face-first against the bulkhead, his wrists zip-tied behind his back.

Vasko clicked the transmitter of a small radio on his hip. "Engine room secure," came the prompt reply.

"Bridge secure," Vasko said. "Give me power to the main engines."

"Affirmative. Five minutes."

Vasko signaled the shore team, who released the ship's berthing lines and hopped aboard. Most of the *Macedonia*'s crew had long since retired to their cabins and the intruders let them be. But they rounded up the midnight crew and a handful of scientists who were working late.

While waiting to get under way, Vasko opened a panel near the helm and disabled the satellite communications system and AIS transmitter, which allowed third parties to track the ship's position. When the *Macedonia*'s engines rumbled to life, Vasko eased the vessel out of the harbor at a crawl, drawing no attention.

Once at sea, he extinguished the running lights and turned north, accelerating to top speed. Stenseth was allowed to remain on the bridge. He mentally recorded the route until he became woozy from blood loss.

After two hours, the ship slowed and turned toward the coastline. Vasko made a cryptic call over the ship's radio and two green lights blinked a mile or so distant. He steered for the lights, which marked the narrow entrance to a small, rocky cove at the base of a high cliff.

Inside the narrow cove, a single pier extended across the water. Under its shaded lampposts, Stenseth could make out a salvage ship that looked like the *Besso* and a black crew boat tied up near shore. An open barge was moored at the opposite end of the pier.

Vasko spun the *Macedonia* around in the tight confines of the cove and slid it against the remaining open dock, backing its stern to the barge. A handful of workmen came out to meet the ship, several carrying assault rifles.

The *Macedonia*'s crew was roused from their cabins, stripped of any phones or electronics, and escorted off the ship under armed guard. As they were marched down the dock, Stenseth saw a pair of workers rigging a tow line from the barge, which was filled with heavy wooden crates.

The NUMA personnel were led into a warehouse and forced

to stand at gunpoint. Satisfied they were secure, Vasko stepped to a main office and housing structure across the compound.

Mankedo didn't bother to look up from his laptop when Vasko sat across the desk from him. "Any problems?"

"None," Vasko said. "We crept out of Burgas without so much as a nod in our direction."

"You made good time. We should have her out of sight of the coastline before sunup."

"She runs about seventeen knots. Is the barge wired?"

"I've placed a small charge in the bilge to sink her. You'll need to manage the munitions blow."

"Semtex?"

"There's plenty left in the explosives locker," Mankedo said.

"What's the plan of attack?"

Mankedo spun around his laptop, revealing a map of Sevastopol Harbor. "We'll set the ship's auto helm to run to a coordinate two miles due west of the harbor entrance. When the *Macedonia* reaches within five hundred meters of that point, it will trigger a detonation of the barge's hull charge. We can use the same signal to initiate a timed detonation of the munitions."

"Twenty minutes should be enough to allow her to sink to the seafloor. What about the tow line?"

"We could blow it separately, but the target depth is only ninety meters, well less than the length of the tow line. Once sunk, it will act as an anchor for the NUMA ship."

"What do you want to do with the crew?" Vasko asked.

"Are they still aboard?"

"They're in the warehouse."

"Lock them in one of the caves for now. We'll dispense with them later." He closed the laptop and rose from his chair.

"I see the *Besso* beat us back," Vasko said. "The reconfiguration went well."

"Yes, the crew worked around the clock to change her appearance. It should be enough to pass a casual inspection. By the way, her new name is *Nevena*."

"I thought by now she'd be headed to the Mediterranean."

"She should be, but another project came up. Something we need to jump on just as soon as the *Macedonia* is on her way."

He opened the door to a small anteroom. A heavyset man was bent over a table inside, poring through a stack of documents. Beside him, a small bowl contained some metal tags. The man looked up with mild disturbance.

"Ilya," Mankedo said. "Say hello to Dr. Georgi Dimitov."

23

na found Giordino refilling a coffee cup in the Burgas Police Department break room. Across the corridor, they could see Pitt arguing with the chief of police.

"How's he doing?" Ana asked.

"Ready to eat someone's liver for breakfast. Beyond notifying the Coast Guard, the chief constable's reaction in searching for the *Macedonia* has been, shall we say, minus four hundred and sixty degrees Fahrenheit."

"Absolute zero?"

Giordino nodded.

"I'm working through Europol to notify coastal towns in Romania, Turkey, and Ukraine. I'm not sure the local police can do a whole lot more." She looked at Pitt, whose green eyes seemed afire. "I've never seen him so intense."

"He doesn't take kindly to anyone messing with his ships—or his people. He has a lot of friends aboard the *Macedonia*."

"Loyalty means a lot to him?"

Giordino nodded. "You better know it. He'd swim the Atlantic if it meant helping a friend. On top of that, he's not one to take no for an answer."

"We better get him out of the chief's hair before he gets himself thrown into a jail cell. I've got the video link with Washington set to go." Ana poked her head into the chief's office and retrieved Pitt.

He shook his head. "I finally convinced him to send some investigators to the dock. Should have been done hours ago. Any word from the Coast Guard?"

"They are organizing their resources and will be initiating search efforts shortly. The wet weather, unfortunately, will hamper an air search."

She led Pitt and Giordino down the corridor to a darkened room with several chairs and a computer in it. A video conference link to the computer monitor showed two men at a table with a NUMA logo on the wall behind them. Hiram Yaeger, the ponytailed head of NUMA's computer resource center, sat next to Rudi Gunn, Pitt's deputy director. Both had a weary look from working into the wee hours of the morning.

"Good morning, gentlemen, and thanks for hanging in with us," Pitt said. "What can you tell us from your end?"

"Our satellite link with the *Macedonia* was severed at 12:05 a.m. local time," Yaeger said. "I checked the regional AIS system, which tracks the position and identity of all commercial vessels via satellite. It was deactivated a few minutes later. Both systems show the ship's last recorded position as the commercial terminal in Burgas Harbor."

"So the systems were disabled even before the ship left port," Pitt said.

"That's what the data indicates."

"Someone knew a thing or two about hijacking," Giordino said.

"Assuming it was a hijacking, every hour counts," Gunn said. "The *Macedonia* is rated at a top speed of seventeen knots. Eleven hours have elapsed, so by now she could be two hundred miles from Burgas. That could place her anywhere from Ukraine to the gates of the Dardanelles."

"We've issued alerts to all regional country Coast Guards," Ana said. "The Bulgarian Coast Guard will be initiating sea searches out of Burgas and Varna, supplemented by an air search once the weather improves."

"Any evidence who may have taken the ship? Or why?" Gunn asked.

"We can only suspect the salvage crew that wanted to sell the stolen uranium," Pitt said. "I don't have a good answer why they would take the *Macedonia*, other than payback for intercepting the HEU."

"We're getting some leads on their salvage ship, the *Besso*," Ana said. "She has been a familiar site in these waters and has been listed as an additional target of the Coast Guard search."

"Perhaps one will lead to the other," Gunn said.

"What other search resources do we have at our disposal?" Pitt asked.

"I've got Max conducting an inventory of all available satellite imagery for the area," Yaeger said, referring to the holographic interface he used to communicate with NUMA's supercomputer.

"These days, the reconnaissance focus is more directed toward Ukraine, so the coverage around Bulgaria may be slim."

"We may have better luck with the Air Force," Gunn said. "I've been in touch with the U.S. commander at Bezmer Air Base, about sixty miles west of Burgas. We have joint forces stationed there with the Bulgarians, including some recon aircraft. They've agreed to assist with the search efforts but also cited the local wet weather as restricting their capabilities."

"Anything we can throw up there will help," Pitt said.

"The Navy also has a visiting cruiser in the Black Sea," Gunn said, "and they've been informed of the *Macedonia*'s disappearance. They've promised to do what they can." Gunn could see the impatient look in Pitt's eyes. "I'm afraid there's not much more that can be done at the moment, boss. We'll have to sit tight while the search resources get deployed."

"Thanks, Rudi, I know you've done all you can."

Gunn's eyes focused through his thick horn-rimmed glasses. "Dirk, I hate to ask, but is there any chance they took the *Macedonia* offshore and sank her?"

Pitt stared at the monitor a long moment. "No," he said in a determined voice. "That's a proposition I simply won't accept."

24

The armor-plated BMW X5 pulled up to an aged white apartment building on the outskirts of Kramatorsk. The building's only distinguishing feature was a multitude of triangular concrete barricades that surrounded it like a ring of dragon's teeth. One of the armed guards patrolling the perimeter directed the luxury SUV to a side parking lot. The driver parked beside a pockmarked armored personnel carrier and opened the rear passenger door.

Martin Hendriks felt the chill of a damp Ukrainian morning as he approached the building's portico. A soldier at the entrance prepared to search him but was overruled by an older armed man who had appeared at the door and greeted the businessman. "It is good to see you again, Mr. Hendriks. This way, please."

The guard led the Dutchman up two flights of stairs to a corner apartment that had been converted into a war room. But it was not the abode of a well-provisioned military leader. The room's few furnishings were old and tattered. Boxes of canned food were stacked in a corner near some army cots.

At the room's center, a bearded man in fatigues was bent over a table, studying a map. His grizzled face warmed at the sight of Hendriks. "Martin, a surprise to see you again so soon after our visit in Kiev." He stepped over and shook hands.

"I had business in Bulgaria, Colonel, and thought I would stop by on my return."

Colonel Arseny Markovich led Hendriks to a pair of over-stuffed chairs near the window. Markovich was commander of the 24th Territorial Battalion, one of several pro-government paramilitary forces established in Ukraine after the Russian annexation of Crimea in 2014. Loosely supporting the government's Armed Forces of Ukraine, the battalion operated in the hotly contested Donetsk and Luhansk regions of eastern Ukraine.

"Do you bring good news on your deal to acquire surface-to-surface missiles?" the commander asked.

"Regrettably not," Hendriks said. "Our stock-in-trade was intercepted by the authorities before we could get it to the Iranians. The deal is now dead. I'm sorry to have let you down."

Colonel Markovich, whose home village was controlled by Russian-supported separatist rebels, accepted the news stoically. "You have provided us a great deal of arms and equipment over the past three years. Our situation would be much worse without your support."

"How is the situation?"

"Relatively calm at the moment, but it is simply a part of the seasonal cycle. A cease-fire gets brokered in the fall and things remain quiet over the winter. Then in the spring the separatists ignore the peace treaties and launch new offensives."

Hendriks shook his head. "Those missiles would have been a nice deterrent."

"They might have even turned the tide. The real problem, as you know, is the Russians. Without their stealth support of the rebels, we could collectively crush the separatist forces and restore unity to Ukraine in a matter of weeks."

"They are still present everywhere?"

Markovich nodded. "I have received reports that plain-uniformed Russian troops are filtering into Luhansk in great numbers. They mean to launch an offensive to the west, perhaps in an attempt to take Dnipropetrovsk. Who knows, maybe even Kiev?"

"Can they be stopped?"

"Not if the West continues to look the other way. We lack the resources to halt the Russians if they wish to take Ukraine. Outside military support would become critical to our survival." He shook his head. "The European nations are too reluctant to help. Our only hope is with America. We need them to step in with weapons support. Or more."

"I have come to the same conclusion. The Americans are cautious, but they can be provoked into action. The natural mistrust between the U.S. and Russia presents an opportunity to be exploited."

"But what can we do?"

"Simply strike a spark between the two. We may in fact draw the Americans in very soon." Hendriks explained the planned attack on Sevastopol.

A smile crossed the colonel's face. "That is striking at the heart of the matter. Maintaining their naval port at Sevastopol was certainly a key to the Russian invasion of Crimea."

"Truth be known, I would prefer a strike at Moscow."

Markovich nodded, realizing Hendriks's hatred of the Russians matched his own. "You may incite a dangerous reaction," he said. "The Russians will have to save face. They might retaliate by sinking an American warship, as they did the nuclear submarine *Scorpion*."

Hendriks gave him a long, cold stare. "That is what I am banking on. The Americans will be angered. It will cause them to fight any further attempts at Russian expansionism, beginning with Ukraine. It would not surprise me to see American troops on the ground here within a few weeks. Then, I trust, you will be able to exterminate the separatists once and for all."

"With delight," the colonel said. "It is a bold, shrewd plan. You have given us a gift greater than missiles. You have given us hope for victory."

"That is what I wish."

"You are a true friend of Ukraine."

Hendriks stood and put on his overcoat, and Markovich escorted him down the stairs. At the door, the colonel turned and asked, "Are you making a visit to Hrabove?"

"Yes." Hendriks looked down at the ground.

"Be careful. And don't drive on the road after dark."

"I will be back to the airfield at Dnipropetrovsk well before then."

Hendriks returned to the BMW, where his driver waited with the engine idling. He climbed into the warm interior and stared out the window as the car headed southeast. Leaving the city, they drove across miles of rolling plains. Scattered plots of maize and beans gave way to large fields of wheat and barley.

Thirty miles on, they neared the town of Toretsk, where they were stopped at a makeshift border crossing that divided government lands from separatist-held territory. As an unarmed businessman from the Netherlands, he was quickly allowed to pass. The BMW drove another forty miles across rural lands before approaching the dusty farm town of Hrabove.

Hendriks, who had been dozing, suddenly grew more attentive. Making note of the local landmarks, he guided the driver out of town and down a dirt road. Gazing at a vacant field that looked like all the others, he had him stop. Hendriks climbed out and walked a few yards to a small pile of stacked rocks. Scattered about its base were the remains of some long-dead flowers. He clawed one of the dried stems from the dusty soil and stepped into the adjacent field.

He walked to its center, stopped, and stared up at the sky. He stood for nearly an hour, lost in another place and time. A cold breeze knifed through his clothes, but it didn't touch his already frozen soul. Standing there in the field, he felt more dead than alive.

After a while, he patted his coat pocket, feeling the familiar metallic object, which gave him a morsel of comfort. He dropped the flower stem, reached down, and grabbed a fistful of the dark, untilled soil. Squeezing it until his hand shook, he released the earth into the sacred confines of his pocket. Words, a curse of some sort, tried to form on his lips but were lost in the wind.

His anguish at last released, the broken man returned to the car, a lone tear dried on his cheek.

25

ummer Pitt shook her head as she approached the *Odin*'s survey shack. Even with the door closed, a heady blues riff from guitarist Joe Bonamassa could be heard blaring from the small room. Flinging open the door, Summer found her twin brother, Dirk Jr., seated in front of a sonar monitor, stomping his feet to the music.

As she entered, he nonchalantly cranked down the volume on a tabletop speaker.

"Really?" she said. "You're waking the fish from here to the North Pole."

He stifled a yawn. "Just needed a little juice to finish my shift." He glanced at a clock on the bulkhead and saw it was a few minutes to four in the morning.

"I should have known you were headed down an all-consuming path when Dad loaned you his Eric Clapton collection."

Dirk smiled. "He knows a thing or two about the blues."

There was no disguising their resemblance to their father, the head of NUMA. Both carried his strong facial features and were tall, lithe, and strong. But while Dirk had the same dark hair, Summer was a redhead. They had followed in his seafaring footsteps, studying marine engineering and oceanography before joining him at the underwater research agency.

"Anything to report on the sonar?" she asked.

"It's been a steady diet of mud and sand."

They were performing a multibeam sonar survey of the northern coastal fjord region of Norway to study its former glaciers. Those glaciers were believed to have extended beyond the current fjord channels, leaving subsea scouring and debris zones when they retreated after the last Ice Age. Deploying a towed array sonar, the NUMA research ship *Odin* surveyed the region, allowing scientists to study the history of glacial retreats in conjunction with changes in global climate.

"We should finish surveying the final search grid on your shift," Dirk said.

"It's been a long, cold, and tiring four weeks," Summer said. "I'll be glad to wrap up this project."

"If we hang around here much longer, we're liable to be dodging icebergs soon."

She motioned for Dirk to give up his seat, but he shook his head. "I've got two minutes left on shift." He motioned toward the clock. "Grab yourself a cup of coffee."

Summer rolled her eyes and stepped to a coffeepot wedged in the corner of the cramped sonar bay. "What are you hoping to find in the last two minutes?" she asked, pouring herself a cup. "Signs of a new glacier?"

Silence.

She turned to her brother, who had his face glued to the monitor.

"Not a glacier," he said slowly, "but a shipwreck."

Summer rushed over to see a dark image scroll down the screen. It had a clearly defined rectangular shape with a pointed prow. A thin shadow protruded off one side.

"A steel wreck, sitting upright," she said. "It looks to be in pretty good shape."

Dirk marked the position, then consulted a nautical chart spread on the table. "Must be an unknown wreck. It's not marked on the chart."

"It's nearly one hundred and fifty meters long," Summer said. "A pretty large vessel."

"Take a look at that." Dirk pointed to a small shadow. "Might be a gun turret."

"If it's a warship, there must be a record of its loss." She waved him out of his seat. "A pretty nice score on the two-minute drill, but we still have a geological survey to complete. I'll take it from here."

Dirk eased out of the chair and refilled his coffee cup.

"Aren't you going to bed?"

"Heck, no. First I have to go to the ship's library and see if I can find out what ship that is."

"And then?"

"And then I have to talk the captain into letting us dive it."

Four hours later, Summer completed her sonar shift, concluding the final search grid without any new geological discoveries. The *Odin* turned around and retraced its path southward toward the site of the shipwreck. As the NUMA survey was ahead of schedule, Dirk had no problem convincing the captain to take an extra day on the journey home to investigate the wreck.

Dirk joined Summer at the sonar station as they made several more passes over the target, gathering detailed images of the wreck while pinpointing its location. In a chilly breeze on the stern deck, they met a brawny underwater technology specialist named Jack Dahlgren, who helped retrieve the sonar towfish.

"It's colder than my ex on an iceberg," Dahlgren said.

Dirk grinned. "Feels like Amarillo in August to me."

"I wish. Y'all want to take a dive on the wreck now?"

"The seas look stable enough." Dirk gazed over the ship's rail. "Let's get the submersible prepped while the captain puts us on position."

An hour later, under darkening skies, a bulb-shaped yellow submarine was lowered over the stern. The light green waters of the Norwegian Sea washed over the vessel as Dirk flooded its ballast tanks. Summer sat beside him at the controls while Dahlgren wedged into a seat behind. They let gravity draw them to the seabed as the waters outside their viewport faded to black.

"So, ancient Viking ship or Norwegian cruise liner?" Dahlgren asked.

"Neither, methinks," Dirk said. "The online records are pretty sparse for shipwreck data in this region. I couldn't find any record of a commercial vessel lost near here, so if it's a freighter or fishing schooner, it might be a challenge to identify."

Summer looked over her shoulder at Dahlgren. "But we don't think it's a commercial ship."

"That's right. The sonar passes show what look to be gun turrets at several locations around the ship. I also found one historical reference to a warship that was presumed lost in the area."

"What was that?" Dahlgren asked.

"The *Canterbury*. A Royal Navy C-class light cruiser built in 1915. She was presumed lost at sea in February 1917, but postwar records indicated she was torpedoed by a German U-boat, the UC-29."

"This is a long ways from Jutland," Dahlgren said. "What were they doing squaring off way up here?"

"The Allies were running guns and munitions to the Russians via Archangel," Dirk said. "Once the Germans got wind of things, they tried to intervene as best they could."

"So the *Canterbury* was an escort ship?"

"Possibly. She was on a return voyage from Archangel, though the records didn't indicate whether she was accompanied by any other vessels."

Dirk eased their descent as they approached the bottom at two hundred meters. Almost directly below them, a long dark shape materialized on the seafloor. Too small for a ship, Summer identified it as a ship's funnel. Lying dented in the sand, it pointed toward a towering black shape at the fringe of their view.

Dirk engaged the thrusters and glided toward the object, scattering a deep school of mackerel. The ship materialized moments later, a forest green mass of steel engulfed in cold deepwater encrustation. Dirk held up a photo of the *Canterbury* he had culled from his research.

Dahlgren glanced at the slab vertical sides of the ship in the image and compared it to the mass in front of them. "Looks like the spitting image."

They approached the wreck from its starboard flank, noting the ship rested on its keel at a slight angle. Moving up the side of its hull, Dirk turned to his right, guiding the submersible toward the forward deck. He could already tell from the size and limited open decking that the wreck was neither a freighter nor a fishing vessel. As they hovered above the starboard rail, he spotted the first indication of the ship's true intent, a corroded light machine gun mounted on a stand. As they moved toward the bow, the submersible's bright lights cast a shadow over a large gun and turret.

"Certainly looks like one of her six-inch guns," Dirk said.

"We need to roll video." Summer reached to a control panel and activated an exterior-mounted camera.

"I'll try to cover as many features as I can," Dirk said.

He slowly crisscrossed the length of the ship, allowing the camera to record the three additional six-inch gun turrets, a stack of torpedoes and launching tubes near the stern, and one remaining funnel. On the port flank, they found a large hole in the lower hull, the handiwork of the U-boat. After filming the damage in detail, Dirk guided the submersible to the *Canterbury*'s forward superstructure, rising to bridge level.

Approaching the top-level bridge, they peered through the empty window frames into the control station. Though the wooden ship's wheel had long since vanished as a feast for marine organisms, the remnants of the brass binnacle and telegraph stood erect near the helm.

Dirk eased the submersible around the side of the bridge until its propulsion fans kicked up a cloud of sediment that obscured their visibility. He descended a level and moved aft, finding a short bank of cabins whose doors had been jarred open by the ship's sinking. Poking the nose of the submersible into each room, he let the camera film until the sediment again flew. He continued moving down and aft until the submersible reached the stern rail.

"That's almost an hour of video." Summer shut down the camera. "If that's not enough detail to document her as the *Canterbury*, I don't know what will."

"I bet there are some descendants of her crew that will appreciate a viewing," Dirk said.

She nodded. "I'll make sure a copy gets sent to the Royal Navy Association."

Dirk took another high-level pass, the ship appearing forlorn in the dark depths. As the submersible began its slow ascent, a silent rumination fell over the NUMA crew, their thoughts on the young sailors who died on the ship a century before.

Their quiet reflection ended when the submersible broke the surface to find a modern Russian oceanographic ship commanding the seas barely a hundred yards away.

26

"They're on it."

Viktor Mansfield grimaced at the words. He looked to the ship's captain, who stood beside a sonar operator's console.

"Are you sure it is the same wreck?" Mansfield asked.

"Our hull-mounted sonar array shows a one-hundred-and-thirty-five-meter steel wreck, possibly mounting guns. We're within a half mile of the German submarine's coordinates of the sinking, in an otherwise remote section of the Norwegian coast. Come see for yourself."

Mansfield stomped across the bridge of the Russian oceanographic survey ship *Tavda* and glanced at the color sonar screen. He didn't have to study the image's details to know it was the *Canterbury*. "How did they know to get here now?"

The hog-faced captain of the *Tavda* chortled. "Why don't you call them up and ask?"

"You talk to them. Tell them the wreck is a sovereign ship of Russia and to stand off."

The captain nodded. "I can do that."

Mansfield gazed at the turquoise survey ship, then focused on a submersible surfacing near its stern. "Before you talk to them, have my demolitions kit brought to the launch deck. I'm going to take care of the wreck straightaway."

Across the waves, the recovery team pulled the yellow NUMA submersible aboard the *Odin*. The lights on the stern deck were fully ablaze under the fading daylight as Dirk, Summer, and Dahlgren exited the craft. Dahlgren set the recovery team to work, inspecting the submersible and preparing it for future dives.

"I'm going to make a copy of the video first thing." Summer hurried toward a nearby laboratory bay, carrying a portable hard drive.

Dirk gave her a wave. "I'll report to the bridge and see what the Russians are doing here."

He made his way to the *Odin*'s pilothouse, where the captain, a bearded man named Littleton, was peering through binoculars at the *Tavda*. "What's up with our nosey neighbors?"

"Good question," Littleton said. "He steamed right up to our position and wasn't very considerate about backing away when I told him we had underwater operations in progress." He passed the binoculars to Dirk. "Nice-looking ship, though."

Dirk admired the Russian vessel, nearly twice the size of the *Odin*. It featured multiple A-frames for deploying equipment, a moon pool, and a covered helicopter on an elevated pad amidships.

"She's called the *Tavda*," Littleton said. "A recently launched oceanographic research ship with icebreaking capability. Apparently, she's also designed to perform deep-sea salvage operations. Or so say the news reports."

"Looks first-rate. I wonder what she's doing here?"

His query was answered a short time later when the ship's radio crackled with a Russian-accented voice. "Research vessel *Odin*, this is the survey ship *Tavda*. You are intruding on a shipwreck of the Russian Federation. Please vacate the area at once."

"*Tavda*, this is *Odin*," Littleton said. "We have conducted a survey of the wreck and ascertained she is the British light cruiser *Canterbury*, sunk in 1917. Over."

There was a long pause. "Negative. The wreck is a warship of Russia. We must insist that you vacate the site at once."

Littleton looked at the *Tavda* again with his binoculars. A small contingent of armed Marines were assembling on the fan deck. He turned back to Dirk. "I think they're serious about the wreck. Could they be right?"

"It's possible but doesn't seem likely. The wreck's dimensions and features match up perfectly to the specs we have on the *Canterbury*. But I guess it doesn't much matter now. We've got the video of the survey. We can turn it over to the British and let them fight the Russians over it."

The captain nodded. "Then I guess we're done here." Littleton radioed the *Tavda* and informed them the NUMA ship would move off the site as requested.

Summer stepped onto the bridge a few minutes later. "Why are we moving?" she asked.

"We don't want to get shot over a rusty shipwreck." Dirk motioned toward the *Tavda*. "Our Russian neighbors claim it's theirs—and seem willing to wage a war over it."

Summer shook her head. "No, I think we need to take another dive on her. There's something on the video I think you should see."

She plugged a flash drive into a computer at the rear of the bridge. Dirk and Littleton crowded around as footage of the *Canterbury* appeared. Summer fast-forwarded to the halfway point.

"At about thirty minutes in, we filmed the starboard cabins just beneath the bridge," she said. "This is the first one coming up."

The video showed the interior of the bridge as the submersible slid around to the starboard side. The submersible then dropped down a level and focused on an open steel door. The camera peered into the small room, showing the corroded remains of a metal desk and porcelain sink on one side and some scattered debris on the floor. The view lingered for a moment, then slowly turned away and out of the cabin as a flurry of silt from one of the submersible's side thrusters filled the room.

"There!" Summer stopped the video.

Dirk and Littleton looked at each other and shook their heads.

"Didn't see anything," Dirk said.

"Look on the floor, near the side bulkhead, just before the silt gets thrown up." Summer replayed the last section of the video, this time at slow speed.

"That?" Dirk pointed at a reflection in the corner.

"Yes."

Summer froze the frame and enlarged the image. Dirk and Littleton stared at it and nodded. There was no mistaking the small object that glimmered on the floor.

It was a bar of solid gold.

27

With a large plastic crate of explosives secured to the submersible's prow, Mansfield could barely see through the forward viewport. Only by raising his head and sitting forward in the pilot's seat could he see past the crate to the stern of the *Tavda*.

He glanced to the right of the cockpit, where a technician completed a predive checklist.

"Clear to proceed?" Mansfield asked.

"Yes, all systems are operational."

Mansfield radioed the deck crew to initiate launch. The large white submersible was hoisted over the ship's moon pool and lowered into the water. Mansfield flooded the ballast tanks and activated a forward-looking sonar system. Before the submersible reached the seafloor, he had a directional bead on the shipwreck.

He approached the *Canterbury* from the stern, then elevated the submersible past one of the ship's massive bronze propellers, which were embedded in the seafloor. Reaching the stern rail, he moved forward along the portside deck. Due to his limited visibility, he kept the submersible well outboard of the ship.

As he passed a gun turret amidships, he discerned the rising shadow of the cruiser's high superstructure. Ascending to the bridge, he inspected it briefly, then eased the submersible down a level. As gently as he could, he parked the vessel on the corroded steel supports of what had been a teakwood deck. A row of four cabins stretched in front of them.

Mansfield nodded to the technician. "Release the explosives here."

Kromer, the Moscow researcher, had provided him a crude plan of the ship and concluded Sir Leigh Hunt most likely would have berthed among the officers' cabins beneath the bridge.

Using an articulated robotic arm, the technician released a strap securing the explosives, then pushed the plastic crate off a forward-mounted skid plate. Mansfield assisted by backing the submersible away from the bulkhead. As the crate slid away, stirring a small cloud of silt, Mansfield noticed a faint light near the top of the bridge.

The technician strained to see through the murk. "It's away, and positioned against the bulkhead."

Mansfield looked for himself, then immediately elevated the submersible. Ascending past the top of the bridge, he was met by the lights of another submersible.

The two crafts faced each other nose to nose, their LED exterior lights blinding each other's pilot. Mansfield made out the blue lettering NUMA on the opposing vessel's stern. In the opposing cockpit, he spotted two men and a woman wearing turquoise jumpsuits.

The two submersibles operated on different communication frequencies, so they could not talk to each other. Mansfield called his support ship to relay a message to the *Odin*. A response came seconds later.

"The NUMA ship reports its submersible left something on the wreck that it needs to retrieve. They will leave the site shortly."

Mansfield shook his head. "I think not," he said to his copilot.

As the NUMA submersible turned and descended on the starboard side of the superstructure, its occupants gave Mansfield a friendly wave. The Russian watched it disappear, then guided his submersible down a parallel path on the port side of the bridge. Returning to the crate of explosives, he eased close and hovered over it. "Activate the timer."

The technician extended the manipulator arm and opened a small compartment door. Mansfield edged close so that they could look down into the opening, where a timer clock sat next to a large toggle switch.

The technician glanced at Mansfield for confirmation, then reached in with the manipulator and flipped the switch. The LED timer illuminated with a preset time of twenty minutes, which began counting down. "Detonation timer activated," he said.

Mansfield nodded and activated the thrusters. Backing away from the *Canterbury*, he purged the ballast tanks and they began ascending toward the surface. Rising above the wreck, he spotted the lights of the NUMA submersible on the opposite side of the *Canterbury*'s bridge. He watched with satisfaction as he distanced himself from the opposing submersible—and the explosives-laden wreck.

28

"Get me a little closer," Summer urged.

Dirk had maneuvered the submersible to the doorway of the first starboard cabin, where Summer extended the manipulator to its full reach. The gold bar, under a thin coating of silt, lay just beyond Summer's grasp.

"I can't get much closer without knocking down a bulkhead or two." Dirk elevated the submersible and pivoted it slightly before bringing the nose against the doorway a second time, then dropping to the deck. A fresh cloud of silt rolled through the cabin, forcing Summer to wait for the water to clear.

Through the easing murk, she extended the manipulator once more and again fell short.

Dahlgren noticed a slim bone handle protruding beneath the bar. "It looks like it's sitting atop the remains of an attaché case. Maybe you can pull it over."

Summer grabbed the handle with the claw. Pulling gently, she shook her head as the handle tore away from the decayed remains of the case. "Nice idea, in theory." She released the handle and gazed at the gold bar. "I'd hate to leave it here for the Russians."

"You just need a rake." Dirk scanned the cabin and pointed to several thin, rusty slats. "Try one of those bits of scrap over there."

Summer used the manipulator to reach one of the steel slats, a remnant of a bed frame. Using it like a rake as Dirk suggested, she dragged the bar a foot or two, then released the beam and wrapped the manipulator's claws around the gold bar. "Got it."

Dirk began easing the submersible away from the cabin when a deep rumble sounded through the water. A second later, they were struck by an invisible shock wave. The submersible was hurled away from the ship, smashing over the side rail and tumbling end over end until driven into the seabed a short distance away. As bits of corroded debris fell through the water in a black rain, the submersible vanished in a cloud of silt.

The submersible's darkened interior echoed with hissing, creaking, and electrical alarms, as well as some human moans. Summer wiped a bead of blood from her eyes that had trickled from a gashed scalp and realized the interior wasn't completely dark. A thin row of panel lights flashed near the helm, filling the interior with red and yellow hues.

Her head felt like a jackhammer was splitting her skull, and when she tried to move, her limbs refused to respond. Someone rummaged around the floorboards and shoved her leg aside, igniting a new agony. She tried to cry out but felt too woozy to speak. She perked up when she realized it was her brother but flinched when he leaned over and she saw his face was red. Was it blood or just the lights?

"Hang on, sis," he said. "The elevator is headed up."

She gave him a smile and then drifted into a cold, deep sleep.

29

Mansfield's submersible reached the surface as the explosives detonated. He and his copilot felt only a slight vibration but watched as a fountain of froth erupted from the sea nearby. The submersible was hoisted aboard the *Tavda*, and Mansfield made his way to the bridge.

"The American ship has inquired about an explosion," the captain said.

"Tell them we know nothing about it but are standing by to assist if needed."

Mansfield listened to the angry voice of Littleton relay that he had a submersible in the water. Smiling, he turned to the *Tavda*'s captain. "Reply that we can assist in the search, but, regrettably, our own submersible requires immediate repairs, which will take several hours."

The *Odin*'s captain ignored the message.

A short time later, Mansfield noticed the NUMA ship had

several spotlights trained on the water. Following the beams through a pair of binoculars, he spotted the yellow submarine bobbing on the surface.

"So they survived," he muttered. He turned to the captain. "The Americans will surely leave the site now. When they do, follow them at the extreme range of our radar system until they give an indication of turning to port."

"What then?"

Mansfield yawned and headed for the door. "Alert your helicopter pilot, then wake me in my cabin."

Across a rising sea, the NUMA submersible was lifted aboard ship and surrounded by an anxious circle of crewmen. Captain Littleton joined them as the hatch was opened. Dirk appeared, battered and bruised, holding the semiconscious body of his sister. Passing Summer to the ship's doctor, he ducked back inside to help Dahlgren, who could stand on only one leg. Dirk accompanied them to the ship's medical ward, then hobbled over to Littleton.

"You all right, son?" the captain asked.

"We got knocked around pretty good down there, but I'm fine. Jack has a compound fracture to his left leg, and I fear Summer has some internal injuries as well as a concussion."

"We've got a good doctor aboard, but we'll make for Bergen at top speed all the same." Littleton gazed at the submersible's dinged and discolored exterior. "What happened down there?"

"I'm not sure." Dirk shook his head. "I'm guessing some sort of large explosion on the port side of the ship. But there's one thing. We met up with the Russians' submersible in the general vicinity just a few minutes earlier."

"They surfaced right about the time of the blow," Littleton said.

"I should have known. They must have set a timed charge. Blew apart the entire superstructure. We were lucky to have had the cabin deck as a barrier or else we would have bought it. Fortunately, the sub maintained internal pressure. I was able to purge one of the ballast tanks with emergency power and we floundered to the surface." He began walking around the submersible, inspecting its damage.

"The Russians offered to help search for you," Littleton said, "but claimed their submersible was down for repairs."

"They must be after something belowdecks on the *Canterbury*."

"More gold?"

"Perhaps."

"Were you able to grab the gold bar you'd seen in the cabin?"

Dirk shrugged. "We had it for a moment. Wasn't a big concern after everything went black."

The two men made their way to the front of the submersible.

"I guess the trip paid for itself." Dirk pointed to the cradled manipulator.

Visible within the clutch of its steel claws was the yellow sheen of the gold bar.

30

"Al, they've found the *Macedonia*."

Dozing in a corner of the Burgas police station's video conference room, Giordino woke with a start. He stood and moved swiftly to the conference table, where Pitt was back in touch with Gunn and Yaeger in Washington. The men showed a sudden sense of vigor that masked the fatigue of the last forty-eight hours.

Giordino took a seat at the table and joined the conversation. "Where is it?"

"North-central Black Sea," Yaeger said, "about forty miles southeast of Sevastopol. We just identified her on a satellite image from the National Reconnaissance Office. It's from one of their Air Force birds, taken about ninety minutes ago."

Yaeger typed at his console and displayed on the screen a grainy photo. The digitally enhanced image showed a small ship trailed by a box-shaped vessel. Yaeger enlarged the photo until a few distinct features on the ship could be seen. "It wasn't a direct satellite pass, and the weather adds degradation, but it appears to be the *Macedonia*. The dimensions match up, the topside structures are correct, and you can even make out a submersible on the aft deck."

"That's her," Pitt said.

"Yep." Giordino nodded. "That's exactly where the submersible was positioned when we came into port."

"Nice work, Hiram," Pitt said. "You found the needle in a haystack."

"Max did all the work," Yaeger said. "I just input the vessel's configuration and sent her to work scanning satellite images."

"What's with the vessel behind her?" Giordino asked. "Is she towing a barge?"

Yaeger readjusted the image and zoomed in on the second vessel. Under magnification, they could see, it was an open-hulled steel barge loaded with crates.

"It's a towed barge, all right," Pitt said. "You can make out the tow line on one of the forward bollards."

"Why would someone hijack a research ship and use it to tow a barge?" Gunn asked.

"There must be a clue in the cargo," Yaeger said.

"Most likely," Pitt said. "Whatever they're towing, it's slowing them down. That will make them more vulnerable."

"If she makes it to Sevastopol, things might get ugly trying to pry her back from the Russians," Gunn said.

Pitt nodded. "Give us her coordinates. We'll contact the Ukrainians and see if their Coast Guard can get to her first. They can at least radio *Macedonia* and see who answers. How about our own Navy?"

"We'll have to check," Gunn said. "The Montreux Convention allows us only a temporary naval presence in the Black Sea, but the Aegis-class destroyer *Truxton* is currently on deployment."

"Get on it," Pitt said. "I'll also need a contact for the Bezmer Air Base commander."

"You going to request a flyby?" Gunn asked.

Pitt gave Giordino a knowing look. "Something like that." He signed off the video call and made arrangements with the Bulgarian police to contact the Ukrainian Sea Guard. In Washington, Gunn contacted a friend who was aide to the Chief of Naval Operations, while Yaeger continued trying to track the *Macedonia* and studying satellite images. Something in the barge photo caught his eye and he examined it under different levels of lighting and magnification. Finally, he saw it. On the top of one crate was a word in black paint. He adjusted the brightness, contrast, and magnification in multiple variations, but he couldn't make out the lettering.

"Max," he called out. "Are you there?"

A holographic image of a woman appeared beyond Yaeger's computer console. She was young and attractive, modeled after his wife, and she looked at him attentively. "I'm here around the clock for you," she said in a seductive voice. "You should know that by now."

"This photo on display from your database," he said. "It shows a barge containing crates. On the port rail, third crate from the stern, there are some visible markings. Do you see it?"

"Yes. Rather blurry from a thousand miles up."

"Do your best to tell me what it says."

Max crinkled her nose as the supercomputer that created her leaped at the challenge. The photographic image was broken down and redisplayed many thousand different ways, as an optical scanner recorded each variation. One by one, each letter was dissected. After less than a minute, Max winked at Yaeger. "You may want to inform the boss."

"What does it say?"

"боеприпаси."

"You lost me," Yaeger said.

"It's Bulgarian." Max gave him an abrasive look. "It's the word for *munitions*."

31

irk stepped onto the *Odin*'s bridge wing as the ship entered Hjeltefjorden, a twenty-two-mile waterway that stretched southeast toward Norway's Bergen Peninsula. Snowcapped hills rose sharply on either side, as the vessel steamed toward Bergen. The sun shone brightly, casting the waters a brilliant sapphire while softening the chill of a stiff southerly breeze.

A thumping caught his attention and he turned to spot a helicopter approaching from behind. Skimming over the fjord, the chopper raced by just off *Odin*'s beam. Dirk didn't recognize the model, and its registration markings appeared to be taped over. He watched the helicopter disappear over the horizon on the route to Bergen, then he descended two flights of stairs and entered the wardroom. In the corner, Jack Dahlgren sat at a table, sipping coffee. His left leg was wrapped in a temporary cast and propped on a suitcase.

Dirk smiled. "They finally kick you out of sick bay, stumpy?"

"I exhausted their supply of painkillers, so there was no reason to stick around," Dahlgren said. The discomfort from his broken leg was evident in the hooded squint of his eyes.

"How's the leg?"

"Mostly numb, except when I move. The doc did what he could, but with a shattered femur, I'm headed for shoreside surgery and a leg full of tin."

"I'm sure you'll get top care in Bergen, along with all the *lutefisk* you can stomach."

"I was banking on it, but I think your sis has other designs." He pointed across the room at Summer, who had just entered and was striding toward them, carrying a leather purse. She limped from a sore ankle and was trying to hide a large bruise on the side of her face by letting her long red hair hang loose.

"The second member of the Walking Wounded Club arrives," Dirk said.

Summer shook her head. "The submersible rolls over—and Jack breaks his leg and I get a new face. Meanwhile, you waltz out without so much as a scratch. Show me the justice in that."

"I think when we tumbled, his skull put a few dents in the submersible," Dahlgren said. "Did more damage to the submersible than to himself."

"Always was hardheaded," Summer said.

"But not the only one in the family," Dirk said. "So what's this about not letting Jack get patched up in Bergen?"

"I just booked tickets for the three of us on an afternoon flight to London."

"Why London?"

"The Royal National Orthopaedic Hospital, the Royal Navy, and Cambridge University."

Dirk and Dahlgren looked at each other and shrugged.

"Okay, I'll bite," Dahlgren said. "What's the significance of those three establishments?"

"Well, for starters, the hospital is where Dr. Steven Miller holds seasonal residency. Miller is a world-renowned orthopedic surgeon from Muncie, Indiana, who happens to be an old friend of Rudi Gunn. At Rudi's request, Dr. Miller is ready and waiting to rebuild Jack's leg as soon as we arrive."

Dahlgren smiled. "Adios, *lutefisk*."

"Nice of Rudi to help out," Dirk said. "I assume a stop at the Royal Navy isn't for Jack's benefit?"

"That will be to return this." Summer raised her purse and set it on the table with a clunk.

"Is that what I think it is?" Dahlgren asked.

"Hasn't left her side," Dirk said. "I think she sleeps with it under her pillow."

"It's not something I care to lose." She unsnapped her purse and retrieved the gold bar from the *Canterbury*.

"May I?" Dahlgren reached out his hands.

Summer passed him the bar.

"Sweetness." He balanced its weight, then held it up to the light.

Summer smiled. There was something intrinsically magical about the heavy yellow mineral that elicited a childlike amazement in everyone who touched it. No wonder there were so many treasure hunters scouring the globe for gold nuggets and coins.

Dahlgren rapped a knuckle against the top of the bar, which

was engraved with various numbers and symbols. "Have you deciphered the hieroglyphics and the two-headed chicken?"

"That's no chicken," she said. "It's actually an eagle, the coat of arms of the Romanov family. It ties with the accompanying Cyrillic lettering, which indicates some sort of tracking number and the smelting date, October 1914."

"Romanov gold?" Dirk asked.

"I'm no expert, but from what I can determine, the markings indicate it came from the Imperial Russian Treasury."

"That might explain the appearance of the *Tavda*."

"The Russians must think there's more gold aboard," Dahlgren said.

"It's possible," Dirk said, "though there was no mention of gold shipments in the *Canterbury*'s history that I found."

Dahlgren looked to Summer. "So you want to rat out the Russians in London?"

"The *Canterbury* is a British naval ship as well as a war grave. The Royal Navy should be notified that the Russians are claiming it as theirs and possibly blowing it apart in a search for gold."

"Sounds like the right thing to do. But how about this?" Dahlgren held up the gold bar. "Going to keep it as a finder's fee?"

"Of course not," Summer grabbed the bar out of his hands and deposited it in her purse. "It will be given to the Royal Navy, along with the wreck's coordinates."

He shook his head. "Always the saint."

"I think I can dispute that," Dirk said.

Summer snorted. "Never you mind."

"So I understand flying to London to fix Jack's leg and to kiss the gold bar good-bye," Dirk said. "But how does Cambridge play into the trip?"

"That's something of a bonus. I tried calling St. Julien Perlmutter in Washington to enlist his help in researching the *Canterbury*. If anyone could find out if there's gold aboard an old shipwreck, it would be Julien. By luck, he happens to be attending a nautical history symposium at Cambridge."

"Summer," Dahlgren said, "I never knew you were such a gold hound."

"It's not the gold itself. I just want to know why it was aboard. And why the Russians are claiming the ship."

"The British Admiralty records might be helpful," Dirk said.

"With Julien's assistance, we're sure to find something."

"I just have one question for you, Summer." Dahlgren eased his leg to the floor and sat upright. "How are you going to carry both me and that gold bar off the ship in Bergen?"

Two hours later, the *Odin* arrived at Norway's second-largest city and docked near the commercial wharves. Without any assistance from Summer, Dahlgren hobbled off the ship on crutches. Dirk hoisted their bags, and the trio squeezed into a waiting Volvo taxi. As they exited the dock facility, the taxi passed a brown sedan idling at the curb with two men inside.

Mansfield folded up a compact pair of binoculars and stuffed them in a pocket of the door panel. "That's our mark. Stay with them."

The nondescript sedan, rented for the occasion by the Russian Consulate, scooted into traffic and followed the taxi a few car lengths behind. The driver was a professional, holding back and hiding in back of the intervening vehicles but bolting forward at traffic signals so as not to be left behind.

The two vehicles swept around the waterfront city, following route E39 south for twelve miles to the Bergen Airport. Traffic was light as the taxi stopped at the departure terminal. The sedan pulled to the curb a safe distance back. After the Americans entered the terminal, Mansfield hopped out to follow. He was dressed in a casual winter jacket and wore fashion-rimmed glasses to draw attention from his unshaven face. He took his place in line at the check-in counter and scanned the departures listed on the monitor.

As Dirk, Summer, and Dahlgren reached the counter and began checking in, Mansfield cut out of line and stepped to an adjacent counter, under the guise of getting a baggage label. With his back to the Americans, he listened as the gate agent checked their bags and told them their gate.

The Russian returned to his place in line, turning the other way as the trio headed for security. When he reached the check-in agent a few minutes later, he politely handed her a French passport.

"Where are you traveling to today, sir?"

"A ticket to London, please. One way, no baggage."

32

"**S**onar contact, bearing two-one-two degrees."

Captain Vladimir Popov nodded at the sonar operator and rose from his seat with a smile. "Helm, steer two-one-two degrees. Let's close on her."

Popov began pacing the cramped combat information center of the Russian Krivak-class missile frigate *Ladny*. The low-lit bay, several levels below the ship's bridge, was filled with electronics and weapons specialists wedged into individual computer stations. But there was nothing futuristic about the layout. The *Ladny* was more than thirty years old, and most of her electronic equipment was older than its operators. Popov retook his seat, facing a video screen that constituted one of the few updates. The screen was dotted with symbols depicting nearby ships and aircraft detected by the ship's radar.

"Sonar, what's your range?" he asked.

"Sir, target is at an approximate distance of eight thousand meters, speed of fourteen knots, depth of eighty meters."

"Excellent. Stay with her. She's ours now."

The sonar operator continued calling out ranges as the frigate, running at nearly double the speed, quickly closed on the submerged target.

"Sir, the target has turned to three-one-five degrees. She's putting on speed."

The radar operator spoke again before Popov could answer.

"Captain, I show two unidentified vessels breaching the western border of the restricted sea zone at a speed of nine knots."

"Acknowledged," Popov said. "Helm, steer three-one-five degrees."

The sonar operator continued tracking the submerged target. Popov sat on the edge of his seat, excitement in his eye as he closed in for the kill. When they were less than a thousand meters away, he gave the order. "Sonar, blast her!"

The operator maximized the power to the frigate's hull-mounted sonar transponder and triggered five extended acoustic signal bursts. Three hundred feet below the surface, the sonar operator aboard the Russian submarine *Novorossiysk* ripped off his headset. "They got us."

Popov leaped out of his chair and danced around the bay, high-fiving the sailors nearby. For six days, he and his crew had been playing a cat-and-mouse war game with the nuclear submarine. Until now, the *Ladny* had been on the receiving end of the simulated attacks. At last, the frigate's crew had turned the tables. "Notify the fleet simulation coordinator that we have de-

stroyed the *Novorossiysk* and await new redeployment," he said
to his communications operator.

As the excitement in the bay subsided, the radar operator
called again to the captain. "Sir, the unknown targets continue to
cross the restricted zone. They will soon be nearing the approach
to Sevastopol."

On the video board, a pair of red triangles cut across the left
side of the screen in tandem.

"Radio the fools and tell them they have entered restricted
waters and must move thirty kilometers to the south before re-
suming course to Sevastopol."

"Yes, sir," the communications officer said. After several minutes, he reported back to the captain. "Sir, I have relayed the message but have received no response."

Popov glanced again at the combat screen. The two vessels
had not deviated from their course.

The ship's executive officer studied the image, then approached
the captain. "A tow ship, sir?"

"Possibly." Popov's joy turned to irritation. "Lay in an intercept course, then request an airborne reconnaissance. I want a
visual on her, one way or the other. Keep communications after
her as well."

"Yes, sir," the exec said. "What's your wager, sir? That she's a
freighter with a drunken captain or a derelict tug with a bad
radio?"

Popov nodded. "In these waters, what else could it be?"

33

"I've got a visual," Giordino said over his radio headset. "About eighty degrees."

Pitt scanned the expanse of open sea beneath their helicopter and spotted a faint gray object to his right. He pressed the pedals that tilted the rear rotor, sending the Bell OH-58 Kiowa in a slight bank to starboard until the distant speck lined up with the center of the windscreen.

Two hours earlier, they had commandeered the light observation chopper at Bezmer Air Base, west of Burgas. Though Pitt and Giordino's Air Force flying days were well behind them, both retained qualification to pilot a variety of aircraft. The rigors of flying a helicopter for an extended period hadn't waned, and Pitt felt his muscles beginning to ache as the chopper reached the limits of its flight range. He established radio contact with the ship ahead and received permission to land as the gray vessel gradually loomed beneath them.

It wasn't the *Macedonia* but the U.S. Navy Aegis-class destroyer *Truxton* that was speeding to the northeast at better than thirty knots. Pitt approached from the stern, where he was guided down to the ship's flight deck, normally reserved for the vessel's twin SH-60 Seahawk helicopters. As he shut down the Kiowa's single engine, the ship's flight crew rushed over to begin refueling.

Pitt and Giordino climbed out to stretch their legs and were promptly met by a pert blond woman, who extended her hand in greeting. "Mr. Pitt, Mr. Giordino, welcome to the *Truxton*. I'm Commander Deborah Kenfield, Executive Officer. The ship's captain sends his greetings from the bridge."

"Thank you for the stopover and fill-up, Commander," Pitt said.

"We're trying to get you as close as we can, but we're still eighty miles away."

"Do you know where the *Macedonia* is right now?" Giordino asked.

"We're tracking her on the Aegis radar. She's about ten miles from Sevastopol and creating a bit of a stir."

"How's that?" Pitt asked.

"The Russians recently established a restricted sea zone west of Crimea. Presumably, it's an area where the Russian Navy performs weapons testing and engages in tactical simulations. It seems the *Macedonia* has sailed into the center of the restricted zone. We've picked up some scattered radio communications and it doesn't sound as if the Russians are too happy."

"The *Macedonia* is towing a barge filled with munitions to Sevastopol," Pitt said, "and the Russians don't know about it?"

"Not from what we can tell. They've identified it as an American vessel but don't seem to be in direct contact. We've informed the Russians that we believe the ship has been hijacked and requested intervention, but they haven't advised us as to their intent." The look in Kenfield's eyes told Pitt there was no reason to expect cooperation.

"Do you think they might sink her?" Giordino asked.

"This close to Ukraine, we believe their missile frigate *Ladny* will be apt to shoot first and ask questions later. For that reason, the captain has respectfully requested you cancel your flight plans, as the *Macedonia* has already crossed into their territorial waters."

Pitt shook his head. "We don't know if the crew is still aboard."

The nearby ground crew pulled away their refueling gear and indicated the helicopter was topped up.

"Tell your captain we appreciate his concern," Pitt said, "but we need to know for certain."

"He suspected as much," Kenfield said. She passed him a slip of paper. "The *Macedonia*'s last coordinates. We'll do what we can to support you. Good luck."

"Thanks, Commander."

Pitt walked over and thanked the *Truxton*'s flight support crew. When he returned to the helicopter, he found Giordino in the pilot's seat.

"Sorry, boss, but the Air Force said we had to split seat time for extended flights before they gave us the keys."

"Guess I didn't read the fine print," Pitt said. Glad for the break, he stepped around and climbed into the copilot's seat.

Giordino lifted off quickly and accelerated toward the *Macedonia*'s coordinates. Thirty minutes later, they spotted the turquoise research ship with its tow barge. The cloud cover had finally thinned and in the distance they could see the hills of the Crimean Peninsula. To the north they could make out the slim gray figure of the *Ladny* under speed.

Giordino brought the helicopter in low over the barge, examining the wooden crates packed into the open hold.

Pitt pointed to some crates on the starboard side. "There's a damaged lid."

Giordino eased the chopper down until they were hovering just above it. The lid of one crate had been worked loose by the jostling seas, allowing a partial glimpse inside. Both men could make out a row of brass cylindrical objects.

"Yaeger was right," Pitt said. "She is indeed loaded with munitions."

"Why would someone steal an oceanographic research ship and use it to haul a barge full of artillery shells to Sevastopol?" Giordino asked.

Pitt shook his head. "For no good reason I can think of."

Giordino pushed the helicopter's cyclic control forward, propelling them past the barge and over the water. He followed the tow line to the *Macedonia*, where he made a wide loop around the ship. No one appeared on deck to watch the thumping chopper skim overhead.

"Must be a skeleton crew," Giordino said.

"Let's see who's on the bridge."

Giordino eased close alongside the port bridge wing, where they had a clear view inside. The entire bridge was empty.

"No wonder she's defying the Russians," Pitt said. "No one's home. She must be on autopilot."

"If the crew's locked belowdecks, that might not be good."

"Get me aboard," Pitt said.

Giordino elevated the Bell to better scan the moving ship beneath him. The topsides were an unfriendly maze of cranes, antennas, and radar masts. Moving aft, he pointed to the *Macedonia*'s submersible, which had been left dangling from a lift crane while under repair. "Not optimal, but if I can get a clear drop over the submersible, you can use it as a ladder."

"Do it," Pitt said.

Giordino brought the chopper around the stern and over the submersible, expertly matching speed with the ship.

As he eased the helicopter lower, Pitt rapped him on the arm. "See you in Varna. First beer's on me." Pitt tore off his radio headset, opened the side door, and stepped down onto the landing skid.

Despite the rotor wash buffeting off the deck, Giordino held the helicopter rock steady.

Pitt took a short leap from the skid, landing atop the submersible while grabbing a lift cable for support.

The helicopter instantly pulled up and away from the ship as Pitt slid down the exterior of the submersible, landing on his feet. He raced forward across the deck and ducked into a covered passageway.

As Giordino watched him disappear, the helicopter radio erupted with a deep voice speaking in heavily accented English. "American vessel *Macedonia*, this is the warship *Ladny*. You are instructed to halt for inspection or turn away and exit the restricted zone at once. This is your final warning. Please respond or be fired upon."

Only silence came from the ship.

34

Popov looked from the large display to a nearby computer monitor, which displayed the distant image of the *Macedonia* through a long-range video camera. The turquoise ship was plodding through the waves as a green helicopter hovered close behind.

"Sir, the American helicopter has repeated its request not to fire." The communications officer had translated Giordino's radio transmission, which was broadcast through the combat information center.

Popov gazed from the camera view to the large screen. "I detect no change in speed or course. Radio the vessel one last time. Tell them to respond at once or be fired upon."

As the message was relayed to the NUMA ship, the *Ladny*'s executive officer rushed up to Popov with a slip of paper. "Fleet Headquarters has approved our defense of territorial waters. We may strike at the vessel with discretion."

Popov read the order, folded the paper, and slipped it into his pocket.

"Status, surface weapons?" he said in a commanding voice.

A weapons officer at a nearby console spoke in a similar tone, as the rest of the combat information center fell quiet. "Sir, forward batteries loaded and armed. Target coordinates have been input to port battery. Torpedoes set to surface running."

Popov nodded. "Ready, port missile one?"

"Port missile one ready, sir."

Popov looked at his communications officer. "Any response?"

The officer returned his gaze with a faint shake of the head. "Still no reply, sir."

The captain took a deep breath. "Fire port missile one."

"Fire port missile one."

The weapons specialist's fingers danced over the console. A loud rushing sound echoed from above and the ship swayed on its keel.

"Port missile one away," he said.

Popov turned to the turquoise ship displayed on the video monitor and watched for it to disappear.

35

itt stepped onto the bridge of the *Macedonia* to be met by Giordino's voice blaring through the radio speaker.

"Dirk, if you're there, radio the *Ladny* that you're aboard. They've got their finger on the trigger."

"Let's get her turned around first," Pitt muttered aloud as Giordino repeated the warning.

He stepped to the helm console and disengaged the autopilot. He set the throttle, then spun the rudder control dial one hundred and eighty degrees to send the ship on a starboard pivot in the opposite direction. As he watched the tip of the bow begin to nudge right, Giordino's voice blared once more through the radio. This time, his voice had an urgent tone.

"Dirk, I've spotted a flash from the Russian ship. They've fired! They've fired! Get off the ship now!"

Pitt coolly glanced at the radarscope, his brain responding in hyperdrive. He was no stranger to life-or-death situations, and, for him, time seemed to slow in those moments. His mind raced back to a pair of Russian warships they had passed in the Bosphorus a few days earlier. They were aged vessels, at least forty years old, showing rust and poor maintenance. Even the sailors appeared slovenly. It signaled to him that Russia's frontline Navy, with its most modern ships and weapons, was deployed somewhere other than the Black Sea. That meant he had a chance.

He calculated that he had two, maybe three minutes tops, as his body began to move ahead of his thoughts. He adjusted the rudder controls, then sprinted toward the door, muttering, "Please let it be a torpedo."

A few seconds later, Giordino brought the helicopter in tight alongside the bridge to give warning. Finding the bridge empty, he elevated the chopper and fell back. Pitt was running across the stern deck toward the submersible.

Giordino swooped in to pick him up, but Pitt waved him off, instead climbing onto the lift crane controls.

With quick precision, Pitt powered up the crane and swung the submersible out over the stern. The sub swayed over the angled tow line pulling the distant barge and splashed into the sea. Pitt reversed the cable spool attached to the lift line, allowing the submersible to fall back of the moving ship. Watching the bobbing submersible recede behind him, he saw the smoky trail of the approaching Russian missile.

He moved to return to the bridge but hesitated when he heard a loud pop. It came from the barge, angled far to Pitt's left. He noted a small puff of smoke rising from the barge's stern, then turned and raced to the *Macedonia*'s bridge.

Five hundred feet above the NUMA ship, Giordino watched

Pitt's defensive measure, then turned to the imminent threat. The incoming missile was skimming above the waves. At a quarter mile away, the missile dropped an object into the water and continued on its flight.

But the missile did not align on the *Macedonia* after Pitt had changed course. Instead, it flew past the ship and continued toward the horizon, where it would expire harmlessly once its fuel was spent.

So far, Pitt's luck was holding. The Russians had fired an SS-N-14 Silex missile, whose payload was an underslung torpedo that was dropped near the target. While free of a missile strike, the torpedo was nearly as deadly.

Giordino searched the water for the torpedo, spotting its white-water tail as it bore down on the *Macedonia*. Pitt had turned the research ship away from the *Ladny*, so the assault would strike from the stern. Giordino watched helplessly as the homing torpedo locked onto the ship and raced toward its transom. The torpedo seemed to gain speed as it drew closer to the research ship until it struck paydirt—and exploded in a towering cloud of spray and debris.

36

The *Ladny*'s long-range camera showed an upheaval of sea and white smoke rising high into the air. Popov and his crew seldom had the opportunity to fire live weapons, let alone against an actual opponent. They stared at the video monitor with a mixed sense of wonder and satisfaction. But Popov's pride turned to confusion as a ghostly image appeared on the screen.

It was the *Macedonia*, sailing past the dissolving smoke. The NUMA vessel was apparently still charging toward Sevastopol, completely unscathed. Popov looked to the combat screen to affirm he wasn't seeing things. The red triangles of the two targets were still moving east, though now positioned parallel to each other rather than in tandem.

"What has gone wrong?" Popov yelled.

The executive officer shook his head. "It must have been a premature detonation."

"Do we have a second missile ready?"

"Port missile two armed and ready," the weapons officer said.

"Fire port missile two."

Seconds after the frigate shuddered under the launch, the *Ladny*'s communications officer turned to Popov with a startled look. "Sir, I'm receiving a call from the American ship."

"What? Patch it through."

Pitt's voice was transmitted through the bay. "*Ladny*, this is the *Macedonia*. Thanks for the warm hospitality, but we've decided to save Crimea for another vacation. We'll be departing your restricted zone shortly. *Do svidaniya!*"

The communications officer turned pale. "Sir, what do I say? The missile has already been launched."

The weapons officer seated nearby looked at a firing clock. "The torpedo is about to deploy, sir. It's too late to stop it now."

Popov turned to the communications officer with a sober gaze.

"There is nothing to say now," he said in a low voice. He turned to the exec. "Have the crew stand down."

PEERING FROM THE HELM of the *Macedonia*, Pitt could see the second Silex missile coming at him. He felt only slightly more confident in this second deadly game of chicken. He could tell the *Macedonia* was faster and more responsive since the barge tow cable had been severed when the first torpedo had struck the submersible tailing behind, exploding well aft of the research ship. And this time he had more than just a tiny submersible to run interference.

Pitt had briefly driven the ship toward the *Ladny* but now

spun the vessel around and away from the oncoming missile. He pushed the *Macedonia* to full speed as he made for a collision course with the munitions barge. The open tow boat was barely fifty yards ahead, sitting low in the water from its keel-shattering explosion.

"Torpedo's away," Giordino said over the bridge radio.

Pitt watched the Silex missile shriek by low overhead after jettisoning its payload. He had just a few seconds for the torpedo's acoustic homing device to lock onto the rumble of the *Macedonia*'s engines and rush in for the kill.

The sinking barge loomed off the bow as Giordino radioed him again from his observation point in the sky. "She's on you. About five hundred meters."

"Got it. You best fly clear." Pitt held the helm steady to the last possible second, then cut to his port side, following the current. The turquoise ship barely slipped alongside the barge, scraping its hull paint in the process.

"One hundred meters," Giordino said, easing the helicopter away to watch from a safe distance.

After he cleared the barge, Pitt wheeled the *Macedonia* back to starboard, centering the drifting vessel in his wake. He counted the seconds, hoping to put as much blue water behind him as possible, when the first explosion sounded. The loud report was followed a second later by the bellow of an exploding volcano.

The barge disintegrated in a massive fireball that rose a hundred feet into the sky. Metallic debris rained down from the plume, peppering a large radius of the sea.

On board the *Macedonia*, Pitt was knocked from his feet. The shock wave blew out the bridge's rear windows and lifted the ship's stern with a billowing wave. The hull and topsides were splattered with shrapnel. Most of the damage was superficial.

Regaining his feet, Pitt found the *Macedonia* continuing to churn away from the maelstrom. He looked back at the remnants of the barge, which was foundering under a thick blanket of black smoke. The Air Force helicopter appeared above, circling around the haze.

"Dirk, are you all right?" Giordino radioed.

"No harm done," Pitt replied. He set the helm on a southwesterly bearing that would take the *Macedonia* out of the restricted zone as soon as possible. "Just tell me our friends are done shooting."

"I guarantee they've holstered their weapons. The *Truxton* just threatened to send them to the bottom if they fire again."

"Jolly good for the Navy."

"From up here, the *Macedonia* looks like a spotted frog. You've got a few smoldering hot spots on the aft deck that could use some dousing."

"I'll get on it shortly." He noticed for the first time some dried blood on the floor of the bridge.

"Have to ask you," Giordino said, "what inspired the idea to turn toward the Russians and invite that second missile attack?"

"The barge," Pitt said. "I saw a small charge detonate on her, away from the stored munitions. I think they intentionally blew out her keel to sink her."

"Why would they drag it three hundred miles across the Black Sea to sink it outside of Sevastopol?"

"I don't know. Maybe they were trying to block the harbor and their timing was off."

"Any sign of the *Macedonia*'s crew?"

"None," Pitt said. "Going to check now."

He set the helm on auto and exited the bridge with a handheld radio. Starting in the engine room and working his way up, he surveyed the entire ship. From open journals in the laboratories, to moldy half-eaten plates of food in the galley, he found numerous indications of a hurried crew departure.

As Pitt returned to the bridge, Giordino was flying point off the ship's bow. The *Macedonia* was nearly clear of the restricted zone and the *Truxton* was now visible on the radarscope. His mind on the missing crew, Pitt stood at the helm and stared at the open waters before him. After a time, he turned to a chart table— and noticed a miniature wireless video camera concealed in the ceiling.

He pulled it down and saw it was actually twin cameras, one pointed at the helm and the other out the rear window. He tossed it on the table, then carefully examined the entire bridge for a clue. He checked the ship's log first, but the most recent entry was days old, from when the *Macedonia* last entered port. Communications records, charts, and all other paperwork lying about the bridge were equally uninformative. But when he took a second look at the dried bloodstains on the floor, he noticed something.

It was a light swirl in a smaller stain by the bulkhead. The smudge had been created by the toe of a shoe while the blood was still liquid. Looking closer, he saw a nearly invisible message that told Pitt what he already suspected. It was a single word smeared on the floor.

Besso.

37

Mankedo and Vasko watched in disbelief as Pitt ripped the camera from the ceiling, sending the satellite-fed video link to black.

Mankedo snapped shut the laptop on which they had watched the last hour's events and shoved it to the side of his desk. "It was nearly there, on its way to a submerged detonation. Instead, destroyed on the surface, to no effect."

"That man!" Vasko said, his voice seething. "He was the same one on the inflatable who aided the Europol agent and took the uranium. How did he find the ship?"

"He must be the head of NUMA that Dimitov dealt with on the *Macedonia*. His name is Pitt. Apparently, he's an accomplished marine engineer."

"Why wasn't he among the captured crew?"

"Dimitov said this Pitt and another man responsible for the submersible were ashore when the ship was taken."

Mankedo rose from the desk and paced his office. "I fear this will bring increased police scrutiny. We must move the *Besso* out of the Black Sea at once. I have a secondary project in the Mediterranean and will send Dimitov to initiate things. But first I will call Hendriks. This may finish our relationship."

"I don't think so," Vasko said. "He knew it was a risky project."

"Perhaps, but we have failed him in the bold strike he desired. That will likely mean an end to future jobs with him."

"You are wrong about that, Valentin. I have seen Hendriks and I have talked to the man. He is operating from a state of high emotion. He's no longer the calculating business virtuoso that made millions. He is in a totally different place, and I believe he will support any grand plan that satisfies his need for aggression. The grander, the better. And we can give it to him. With the bomber."

"The bomber," Mankedo said softly.

"I've been working on it with Dimitov. He told me about the Ottoman wreck and the pilot's body. The identification tags, as we know, confirm he was a flight engineer on the missing Tupolev bomber. It reminded me of some data we obtained from a fisherman in Balchik years ago. We purchased his snag records of underwater obstructions, hoping to find a salvageable wreck. He mentioned an odd tire assembly he pulled up in the area. It was back in the 1990s, so he may have forgotten or he didn't know about the lost bomber."

"It could have been from another aircraft or something else entirely."

"Perhaps, but I checked his records. The fisherman described it as a nose wheel assembly, and his notes indicate it was found only three kilometers from the Ottoman wreck site. Dimitov and I have put together a compact search grid based on his coordinates. It's worth a look."

"We don't know if the rumors about the aircraft are even true."

"We also don't know if they're not. Just think about it, Valentin. We'd have something in our hands for which Hendriks would pay us dearly. If the plane is where we think it is, in relatively shallow water, we can find the truth easily enough."

Mankedo contemplated the idea and nodded. "Yes, it may soften the blow with Hendriks. But we'll have to work fast. I'll allow twenty-four hours to find it before I send Dimitov and the *Besso* off to the Mediterranean."

Vasko rubbed a hand across his bald head and smiled with confidence.

"Consider it done."

38

The distant glow of lights from London greeted Dirk, Summer, and Dahlgren as they exited the terminal at Heathrow Airport. The trio squeezed into a black taxi-cab for the twenty-mile ride into the city. An off-duty cab tucked in behind them, while Mansfield followed several car lengths back in a plain white panel van driven by a female agent.

Reaching the city center, the lead cab turned north, passing through Soho, before pulling into the entrance of the Royal National Orthopaedic Hospital. Summer helped Dahlgren hobble into the lobby and check in. A nurse arrived with a wheelchair and carted him off for a battery of tests and X-rays ahead of his scheduled surgery the next morning.

Summer waved to him. "We'll pick you up tomorrow night for dancing at the Savoy."

"I hope they'll permit a peg leg in to mar the ballroom floor," Dahlgren said.

Dirk and Summer returned to their waiting cab, which back-tracked south and west through London. The panel van took up a tailing position this time, maneuvering aggressively through the city's heavy traffic to remain on the cab's rear bumper. They entered Kensington, and the cab pulled into the entrance of The Gore, a four-star hotel just off Hyde Park.

The panel van drove past the hotel and pulled to the curb a half block later. Mansfield looked to his driver, a cool, serious woman named Martina who wore her dark hair cut short. "Do you have system access to The Gore?"

Martina retrieved a small electronic tablet hidden beneath the seat and consulted a long list of London hotels. She found a mark highlighted next to The Gore's name and nodded. Never known for their high degree of security, the reservation systems of most hotels in major cities were long ago hacked by foreign intelligence agencies in order to track people of interest.

"We'll have their room number the instant they check in," she said. "Ivan in the taxi will keep watch in the lobby until my surveillance team can be put in place."

"How long will that take?"

"Less than an hour."

Mansfield looked across the street at a small hotel called the Queen's Gate.

"I'll take a room there and wait for your surveillance data. Perhaps we can have a drink together afterward?" he said with a charming raise of the brow.

Martina gave him a glacial stare. "The data will be delivered once it is acquired."

Mansfield chortled and exited the car.

Inside The Gore, Dirk and Summer checked in at the front desk, where a message was handed to them.

"It's from St. Julien," Summer said. "He'll be by in an hour to take us to dinner."

"Knowing Julien, we better dress for fine dining."

They settled into adjacent rooms on the third floor and returned to the lobby an hour later. Summer was dressed in a soft, beige cashmere sweater and boot-length skirt, while Dirk wore a dark blue sport coat and gray slacks.

Standing behind a porter's cart and pretending to study a tourist map, the agent named Ivan discreetly watched their movements.

They made their way out to the portico, where right on time an elegant Rolls-Royce Phantom III Town Car pulled to the entrance. Dirk recognized it as a 1937 Sedanca de Ville.

The driver, a man of Pakistani descent in a chauffeur's uniform, hopped out and opened the rear door. "Ms. Pitt? Mr. Pitt?" He waved a gloved hand toward the interior.

Summer climbed in first and found a massively rotund man occupying the bulk of the rear seat. He patted the Connolly leather beside him. "Plenty of room here, my dear. We'll give Dirk the jump seat."

Summer gave him a hug and squeezed in beside him.

Dirk wriggled in and parked himself on a fold-down seat, then reached across and shook the big man's hand. "Traveling in style, I see."

"Coachwork by Barker," Perlmutter said, stroking his long, full beard. "A bit roomier, you know. I will say that it does earn high marks for styling."

"It's gorgeous," Summer said, "especially for an eighty-year-old car."

Perlmutter reached forward and wrapped a knuckle against the window to the driver's compartment, then lowered the glass an inch. "To Le Gavroche, James."

The chauffeur nodded, dropped the car into gear, and silently pulled forward as Perlmutter rolled the window back up.

"A chauffeur named James?" Summer asked.

Perlmutter shrugged. "I believe his name is actually Ravi, but he kindly answers to James."

Summer laughed. "It's wonderful to see you again, Julien. How was your nautical history conference?"

"Smashing. There were some excellent papers on early wrecks being investigated in the Mediterranean, as well as some exciting research topics here in England. My presentation on the Aztec sea canoes you and your father discovered in the Caribbean was quite well received."

As one of the world's leading maritime historians, Perlmutter was a walking encyclopedia of shipwreck knowledge. A longtime friend of the Pitt family, he had been a trusted resource on many NUMA projects, as well as being a reliably jovial dining companion. Aside from his passion for nautical history, Perlmutter was a dedicated gourmand.

"I almost forgot." Summer handed over a bottle in a felt bag. "A gift from Norway."

Perlmutter opened the bag to reveal a dark green bottle. He studied the label, then chuckled. "Aquavit, of course. Why, thank you. It makes for a delightful cordial." He slid open a walnut compartment beneath the driver's window, exposing a small bar set. Cracking the seal on the bottle, he poured three glasses and passed them around.

"*Skål!*" he toasted.

Summer sniffed the harsh-tasting liquid with a grimace.

Dirk noticed her reaction and smiled. "At least it will keep you warm if the London fog rolls in."

As they sipped their drinks, the Rolls driver slithered around the east end of Hyde Park before pulling up to a corner brick building. Perlmutter led his guests into a side door beneath a brass plate engraved *Le Gavroche*. A historic training ground for London's top chefs, Le Gavroche was easily the city's best French restaurant.

Perlmutter had a spring in his step as they were guided downstairs and seated in a green velveteen tufted booth. Ordering a lobster mousse appetizer, he sighed with delight. "I recall when a pork pie was considered haute cuisine in London. My, how times have changed for the better."

"Tell the truth, Julien," Summer asked. "Was it the nautical conference or London's fine dining that enticed your visit from Washington?"

"I refuse to answer that on the grounds it may prove incriminatory." He patted his stomach and laughed.

Ordering a roast duck in port jus to Dirk's turbot and Summer's Dover sole, he forced himself to turn his attention from food. "Now, tell me about this Norwegian shipwreck of yours."

"It's British, actually." Dirk described their discovery of the *Canterbury* and their encounter with the Russian salvage ship.

"My word, that is most aggressive behavior," Perlmutter said. "Any idea why the Russians would take such a keen interest in a rusty Royal Navy cruiser?"

Summer reached into her purse and retrieved a photo of the gold bar. "We found this in a cabin near the bridge."

Perlmutter's eyes lit up. "Perhaps there is more in the hold, though a light cruiser makes for a poor cargo ship."

"We suspect that's what the Russians are after," Dirk said. "Note the stampings on the bar."

Perlmutter had already focused on the imprint of the double-headed eagle. "House of Romanov," he whispered. "Small wonder the Russians claimed the wreck as their own. Tell me again, when was the *Canterbury* sunk?"

"February twenty-sixth, 1917," Dirk said. "She had left Archangel a few days earlier."

The wheels began churning in Perlmutter's head, taking him far from the French restaurant. "Most curious." He placed the photo on the table. "My land-based history may be a bit rusty, but, as I recall, the Russian monarchy possessed an enormous inventory of gold at the beginning of World War I. What they didn't have, however, was an adequate supply of weapons and ammunition for their troops. They shipped gold bullion to the Allies in exchange for munitions, first via Archangel, then from Vladivostok after the Germans wised up and laid mines in the west. An attempted gold shipment from Archangel in 1917 would have been both dangerous and somewhat extraordinary but not impossible."

"How can we find out more about the *Canterbury*'s last voyage?" Summer asked.

"Dr. Charles Trehorne, Emeritus Professor of Nautical Archaeology at Oxford. He's a colleague and an expert on Royal Navy shipwrecks. I'll ring him this evening and see if we can meet with him tomorrow." He twirled the wineglass with his thick fingers.

Savoring the aroma of the Bordeaux, he slipped the photo of the gold bar back to her. "What did you do with the gold itself?"

"We brought it with us," Summer said. "It's in the room safe at the hotel. I'm sure no one would suspect I have anything of value there."

Perlmutter nodded and took another sip. He had no way of knowing, but at that very moment, Summer's room safe was both open and empty.

DRESSED IN A HOUSEMAID'S UNIFORM, the Russian agent Martina had entered The Gore's rear service door, concealing an assortment of electronic infiltration devices in a bucket of cleaning supplies covered by a towel. She climbed a stairwell to the third floor and found the room numbers to which she'd been directed by a hacker at the Russian Embassy.

She started with Dirk's room, slipping a card key into the door lock, which had been precoded by the hacker with the correct security code. Dirk hadn't bothered unpacking, which made her mission simpler. She started with his unlocked suitcase, rifling through it and finding nothing of intelligence value. Moving to the room telephone, she attached a tiny wireless transmitter to its base, supplemented by a signal booster she attached to the back of the window curtains. The device would transmit all phone and room conversations to a listening station in the panel van parked down the street, at least until its batteries expired in a week or so. Finally, she dug out a ring of keys and found a master that matched the hotel manager's emergency key to the room safe. Inside, she found only Dirk's passport. She ignored that, closed the safe, and hurried to the next room.

She repeated the procedure in Summer's suite, at least to the point of opening the room safe. Startled by the gold bar, she removed it and set it on the bed, along with Summer's passport, laptop, and a flash drive. Using her small electronic tablet, she photographed the bar from all sides, then returned it to the safe with the computer and passport. She inserted the flash drive into the tablet and copied its files, then returned it and closed the safe.

Martina placed her devices at the bottom of her bucket and was turning to leave when she heard a knock at the door and a click of the lock. She froze as the door swung open and a house-keeper entered, carrying a jar of mints. The housekeeper stopped and stared at the Russian. "Are you turning down this room?"

"Naw, they just wanted a'nuther towel," Martina said in a practiced East Ender accent. She pointed to the towel in her bucket and made for the door, slipping past the night housekeeper and walking briskly down the hall. She didn't look back until she had left the hotel and walked two blocks south.

Satisfied she had drawn no further interest, Martina circled around the neighborhood to Mansfield's hotel and knocked on the door of his street-view room. He pushed aside a room service table topped with a half-eaten steak and a bottle of Montepulci-ano and invited her in.

"Any trouble?" He poured her a glass of wine.

"No." She took the glass and set it down without drinking. "The listening devices are in place and activated."

She reached into her bucket and handed him a disposable cell phone. "The van will record all conversations and notify you of any potential transmissions. You are welcome to join the technicians for eavesdropping."

"I'll just wait for the call." He gave a smug grin. "Were you able to arrange a meeting with the financial expert?"

"Yes. Ten o'clock tomorrow." She handed him a folded note with an address.

"Joining me?"

"No, I will be on surveillance duty at that time."

"A pity. You sure you won't stay for a drink?"

Martina shook her head. "I wouldn't want to disrupt your studies." She handed him the tablet. "I downloaded the contents of a flash drive the woman had stored in her room safe. You'll also want to check the photographs I took of another object I found in the safe. Good night."

Martina turned on her heels and let herself out the door. Mansfield activated the tablet and pulled up the file copied from Summer's flash drive. It was her underwater video footage of the *Canterbury*. Mansfield watched the sixty-minute recording of the shipwreck, which concluded with a surface shot of the *Tavda* at dusk near the wreck site.

He started to set aside the tablet, then remembered Martina's parting comments. He opened the digital folder marked PHOTO-GRAPHS, and out sprang a half dozen images of the gold bar. With eyes wide, he stared at the Russian Imperial Seal engraved on it, then reached over and picked up the in-house telephone.

"Room service? I'm going to need another bottle of wine, please."

39

At precisely eight in the morning, Perlmutter collected Dirk and Summer in his rented Rolls-Royce. It was only a short drive to the hospital, where they caught Jack Dahlgren a few minutes before he was wheeled into surgery. They waited in the cafeteria drinking coffee until Dahlgren cleared the recovery room a few hours later. Groggy from the medication, he laughed with his friends after being told he would make a full recovery. Dirk promised to smuggle him a beer on their next visit, and they left him in the watchful care of a nurse who resembled the singer Adele.

The Rolls was soon on the move again, tailed discreetly by a silver Audi sedan. Their destination was Churchill Gardens and a penthouse flat in a large gray stone building that fronted the Thames River. A cramped elevator carried them to the top floor, where Perlmutter rapped a miniature anchor knocker affixed to a polished hall-end door. A large sandy-haired man holding a pot of tea welcomed them in.

"Just off the boil," Charles Trehorne said in a soft, upper-schooled accent. "My wife Rosella set it just before slipping out to run some errands. Please do come in."

The flat resembled a private library. Walnut shelves stuffed with nautical books filled the open floor plan, accented with oriental carpets, antique ship prints, and modern leather furniture. Dirk and Summer looked at each other and smiled.

"Your residence bears a striking resemblance to St. Julien's home in Washington," Summer said.

"Yes, the books," Trehorne said. "An occupational hazard. But I believe Julien has a more exquisite collection."

"Only in numbers," Perlmutter said. "We'd make a formidable maritime repository if we consolidated resources."

"Best in the English-speaking world, I daresay. Please sit down." He ushered them to a round table beside a glass wall that overlooked the river.

Summer watched a small dredge move by. "Stunning view of the Thames."

"Inspiring and distracting at the same time," Trehorne said. He poured tea while Perlmutter helped himself to a plate of scones. Trehorne reached into a nearby book cabinet and produced a bottle of Balvenie single malt Scotch hidden in back. He poured a stiff shot into his cup of tea and passed the bottle to Perlmutter. "A pleasant fortifier, if you like." Trehorne sampled the results with satisfaction and set his cup back on the table. "So, tell me about this Yankee interest in a Royal Navy C-class cruiser."

"We located the *Canterbury* by chance off the coast of Norway," Dirk said, "then found we weren't the only ones interested in her."

"Julien told me about your scrape with the Russians. It leads me to believe there was more to her last voyage than meets the eye."

"What can you tell us about the *Canterbury*?" Summer asked.

Trehorne opened a file that he had prepared. "The *Canterbury* was commissioned in October 1914, the second in the Cambrian class of light cruisers built by John Brown and Company. She was assigned to the Harwich Force early in her career, defending the eastern approaches to the English Channel. She saw light action in the Mediterranean in 1916, then was assigned convoy duty near the end of the year. She was lost off the coast of Norway in February 1917, later determined to have been sunk by the German U-boat UC-29."

"Nothing out of the ordinary there," Perlmutter said. "What do you know of her last voyages?"

"Convoy duty." Trehorne dug deeper into the file. "She made a convoy run to Archangel in November 1916, accompanying a munitions shipment, and returned to Scapa Flow for minor repairs a few weeks later. In the middle of February, she helped escort a second convoy, arriving in Archangel on the eighteenth. But that's where things turn interesting." He looked up at Perlmutter and smiled. "She sailed on convoy with three other Royal Navy ships: the *Concord*, the *Marksman*, and the *Trident*. Those vessels returned with the convoy, arriving in Scapa Flow on February twenty-fifth. The *Canterbury* wasn't among them, but German records indicate she was sunk by the UC-29 on February twenty-sixth."

"A day after the convoy had returned to England?" Perlmutter's lips drooped in skepticism.

"Exactly. It doesn't make any sense. Of course, the Germans could have been off on their dates, but I did some digging at the National Archives and found this." He handed Perlmutter a photocopy of a typewritten order from the Office of the British Admiralty to the captain of the *Canterbury*. Buried within the sailing and refueling orders, Perlmutter found directions for the captain to hold his ship in port for the return of Special Envoy Sir Leigh Hunt.

"Who's Hunt?" Perlmutter asked.

"At the time of his death, he was Special Envoy to Prime Minister Lloyd George. Up until 1916, he had served as Consul General to the British Embassy in St. Petersburg. His biography indicates he had a strong personal relationship with the Tsar."

Dirk turned to Trehorne. "So he returned to St. Petersburg in the waning days of the monarchy and held up the *Canterbury* for a ride home?"

"It would seem so. But I find it unusual that the *Canterbury* abandoned the return convoy to wait for Hunt and make the voyage alone."

"You're certain the ship did in fact wait for Hunt?" Perlmutter asked.

"Yes. He is listed as having perished aboard the *Canterbury*. I made some inquiries and found that Hunt's personal papers are stored at the National Archives. They may shed some light on what he was doing back in Russia. But for the moment, it is all a bit of a puzzle."

"Dr. Trehorne," Summer said, "I have an additional clue to

the mystery." She reached into her handbag and retrieved the gold bar, which she clunked on the table.

Trehorne regarded it with mild curiosity. "An attractive girl like yourself shouldn't be prancing around Westminster with such a treasure."

Dirk smiled. "I'd pity the fool who would try to take it from her."

"I will be more than happy to be rid of it," she said, "if you can advise an appropriate recipient."

"I have plenty of contacts in the Royal Navy who would be thrilled to have it. It will probably end up in their fine museum in Portsmouth." He slipped on a pair of reading glasses and studied the bar. "The Romanov crown markings, if I'm not mistaken."

"That's our interpretation," Summer said. "Do you think the *Canterbury* might have been carrying a large shipment of gold from Russia?"

Trehorne set down the bar and stroked his chin. "Anything is possible, but I would be skeptical. Gold shipments, even in World War I, were very well documented. There's nothing in the ship's record that suggests as much. By that time, Russian gold shipments to the Bank of England for munition purchases had already been rerouted to the Pacific." He shook his head. "Perhaps the Russians know something we don't. Where exactly aboard ship did you locate this sample?" He passed across the table a black and white photo of the *Canterbury*.

Dirk pointed to the squat cabin deck beneath the bridge. "The first cabin there on the starboard side."

"A likely accommodation for a diplomat such as Hunt," Trehorne said.

Summer frowned. "Destroyed now, thanks to the *Tavda*."

"Perhaps by design." Trehorne's voice trailed off. He stood and carried the whiskey bottle to the cabinet. "Well, Julien, you best dispose of that gold bar before every Artful Dodger in London gets on your tail. In the meantime, I'll make an appointment with the National Archives to take a look at Sir Hunt's papers."

"Very kind of you to help us," Summer said. "Is there anything we can do to repay you?"

"There most certainly is." He glanced about the room, then stuffed the bottle back into its hiding place. "You can kindly not inform my wife how I took my tea."

40

Across London in the East End neighborhood of Whitechapel, Viktor Mansfield stepped into a dark pub called the Boar's Head. Wearing a navy Prada sport coat, he was notably overdressed among the sparse crowd drinking at the bar before noon. Only a gray man in a gray suit, seated at a rear booth, appeared similarly out of place. Mansfield ordered two pints of Guinness at the bar and took them to the man's table.

"Mr. Bainbridge?" he asked.

"Yes." The single syllable was uttered in the dry monotone of a banker reviewing a loan application. He gave the beers a derisive look. "A bit early for me, I'm afraid."

"No worries." Mansfield took a long draw on one of the pints, set the glass aside, and leaned forward. "I need information on a gold shipment from Russia to Britain in early 1917."

"Yes, that is what I was told," Bainbridge said. "The Bank of

England archives, to which I have full access, are quite clear on the matter. There was a single recorded transfer of twenty million pounds placed into the Bank of England repository in Ottawa in April 1917."

"Ottawa, Canada?"

"Between 1914 and 1917, there were four major shipments of gold to Britain on agreement for war material. The first occurred in October 1914, when two British warships, the HMS *Drake* and the HMS *Mantois*, received a nighttime transfer of eight million pounds' worth of gold at a rendezvous point thirty miles off Archangel. Despite the attempted secrecy, the Germans learned of the shipment and nearly sank the vessels before they could safely reach Liverpool. Subsequent shipments were sent overland to Vladivostok, where Japanese warships carried the gold to Vancouver. The bullion was transferred to a Bank of England emergency repository in Ottawa, where it was held for safekeeping. There were shipments of ten million in 1915, thirty million in 1916, and the twenty million mentioned in 1917."

As the banker spoke, Mansfield found the bottom of his Guinness and set the empty glass down. "It doesn't sound like a substantial amount of gold was actually transferred," he said, reaching for the second beer.

"Well, sixty-eight million doesn't sound like a great deal today, but that represents almost thirteen billion in today's gold and currency values."

"Thirteen billion?"

Bainbridge nodded indifferently.

"You indicated those shipments were for war material,"

Mansfield said. "Are you aware of any transfers on behalf of the royal family or the Tsar personally?"

Bainbridge shook his head. "The shipments were payments for military aid. The first consignment was arranged by the Russian Ambassador to England, Count Benckendorff. The remaining shipments were by agreement of the Russian Finance Minister and Prime Minister Lloyd George, after a meeting in Paris in 1915. Some more distant Romanov family members had holdings in England, but late in the war Nicholas II made a show of bringing home all foreign deposits. By the time of his abdication, he and his immediate family had no assets in the Bank of England."

Mansfield leaned forward. "I am interested in another transfer that occurred, or may have been scheduled to occur, in 1917 via the Mediterranean."

Bainbridge stared back. "I am a banker and a banking historian. I deal in records and documents archived at the Bank of England. If there were additional gold shipments received by the bank in 1917, there would be evidence. My search revealed neither an additional deposit, nor evidence of a pending deposit, originating from the Mediterranean or elsewhere. If there had been an additional gold shipment made to England, it didn't involve the Bank of England."

"Would there be others, outside of the military, who would have advance logistics information of a proposed gold shipment, whether it went to the Bank of England or some third party?"

"The diplomatic corps might, but security and transport would in all likelihood be handled by the military." Something tugged at Bainbridge's mind and he looked out the pub window.

Across the street, plastered on a bus stop bench, was an advertisement for a Lloyd's of London insurance office.

"There is one other avenue you may consider investigating," he said. "The initial shipment from Archangel in 1914. It was carried on Royal Navy vessels. The War Risks Insurance Office in London insured the shipment and charged the Russian government a premium, along with the transport fee, totaling one percent of the shipment. If your phantom shipment was to be carried on a Royal Navy ship, there's a fair chance the Insurance Office would have known something about it."

A wide smile crossed Mansfield's face. "I knew that you would be of great service." He stood and bowed. "Thank you, Mr. Bainbridge, for the information and for the beer." He turned and left the pub, leaving Bainbridge to stare at the twin empty glasses.

41

"Good morning, Summer," Julien said on the telephone. "I have some intriguing news."

"Good morning, Julien." With her free hand, Summer pulled open the curtains of her hotel room and glanced at the cloudy weather. "What kind of news?"

"Charles Trehorne just called me from the reading room of the National Archives, where he got an early start this morning. He says he found an extraordinary document in the papers of Sir Leigh Hunt. He didn't elaborate but encouraged us to meet him there."

"Do you think it's information about the gold?"

"All he said was that it might explain a few questions about the *Canterbury*. I'm on my way over now and can pick you up in about ten minutes."

"I'll grab Dirk and see you downstairs."

The Rolls was waiting at the curb when the twins exited the

hotel. Dirk and Summer climbed in back, where Perlmutter was reading a copy of the London *Times*.

"Trehorne worked pretty fast," Dirk said.

"He practically lives at the National Archives. Plus, it doesn't take much of a historical mystery to get him fired up."

As the Rolls began to exit the hotel drive, they heard a loud-revving car. The Rolls jolted to a stop, amid a crunch of gears, and its occupants were flung forward as the old car suddenly sped in reverse. An instant later, a black car burst by, its side door careening off the Rolls's front bumper amid a squeal of tires. The speeding car hopped the curb, plowed through a small garden, and slammed into the brick façade of the hotel's gift shop.

Ravi rolled down the divider window. "Is everyone all right?"

"Yes, thank heavens," Perlmutter said. "The blasted fool nearly sent us to our demise."

"Ravi, that was a fine bit of accident avoidance," Dirk said. "How did you know he was going to strike us?"

Ravi smiled. "Private security driving school. We were taught how to minimize a collision. I heard the loud engine, saw his driving angle, and had an inkling he was headed our way. Fortunately, this old car dropped into reverse in a flash."

"Do you think he survived?" Summer motioned toward a cloud of smoke around the smashed car.

They exited the Rolls and approached the car, an old black cab whose front end looked like an accordion. The driver's door was wedged open but the interior was empty. A crowd surrounded the car. There was no sign of a driver.

Examining the car, Dirk noted a racing-type four-point safety harness in the driver's seat and the absence of a license plate. He scanned the crowd, but whoever was driving had melded into the onlookers, then escaped.

"A missing driver," Perlmutter said. "That's odd."

"Probably wasn't a registered driver and wished to avoid a jail sentence," Ravi said, before walking back and examining a long crease on the Rolls's bumper. Soon the police arrived, an accident report was completed, and they were permitted to leave.

"I hope that concludes the excitement for the day," Perlmutter said as the Rolls got moving again. "And I hope it doesn't make us late for lunch."

"I'm sure the National Archives building has a cafeteria," Summer said. "We can grab a bite after we meet with Dr. Trehorne."

"Don't trifle with me, young lady. There's a Michelin-rated Korean restaurant near the Archives that I insist we sample."

She gave him a stern look. "Business before pleasure."

It was less than a fifteen-minute drive to the National Archives in the west London borough of Richmond upon Thames, where a thousand years of British historical documents were housed. Perlmutter led Dirk and Summer up a flight of steps to the entrance of the modern glass structure and into its atrium. While Dirk eyed an attractive woman in a leather jacket who was studying the floor plan, Perlmutter asked at the front desk about Trehorne.

The receptionist perked up at the mention of his name. "I'm sure Dr. Trehorne is at his usual table in the Document Reading Room. I'll have someone take you there."

A research assistant escorted them through a security checkpoint and into the expansive room. "He's in the far back." She pointed to a distant corner.

The trio made their way past dozens of students and researchers at small wooden desks, quietly examining ancient documents. Threading their way to the corner, they found Trehorne wedged behind a long table sided by sliding bookshelves. Two thick document files and some loose pages were stacked on the table, but his focus was on a slim blue binder opened before him.

He looked over the top of his reading glasses and smiled. "Good morning, all. You found me without trouble, I hope?"

"That was the least of our difficulties this morning," Perlmutter said. "You have quite a reputation in these parts."

"I apologize for troubling you with a visit, but I thought you would like to see the original pages of the documents I found. They are quite fascinating."

"We're glad you called," Summer said. "What is it that you found?"

"I had the papers of Sir Leigh Hunt pulled for the period of 1916 to 1917." He patted the binder. "It was in his last set of documents that I found—"

His words were cut off by a loud siren.

"Oh, dear," he said. "That sounds like the fire alarm."

As people began evacuating the reading room, a woman approached the table. Dirk was surprised to see it was the dark-haired beauty he had noticed in the lobby. She ignored him and addressed Trehorne.

"I'm afraid you must evacuate the building," Martina said in an authoritative voice. "I must collect the documents you have checked out."

"Edith in Foreign Service Records provided me these documents," Trehorne said.

"I'll need to return them." Martina slid past Perlmutter to the side of the table.

"This is most unusual," Trehorne said, setting down the blue binder.

Martina leaned across the table and collected the two thick folders, then the binder. Dirk watched as her leather jacket flapped open, revealing a small automatic pistol tucked into a shoulder holster. He realized that unlike the other library assistants, she wasn't wearing a name badge.

Standing between Summer and Perlmutter, he elbowed his sister and motioned at a door along the back wall. He discreetly moved his foot to the side and slipped it around Perlmutter's ankle.

"Forgive me, Julien," he said, then shoved him toward the woman.

The big man stumbled and fell to the side, colliding hard with the Russian. The documents in her hands went flying across the table as she was knocked to the floor.

"I'm terribly sorry," Perlmutter said. Catching himself on a chair back, he leaned over and pulled Martina to her feet.

"Clumsy fool!" She jerked away from his helpful hands.

The nearby door clicked closed, and she wheeled around. In an instant, her trained eyes registered that Dirk, Summer, and the blue binder were gone. Boxed in by Perlmutter and Trehorne, she dove across the table, rolled onto her feet on the opposite side, and drew her gun. She rushed to the door, flung it open, and charged in.

The door opened onto a stairwell landing. She heard the clatter of footfalls and looked over the rail, catching a glimpse of

Dirk and Summer on the floor above. She raised her gun and fired a single shot, which reverberated like a cannon in the stairwell. An instant later, a door slammed.

Martina hesitated, then pulled a two-way radio from her pocket. "The two younger ones have entered the second floor, east side," she said in Russian. "They have the documents."

42

"Why is she shooting at us?" Summer asked as they burst onto the second floor.

Dirk pushed his sister ahead. "Let's not stop and ask her."

They had stepped into a small map room whose occupants had already cleared out. A doorway at the far end led to a larger map and document reading room. Dirk looked to the far room, then pushed Summer toward a side door marked EMPLOYEES ONLY.

They found themselves in a large, dimly lit bay. They took a second to let their eyes adjust, thankful that the alarm blaring throughout the building was muted inside. The bay contained one of the Archives' many large book depositories. Wedged into the cavernous bay were row upon row of sliding bookshelves standing eight feet high. As they padded down a narrow opening between shelves, Summer noted the books contained Britain's tax collection rolls. They reached the end of the shelf only to find more rows beyond.

Dirk gazed at a back wall to his left, then turned to Summer. "Stay here and keep an eye on the door—and a tight grip on that binder. I'll run down and see if there's another exit at that end."

"Okay. I'll follow if we have company."

As Dirk ran off, Summer stepped a few feet in the opposite direction, keeping an eye down the aisles toward the door they had entered. The next row of shelves to her left ran short, ending at a wall with a large canvas cart filled with books. Curious, she scurried down the aisle and found a freight elevator just beyond. She pushed the call button, then hurried back down the row to regain her view of the entry door. It still seemed quiet.

But as she resumed her watch position, a voice called from nearby. "I believe the Archives are now closed."

Summer nearly jumped out of her shoes as she turned and faced a familiar man with blond hair.

"I'll take the documents," Mansfield said in an easygoing voice.

Summer noticed he was nicely dressed in a sport coat and slacks, and held a Beretta aimed at her midsection. It took a moment for her to place his face. "Wasn't it enough to blow up half of the *Canterbury*?" She intentionally spoke in a nervous, high-pitched voice.

"Not when there are still tales to tell. Your brother?" he asked, waving his gun from side to side.

"Coming on the elevator with security." She took a half step back as she motioned over her shoulder at the freight elevator.

They stood facing each other in a narrow track between bookshelves, but Summer had eased past the end of the rack. "What is so important in the files?"

Mansfield could see she was stalling for time. He reached out his free hand. "Give me the folder. Now."

A loud ding announced the arrival of the freight elevator. Mansfield turned and peered over Summer's shoulder toward the opening doors. A second later, a rumbling emanated near his feet. He looked back to see Summer leaping to the side as one of the towering bookshelves toppled toward him.

Two shelves over, Dirk had his shoulder pressed to a center rack and was shoving against it like a charging rhino.

Before Mansfield could brace himself, the twin sliding shelves slammed into him. His chest caught a high shelf that jammed his ribs. He winced as a collection of dusty tax books cascaded onto him, dropping him to the floor as the shelves bounced off him.

Dirk let go and sprinted toward the elevator, shouting to his sister, "Lift!"

Summer was already on the move, reaching the open elevator ahead of him. She jabbed the lowest-floor button and glanced back at the bookshelves. The two mashed shelves around Mansfield began to part. A hand emerged from the pile of books, aiming a gun in her direction. Dirk was still several paces away.

"Get down!" she said, ducking to the side of the elevator door.

Dirk took a step and leaped, sliding headfirst into the elevator. As the twin doors rattled to a close, two shots splattered into the elevator's back wall.

"You all right?" Summer asked.

"Yes." Dirk climbed to his feet. "Where'd he come from?"

"Either slipped in when I was checking the elevator or found another entrance. The woman must have tipped him off." She watched the lights of the floors flash by. "I'm glad you were able to sneak back quietly."

"I heard you speak up and figured it wasn't a good thing."

Summer gave her brother a concerned look. "He was the pilot on the Russian submersible."

"What?"

"I'm certain of it. He's from the *Tavda*. And he didn't deny it."

"Apparently, it's more than gold they're after." His eyes fell to the blue binder that Summer clutched with an iron grip. "We need to find security."

"The front entrance is our best bet. Where are we headed?"

The elevator doors opened. They had dropped into the building's warehouse and loading dock. Packages of dry foodstuffs for the Archives' restaurant were stacked near shrink-wrapped crates of books and calendars for the gift shop. They walked past orderly stacks of plastic containers of contemporary government records fresh from Parliament. They continued along an empty loading dock, framed by a large drop-down garage door. A nearby fire alarm, one of many clanging throughout the building, suddenly stopped.

Summer hesitated and grabbed Dirk's arm. "Someone's coming."

Dirk heard it, too, someone running down a flight of stairs. He glanced away from the sound to his right, where an exit door stood beside the loading dock. At the opposite end of the bay, another door burst open. Martina came flying out, her eyes locking onto the twins.

Dirk was already on the move, dragging Summer to the exit door and flinging it open. The door led outside. They raced down a flight of steps to the base of the loading dock. They were at the rear of the Archives, whose blank walls stretched in either direction. A short delivery driveway extended from the dock to a narrow side lane. Otherwise, they were surrounded by open asphalt.

"Nothing like a distinct lack of cover," Dirk muttered as he led Summer at a full run to the road. Just across the paved lane, a large open field rolled down to the banks of the Thames. The field was flanked by a pair of industrial buildings positioned a healthy sprint away. As the warehouse door banged open behind them, Dirk looked to the river.

Upriver from the bustle of central London, the Thames was relatively serene, a haven more for sport rowers than commercial boats. From their vantage, the river was empty except for a lone tugboat chugging downstream.

Dirk led Summer into the field, angling toward the nearest industrial building. They could see some teens near the water's edge, along with a long, lean object resting on the bank.

"It's too far." Between gasps for air, Summer motioned to the building ahead.

But Dirk had an alternate plan. "This way. To the river."

"Swim for it?"

Dirk just pointed to the riverbank.

With their head start, the downward sloping field gave them a hint of cover from Martina's pistol. The Russian woman reached the top of the field as Dirk and Summer approached the riverbank.

As they drew near the water, Summer shook her head. "You can't be serious."

She stared at a four-man rowing scull beached on the rocks. Its owners, four teen boys who had stopped for a break, were upriver exploring the reeds.

"We don't have to go far," Dirk said.

He muscled the scull off the bank, hesitated a second for Summer to take a seat, then shoved it into the water and hopped aboard. The rail-thin scull would have capsized, but Summer was quick to steady it with a pair of oars. Dirk took to another set and they were quickly stroking toward the center of the river.

Pursuing them at a run, Martina reached the middle of the field. She pulled to a stop and raised her pistol. But the teen boys had noticed the boat thieves and raced along the riverbank, shouting at the two rowers. One took to hurling rocks and the others followed suit. With four witnesses directly in front of her, Martina lowered her pistol and slid it into her shoulder holster.

She stood for a moment, watching the scull cross the bow of the small tug, then turn along its opposite side.

"Martina!" Mansfield called from the road, where he stood watching the scene.

She hurried back across the field and reached him just as a silver Audi driven by Ivan screeched to a halt in front of them. Mansfield jumped into the front seat, and she climbed in back a second later.

As Ivan hit the gas, Mansfield turned to her with his blue eyes ablaze. "We need a boat." His voice was calmer than his expression. "And we need it right now."

The green vessel blew its horn at the rowers crossing its path and cut sharply to starboard to avoid slicing through the forty-foot rowing shell. It wasn't a tugboat, Dirk could now see, but a stout fishing boat. Built in the fashion of a North Sea trawler, the steel-hulled vessel had been designed for endurance in all-weather climates.

After cutting across the trawler's path, Dirk and Summer shelved their portside oars and dug in with their starboard blades. They swung the scull alongside the fishing boat until Dirk could grab a side tire fender. Summer rose and stretched for the side rail and pulled herself aboard. She quickly reached back and snared the blue binder that had been at her feet. Dirk followed her aboard, kicking the scull toward shore as he pulled himself onto the deck.

They were greeted by a black and tan dachshund that approached with its tail wagging, offering an ominous howl. Summer knelt in surrender, eliciting a lick and a melodious greeting.

The dog was followed by a tall silver-haired man who gazed at them through curious coral-sea green eyes. "Are you a boarding party?"

"No, just hitchhikers." Summer rose to her feet. "Sorry to board without asking, but they were trying to kill us." She pointed at the opposite riverbank.

The old man looked across the river. He ignored a silver Audi speeding down the road and focused on the four boys wearing spandex and hurling rocks and insults from the shoreline.

"Killers, eh?" He shook his head. "I guess they do look slightly hostile. I would be, too, if someone stole my boat."

"You don't understand—"

"Excuse me, but I need to get back to the wheel." He turned and stepped to the pilothouse, trailed by the dachshund.

Following behind, Dirk and Summer noticed a life ring outside the wheelhouse identified the boat's name as *First Attempt*.

"Is there a river police station on the Thames?" Dirk asked.

"I think the Brits have some sort of patrol station up near the London Eye. It's along my way, so I can drop you."

"We'd be very grateful." Summer noticed the boat's owner was drinking coffee from a mug inscribed with *Balboa Yacht Club* and the initials *CC*. "What's a fellow Yank doing sailing on the Thames?"

"Mauser and I decided to see the world by boat." He nodded toward the dachshund, now curled up on a pillow near his feet. "We're coming down from a side trip to Oxford." He waved a hand at the windscreen, beyond which the tall landmarks of central London could be seen in the distance. "I always found that you see the worst side of a town driving past it on the highway. The great old cities seem to preserve their best face for the waterfront. We've enjoyed London and are off now to cross the Channel for the Seine River and Paris."

"Did you cross the Atlantic in the *First Attempt*?" Dirk asked.

"Oh, yes, we sailed her across. She's built like a battleship, and just as stable. I've got extra fuel tanks below that give us a range of over three thousand miles."

"How fast can she go?" Summer gazed the shoreline for signs of the two Russians.

"With a friendly breeze and a favorable current, she's good for nine and a half knots." He rapped the throttle forward to its stops. "Don't you worry, miss. I'll have you to the police dock in about twenty minutes."

LESS THAN TEN MINUTES LATER, Mansfield found a boat. By luck, the Chiswick Pier Marina a mile downriver had a handful of boats for hire. Martina arranged a rental by phone seconds before the Audi skidded to a stop out front.

"Keep downriver, and track them as best you can," Mansfield told the Audi's driver.

Ivan had a bruised cheek and a fresh cut on his hand from his collision in the old taxi but brushed off any pain and nodded at Mansfield.

Martina followed Mansfield as he jumped out of the car and hurried to a wiry man wearing coveralls and carrying a gas can.

"You here for the boat?" he asked with a friendly grin.

"Yes."

"The fastest we have, per the lady's request." He pointed past a row of sailboats to a small powerboat at the end of the dock. "A Seafarer 23. She's no cigarette boat but a fine old runner nevertheless, all fueled up and ready to go. I'll just need your driver's license and a credit card."

Mansfield handed him his phony French passport with several hundred-pound banknotes protruding from the cover. "I presume this will suffice?"

The boatman's eyes grew wide. "The keys are in the ignition. Just have it back before it gets dark. Cheers." He watched with curiosity as the attractive, nicely dressed couple sprinted to the boat and roared off into the Thames.

44

The trawler had followed the meandering path of the Thames through west London and reached a northerly turn near Battersea Park when the pursuing speedboat raced into view. Dirk was the first to spot it, recognizing Mansfield and Martina in the front seats. "Can you drop us somewhere quick?" he asked the old man.

"There's nothing close ahead. We just passed St. George Wharf a bit ago," he said. "Do you want to go back?"

Dirk eyed the closing speedboat. "No, let's just keep on."

The sedate old Thames grew busy as they neared central London, the waterway bustling with tourist boats and the occasional small barge. The *First Attempt* held to the center of the river to avoid the growing traffic, the old man holding a steady hand on the wheel. While he was looking ahead, Dirk and Summer stared out the rear window at the approaching boat.

Mansfield brought his boat alongside the *First Attempt*'s starboard beam and slowed to match speeds. He tapped his horn to get the old man's attention, then drew his hand horizontally beneath his chin.

"This fellow seems to want me to stop," he said. "Is he the one who tried to kill you?"

Summer gave him an earnest look and nodded.

The old man smiled and waved at Mansfield, then turned away, keeping the throttle set at full.

Mansfield moved in tighter and displayed a pistol beneath his jacket.

The old man repeated his wave and smile.

"I believe he may use that piece." He looked to Summer and stepped away from the window. "You might want to keep your head down."

Mansfield didn't shoot but dropped behind the *First Attempt*, then eased up to its port flank. Martina stood on her seat cushion and reached for the trawler's rail.

"The woman is trying to climb aboard," Summer said.

Dirk scanned the pilothouse and spotted a half-empty wine bottle on a wall rack. He grabbed the bottle by the neck, stepped out of the doorway, and tossed it rearward. The bottle skidded across the deck and struck Martina in the chest. More startled than injured, she fell back into the boat.

Mansfield replied by pumping three shots from his Beretta into the wheelhouse as Dirk dove for cover.

"I think you got them angry now," the old man said, wheeling the trawler to port.

"They weren't too happy to begin with," Summer said.

Rising to his feet, Dirk scanned the river ahead. There was a pier a half mile downstream, but until then shore access was non-existent. On the river itself, a small barge was approaching along the shoreline, while ahead a triple-decked tourist boat cruised slowly off their starboard bow.

He had to catch his balance as the old man spun the wheel hard over, sending the boat careening. A second later, he reversed the helm and the boat swerved back. He was trying to dodge the speedboat as it attempted another boarding.

"If you can get us alongside that tour boat," Dirk said, "we'll get out of your hair."

"I can try."

The old sailor continued corkscrewing his trawler, torment-ing Mansfield's attempts to transfer a now cautious Martina aboard. "When I give the word," he said, "slip in front of the wheelhouse and stay low." He swung the trawler in a hard turn to starboard and held the wheel until the side doorway was out of view of the speedboat. "Now!" he yelled.

Dirk and Summer bolted out the door and crouched on the bow as the boat heeled back to port. A few seconds later, the *First Attempt* caught up with the tour boat.

The old man could see that the tourist boat's rear deck of-fered the easiest point of access, so he pulled parallel, then rapped on the windscreen to alert Dirk and Summer.

As the speedboat approached on his port flank, the old man swung the trawler hard right until it slapped the side of the tour boat.

Dirk and Summer leaped without hesitation and scampered up and over the side of the tour boat, blocked from Mansfield's view by the *First Attempt*.

"Sorry for the troubles, but thanks for the lift," Dirk called out.

The old man stuck his head out the side window and waved. "No worries. But you do owe me a half bottle of Bordeaux."

He killed the throttle and let the tour boat slip ahead as the trawler drifted with the current. Mansfield caught the move late but slowed and pulled alongside and Martina easily jumped aboard.

With gun drawn, she sprinted to the wheelhouse. In the doorway, she leveled her weapon at the old man as the dachshund erupted in a howling frenzy. "Where are they?"

The old man smiled and said nothing. Martina looked over his shoulder and noticed the tour boat pulling ahead. She looked back at the old man and shook her head. "Today, you are lucky." She aimed a kick at the barking dog and ran back to the speedboat.

Mansfield stood at the wheel with an anxious look. "Well?"

Martina pointed up the river. "They're on the tour boat."

45

The *Sir Francis Drake* was one of the larger boats to ply the Thames River tourist trade, covering the waterway from Kew Gardens in west London to Greenwich in the east. Featuring an indoor café and a topside bar, the triple-deck tour boat could seat a thousand sightseers. But on this cloudy summer weekday, she carried fewer than three hundred passengers.

An inebriated holidaymaker from Yorkshire helped pull Summer onto the open stern deck.

"Welcome aboard, love," he said, giving her a lecherous gaze. "Join me for a drink?"

Dirk was quick to intervene. "Come along, dear." He took her by the arm that still clutched the blue binder and pulled her forward.

Summer feigned disappointment for the drunk's benefit. "Perhaps another time."

She followed her brother through a swinging door that led

into the lower deck's enclosed salon. They ignored a *Private—Reserved for the McIntyre Company* placard at the entrance and stepped down the main aisle. The bay was filled with workers from a local high-tech firm enjoying an excursion on the founder's birthday. Well-dressed employees ate cake and drank beer and wine while looking out the window as the Palace of Westminster came into view. A hired photographer snapped a flash photo of Dirk and Summer as they tried to pass a standing throng and make for the forward stairwell.

While everyone was looking forward out the portside window toward Big Ben, Dirk peered upriver. The *First Attempt* still drifted in the center of the river. But the speedboat was accelerating past her bow toward the tour boat.

Summer hailed a passing busboy. "Can you tell me when the boat will stop next?"

The busboy glanced out the window. "We should tie up to the London Bridge City Pier in about five minutes."

"And where will we exit the boat?"

"The Lido, or second-deck level. I think it will be the portside gangway."

Summer considered the corporate group, then turned to her brother. "I have an idea. Get up to the top deck and make yourself seen by the speedboat. Then slip down to the Lido deck and meet me at the gangway when we dock."

Dirk nodded. "Save me a piece of cake."

"I had a beer in mind."

He ran up the forward staircase to the open top deck, then worked his way to the aft rail and watched the speedboat approach the side of the *Drake*.

Martina made eye contact with him as she stood on the speed-boat's passenger seat. Mansfield bumped the boat against the *Drake*, and Martina leaped for its side rail.

The drunken Yorkshireman was still there to grab her arm and help her across the rail. "My heavens, a second angel from the deep. What's your name, my lovely?"

Martina's answer was a knee to the groin that sent the man and his beer sprawling across the deck. By the time he regained his feet, Martina was scampering up the external stairwell. She stepped onto the upper level as the *Drake* sounded its horn.

The deck vibrated beneath her feet as the tour boat briefly reversed power, slowing its approach to a wooden dock that extended into the river. Half of the seated tourists rose to their feet and crowded toward the stairs as a loudspeaker announced their arrival at London Bridge City Pier.

Martina filtered her way through the crowd, searching for the tall dark-haired man, but Dirk was nowhere to be seen.

She descended the forward stairwell and met a mob of tourists and McIntyre employees who crowded against the portside rail, waiting for the boat to dock. Near the front of the line, she spotted Dirk and Summer, both standing nearly a head taller than the elderly passengers around them. She retrieved her hand-held radio and pressed it to her lips. "They are exiting the boat. Get to shore."

Mansfield was already scouring the pier for a place to tie up. He found an open berth and drove the speedboat alongside.

A dockworker in a blue jumpsuit saw him approach and ran to the water's edge. "I'm sorry, sir, but no private mooring is allowed. This pier is for licensed tourist boats only."

Mansfield ignored the man's comments as he tied up the boat and climbed onto the dock.

"I'm with Scotland Yard on a security matter," he said. He reached into his pocket and extended to the man a hundred-pound note. "Can you watch my boat for a few minutes?"

The dockworker looked up and down the pier to make sure he wasn't being observed, then snatched the bill. "Glad to, sir. She'll be waiting right here for you when you return."

Mansfield ran toward the *Drake* but was a few seconds too late. The gangway had already been extended and the initial throng of tourists had swarmed off. He spotted Martina near the back of the pack, trying to push through the line.

Martina waved for him to join her. The remnants of the crowd were diverging, some exiting straight off the pier, while most followed a raised walkway along the river's bank.

He wormed his way beside her. "Where are they?"

"Near the front," she said, "but we have them now. They're headed aboard the *Belfast*."

Mansfield looked ahead. The walkway fed into a ramp that extended over the water to a large gray warship. The HMS *Belfast* was a Royal Navy cruiser built in 1938 that had seen extensive action in World War II. Preserved as a museum, she was now permanently moored in the Thames, across the river from the Tower of London.

At the ship's entry ramp, Dirk stopped and turned to Summer. "You sure we want to board her?"

She moved ahead. "We need to buy some time waiting for the tour boat."

They led the pack of tourists to the ship's entrance, keeping tabs on Mansfield and Martina following behind. Boarding the old cruiser on her lower deck, they were given free rein to explore most of the ship's inner workings. Summer and Dirk immediately headed aft, walking briskly to the quarter deck and crossing to the starboard rail. A ladder led up to an open hatchway to one of the ship's triple-gun turrets. They climbed two levels and ducked inside. The breeches of three massive six-inch guns filled the circular turret. Peeking through a cutout on the opposite side, Summer could see Martina standing watch on the gangway.

Dirk looked through another viewport as Mansfield pushed past some tourists to skirt around the aft base of the turret. "He's on us."

"Let's get forward and go as high up as we can."

"We'll need to drop down before we can go up," Dirk said.

They scurried down a ladder and entered a bay leading forward, then passed through an exhibit of the ship's laundry station, complete with a mannequin loading an industrial-sized washer. Dirk found a companionway out a side hatch and they descended several more levels, arriving at one of the *Belfast*'s twin engine rooms. They made their way forward as quickly as they could, maneuvering past a maze of pipes and machinery surrounding one of the ship's boilers, as well as past a few slow-moving tourists.

When they reached the forward-most bulkhead, they climbed up the nearest ladder. Dirk hesitated on the steps and peered down the passageway from where they had just come. At the far end of the engine room, Mansfield was hurrying through the bay.

They continued the cat-and-mouse chase, pushing forward and higher through the ship. Dirk and Summer passed the crew's mess on the lower deck before finally reaching the forward super-structure. From there, they clambered up several decks to the narrow confines of the *Belfast*'s bridge. Summer hesitated, checked her watch, then peered out the forward windows. A horn sounded ahead of the ship and she nodded. "That's our tour boat, departing right on time. Let's go up to the flybridge."

They climbed another level to the exposed flybridge, which offered a stunning view of the river and the Tower of London on the opposite bank. They stepped to the port side and briefly looked down at Martina, still guarding the gangway. Then they crossed the bridge to the starboard rail and gazed at the river.

Mansfield arrived less than a minute later. He approached them casually but somewhat out of breath. "Well, we could certainly have dispensed with the ship calisthenics."

"You could have sent your girlfriend," Summer said.

Mansfield smiled. "She's not my girlfriend, but you are correct. She is probably in better shape than me. Now, if you don't mind, I'll have the folder."

Summer held out her hands, both empty. "We don't have it."

Mansfield frowned. "Yes, very clever to have hidden it somewhere on this ship." He gazed around the flybridge, which was shared at the moment by a young family admiring the view. Mansfield turned back to Dirk and Summer, speaking in a low tone. "Siblings, aren't you?" He addressed Summer. "When the family departs, I will shoot your brother unless you produce the folder. And if not, I will shoot you, too." The calm coldness to his voice left no room for doubt.

Summer watched as the family migrated to the stairwell after taking several pictures. "Who are you?" she said. "And why are you claiming the wreck of the *Canterbury* when it's clearly a British ship? Is it the gold?"

Mansfield laughed. "There's no more gold aboard, so I have no interest in the ship now. My name is Viktor Mansfield, if you must know, and I will take that file, please." He tilted his head toward the family, which was now descending the stairwell.

"I didn't hide it aboard the *Belfast*," Summer said. "I left it on the tour boat." She motioned toward the *Drake*, which was passing alongside the warship on its way to Greenwich. "If you look closely, you can just make it out on the lower aft deck."

Mansfield peered over the rail at the passing boat, focusing on its stern. A heavyset man leaned against a tall table drinking a beer, but the small open area was otherwise empty. Then he saw it. The blue binder sat on the center of one of the empty tables, weighted down by a pint of beer.

"I wondered where my beer went," Dirk said.

Mansfield pulled his radio and called to Martina, in Russian, "Get the boat!" He turned to Dirk and Summer as an elderly couple stepped onto the flybridge. "It could be unfortunate for you if this is a trick."

"It isn't," Summer said.

Mansfield nodded, trusting her body language that she was telling the truth. "I trust we shan't meet again." He turned and left the bridge.

Summer sagged in relief as Dirk watched the *Drake* disappear under the Tower Bridge.

He shook his head. "I can't believe you gave it up without finding out what was in it."

"Not exactly," she said. "We'll find out everything that was in that binder tonight. But it's going to cost us fifty pounds and another dinner at La Gavroche."

"La Gavroche again? Are you trying to break the bank?"

Summer shrugged. "Sorry. It's the only restaurant in London I know."

46

he second meal at La Gavroche was just as delicious, and just as expensive, as the first. But the company was decidedly less captivating. Dirk had immediately recognized the photographer from the tour boat as he approached their table, underdressed and unkempt. For his part, the photographer was also disappointed, having expected a private dinner date with Summer.

"Hi, Terrence. I'm glad you could join us," she said. "I'd like you to meet my boyfriend, Dirk."

The men reluctantly shook hands and took a seat on either side of Summer.

"I . . . I thought we might be dining alone," Terrence said.

"Don't be silly," she said. "I see you brought the photographs. How did they come out?" Before he could answer, she plucked the large manila envelope from his hands and passed it to Dirk.

"A moving boat wasn't the best platform on which to photograph documents," Terrence said, "but they came out fine, every page readable."

"That's wonderful. Now, what would you like to eat?"

Dirk and Summer hurried through their exquisite meals at high speed, and Terrence followed suit when the remaining conversation fell away. After skipping dessert, they bid farewell. Summer rewarded the photographer with a peck on the check, along with a fifty-pound note.

"That was a bit cruel," Dirk said as he hopped into a cab with Summer.

"I think he was pretty well compensated for just taking a few photographs."

"True, but I don't think it was quite the compensation he had in mind."

They refrained from opening the envelope until they arrived at Charles Trehorne's residence. They found the historian drinking tea with Perlmutter, served by Trehorne's vivacious wife, Rosella.

"You two don't look the worse for wear after your escapades this afternoon," Perlmutter said. "You gave us quite a scare after you disappeared with that armed woman in pursuit."

"We realized the fire alarm was a staged diversion so someone could get their hands on the file that Dr. Trehorne discovered," Summer said.

"Who on earth would go to such extremes for some dusty old documents?" Trehorne asked.

"The same people who blew apart the *Canterbury*," Dirk said. "The Russians."

"I wish I'd have known that when I gave my report to the police," Trehorne said. "Julien tells me you were forced to hand over the Archives' folder on Sir Hunt."

"I'm afraid so," Summer said.

"That's a pity. I didn't have a chance to review the entire contents. I phoned Julien when I came across a report of Hunt taking a top secret document to St. Petersburg and I presumed we would find our answer." He set down his tea and looked out the window at the lights across the Thames. "My friends at the Archives won't be pleased, either."

"We may have lost the original, but we do have this," Summer said. She opened the manila envelope and pulled out a thin stack of page-sized photos.

Trehorne gazed at the top photo, of a letter handwritten by Hunt. "That was the first document in the binder."

Summer nodded. "I found a photographer on the run who snapped pictures of the binder's contents. Hopefully, he didn't miss any pages."

"Wonderful thinking," Julien said.

"Oh, it cost us." Dirk cast a sideways glance at Summer.

Trehorne held up the first photo and smiled. "This is almost as clear as the document itself. Let's see what else we have in here."

It didn't take them long to filter through the photos, most of which captured mundane administrative documents. Then they came to one marked *Proposed Treaty of Petrograd*. Trehorne skimmed the three-page draft, then passed it to Perlmutter with a shaky hand.

"Take a look at this, Julien. Quite remarkable. I think I may require a drink." He rose to locate his bottle of Balvenie.

Perlmutter began reading the document aloud. It was a draft copy of the treaty transferring Russian mineral rights to Great Britain in exchange for securing the Romanov family wealth. The room remained silent as Perlmutter read to the end.

"That's unbelievable," Dirk said. "The Romanovs shipping their gold to the Allies is one thing, but assigning a piece of their mineral rights for a century to come . . . ?"

"Tsar Nicholas must have considered it a last-ditch effort to save the crown," Trehorne said. "Turning to Britain for help wouldn't have been unusual. After all, King George V and Nicholas II were cousins. But it is still a remarkable proposal."

"Could the treaty still be enforced after all these years?" Summer asked.

"I'm sure an army of the Queen's best attorneys would try to find out, particularly if they could beat the expiration date," Trehorne said. "With billions potentially at stake, there would certainly be an incentive to try."

"But that's only if the deal was signed," Perlmutter said, "and the Romanov gold was actually transferred to Great Britain."

Trehorne retrieved four glasses and poured a tall shot of Scotch in each. Downing his own glass, he picked up the first photo and studied it again.

"It's dated February tenth, 1917," he said. "That's two days before Hunt set foot on the *Canterbury* in Liverpool and sailed to Archangel. Seems likely he took it to the Tsar to sign. I found a Foreign Office report in another file that Hunt did in fact have a meeting with Nicholas, but no details were provided."

"There seems to be no record of such a treaty," Perlmutter said, "so Nicholas must never have signed it."

"I disagree," Dirk said. "I think the treaty was in fact signed and that Hunt was returning to England with a copy on the *Canterbury*."

"No way to prove that," Trehorne said.

"We already have the proof," Dirk said, "and that's with the Russians. They arrived at the wreck site of the *Canterbury*, claimed it was theirs, and proceeded to blast it apart."

"They might have believed the ship was carrying gold," Summer said.

Dirk shook his head. "There's three reasons why they didn't. First, they set their explosives to blow up the ship's superstructure. Any quantity of gold would have been carried in the lower holds, so they should have been blasting open the deck or a side hull."

"They may have been working their way there," she said, "or just wanted to eliminate us first."

"True, and they might still be there blasting it open as we speak. But I think not, for the second reason. The Russian on the submersible who handled the demolition is now here in London. He's tracking our movements and stealing historical documents from the National Archives." He tapped the stack of photos.

"There's logic to what you say," Perlmutter said. "The Russians may have blown up the *Canterbury*'s superstructure because that's where Hunt would have been berthed. If he was carrying a signed treaty copy in a diplomatic pouch, or even a heavy leather valise, there is at least a possibility it could have survived the sinking." He looked at Dirk and Summer. "They know you two were suspicious about the wreck and may have been trying to circumvent your discovery of the treaty."

"And the associated Romanov treasure that was to be sent to England," Trehorne said.

"Indeed," Perlmutter said.

Summer looked to her brother. "You said you had three reasons. I counted only two."

"Our encounter with Viktor Mansfield today. Do you remember what he said when you mentioned the *Canterbury*'s gold?"

"He said there is no more gold aboard her. But if the treaty was signed and no gold was shipped on the *Canterbury*, then where did it go?"

"Probably captured by the Bolsheviks, along with the rest of the Romanov assets, when they overran St. Petersburg a short time later," Perlmutter said.

Trehorne cleared his throat. "Perhaps not." He held up the final photograph. The image depicted a typewritten letter from Hunt to an Admiral Ballard. The letter was red-lined, with a few handwritten word changes, indicating a draft copy.

"Please read it to us, Charles," Perlmutter said.

"It's a letter dated February eleventh, 1917, addressed to Rear Admiral George Ballard, Commander, Malta Dockyard," Trehorne said.

"Dear Admiral.

"With approval from First Sea Lord Jellico, please station HMS Sentinel *off Epanohoron Cape by 27 February, 06:00, for possible rendezvous with* Pelikan. *Transport to Liverpool via G to follow, at RN discretion.*

> *"Yours obediently,*
> *"Sir Leigh Hunt, Special Envoy to Russia,*
> *"The Foreign Office"*

"My, my," Perlmutter said. "That certainly sounds like they were up to something, if this *Pelikan* is a Russian vessel."

"Quite so. Let me see what I can find on these two ships." Trehorne walked to the other room, perused his library for a few minutes, and returned with a pair of hardcover books and an old atlas of the Mediterranean.

"Let's start with vessels of the Russian Imperial Navy." He opened the first book. "The *Pelikan*. Yes, here it is. It was actually a submarine. One of the Bars class, the largest of the Russian subs, at sixty-eight meters and six-hundred-and-fifty-ton displacement. Her hull was laid down in September 1915 and she entered service the following April, assigned to the Black Sea Fleet. The *Pelikan* supported the Caucasus Campaign and saw action off the Danube in 1916. She was listed as missing in action and presumed sunk by Turkish warships off Chios in February 1917."

"Chios, Greece?" Perlmutter said. "She must have snuck through the Bosphorus and the Dardanelles."

"A risky move during the war," Dirk said. "Prompted by special cargo?"

"She was a large boat for the day, so theoretically she could have carried a sizable cargo of bullion," Trehorne said. "A crafty move, if that's what it was, sliding it right under the nose of the Ottomans."

"Nicholas may not have had much choice," Perlmutter said. "The Imperial gold reserves were held in Moscow and St. Petersburg. Perhaps he knew that St. Petersburg was about to fall, and that it was too risky to send the gold north. There was still the overland route to Vladivostok, but I believe his loyalist forces were strongest in the south."

"That is true," Trehorne said. "The rise of the loyalist White Army was centered in what is now Ukraine. So in the waning hours of Nicholas's reign, that may have been the safest route."

"Where is this Epanohoron Cape, the designated rendezvous point?" Summer asked.

Perlmutter consulted the atlas. "It's the northern point of the Greek island of Chios. The same region where the *Pelikan* was listed as sunk," he said with a raised brow.

"If she sank in February, then it is questionable whether she made her rendezvous with the *Sentinel*," Dirk said.

Trehorne opened the second book. "Let's see what the Royal Navy has to say about our second vessel. Here it is. The HMS *Sentinel* was a scout cruiser built in 1904. She served in the Mediterranean Fleet during much of the war, based out of Malta. She struck a mine and sank off Sardinia in March 1917."

"A couple of unlucky vessels," Summer said.

"She sank in March," Dirk said. "That means she came nowhere close to sailing to Liverpool after the rendezvous."

"Quite right," Perlmutter said.

"Which means the gold is still on her—or, more likely, the *Pelikan*," Summer said, excitement in her voice.

Trehorne nodded. "It would seem to be a strong possibility."

Summer looked at her brother. "What do you say? It's a nice time of year to take a visit to the Mediterranean."

"That sounds good to me, but there's one problem." Dirk gazed at the picture of the Russian submarine. "We're not likely to be the only ones making the trip."

47

Sixty miles east of Odessa, a mud-splattered pickup turned off a narrow dirt road and into a pasture. The flat property was no different than the neighboring farms that stretched as far as the eye could see except for two vehicles parked behind a strand of trees. One was a large green semi-trailer truck, the other a sleek Peregrine unmanned aerial vehicle.

Martin Hendriks emerged from the trailer with an assistant and greeted the driver. "You are right on time."

"Colonel Markovich sends his regards."

"Was the delivery made without incident?"

The driver, an overweight man with a thick beard, nodded. "Yes, the Russians handed them over to us in Sochi. They thought we were dockworkers putting them on a ship to Africa." He laughed. "They have no idea that they'll be seeing them again."

He walked to the back of the pickup, removed a tarp, and

uncovered four Vikhr laser-guided antitank missiles, commonly deployed on Russian attack helicopters. "We accepted delivery of twelve missiles and, per your directive, kept eight for our use."

"Can you help load two onto our trailer," Hendriks said, "and the other two onto the drone?"

"Of course."

The driver and Hendriks's assistant loaded two of the one-hundred-pound missiles into a hidden storage compartment on the trailer, then attached the remaining two on the Peregrine's underwing launch racks.

As the driver climbed back into his pickup, Hendriks stuffed a wad of Ukrainian currency into the driver's hands. "Tell Colonel Markovich to put the other eight to good use."

"We will," the man promised, then drove away.

Hendriks inspected the armed drone, then turned to his assistant. "Gerard, let's launch the Peregrine."

Gerard wheeled out a radio control console, which Hendriks used to start the drone's motors. The vehicle rolled forward and easily took to the air under its wide flared wings. Hendriks had it circle the field a few times, then sent it south. He switched off the local radio signal and transferred guidance control to a commercial satellite system relay. By the time the drone reached the Black Sea coastline a few miles away, it was cruising at twelve hundred meters.

Gerard opened a laptop and pulled up a map of the Black Sea showing green triangles that marked the locations of GPS-monitored commercial ships. He zoomed in on the coastal region near Odessa and studied a myriad of vessels.

"Mr. Hendriks, I show two Russian-flagged ships. One is a tanker, the *Nevskiy*, near the mouth of the Dnieper. The other is a freighter, the *Carina*, which appears en route to Istanbul."

"Let's take a look at the freighter. How far off is she?"

"Just under fifty kilometers. We'll catch her before dark."

Hendriks nodded.

Gerard programmed the freighter's speed, direction, and co-ordinates into the flight control system. A half hour later, a red freighter appeared on the drone's long-range camera. Hendriks took over manual control and approached the ship from the stern while maintaining a covert distance.

The Peregrine's camera showed a small bulk carrier riding low in the water, its white, blue, and red Russian flag flapping at the sternpost. Hendriks turned the drone away and let Gerard program the vehicle to fly in a slow holding pattern.

"That will make for an acceptable target," Hendriks said, stepping from the console. "Let's engage in about five hours."

The Dutchman retired to a small cabin that stood at one end of the trailer. At two in the morning, he awoke and returned to the console. The Peregrine was trailing the *Carina* by three kilometers, but it was close enough for Hendriks to lock on the drone's laser targeting system to the freighter's bridge.

"How is the surrounding traffic?" he asked.

"I'll check." Gerard yawned and consulted his computer. "The nearest vessel is twenty kilometers away, heading north."

Hendriks nodded, then pressed a pair of red buttons. A hundred kilometers away, the two Vikhr missiles whooshed off the Peregrine and rocketed toward the ship. Hendriks held the camera tight on the freighter as the missiles struck in tandem at the rear of the *Carina*'s blockhouse. The bridge structure disintegrated in a bright fireball that was quickly swallowed by the night sky.

Hendriks watched for several minutes, then passed the controls to Gerard. "It will appear as an internal accident. Move the Peregrine off thirty kilometers to a remote section of sea. At dawn, bring her back to the area at low altitude and search for survivors. Be sure and run video when you find them. Hopefully, we'll be the first to call it in to the Ukrainian Coast Guard."

Gerard quietly nodded, then stared with discomfort at the sinking ship.

Hendriks felt no such sensation. He returned to his cabin bed and slept like the newly dead until morning.

48

The two ships slogged through a heavy rain, running parallel courses. Each towed a side-scan sonar towfish on two hundred meters of electronic cable. Working together, they took less than twelve hours to survey thirteen square kilometers of seafloor—and locate the remains of Alexander Krayevski's aircraft.

Valentin Mankedo stepped to the sonar station wedged into a corner of the *Besso*'s bridge. Renamed the *Nevena*, the salvage ship looked like a different vessel. Several deck cranes had been removed and her moon pool covered with a temporary cover. Plywood bays had been added about the main deck to alter her topside appearance, plus a fake funnel was added well aft of the functioning one, which had also been altered. A re-spray of paint from gray to blue completed the *Besso*'s transformation. Mankedo knew it would deceive any casual observer.

"She should be coming up any second now," Vasko said from a seat in front of the sonar monitor.

Archeologist Georgi Dimitov joined Mankedo in watching the screen. Dimitov moved unsteadily, his ghost-pale complexion revealing a losing fight with seasickness.

On the monitor, a gold-tinted image of the seafloor scrolled by, the signal fed from the towfish. Gradually, a black linear object appeared on the screen, taking the shape of a thick letter т. It took little imagination to see the shadow as the remains of a large airplane. One wing and part of the tail were absent, but the rest of the aircraft appeared intact, sitting upright on the bottom.

"What do you think, Georgi?" Mankedo asked.

"Twin motors on the remaining wing is a positive indicator." Dimitov tried to focus on the moving image. "Can you determine the dimensions?"

Vasko used a computer mouse to drag a line along the image.

"Fuselage is thirty meters long. The wing looks to be about twenty meters."

Dimitov nodded. "Those are the correct parameters."

Mankedo stared at the monitor as the plane's image scrolled past, deep in thought. "I had heard stories from the old-timers about a lost Russian bomber that supposedly went down near Durankulak in the 1950s. Apparently, the legend is true and only the location is wrong."

"Do you think its payload remained intact?" Dimitov asked.

"The fuselage appears whole," Vasko said, "but no telling if it was jettisoned. We'll have to take a closer look to find out."

Mankedo ordered the *Besso* to drop a buoy to mark the position, then turn around and make another pass.

"The history I found is that local fishermen in Durankulak were quietly hired by the Russians to search for debris from the aircraft," Dimitov said. "My uncle was a young crewmate on one of the boats. That's why I knew the significance of the body found on the Ottoman wreck. My uncle said they never found any sign of the plane, only the rumor of an oil slick spotted in the sea near the Romanian border."

Mankedo shook his head. "A false lead that sent the searchers too far north."

"I guess we have the Americans to thank," Vasko said.

The salvage operator in Mankedo took over and he turned his attention to the operation to retrieve the old bomber's payload. A remotely operated vehicle was sent to video the wreck site and from there he developed a plan for extraction.

Mankedo personally led the first dive team to the site, carrying an assortment of torches, cutting tools, and small explosives to gain access to the fuselage. Topside, Vasko assembled a sling and harness lift system to use with the stern A-frame.

When Mankedo returned to the ship from his dive, he was all smiles. "A nice fat baby ready for delivery," he said, then gave Vasko measurements for the lift system. "Side access is wide open. A block pulley should work to pull it out."

Vasko led the next dive team to the plane, taking the cabled sling and harness and a framed pulley. Working more deliberately than usual on a salvage job, he secured the lone weapon in the bomb bay with the harness. Then he used the pulley affixed to the fuselage frame to slide it horizontally from the bay. Once it was clear of the plane, he activated the ship's cable and raised the weapon slowly to the surface.

Vasko swam alongside the behemoth until nearly reaching the surface, then returned to the ship. Standing in a dripping wetsuit beside Mankedo, he watched as the bomb was hoisted from the sea and set on a wooden deck rack.

Dimitov approached and looked at the weapon with astonishment. "It appears nearly new. Hardly any corrosion."

"A gift of the anoxic seas," Mankedo said. "If it has remained watertight, then it should still be able to go *bang*."

The thought made them all a bit nervous and they studied the weapon with reverence. Vasko directed some crewmen to secure the device and cover it with a tarp.

"I'm not sure that keeping it aboard the *Besso* is the safest move."

"True," Mankedo said. "The weather is lifting, and I want to get the ship to the Mediterranean as soon as possible. We'll drop it at the facility and see if our Dutch friend has an interest."

"There's no question he'll have an interest. The question will be whether he has the money."

Mankedo smiled. "Exactly."

49

Viktor Mansfield sat in the passenger seat of the silver Audi rereading the blue binder he had recovered from the tour boat.

To his right, Martina nervously tapped the steering wheel with her long manicured fingernails. "We should have taken another car," she said.

Mansfield gazed out the windshield, past the church parking lot, to the concrete and glass National Archives building two blocks down the street. "No, we're safely out of view. Besides, there was no time to change cars. I need the data on the British ship before the Pitts or their cronies find it."

They waited another hour before Ivan appeared with a folder under his arm. He glanced around to ensure he wasn't being followed, then made a beeline for the Audi and climbed into the backseat.

"Any suspicions?" Martina asked.

"None." His deep, clipped voice revealed his Muscovite roots. "There were no questions about my data request. There may have been a different research librarian than before."

"What were you able to find?" Mansfield asked.

Ivan passed him the folder, which contained a handful of photocopied papers. "Very little on the HMS *Sentinel*, I'm afraid. They had some build specifications and sea trial data, which I grabbed, along with a brief history. She apparently sank off Italy after striking a mine in March of 1917. The librarian said the Portsmouth Naval Museum might possess a greater operational history of the ship."

"What about the risk insurance?" Mansfield asked.

"That's what took some time. The original War Risks Insurance Office records were absorbed into the Ministry of Transport in 1919. I checked the data and found one payment in 1917 from Russia."

He pointed to a page in the folder and Mansfield held it up. It was a statement of accounts for the full year 1917. Amid a long list of payments for merchant ships and cargoes lost at the hands of the German naval forces was a large credit posted from the Imperial Russian Treasury. The notation listed an April payment of two hundred thousand pounds drawn from an account in Ottawa.

Mansfield shook his head. "That was for an earlier shipment of arms valued at twenty million pounds."

"Look on the next page," Ivan said.

The following page held a short list of uncredited receivables. An additional entry was shown for the Imperial Russian Treasury in the amount of one hundred and twenty-five thousand pounds.

"It says a pending shipment to Liverpool," Ivan said. "But it was never paid."

"From the submarine mentioned in the other file?" Martina asked.

"Yes, it must be the *Pelikan*," Mansfield said. "My Moscow historian indicated it was lost in the Aegean in late February 1917. They evidently made it that far with the gold."

"But the British government didn't collect the insurance premium. They must not have received the gold."

Mansfield noted the payment amount and whistled. "The Tsar paid one hundred and twenty-five thousand pounds to insure the shipment."

"That sounds like a healthy amount in 1917," Ivan said.

Mansfield thought back to his meeting with Bainbridge. The banker said the earlier gold shipments were insured by a one percent premium on the shipment value. If the same formula held for this shipment, it would place the value of the gold aboard the *Pelikan*, at today's prices, at more than two billion pounds. "There were no other indications that the premium was paid?"

"No," Ivan said. "If you look at the other documents, you'll see it was carried in their records for several years and ultimately written off as an uncollectible in 1925."

Martina started the car and backed out of the church lot. "Is that the answer you were looking for?"

"It's a data point. Not the concrete evidence I would prefer, but it provides strong inference."

"What about the Americans?" she asked. "Are you satisfied they can cause no further trouble with what they know?"

"I am satisfied there is no signed copy of the treaty in England to worry about. As for the Americans, they can be a persistent bunch, so we must act to preserve what is ours."

"What did you have in mind?"

He gave her an assured smile. "Tell me, Martina. Have you ever been to Greece?"

50

The *Macedonia* crept into Burgas Harbor just after dusk, the waters calm and glowing from the lights of the waterfront shops. The NUMA vessel's lone crewman expertly piloted the ship alongside an open berth, where Giordino and a handful of dockworkers secured it to the wharf. Ana watched from nearby with a police escort, noting the speckled damage to the ship's exterior.

"Ready to go aboard?" Giordino asked her.

"Yes, of course."

He led her onto the *Macedonia* and up to the bridge, where they found Pitt shutting down the engines. His face was furrowed with exhaustion, but his eyes sparkled at the sight of the two visitors.

Giordino grinned. "How's our zombie captain holding up?"

"Ready to sleep like Rip Van Winkle." He lightly stomped his feet, cursing the pain in his knees that seemed to strike with more frequency as the years rolled by.

"How long were you at the wheel?" Ana asked.

Pitt eyed a bridge chronometer. "About twenty hours. Nearly drained the galley's supply of coffee and peanut butter and jelly."

"Rudi has a backup skeleton crew en route from the States that should arrive tomorrow," Giordino said. "And Ana has arranged round-the-clock security from our friends at the Burgas Police Department."

"Glad to hear. I wasn't looking forward to standing watch tonight."

"We better get you off your feet," Ana said. "Is there a place we can sit?"

They relocated to the wardroom, where they found comfortable chairs around a conference table.

"Al told me about your ordeal with the Russian warship," Ana said. "I still don't know how you could have survived such an attack."

Pitt patted the top of the table. "The *Macedonia*'s a pretty responsive old gal when she wants to be. The question is, who would instigate such an attack on Sevastopol—and why?"

"I can't answer the why, but we may have a lead on the who," she said. "Forensics came through for us on one of the two men killed on the docks here. He was a Ukrainian national from Mykolaiv. A police interview with his family indicates he took a job just a few months ago with a salvage company near Burgas. We canvassed the area and found only one salvage operation of any size. Thracia Salvage is located on a remote section of the coast between Burgas and Varna."

"What do you know about them?" Pitt asked.

"They've been around almost thirty years, run by a man named Valentin Mankedo. He may be an ex–Romanian Navy diver. Apparently, the company works throughout the Black Sea, though it isn't particularly well known in Burgas. Local authorities report that in recent years, expensive cars and boats have been seen near his yard."

"That doesn't sound like the lifestyle of any salvage operators I know," Pitt said.

"Although it appears he's involved in something more financially rewarding," Ana said, "the regional police have no record of any illicit activity."

"So we don't have a lot to go on," Giordino said.

"Except for this." Ana pulled a photo from her purse and laid it on the table. It was a grainy overhead shot of a ship and boat docked in a narrow cove.

"Satellite photo?" Pitt asked.

"From NATO, taken about six months ago. It's a blowup of an image of the coastal area that includes the Thracia salvage facility. It is a bit fuzzy, but we believe the ship is—"

"The *Besso*," Pitt said.

Giordino nodded. "That crane configuration is what we saw at the site of the *Crimean Star*."

"Authorities in the nearby town of Obzor confirm sightings of the *Besso*. She's registered in Cypress to an entity that may be a front for Thracia Salvage."

"Is the *Besso* there now?" Pitt asked.

"No. I have the yard under surveillance and she's not there. I'm afraid we don't know her whereabouts."

"Why don't you shake down this Mankedo character?" Giordino asked.

"I obtained a warrant this afternoon to pick him up for questioning. I also have approval to search his salvage yard." She looked to Pitt. "We don't have any evidence they were responsible for the *Macedonia*'s hijacking. But like you, my suspicions are high. I'm going in with a small team first thing in the morning. I thought you might want to be there."

Pitt glanced around the empty wardroom, wondering about the crew's fate. A deep resolve overshadowed the fatigue that marked his face. He gave Ana a firm nod.

"You thought right."

51

Some one hundred and twenty miles to the southeast, the *Besso* received radio permission from the Turkish Control Station at the Türkeli lighthouse to enter the Bosphorus Strait. Only she was no longer the salvage vessel *Besso* but the oil supply ship *Nevena*. Renamed, repainted, reconfigured, and littered with a stack of drill pipe on her deck for good measure, she bore little resemblance to her former self.

Joining the other southbound traffic that was permitted entry from noon to midnight, the *Nevena* churned past the Türkeli light and entered the narrow passage. Two hours and sixteen miles later, the ship crept past the Golden Horn. Georgi Dimitov buttoned up his jacket as he stood on the bow, watching the lights of Istanbul twinkle by on both Asian and European shorelines. The city lights gradually faded as the ship entered the Sea of Marmara a short time later and the *Nevena* increased speed.

The archeologist made his way to the bridge, where the helmsman breathed a sigh of relief.

"Difficult passage?" Dimitov asked.

"It's always a challenge, but especially at night. I don't know how the big tankers manage it. There are tight turns, strong currents, and endless traffic to contend with."

"A pilot is not required aboard?"

"Only for Turkish ships. We have a Cypriot registry."

Dimitov stepped from the window and studied a digital map of the sea ahead on a monitor.

The helmsman read his mind. "Chios Island?"

"Yes."

"About eighteen hours, if we sailed direct."

Dimitov nodded and stared out the forward window. Although there was nothing but blackness ahead of the ship, all he could see was gold.

52

The battery-powered drone flitted above the salvage yard like an overgrown butterfly. Nearly invisible in the dawn light, the device flew high enough that the whine from its four rotors could barely be heard. Crisscrossing over the facility, the drone eventually flew past the entrance and down the road a hundred meters, then landed behind a large hedge.

Ana glanced from the video monitor to the device itself as it landed a few feet away.

The drone's operator, a cadet with the Bulgarian National Police Service, retrieved the device and began packing it in a case. "See everything that you needed to?" he asked her.

"Yes, as much as we could with the minimal light."

Pitt and Giordino eyed the drone before it disappeared into its case. "If those things can deliver a pizza," Giordino said, "I might have to invest in one."

Ana ignored the comment and joined five other heavily armed agents who stood by the hood of her car, examining satellite photos of the Thracia Salvage Company's compound.

"The photos were taken some time ago," she said, "but the drone view looks little different. The large salvage vessel is gone, but two other vessels are still at the dock, a workboat and a passenger craft." She nodded to two men to her left. "Mikel and Anton, you'll secure the dock in case anyone decides to leave by boat. The rest of us will cover the main compound building, which appears to contain on-site residences and offices. Any questions?"

"Do we approach on foot or in our vehicles?" one of the policemen asked.

"We'll leave our cars at the front gate and enter on foot. The drone shows that the street gate and a heavier, second gate farther in are both open." She pointed to one of the photos. "There's a long walled corridor after the second gate that we must pass through to enter the compound. It opens up near the dock. From there, we'll have to backtrack to the main building. It's the only entry point, aside from the narrow cut from the sea, so let's move through it quickly. Remember, the suspects are likely armed and apt to resist."

As the teams broke to prepare the raid, Pitt approached Ana. "Al and I spotted a small boat just down the road. Spare us a weapon and we'll cover the sea approach."

Ana considered the offer and decided it would keep Pitt and Giordino out of harm's way. They really shouldn't even be there, but she owed them the opportunity to discover the fate of the *Macedonia*'s crew. "All right. One weapon, for defensive use only." She handed Pitt her SIG Sauer handgun. "No entering the facility until we have it secured."

"We'll just hang out beyond the shore, sailing a sea of discontent," Giordino said.

As Ana and her team slipped into tactical vests and checked their weapons, Pitt and Giordino strode down the road to a pebble-strewn beach. They headed to a small wooden skiff lying hull up on the gravel. They flipped the boat over and found a mast, sail, and oars wedged under its three bench seats.

"I wouldn't sail her to Fiji," Pitt said, "but she looks like she can make it around the breakwater."

They dragged the boat to the water's edge and pushed it through the small breakers and climbed aboard. Giordino raised the mast and rigged the single lateen sail. Pitt tied off the boom, took a seat at the tiller, and turned the boat leeward. The sail rippled tight from the offshore breeze, and the small boat jumped ahead through the waves.

Pitt tacked to the north, aiming for a short-walled breakwater. As they sailed past it, they gazed into the narrow sea entrance of the salvage yard. As the gray dawn washed over the shoreline, Pitt could appreciate the site's seclusion. To the north and west of the complex, steep rocky cliffs provided a natural barrier. A high rock wall ran along the southern barrier, melding into the breakwater.

Pitt dropped the sail and allowed the boat to drift toward the narrow opening between the seawall and a mound of high rocks. Giordino shipped the oars and rowed into the entrance. The boat came to a sudden halt with a scraping metallic sound.

"Run aground?" Pitt asked, although they were in the center of the slender channel.

"No, a chain." Leaning over the bow, he could see a submerged chain curtain, its top strand stretched just beneath the surface. The barricade extended from the side boulders to the seawall.

"Guess they like their privacy." Pitt nodded to a video camera on a pole amid the rocky border.

From the barrier, they had a clear view of the compound. On their right a long warehouse faced the water, while a two-story brick building stood at the far end of the cove. Both appeared to have been built into the cliffside, and both looked more than a century old. Between the structures, open paved grounds were dotted with crates and equipment. Ahead and to their left was a thin wooden dock and the two boats Ana had seen with the drone. Left of the dock was another wall, creating a high corridor with the seawall as the facility's lone shore entry.

Their vantage on the water allowed Pitt and Giordino one other sight. Peering through the gray, they could see a low rock outcropping just past the corridor. Crouching behind the rocks were two men with automatic weapons, waiting in perfect ambush for Ana and her men.

53

The two police cars approached the salvage yard with their headlights dimmed, stopping just short of the entrance. Ana led the team on foot to a rickety chain-link gate beneath a battered sign proclaiming THRACIA SALVAGE. A large anchor beside an old fishing net strewn across a boulder created the desired image of a low-budget operation. Had the law enforcement agents looked closer, they might have found a motion-activated video surveillance camera hidden in the net.

Mikel opened the gate and the team moved down the shrub-lined entry, not knowing they had activated an alarm that was sounding deep within the facility. The road curved as they approached the compound's true entrance, which the foliage had concealed from the main road. Ten-foot walls bordered a paved drive that ran toward the sea.

The team moved past a thick steel gate that was standing open, the men accelerating their pace at Ana's lead. Not until they had gone another twenty yards and the steel gate silently closed behind them did Ana realize they were into more than they had bargained for.

She knew from the drone video that the corridor ran nearly to the water before opening left onto the dock, where they would have to backtrack inland to the shore facilities. The opening was in sight, just a few yards ahead, when a single gunshot split the dawn air. It was nearby but seemed to come from the sea and be aimed elsewhere.

Ana froze and crouched low to the ground, as did the five-man assault team that had fanned out behind her.

She didn't breathe, feeling her heart thump, before the dawn erupted in gunfire.

The hidden figures behind the rocks ahead opened fire on them. Ana dove to the ground as the chatter from a pair of AK-47s reverberated off the walls. Three of the men behind her went down hard and the other two scrambled to return fire. Ana did the same, pulling up a Heckler & Koch MP5 submachine gun and firing a short burst at the rocks.

"Keep moving!" she yelled at her team. They were sitting ducks in the confined corridor. She squeezed off another burst, then leaped up and sprinted a few yards before again diving to the ground. A second later, two of her comrades followed suit and slammed to the ground behind her. She saw it was Anton and Mikel.

"Give me cover to get around the near wall and I'll do the same for you," she said. Not waiting for an answer, she popped up and bolted to the end of the wall. The opposing fire was reduced by half, and Ana saw it was now directed toward the sea entrance.

As Anton and Mikel scrambled to her side, she took careful aim at a lone shooter visible behind the rocks and emptied her clip. The distant muzzle flashes ceased.

She paused to reload. "Where are the others?" she asked Anton.

"They're all down."

Thoughts of tending to her team vanished when gunfire erupted from the main building ahead of them. Two or three figures emerged from the structure and scattered behind some heavy equipment. One of them looked heavy, muscular, and bald.

The agents were exposed as they faced the compound, but cover presented itself in the form of a storage shed wedged against the wall. The trio sprinted for it but came under fire from someone on the dock. Mikel hit the ground, and Ana felt a stinging in her calf, followed by a hard blow to her side.

She gasped and fell. As she tried to get up, Vasko approached from ahead and lobbed a rock-sized object in their direction. The shed was just ahead, so she tried crawling toward it, hugging the wall beside her.

The ground near her erupted, showering her with rocks and debris. Her ears rang, blocking the sounds of battle. She coughed out the dust in her lungs and looked up to see a figure emerge through the haze. It was the gunman from the dock, firing his assault rifle. Ana tried to raise her gun, but her arm was too numb.

The gunman stepped closer and centered his weapon on her

face. As she waited for the gunshot, his dark eyes rolled back in their sockets when a red spot appeared on his temple. He dropped his gun and crumpled to the ground.

An instant later, Pitt was at her side, gripping the smoking SIG Sauer. Giordino arrived beside him and they dragged her to the safety of the shed.

The ringing in her ears lessened enough to hear Pitt say, "My mother's not going to allow us to be friends if you keep getting us into trouble."

Despite the pain in her leg and side, she smiled as he emptied the clip at a distant figure.

Gunfire converged on them from all directions. Then the ground shook under another concussion grenade, more powerful than the first. This one struck at the base of the wall, just ahead of the shed. It was followed immediately by a second explosion that obliterated the shed, along with a section of the rock structure beside it. Ana felt an avalanche of rocks and mortar rain down upon her. First the pain, then the noise, and finally the light around her slipped away to nothingness.

54

The ache began in Ana's wrists and extended through her elbows to her shoulders. She shook her hair from her eyes and the fog from her mind—and the other pains returned. Worst was the hammering bruise to her side where her tactical vest had repelled a slug from an AK-47. A flesh wound to her calf still throbbed, but that was the least of her agonies. The ringing in her ears had been replaced by a headache. It was her wrists and arms, however, which vied for her primary attention. As she regained her focus, she saw why.

Her wrists were tied with a rope that stretched over her head to a warehouse rafter. Somehow she found the balance to put her weight on her feet and she stood erect, relieving the tension on her arms. With that minor relief, she gazed around the dimly lit warehouse. She wasn't alone. A few feet to her right, Mikel hung from his wrists, unconscious. To her left, Giordino and Pitt were similarly bound.

"Welcome back," Pitt said, "although sleeping it out like your friend would appear the wiser strategy."

"How . . . how long was I out?" The words were scratchy from her dry throat.

"We've been stretching our arms for about twenty minutes," Giordino said.

Ana stared at the two men. They were covered with dust from head to foot, and their clothes were torn and spotted with blood. She looked down and saw her own appearance was little better. "What happened?"

"A pair of grenades uprooted a section of the wall," Pitt said. "Collapsed on top of us."

"What about Anton?"

Pitt shook his head.

"I remember now," Ana said. "The wall came down right after you saved me from that gunman." She shook her head at the memory. "You were supposed to stay in the boat."

"We saw two armed men setting up an ambush," Giordino said. "Dirk tried to warn you."

"Yes, they caught us in the open."

"We had to contend with getting the boat over a chain barricade, otherwise we would have gotten to shore sooner."

"All you had was my pistol." She looked at the men. "I'm sorry. I wish you had stayed in the boat and gotten away."

"And miss the chance to hang out together?" Giordino asked.

Ana shook her head at the Americans.

A door slid open at the end of the building and a lone figure entered the warehouse. A ray of light glinted off his shaved head. Vasko carried a capstan bar, using it as a walking stick. The wooden pole, once used by sailors for leverage on manual capstans to weigh anchor, clicked on the concrete floor as he strode toward his prisoners.

He approached his first victim, Mikel, who hung like a side of beef in a meat house. Vasko eyed him, then swung the bar like a baseball bat, striking him in the ribs. The unconscious man gasped reflexively but otherwise hung limp.

"Apparently, he is indeed asleep." Vasko turned to the others and looked them up and down. "My three old friends, dropping in for a visit? You should have told me you were stopping by. I would have planned a warmer welcome."

"It was plenty warm, thanks all the same," Giordino said.

"Did I ask for you to answer me?" Vasko plunged the end of the bar into Giordino's stomach. Most men would have gasped in agony, but Giordino looked down at the man and smirked.

Vasko took another step and approached Pitt. "How about you? Do you have anything to add?"

"Cut me down from here and I might."

Vasko turned the rod and swung it into Pitt's midsection. Pitt tightened his stomach muscles and twisted to catch the blow beneath his ribs. He nearly lost his breath, but he mimicked Giordino and glared at Vasko with a tight grin.

"Seeking to make things difficult, I see," Vasko said. "We'll see how tough you are after a thorough tenderizing." He swung the rod within a whisker of Giordino's face, then tossed it aside.

He walked past the two men and slowly approached Ana.

"And you, Agent Belova," he said, reading a name badge clipped to her vest. "You must have missed me, to return so soon." He slipped an arm around her back and yanked her toward him.

Ana turned away, holding her breath as he pulled her tight. The bearded stubble of his face grazed her cheek.

"Once I have finished with your friends, we'll have some fun together," he said. "Just the two of us."

The blindside blow struck Vasko in the kidneys, sending him sprawling across the floor. He sprang to his feet and spun around as Giordino swung backward on the rope after landing a flying kick. Vasko charged into him, arms flailing.

Defenseless, Giordino absorbed half a dozen body blows to his midsection. His only weapon was his feet. He kicked when given the chance, eventually landing a counterblow to his attacker's knee.

Vasko staggered back, then reached to his hip. He produced a large folding knife and snapped the blade into place. He held it in front of him and flashed the serrated edge at Giordino. "Your time is over, my friend."

He turned an eye toward Pitt to ensure no interference from him, then crouched low and sprang forward. The tactic worked against him. Giordino braced and timed a counterkick that caught Vasko in the wrist. The kick threw off Vasko's lunge and the knife skirted past Giordino's leg. Vasko immediately jumped back, pulling the knife with him. He caught the side of Giordino's leg on the backstroke, slicing his pants and sending a trickle of blood down his leg.

Vasko learned his lesson and stood upright, turning his side toward Giordino. This time, he would rush high and deliver a quick, fatal blow where it could not be deflected. Raising the knife, he took a step forward—as a call sounded. "Ilya!"

The low, measured voice stopped him in his tracks. He glanced at Giordino, then stood back and gazed toward the open door.

The tall figure of Valentin Mankedo approached quickly. He wore an anxious look. "This is no time to be playing games."

"She is the Europol agent who boarded the *Besso*." Vasko pointed the knife at Ana. "And her two friends are the ones from the NUMA ship who disrupted our Sevastopol operation."

Mankedo regarded Pitt and Giordino with curiosity, then approached Ana. "Why did you come here?"

"To arrest you, Valentin Mankedo," she said in a firm voice.

He noticed a folded paper in her vest pocket and pulled it out. "My arrest warrant?"

Ana tilted her head in a faint nod.

He opened the paper and read it while walking away from the prisoners.

Vasko followed at his heels.

"What do they know?" he asked in a low voice.

"Most everything." Mankedo shook his head. "We're suspects in the sinking of the *Crimean Star*, the hijacking of the *Macedonia*, and a possible attack on Sevastopol. Not to mention possible involvement in the trafficking of restricted nuclear materials."

"They must have identified and tracked the *Besso* to the yard." Vasko spat on the ground. "It's that female police agent."

"More will be on the way," Mankedo said. "We'll have to evacuate the yard at once." His dark eyes narrowed. "I need you to dispose of the bodies and the police vehicles while I eliminate our records."

"We can't leave that here." Vasko motioned toward the end of the warehouse, where a flatbed truck held the weapon from the Tupolev bomber. The device was covered with heavy tarps.

"The Dutchman is the only person with the resources to help us with that now."

"Does he know about it?"

"Yes," Mankedo said. "He was quite intrigued and was organizing the expertise to do something with it. I'll call him now and see if he can arrange immediate transportation. When the yard is clear, drive it somewhere remote. If he can come through, it will be your ticket out of the country."

He looked out the warehouse as one of his men dragged a body past the door. "I'll take the rest of the men on the workboat to Turkey and we'll make our way overland to meet the *Besso* in the Aegean. We still have two large opportunities in front of us, and plenty of work in Ukraine when the heat dissipates."

"The heat." Vasko turned and waved a meaty arm at the four prisoners. "What about our guests? We lost three men, on account of them."

Mankedo checked his watch, then glanced at the prisoners.

"Don't waste any more time. Bury them with the others," he said, then turned and strode into the sunlight.

55

The four prisoners dangled by their wrists for another hour as the salvage yard workers scrambled to evacuate the compound. Mikel regained consciousness, only to moan continuously in pain. Pitt watched as a workman started the flatbed truck and let the engine run for several minutes before shutting it off.

"How soon before the cavalry arrives, Ana?" Giordino asked.

"The Bulgarian police are probably formulating a response now after our failure to report. Given our remote location, it may be a few hours before they can assemble and position a team."

"By which time, it would appear, Mankedo and company will be long gone." Pitt struggled with his wrist bindings. "Anyone have a chance of slipping free?"

"It must have been a former Boy Scout who strung us up," Giordino said. "I can't move a millimeter." He flexed his powerful arm muscles to exert pressure on the ropes, but they refused to budge.

Vasko entered the warehouse holding an assault rifle and accompanied by a young bearded man. He passed his folding knife to his accomplice. "You will remain positioned apart and walk in single-file. If anyone tries anything foolish, I will shoot every one of you." He smiled as if hoping to be given the opportunity.

Pitt watched as first Mikel, then Ana and Giordino were cut down. The bearded man had to stand on his tiptoes to reach above Pitt's wrists and cut the thick line. He immediately jumped back, keeping the knife at the ready, as Pitt lowered his arms.

The knife wielder moved back to Mikel and led the captives forward, with Vasko taking up the rear behind Pitt. Mikel tripped and fell several times, and Giordino was allowed to assist him along. As they approached the warehouse entrance, Pitt eyed the flatbed truck. He pretended to stumble, dropping to one knee to try to get a glimpse under the tarps. He saw just a rounded metal skin, the surface dark and smooth, before Vasko's work boot landed between his shoulder blades.

"On your feet."

Pitt stood and followed the others into the daylight. With their wrists still bound in front of them, they walked across the open yard toward the other building, then were led into an opening in the rocky cliff. A pair of rusty rails set in crumbling concrete led from the tunnel, and Pitt recognized the remnants of a mining operation, confirmed by a nearby slag heap. The site was a small tin mine that dated to the Byzantine Empire. Limited commercial operations had continued into the 1930s, until the main ore deposits were deemed tapped out.

The tunnel soon opened into a wide cavern illuminated by dangling overhead lights. Pallets loaded with wooden crates, like the munitions stores Pitt and Giordino had seen on the barge, filled the center. Along the side walls, an assortment of boulders remained from the mine's final days of blasting.

Vasko guided them to a large front-end loader parked between two massive boulders, its blade to the wall. The bearded man climbed onto the rig and started its clattering diesel engine. He raised the steel blade and backed the loader away from the wall, exposing a low opening that led to another room.

Vasko motioned toward the opening with his rifle. "It is time to say good-bye."

Pitt and Giordino eyed each other, but Vasko intervened, leveling his gun at Giordino.

"You first, shorty."

Giordino glared at him, then ducked through the opening, followed by Mikel.

Vasko motioned at Pitt next. "I'm sure you'll have a tearful reunion. Now, go."

Pitt lingered near Ana, but caught Vasko's gun muzzle to his back, and reluctantly ducked through the opening.

Vasko lowered his weapon and stepped close to Ana. "You have created quite an inconvenience for us." He leaned into her. "I wish I had the time to repay you for the troubles you've caused." He grabbed her in a bear hug and kissed her hard on the mouth.

Ana fought the urge to struggle against the vile assault and instead stood limp and cold. It had the desired effect.

"No love today? Then that tears it." He yanked her off her feet and tossed her through the opening. She had barely left his arms when he turned to the man on the front-end loader. "Seal it up. For good."

Ana would have nose-dived onto the rock floor but for Pitt. Waiting on one knee, he caught her as best he could with bound hands. Ana leaned over and spat, trying to remove the taste of Vasko from her mouth, before thanking Pitt.

The front-end loader started forward on the other side of the wall, its steel blade grinding against rock. Rather than seal the cavern with just the machine, the driver used it to shove one of the boulders into place, blocking the opening with a twenty-ton chunk of granite.

All fell quiet as Pitt helped Ana to her feet. They stood and turned to face a second cavern, about half the size of the first. A battered gas lantern, perched on a rock several yards away, cast a dull amber glow. It gave off just enough light to reveal the three dozen haggard, anxious faces of the *Macedonia*'s crew, crowding close around them.

56

Thirty minutes later, the salvage yard was abandoned. Mankedo loaded a cache of weapons, explosives, and research materials onto the workboat, then supervised the final, gruesome cleanup. The bodies of both the police and his own men were placed inside the two police cars, which had been driven alongside the quay. Using a dockside loading crane, each car was hoisted over the side and sunk in twenty feet of water.

Mankedo watched the bubbles rise from the second vehicle as Vasko approached from the crane controls.

"That should keep the next batch of police at bay," the bald man said.

Mankedo motioned toward the damaged stone wall. "There are still signs of the firefight. Nearby residents may have heard the shooting."

"I'll make a pass down the drive with the front-end loader

and clean things up. But if they don't find the bodies, they will have nothing."

"The others are secured?"

"They're sealed up in the side cavern. Unless someone reopens the mine a hundred years from now, they'll never be found." Vasko nodded toward some crates near the tunnel. "Do you want to blow the remaining munitions on the way out?"

Mankedo looked about the compound like an aggrieved parent. "No. I've already loaded the explosives. This has been our home as well as our base for over ten years. I hope to be back."

"With that agent Belova gone, their case will be, too," Vasko said. "Things will blow over, as they always do, and then we can resume operations here."

"Yes, but we best leave now. I reached Hendriks and he said he will try to arrange transport out of Stara Zagora before midnight. He asks that you accompany the device until it's in a safe place. Do your best to stay invisible until then. Once you've made delivery, you can join us in Greece."

"Have you negotiated a price?"

"Twenty million, if it is still operational."

Vasko smiled. "That should buy us a nice base in the Aegean."

Mankedo took the remaining crew and boarded the workboat. They opened the barrier chain, motored into the Black Sea, and heading south toward the coast of Turkey.

Vasko ran the front-end loader down the entry road, obscuring any tracks while scraping up shell casings and wall debris. He guided the pile across the dock and shoved it all into the lagoon. Then he started the flatbed and exited the compound, locking the gates behind him.

A few miles down the road, he passed a string of police cars headed toward the salvage yard. None of them paid any attention to the well-worn truck. Vasko exited the coastal road at the first opportunity and drove inland at a moderate speed.

He drove for several hours, crossing the eastern plains of Bulgaria that were filled with checkerboard swaths of barley and wheat fields. Near Stara Zagora, a prosperous industrial center, he turned south toward the regional airport. A short time later, he parked the truck off a remote section of the runway and watched a sporadic mix of private planes and small commercial flights take off and land.

At half past nine, a huge cargo jet touched down and pulled to a stop well short of the terminal. With the runway lights, Vasko could see a small flag of Ukraine painted on the side. He started the truck and passed through an open security gate that stood unguarded.

He drove to the rear of the aircraft, which was lowering a drop-down landing ramp.

A man in a flight suit approached with a suspicious air. "Name?" he asked through the open side window.

"Vasko. I'm with Mankedo."

The man nodded as he eyed the truck. "I'm the flight engineer. You'll do as I say. We're going to take the whole truck. Drive it up the ramp."

Vasko drove into the cargo compartment of an Antonov An-124, one of the world's largest commercial transports. The truck was carefully secured to the deck by the flight engineer, then Vasko was guided forward to a spartan row of bench seats just behind the cockpit. By the time he took a seat and buckled in, the plane was already moving. He could peer into the open cockpit and watch as the runway rolled beneath them and the big jet took to the sky.

Once the plane reached cruising altitude, the flight engineer reappeared with a cup of coffee, which he handed to Vasko.

"Thanks," Vasko said. "How soon do we land?"

The flight engineer glanced at his watch. "About eleven hours."

"Eleven hours!" Vasko nearly spilled his coffee. "Aren't we just hopping over to Ukraine?"

The man shook his head. "Nowhere near, I'm afraid. We're headed west, with orders to deliver your cargo to Mr. Hendriks's private compound."

"How far west?"

"Halfway across the Atlantic," the man said, grinning. "To Bermuda."

57

The cavern was cold, dark, and silent. As Pitt's eyes adjusted to the dim light, a trim man in a dirty white uniform approached. It was Chavez, the *Macedonia*'s third officer.

"Welcome to our dark little corner of the world." He reached out to untie Pitt's hands.

"We'd feared the worst," Pitt said. "Is the entire crew accounted for?"

"We're all here, doing as well as can be expected. Except for Second Officer Briggs. He was killed in the assault. And the captain's in a bad way." He motioned toward the rock that supported the lantern.

A prone figure lay with a jacket draped over his torso. Even from a distance, Pitt could see the man's labored breathing.

The rope fell free from Pitt's hands and he rubbed his wrists, then turned to untie Ana's bindings while Chavez went to work on Giordino's. Mikel was next. The injured Bulgarian officer lay on the ground, drifting in and out of consciousness.

"Tell us what happened," Pitt said.

"It wasn't long after the three of you left the ship in Burgas. That archeologist was ashore also. An armed assault team came out of nowhere and took over the ship before anyone knew what was happening. They killed Briggs and shot the captain in the arm." His voice trailed off briefly. "They sailed the *Macedonia* out of Burgas straightaway. Brought us to this lovely pit. Nobody's had anything to eat in several days, but they did leave us plenty of water."

Pitt finished untying Ana's hands. "I want to see the captain."

Chavez guided them past the NUMA crew and scientists, who looked gaunt but were encouraged by Pitt's presence. Captain Stenseth seemed to be sleeping, but when Pitt knelt beside him, his eyes popped open.

"How are you feeling, Captain?"

"Arm's giving me fits," he said in a raspy voice, "but otherwise good."

Stenseth's right arm was crudely bandaged just above the elbow. More alarming, it had swollen to nearly twice the size of his other arm. Obviously infected, the wound had become life-threatening.

"Are you here to get us out of this cave?" he asked.

"Yes," Pitt said. "In just a short while."

A faint smile crossed Stenseth's lips before he closed his eyes and drifted into unconsciousness. Pitt stepped away from the captain, joined by the others.

"That arm doesn't look good," Giordino said in a low voice.

"He needs immediate medical attention," Ana said. "As does Mikel."

"Then we need to find an exit, sooner rather than later." Pitt turned to Chavez. "Have you explored the perimeter?"

"Solid rock all the way around, as far as I could tell, except for the gap they shoved us into." Chavez grabbed the lantern and passed it to Pitt. "Have a look."

With Ana and Giordino at his side, Pitt walked the perimeter of the cavern. The walls were as Chavez had indicated, chiseled and grooved stone that rose ten feet high. Above the walls, solid rock tapered to a cathedral ceiling some fifty feet overhead. A shaft of light at the very crest provided a faint supply of fresh air—and a glimmer of hope.

Giordino gazed up at the opening and shook his head. "Even Spider-Man would have a tough time making it out that way."

Pitt continued the circuit until they reached the lone entrance, which was sealed by two massive boulders. Pitt stood in front of the rocks, studying them a long while. "That's our only way out," he said finally.

"Going to be a little tough without a drill bit and some explosives," Giordino said.

Pitt looked to Chavez. "Are there any tools in here?"

"Nope. Just an old car engine and some wreckage behind those rocks." He pointed to the center of the cavern and a low pile of ore tailings. Some rusty pieces of metal protruded from the opposite side.

Pitt held up the lantern. "I'd like to take a look."

Giordino followed him to the rock pile. Skirting a stack of

tunnel support timbers, they found the skeletal remains of an antique car. Pitt waved the lantern over a bare chassis that supported its engine and radiator in front and a fuel tank in back. Stacked in a heap beyond were the rusty, dust-covered remains of the car's body. The chassis had carried a convertible body, Pitt could see, with fenders that were highly flared.

"Odd place to open a body shop," Giordino said.

"They stripped it down to use the engine," Pitt said. "Looks like it dates to the 1920s." He stepped close to the engine, a big straight-eight painted black, and examined the rear mounting. The transmission and driveshaft had been replaced by a makeshift pulley system attached to the flywheel.

"They drove or rolled it in here and used the engine as a power source," Pitt said. "Probably to drive a pump for draining water out of the mine's lower levels."

"Quite a power plant," Giordino said. He walked to the front of the chassis and admired the large nickel-plated radiator. With his palm, he wiped away a layer of grime on the top of the shell, revealing the white letters IF against a blue background.

"You know what it is?" Giordino asked.

"An Isotta Fraschini." Pitt smiled. "A high-end classic car that was built in Italy. Rudolph Valentino drove one."

"I'll remember that the next time I need a lift in the Sahara. Wish we could drive it out of here." Giordino blew a coat of dust off the chassis, revealing a rusty surface. "Looks a little rough, even for your collection."

Pitt said nothing. He owned a warehouse full of antique cars back in Washington, D.C. But he wasn't considering the car for its collector appeal. He leaned over the engine block and pulled out its dipstick, noting the crankcase was full of oil. He replaced it with a nod of satisfaction.

Ana looked at him and shook her head. "I don't think this relic can help us any."

"On the contrary," Pitt said. "This old beast is our ticket out of here."

Ana looked at him like he was crazy. "How can this pile of junk get us out of here?"

Pitt gave her a knowing wink. "Quite simple, actually. We just need to use an old trick that once worked for Hannibal."

58

The *Nevena*, formerly the *Besso*, lay anchored in the Turkish harbor of Kabatepe. An offshore current pulled at the vessel until she floated perpendicular to land. A short distance away, the town's central dock was filled with small, sun-beaten fishing boats. A delivery truck emblazoned with IRMAK PRODUCE motored to the end of the dock and stopped with a squeal of its brakes. Valentin Mankedo hopped out of the cab and opened the rear of the truck, releasing three crewmen who had been wedged between crates of tomatoes.

Mankedo returned to the cab, pulled out a thousand euros from his wallet, and handed the bills to the driver. "Be gone, Irmak. And remember, you didn't bring us here."

"Of course, of course, Valentin," the driver said with a smile. "Good luck with your treasure hunt."

As the truck drove away, a small launch was released from the

Nevena. The boat sped quickly to shore and collected Mankedo and his men.

Returning to the ship, Mankedo climbed up to the bridge, where Dimitov and the ship's pilot welcomed him.

"Any issues passing the Bosphorus?" Mankedo asked.

"None," the pilot said. "We registered as the *Nevena* and passed without question."

"Good." He turned to Dimitov. "Now, where are we with the *Pelikan?*"

"Some positive developments. As you know, available Russian war records only indicate she was lost in the Aegean. Turkish naval records have no information. But I did find a reprimand in March 1917, issued to the commander of a shore battery in the Dardanelles for allowing an enemy submarine to slip past the nets at the southern end of the Sea of Marmara."

"That doesn't sound encouraging. If the Turks sank her but have no record of it, that doesn't leave us much to go on."

"Actually, they didn't sink her," Dimitov said. "It was the Germans. While they had no real surface fleet in the Mediterranean, they did have an active submarine fleet. One of their U-boats, the UB-42, reported attacking and sinking a suspected Allied submarine in February 1917. It can only have been the *Pelikan.*"

"Do we know where?"

"Navy records indicate the engagement took place twenty kilometers off the northwest coast of Chios, within sight of Epanohoron Cape."

"That narrows things down a bit."

"But wartime records are notoriously inaccurate. We might have a weeks-long search on our hands."

"No matter. Let's get under way and out of Turkish waters."

The *Nevena* raised anchor and sailed south, drawing within sight of Chios eight hours later. One of the larger Greek islands, Chios lay in the central Aegean, just four miles from the Turkish mainland. They approached the northern tip of the island and angled to a point twenty kilometers offshore. A towed side-scan sonar array was lowered off the stern, and the ship began sweeping across a search grid of three-mile-long lanes.

They quickly disproved the conventional wisdom of underwater explorers that lost shipwrecks are never where they're supposed to be. On only its second survey lane, the *Nevena* located a prime target. Barely six hours into the search, a lowered ROV confirmed that they had found the *Pelikan*.

59

"Hannibal?" Giordino said. "I don't see any elephants. This old car doesn't even have a trunk."

"If you'd stayed awake in history class," Pitt said, "you might remember how Hannibal solved a problem in moving his elephants, and the rest of his army, across the Alps."

In 218 B.C., Hannibal Barca had led the one-hundred-thousand-man Carthaginian Army in a surprise attack against the Roman Empire, launching what would later be called the Second Punic War. History remembers his epic trek across the Alps from Gaul in the company of thirty-eight war elephants to make a bold strike from the north. But while his army descended the rugged slopes into Italy, its path was blocked by a massive landslide.

Bottled up in the mountains, Hannibal turned his army into laborers, clearing away the loose rock. But several enormous boulders still blocked their way. So the Carthaginian leader turned to an old mining technique that dated to the ancient Egyptians. He set fires beneath the boulders, then doused them with vinegar, which caused them to fracture into smaller pieces that could be hauled aside. With their way now clear, his army proceeded to attack and defeat the Roman forces protecting Milan. Though ultimately repelled by the Romans, Hannibal's march over the Alps remains a classic case study in military strategy.

Pitt knew the fire-setting technique could still work without vinegar. With Giordino's assistance, he hauled several of the support timbers to the base of one of the boulders that sealed the cavern. He then turned to the Isotta Fraschini for a way to ignite the wood. Prying and pounding the crankcase drain plug with rocks until it spun free, he collected the engine's syrupy oil in an empty gravel bucket. He punctured the car's fuel tank with a tire iron, adding some stale gasoline to the mix, and applied it to the boulder and timbers.

"Everybody stay back," he told the NUMA crew. Using the lantern's flame, he ignited the formula. At first the oil and gas mixture burned with a low, smoky flame, but the dry timbers eventually produced a roaring fire.

As the flames danced up the face of the boulder, Pitt stood aside with Ana and Giordino.

"I'm a little worried about the fumes," Pitt said, pointing at the small opening above their heads. "Ventilation is on the weak side."

"Beats shivering to death in a cold, black cave," Giordino said.

The two men kept the fire raging for nearly an hour before testing their thermal shock theory. Pitt filled the bucket with drinking water left by their captors, then flung the contents onto the boulder. The water struck the rock with a crackling sound, sending off a cloud of steam. But the boulder held intact. A few minutes later, a flat sliver cracked off and fell to the ground.

Pitt kicked at the small piece. "Not the avalanche I had in mind."

"At least it proves your theory is working," Ana said.

In the lantern light, Pitt saw she appeared sleepy, and her eyes were unfocused. "Are you feeling all right?"

"I'm just feeling very tired."

"Why don't you go sit with the others and keep an eye on the captain for me?"

Ana nodded, and Pitt guided her to the back of the cavern, where Stenseth and Mikel had been moved. The captain briefly opened an eye at their arrival, then drifted back to his labored breathing. Ana sat down next to him, thankful to be off her feet, and stared off into the fire.

Returning to the blaze, Pitt could see the cavern was filled by a hazy layer of smoke. The scent of burnt wood hung heavy in the air. He approached Giordino, who was dragging another timber toward the blaze. "We've got a problem," Pitt said.

Giordino muscled the wood onto the flames, brushed his hands clean, and turned to Pitt. "Are we all out of marshmallows?"

"Yes. And we have a hefty dose of carbon monoxide to make up for it."

"That might explain my pounding headache." Giordino looked up at the small overhead opening, which was gathering most of the fire's smoke. "Any kind of opening down here would aid the ventilation."

Pitt eyed the massive boulder and frowned. "We need to make it happen fast."

The two men redoubled their efforts, hauling timbers to the fire and dousing the rock with water at regular intervals. Standing close to the fire, they both experienced symptoms from the invisible carbon monoxide gas: dizziness, blurred vision, shortness of breath, and dull headaches. Willing themselves past the poisoning, they attacked the boulder for another hour.

Pitt used the Isotta Fraschini's tire iron to chisel and pound at the rock. Small chunks split from the boulder, but the large mass remained intact. Pitt felt his strength ebb and he stopped and sat to catch his breath. He saw Giordino dragging a timber across the floor in a drunken stagger and he rose to help.

Barely able to stand, both men dragged and rolled the wood to the slowly dying fire.

"That's the last timber." Giordino gasped and fell to the ground, holding his hands to his aching head.

Pitt wanted to lie down and go to sleep, but he forced himself to carry the bucket to the crate of bottled water. He dug through dozens of empties before finding a full bottle. Like the timbers, it was the last one. He poured it into the bucket and staggered back to the fire. Every step seemed to magnify his dizziness, and he nearly tripped and fell onto the fiery rock.

He stopped in front of the rock and turned to Giordino. His old friend was no longer sitting upright but sprawled across the ground, his eyes closed.

Pitt turned back to the boulder and cursed. "Break, you bastard."

With his last ounce of energy, he flung the bucket at the crown of the rock. The rusty pail clanged against the boulder, its contents spilling down the heated granite. Pitt stumbled back as a cloud of steam rose from the surface in a searing wave. He swayed on his feet, ready to collapse, as his burning eyes stared at the rock. "Come on!" he yelled, though his voice was raw and weak.

Above the crackling fire he heard something. It was a deep rumble that sounded far away. The sound grew in intensity, then fell silent. Pitt stood, still swaying, and looked up.

With a crack like a thunderbolt, the boulder gave way. Fracturing into a half dozen large chunks, the massive rock crumbled in front of him. The thundering collapse knocked him off his feet and doused the fire with a cloud of pulverized rock. The cavern grew deathly silent as the light was snuffed out and dust floated to the ground like snowflakes.

Coughing and rubbing his eyes, Pitt rolled over and pushed himself to his knees. He sat for a moment and waited for the dust to clear. Through the haze, he saw a large opening in the wall and smiled as a steady blast of fresh air blew over him.

60

The water surrounding St. David's Island sparkled in the sunshine as the Antonov transport touched down on the single runway of L.F. Wade International Airport. The plane taxied to the cargo terminal and shut down its engines. A waiting ground crew had already filed a phony duty record with the local customs inspector and went to work offloading the Bulgarian flatbed truck, after ensuring its cargo was still concealed.

Vasko shook off a few hours of fitful sleep as he was escorted to a white pickup truck, which followed the flatbed off the airport grounds. The convoy crossed a causeway to Bermuda's Main Island, then traveled a short distance to Tucker's Town, a private enclave of imposing mansions where Hendriks maintained his beachfront estate.

Entering a high-walled gate, Vasko was duly impressed. After ascending a long winding drive, the vehicles arrived at a gleaming white house overlooking the ocean. The trucks drove past a fountain to a garage tucked away on the side, which matched the house with its high-gabled roof. As the trucks entered the garage, a drop-down door closed behind them and a bank of overhead lights flicked on.

Vasko could see the garage was a huge structure, much larger than it appeared from the front. It also contained a working laboratory. Rows of CAD/CAM stations stood across from stainless steel lab benches backed by racks of test equipment. Above one table hung a large drone aircraft, suspended by wires from the ceiling. Hendriks stood by a side door watching the trucks enter, accompanied by two older men. A handful of technicians in lab coats waited behind them.

Vasko jumped out of the pickup and approached Hendriks as he led his entourage toward the flatbed.

"Let's see what you brought us," the Dutchman said.

The two truck drivers removed the tarps, exposing a large, zeppelin-shaped atomic bomb.

Hendriks slowly walked around the platform, his eyes glued to the Cold War–era weapon. He climbed onto the truck bed and ran his fingers over its cold steel skin. Approaching the nose, he stared into a small glass sensor that was coated with dried silt. He finally climbed down, spoke quietly to the two older men, then approached Vasko.

"Fine work, Ilya," he said without emotion. "You and Valentin have delivered something special. Come, let's have a drink while my scientists look it over."

He guided Vasko along a cobbled path to a veranda at the rear of the main house. He mixed them each a rum gimlet, then sat down at a shaded table overlooking the Atlantic.

"Bermuda is quite beautiful," Vasko said. "But I was expecting a shorter flight, to Ukraine or Romania."

Hendriks took a sip of his drink and nodded. "Ukraine was my first inclination, but I decided that security there was too unreliable. There are pro-Russian agents everywhere. When Valentin told me the weapon appeared in good condition, I chartered a long-range aircraft to give me some options. Bermuda made sense, as it is a trusting locale, and I have a special relationship with the customs officials."

"And an impressive working facility," Vasko said.

Hendriks waved toward the garage. "Yes, I have a research lab that I have used for some of my avionics projects. Much of my Peregrine surveillance drone was developed here. The facilities should prove useful for revitalizing the weapon." He leaned forward. "Valentin indicated your Bulgarian salvage yard was raided by police agents."

"Yes, we had to abandon the site."

"And the weapon was transported to Stara Zagora Airport without detection?"

Vasko smiled. "The intruders were dealt with before we departed."

"And Valentin?"

"He should be on our salvage vessel in the Aegean by now, searching for a submarine he believes contains treasure. I am to join him."

They were interrupted by the arrival of one of the white-haired men, who was accompanied by a security escort. "Mr. Hendriks," he said with a Slavic accent. "We have performed a cursory examination of the weapon. The condition appears exceptional, for its age. Aside from some water leakage and corrosion in the tail assembly, the remainder of the device has remained watertight and appears undamaged. We removed the arming mechanism and it looks pristine."

"You are familiar with this weapon?"

"My colleague had early training experience with the RDS-4 and RDS-5 bombs. They are less powerful, but also less complicated, than the later hydrogen weapons, which is what we had expected to receive."

"I just need to know," Hendriks asked, "is it still functional?"

"Its components are quite primitive, by modern standards. We would propose updating all of the electrical components with microchip circuitry and replacing the arming mechanism and detonator with modern electromagnetic devices. But its radioactive elements are still quite potent. And we can provide additional stabilization and monitoring capabilities as part of the refurbishment." He gave Hendriks a firm nod. "In answer to your question, yes, we can make it both functional and more reliable."

Hendriks maintained his look of indifference. "How long will it take you to refurbish the weapon?"

"Less than a week, assuming we can obtain the needed components here."

"I'll have anything you need jetted in. Thank you, Doctor. Please proceed with the effort."

The old man nodded and shuffled back to the garage.

Hendriks watched him go, waiting until he was out of earshot. "He and his partner were two of the top Russian nuclear weapons scientists in the 1970s. They emigrated to France when the Soviet Union dissolved and took up with the French Air Force. They've worked for a few years on a satellite-related contract with my firm."

"Can they be trusted?"

"Every man has his price," Hendriks said. "I told Valentin I would pay him twenty million dollars if the weapon was usable. And so it seems." He gave Vasko a hard stare. "I will pay you an additional ten million dollars if you will deploy it for me."

"I'm no bomber pilot," Vasko said.

Hendriks shook his head. "The attack will be launched from the sea. I intend to use what you've learned in the Black Sea."

"For another attack on Sevastopol?"

"No, I have a different target in mind." He described his design for deploying the vintage atomic bomb.

Vasko had an inkling that the billionaire was mentally unstable, and his plan confirmed it. He stared at his drink, then took a sip. "That's liable to cause quite a reaction."

Hendriks stared out at the ocean. "Yes, it is my intent. You and I are not strong enough to purge the separatists and Russians from Ukraine, but others are. If we are successful, a wrath of fury will rain down upon the invaders in response to our actions."

"I can see that," Vasko said with a nod, "but why not use your own men?"

"Because I see no fear in you," Hendriks said. "My staff people are scientists and engineers. They might be able to construct weapons of death, but they don't have the mettle to use them. I need someone who is not afraid to pull the trigger."

"There will be great risks involved."

"Risks that can be mitigated with a direct and simple plan of deployment. Ten million dollars, I should think, will also buy you a great deal of security."

Vasko thought of Mankedo and the search for the submarine. Maybe he could pull off the job alone. If things went awry, he could still join Mankedo in the Aegean.

"I want half the money up front," Vasko said. "There's to be no mention to Valentin. And I'll call the shots on final deployment, since my neck will be on the line."

"Agreed," Hendriks said. "But first I will need for you to go to Ukraine."

Vasko didn't relish a return flight so soon. "For what purpose?"

"For an important delivery," Hendriks said. "And for the plan's ultimate success."

61

Ana awoke with a shiver, the cold stone floor sapping her body heat. The headache that had rattled her skull was back, now at exponential strength. Even opening her eyes caused a stab of pain.

But the light was different, much brighter. She looked up at a string of overhead bulbs. She heard a murmur of voices and slowly leaned up on her elbows. The movement sent a spasm of pain and a curtain of black spots before her eyes. When her vision returned, she saw a haggard group of people climbing out through a tunnel-like opening in a side rock wall. It was the crew of the *Macedonia.*

Ana watched as the crewmen and scientists emerged from the cavern one at a time. Her colleague Mikel lay nearby. She saw the ship's third officer, Chavez, crawl out, but there was no sign of Pitt and Giordino. Finally, when it seemed there was nobody left, the two NUMA men exited the smoke of the smaller cavern, carrying the limp body of Captain Stenseth. The captain's eyes were open, and he winced as they lay him beside her. Pitt and Giordino smiled at seeing she was now alert.

"Well, Sleeping Beauty has awoken," Giordino said.

"What happened?" she asked.

"You nearly slept the big sleep," Pitt said.

Giordino motioned a thumb toward Pitt. "His Boy Scout fire gave us all a good dose of carbon monoxide poisoning. A tanker full of aspirin would definitely be in order."

Ana glanced at the opening in the wall, where a tumble of rocks were piled at its base.

"The fire broke the boulder?"

"Not as fast as I would have liked," Pitt said, "but Hannibal didn't let us down."

She moved to a sitting position. "Is everyone okay?"

"Seems to be," Pitt said. "I think you took the worst of it, hanging close to the fire with us."

"Are Mankedo and his men gone?"

Before Pitt could reply, a sharp cry came from the cavern's main entrance. "Nobody move!"

Two uniformed men carrying automatic rifles stepped into the room, their weapons held high.

"Put those guns down," Ana yelled back, then winced. "I'm Agent Belova."

She slowly raised her hand and pulled out an identification badge from a front pocket. The two Bulgarian police officers approached close enough to read her badge, then noted the weary appearance of everyone in the cavern. They looked at each other and lowered their guns. "Are you safe?" one of them asked.

"We are now." Ana glanced toward Pitt. "What happened outside?"

"There's nobody here. Where's the rest of your team?"

Ana pointed to Mikel, who was now sitting upright in a dazed state. "That's it."

"Officer," Pitt said, "we have two men here who need immediate medical attention. Everyone else could use some fresh air."

A paramedic team waiting outside the compound was called in to treat Stenseth and Mikel. They carried the two out on stretchers and took them to the hospital in Burgas, along with a few of the *Macedonia*'s crew members suffering the worst effects from the carbon monoxide poisoning. Ana, Pitt, and Giordino should have been among that group, but they refused treatment, helping the remaining crew outside and taking relief in the fresh sea air.

As Ana briefed the lead relief officer, Pitt walked over to the warehouse. He noted the flatbed truck was gone. A panel of corroded aluminum rested against the wall where the truck had been parked, and he studied it with curiosity. Pitt recognized it as a cargo door from an airplane.

He returned to Ana, who was speaking with the officer about the disappearance of her colleagues and vehicles.

"You might check the lagoon." Pitt pointed to the newly graded road and the nearby front-end loader. "Did everyone make a clean getaway?"

Ana nodded with a scowl. "We'll search for the workboat, but it could be in three different countries by now."

"Don't forget the flatbed truck. It's missing from the warehouse, and they seemed to value the object it carried."

"Yes, that might be easier to track down." She gave a detailed description to the officer. When he stepped to his car to call in the data, Ana approached Pitt. "Do you think they knew we were coming?"

"No, but they were prepared."

"We'll find them." She looked at the *Macedonia*'s crew, huddling around the building. "They've called in some buses to transport everyone down to Burgas. Are you and Al going to stay in Bulgaria much longer?"

"I'm due back in Washington shortly, but there's one thing I need to do first."

"What's that?"

Pitt gazed at the empty warehouse with a resolute look.

"I need to make one more dive in the Black Sea."

62

A stiff breeze from the northwest rippled the waters around Cagliari as Dirk and Summer climbed out of a cramped airport taxi. While Dirk collected their bags and paid the driver, Summer looked across the boulevard at Sardinia's capital city. A blanket of rustic brownstone buildings rose up the hillside, enveloping the old Italian port that had changed ownership more than a dozen times through the centuries.

"I don't see our ride," Dirk said. He was looking in the opposite direction at the bustling port, one of the largest in the Mediterranean.

"The *Iberia* isn't due for another couple of hours. Let's go find a coffee somewhere."

They walked off their flight from London by strolling along the waterfront to a cozy sidewalk café. Though she didn't need the jolt, Summer joined her brother in ordering an espresso, having learned on a trip to Milan that proper Italians never drink latté after noon.

"I still say we should have gone to Greece and searched for the *Pelikan*," she said, dousing her espresso with sugar.

"We've been over this," Dirk replied. "It came down to logistics. There are no NUMA vessels available in the Aegean for at least a week. We might have been able to charter something out of Athens, but that would have taken a few days to organize. Instead, we've got the *Iberia* available right now in Sardinia, close to where the *Sentinel* went down."

"What about Mansfield?"

"We can't control his moves. He may well be looking for a boat in Greece, too. Besides, there are no guarantees that the gold is on the *Pelikan*. Julian and Charles are back at the National Archives hunting for new leads on both vessels. They might find the truth before anyone else does."

From his vantage by the window, Dirk kept a lookout to sea, eventually spotting a blue-green dot sliding across the horizon. The turquoise-colored *Iberia*, an intermediate-sized NUMA oceanographic ship studying subsurface currents in the southern Mediterranean, slowly sailed into the harbor and docked at Cagliari's inner port facility. An energetic captain by the name of Myers welcomed them aboard a short time later.

"Thanks for swinging by and grabbing us here," Dirk said.

"No trouble at all," Myers said. "We were running low on fuel and water and needed to make a port run anyway." The captain swayed on his feet, feeling the leftover effect of some bumpy seas. "The crew is quite excited to be participating in a shipwreck search." His eyes were bright. "Everybody is wondering what it is. A Phoenician trader? Maybe a Roman galley?"

"Nothing that exotic," Dirk said. "Just a rusty World War I cruiser named the *Sentinel*."

As the *Iberia* finished refueling, a black sedan sped onto the port facility, then slowed as it neared the NUMA ship. A passenger snapped photos of the research ship with an electronic tablet, which went undetected through the tinted windows. The car motored to the end of the dock and parked near some containers, facing the port's exit to the sea.

Dirk made his way to the bow and watched the deck crew retrieve the mooring lines. Summer joined him as the *Iberia* got under way. They stood at the prow as the *Iberia* eased out of the harbor, watching the historic city slip away behind them.

"Do you think he might have followed us here?" Summer asked.

"Your blond friend? I doubt it. We have insurance this time even if he does show. But he probably took the blue binder and ran back to Moscow. I bet he's two thousand miles from here."

"I hope so," Summer said.

But intuition told her that wasn't the case.

MANSFIELD WASN'T two thousand miles away but instead nine hundred. The Russian stood on the bridge of a dilapidated salvage ship he'd boarded six hours earlier in Athens. But the vessel's shabby appearance was only a disguise, concealing its true purpose as a spy ship. Diverted from tracking NATO ship maneuvers in the Adriatic, the ship sped east across the Aegean, crossing above the Cyclades chain of Greek islands.

Mansfield stared at the expanse of blue water off the bow, then turned to a grim-faced man near the helm. "Captain, how much longer until we reach northern Chios?"

"About three hours."

A GRU intelligence officer like Mansfield, the captain resented being pulled off his assignment in the Adriatic to chase a shipwreck. "How accurate is your target position?"

"I can't say. They're German coordinates from the vessel that sank her. It's all we have to go on." Mansfield ignored the captain's frown. "What do you have on board in the way of survey equipment?"

"We have an older towed array side-scan system, but the hull-mounted sonar is far superior. I'll lay in a survey grid around your coordinates." He stepped to a computer terminal at the rear of the bridge, leaving Mansfield standing there.

The agent stared at the horizon, making out the faint shape of land in the distance, then retired to his cabin two decks below.

The blue binder lay on his bunk. He picked it up and reread it for the tenth time. The data suggested the *Pelikan* sank with the gold, yet something about the timing of the events bothered him. The scheduled rendezvous and the submarine's sinking had occurred very close together. Still, it was all the information he had. He felt like he was assembling a jigsaw puzzle with half the pieces missing.

He dozed off while studying Hunt's letters only to be awakened by a sharp rap on the door. He shook off the sleep and opened the cabin door, surprised to find the captain.

"We have arrived at the coordinates," he said.

"Thank you for alerting me. Are you prepared to initiate the survey?"

"That won't be necessary."

"And why is that?"

The captain gave a sly smile. "It appears that someone else has already beaten you to the wreck."

63

Mansfield followed the captain to the bridge and looked out the windscreen. A half mile off the bow lay a blue-colored salvage ship. "Who is she?" he asked.

"A Croatian-flagged ship named *Nevena*," the captain said.

"Is the hull-mounted sonar activated?"

"It can be momentarily."

"Activate the system and take a tight pass across their stern."

Mansfield moved behind a computer station where a crewman activated the multibeam sonar system. A colored image of the seafloor appeared, scrolling as the ship moved. The captain followed Mansfield's directions, taking the vessel within fifty meters of the *Nevena*.

As they drew near, the *Nevena* radioed the Russian ship. "We are engaged in underwater operations, please do not approach."

"Affirmative, passing clear." The Russian captain nodded at the helm to hold course.

A pair of tough-looking crewmen scowled from the *Nevena*'s stern deck as the spy ship glided past.

Mansfield studied the sonar monitor as a dark line appeared and expanded into the cigar-shaped image of a submarine.

The captain ordered the helmsman to proceed another mile and stop engines, then stepped to the sonar station. He glanced at the wreck's image captured on the screen. "Looks like your submarine."

"Can't be anything else."

"What do you intend to do now?"

"Only one thing we can do," Mansfield said. "Take it from them."

64

Mankedo stood on the bridge of the *Nevena*, studying the Russian vessel through binoculars as it took up a holding position in the distance.

"Any trouble?" Dimitov asked.

Mankedo lowered the glasses and gave a faint nod. "Possibly. I've never seen a salvage ship configured with so many communication antennas."

"Are they with the Greek government?"

"They would have let us know. The Greek flag they're flying is probably as legitimate as our Croatian flag."

"Perhaps we should pull off the site?" Dimitov said.

"No!" Mankedo said. "We're on the *Pelikan*—and we'll finish what we started."

He instructed the helmsman to keep a sharp watch on the other vessel, then climbed down to the stern deck with Dimitov.

At the edge of the moon pool, he found two crewmen working over a small yellow ROV. "Are we ready to deploy?"

The nearest crewman said yes.

"Then lower away."

Mankedo stepped into a bay that housed the ROV's control station. He took a seat and activated the camera, which briefly displayed a crewman's feet before the device was lowered into the moon pool. Mankedo powered on the unit's lights and waited as it descended. At a depth of sixty meters, the seabed came into view and he engaged the ROV's thrusters.

A healthy current had pulled the ROV off its intended drop position, and Mankedo pivoted the device to obtain a view of the surroundings. The dark shape of the *Pelikan* was just visible to the north, and he steered the ROV in that direction.

The Russian submarine lay upright but partially buried in the sediment. After a hundred years underwater, a thick layer of concretion coated its surface. The ROV approached from the stern and cruised along the sub's starboard hull, revealing several large rectangular openings in the side cut by Mankedo and his divers to gain access to the interior.

The ROV skimmed over the cut steel slabs that lay on the seafloor, fresh torch burns visible around their perimeters. The ROV continued forward, past the conning tower and a deck gun, to a final cutout close to the bow. Next to the hole lay a large mesh tray filled with gas tanks and cutting equipment the divers had used to slice into the hull.

Mankedo sat forward in his chair. With a light touch on the toggle controls, he guided the ROV into the forward opening.

The vehicle immediately bumped into a rack of silt-covered torpedoes. Mankedo pivoted the ROV right, displaying the sub's two forward torpedo tubes. Maneuvering in the opposite direction, he guided the ROV across the torpedo room and through an open aft hatch.

Dimitov edged close to the monitor. "A fortunate break that the hatch is open. The crew quarters should be just beyond, which represents an additional storage area."

Mankedo maneuvered the ROV past some damaged pipes and overhead valves, then guided it into the next compartment. There was little to see in the small room to suggest it was once the living quarters for thirty enlisted men. Metal frames from the bunks that lined one side of the bulkhead were the most significant feature.

Mankedo scoured the bay with the ROV, peering into rusty lockers and poking through strands of debris. Satisfied there was no gold, he guided the ROV back to the torpedo room and out the opening. Below the torpedo room was an additional compartment in which the ROV barely fit. Mankedo piloted the vehicle over an open bilge and arrived at a mass of large, metal-encased batteries. "That would seem to do it for the forward compartment."

Dimitov nodded. "Yes, I believe we have covered the available cargo areas."

Mankedo threaded the ROV back through the compartment. As it exited the submarine, a bright flash of light whisked past its lens.

"What was that?" Dimitov asked.

Mankedo turned the ROV to follow, but the object was traveling much faster. The glow from its light dimmed near the stern, then began to grow brighter.

"It's turning back and coming up the port flank," Dimitov said.

Mankedo elevated the ROV just above the sub's deck level, then killed its lights. Guiding the probe by compass, he thrust it forward and across the *Pelikan*'s deck and halted it in the darkness somewhere above the port bow.

The lights approached slowly from the stern. Mankedo waited until the object was just below, then flicked on the ROV's lights.

A vehicle resembling a Jet Ski appeared, ridden by two men in scuba gear. The pilot, a blond-haired man, gave the ROV a nonchalant glance while the passenger aimed a video camera at the sub. The manned vehicle continued on its way around the nose of the *Pelikan* and vanished into the darkness.

A pained smile crossed Mankedo's lips. "I don't know who you are, my friend, but you are a little late to the party."

65

They came in two silent boats, a few hours after nightfall but ahead of a rising moon. Mansfield led three armed men in the first boat, approaching the *Nevena* from her port beam, while the second boat targeted the stern. But what was expected to be a quiet and bloodless seizure erupted in a fury of gunfire before any of the Russians had even set foot aboard.

One of Mankedo's armed crewmen, on watch and patrolling the deck, had spotted two men in black scaling the stern rail. He opened fire, killing one of the intruders and wounding the other. The two other Russians in the boat returned fire, pinning the crewman behind a winch.

Mansfield quickly climbed aboard the port deck. Sending two of his team to take the bridge, he moved aft with the third man. They reached the open moon pool, across which the crewman was firing toward the stern. Mansfield raised an automatic pistol at arm's length and dropped the crewman with one shot.

He spoke into a radio headset. "Team two status?"

"Two down," a grim voice said.

"Cover the starboard deck," Mansfield ordered. He sent the man next to him, a young agent named Sergei, to cover the port deck.

He couldn't believe their bad luck. It wasn't a great surprise that a salvage ship working a treasure wreck would have an armed crewman standing watch. But for his team of boarders, all highly trained GRU Spetsnaz special forces members, this assault should have been child's play. They were to capture the ship, transfer the gold, and be on their merry way. Not only was the element of surprise now lost, but they were already down two men.

The brief firefight had awoken the ship. Crewmen appeared everywhere. To Mansfield's dismay, most were armed. Yet that wasn't to prove his biggest disappointment.

As the stern team met further resistance on the starboard deck, Mansfield ducked into a prefabricated bay next to the moon pool. It was a combination laboratory and repair shop for the underwater equipment. An overweight man with a black mustache cowered behind a table strewn with books and charts. Mansfield stepped closer and raised his pistol as he evaluated the man. He was too old, too flabby, and too well dressed to be a working crewman. Much better than Mansfield had even hoped.

"Stand up," he ordered.

Georgi Dimitov rose to his feet and raised his hands in the air.

"Where's the gold?" Mansfield asked.

"What gold?" Dimitov said.

Mansfield lowered the barrel of his pistol and fired a shot at the archeologist's left foot. It purposely grazed the outer edge.

Dimitov stared, dumbfounded, as a trickle of blood oozed out of the hole on the side of his shoe, then grunted in pain.

"There is no gold," he pleaded rapidly.

Mansfield took aim at his right foot.

"I swear it. There is no gold. The submarine was empty."

"Did somebody beat you to it?"

"No, the vessel appeared undisturbed." Dimitov collapsed into his chair, weakened by the sight of his own blood.

"You've examined the entire vessel?"

"Yes. Every potential cargo area was accessed. We found nothing."

Mansfield stared at the archeologist. Shaking his head in disgust, he left the bay to reassemble the remnants of his assault team.

In a cabin behind the bridge, Mankedo had been studying a chart of the Aegean when the first gunshots sounded. He dropped the chart and pulled a case from beneath his bunk that contained an AK-47 and several ammunition clips. He jammed in a loaded clip, released the safety, and stepped to the cabin door.

He heard the shouts of the two assault team members as they stormed onto the bridge and threatened the lone crewman standing watch. Mankedo stepped back from the door, raised his weapon, and waited.

It took less than thirty seconds for one of the Russians to spot the wooden door at the rear of the bridge and fling it open. Mankedo fired a single shot into the man's forehead and stepped through the door before the man hit the deck. The other assailant stood across the bridge with his weapon trained on the crewman but turned at the sound of the gunshot. He was a second late, and Mankedo pumped three shots into him. The Russian fired a wild burst into the ceiling as he collapsed against the bulkhead and slid to the deck.

"Grab his weapon and guard the bridge," Mankedo ordered the crewman, then raced out the bridge wing door.

Had he exited the port wing, he might have spotted Mansfield retiring to the inflatable tied amidships. But he exited the starboard door, toward the sound of gunfire.

With most of its deck lights shot out, the *Nevena* was now as black as the sea. Only the underwater lights of the moon pool burned brightly, casting a warbly green glow about the stern deck. Dropping down a companionway to the main deck, Mankedo found two of his crewmen huddled behind a steel storage bin, firing aft. "How many are there?"

"Two or three on the stern," a crewman said. "I think they're pulling back."

As if in retort, a short muzzle flash appeared on the aft deck, and a corresponding spray of bullets peppered the underside of the bridge wing above Mankedo's head.

"Cover fire and advance," Mankedo yelled.

His two crewmen popped up and fired toward the muzzle flash. As they did, Mankedo hugged the bulkhead and ran aft, advancing nearly to the moon pool. He stopped and initiated covering fire, shooting at some shadows near the stern rail, as his two crewmen advanced to his side. This time, there was no return fire. As they caught their breath, Mankedo gave instructions for a final charge at the transom.

On the opposite side of the ship, Mansfield had dropped into the inflatable and radioed both assault teams to evacuate. He had lost contact with the men sent to the bridge and assumed the worst. The heavy resistance they had encountered began to weigh against the archeologist's testimony. Perhaps the gold had been recovered and stowed somewhere on the ship. There was only one way to find out.

He reached beneath one of the bench seats for a heavy duffel bag and withdrew an electronic timer attached to a detonator and twenty pounds of plastic explosives. He set the timer for ten minutes and heaved the bag onto the deck.

The sound of someone approaching at a run sent him reaching for his gun and he looked up to see Sergei approach the inflatable.

"Quick," Mansfield said, "toss that bag into the engine room."

Sergei grabbed the bag and ran to an open hatch a few yards away. He heaved the bag inside and sprinted back to the inflatable as Mansfield started the electric motor and cast off. Mansfield gunned the motor and darted away from the side of the ship, sailing in a wide arc around the *Nevena*'s stern. He was just in time to watch the final firefight.

The two remaining Russians were climbing into the other inflatable when Mankedo and his men stormed across the deck, their guns blazing. One Russian tried to return fire but was cut down. The other managed to get the boat under way as bullets whizzed over his head.

From the other inflatable, Sergei knelt and swept the deck with a long burst of covering fire. Mankedo caught a grazing wound to his elbow, but that didn't slow him. He ran to the rail and emptied his clip into the two black boats, which quickly melded into the darkness.

One of the crewmen approached Mankedo at the rail. "You're wounded, sir."

Mankedo ignored the blood dripping from his arm and stared at the lights of the distant spy ship. He spat over the side. "I want to know who they are!"

He was to never find out.

The two inflatables were nearly back to the spy ship when the detonator went off. A massive fireball erupted from the center of the *Nevena*, then a thunderclap sounded across the waves. The shock wave could be felt even at the distance of the small boats. Mansfield stopped the motor and watched as the salvage ship disappeared in a tower of smoke and flames. In minutes, the Bulgarian salvage ship broke in half and plunged beneath the waves.

The two inflatables eased back to the spy ship, where her captain stood on the deck fuming. Once the boats were hoisted aboard, he pulled Mansfield aside. "Four men! You killed four of my men and wounded a fifth!"

"I didn't kill them, they did," Mansfield said, motioning toward the *Nevena*'s former position.

"And a very subtle exit as well, not likely to draw any attention at all," the captain said sarcastically. "I thought you were simply going to take the gold at gunpoint from some salvage thieves. Aside from potentially blowing our cover, you made that task a far sight more difficult."

"I don't think the ship has recovered any gold," Mansfield said calmly. "I'll dive it in the morning to be sure. If you have any further complaints, I suggest you take them up with the President."

He turned on his heels and walked away, leaving the captain

stewing. Reaching his cabin, he set his pistol on a bureau and rummaged through his suitcase for a bottle of Chivas Regal he kept wrapped in a sweater. He twisted off the cap and started to pour himself a glass, then thought the better of it, knowing in a few hours he would make another deepwater dive. He set the bottle next to a laptop computer, which he flipped on. An e-mail from Martina was waiting for him.

Captioned *Cagliari*, it contained a photo of a turquoise NUMA ship leaving the dock in Sardinia. The photo was centered on the ship's bow, and Mansfield zoomed in to see the ship's name. As he did, the figures of Dirk and Summer standing at the rail popped out at him.

Eyeing the twins, the normally restrained agent flung the laptop across the room, then proceeded to pour himself a double shot of Chivas.

66

The Black Sea was as flat as a billiard table when the two divers splashed into the dark green water. Neither hesitating at the surface, Pitt and Giordino descended within sight of an anchored shot line. The calm waters aided visibility, and they reached the one-hundred-and-twenty-foot mark before turning on their lights. A coarse, sandy bottom appeared thirty feet later.

Pitt checked a compass on his dive console and swam to the east, with Giordino following close by. A small school of sturgeon cruised past, then the dirty silver outline of an airplane materialized.

After returning to the site of the Ottoman frigate *Fethiye*, Pitt and the crew of the *Macedonia* had needed only a few hours to locate the plane with sonar. So far, Pitt's growing list of hunches had been borne out. The body of the Russian airman had indeed come from a sunken aircraft, which he had predicted after the

Bulgarian archeologist Dimitov suddenly disappeared. The cargo door at the salvage yard, if from the same plane, revealed a link to Mankedo.

The polished aluminum skin had tarnished, collecting a thin layer of silt. But under the glow of their flashlights, the aircraft was still impressive. It was huge, the fuselage extending nearly a hundred feet, while its lone remaining wing stretched another sixty feet.

The two divers approached the port wing, floating above its twin eighteen-cylinder radial engines. The outer engine's propeller was absent, while the interior's was bent from impact. The divers reached the fuselage and swam aft until reaching the large tail assembly that still rose skyward. Pitt brushed the silt off the vertical stabilizer, revealing a large red star. Beneath the star, in black paint, was the number 223002, which Pitt committed to memory.

He and Giordino swam to the other side of the plane and found a completely different scene. As Pitt knew from the sonar survey, the right wing had been sheared off and lay a hundred yards to the east. Astern of the missing wing's mounting was a gaping hole in the side of the fuselage. The breach, Pitt saw, hadn't come from the plane's crash.

The two men examined its clear rectangular cut and the telltale torching along the borders. Aiming his flashlight at the seabed, Pitt spotted the removed aluminum section a few yards away. Missing from its center was a cargo hatch of the size Pitt had seen at Mankedo's salvage yard.

The two men entered the bomb bay, which was empty of ordnance. Pitt examined a single large support rack on the floor of the bay. Like the rest of the interior, it was well preserved in the oxygen-deprived water. Giordino spread his arms across the rack, showing it carried a weapon about five feet wide.

They moved forward inside the plane, scaring away a small eel, before they were halted by a wall of charred debris and twisted metal that blocked the passage. Judging by the ruins and a soot-coated ceiling, Pitt could see that a fire had brought down the plane. Given the amount of destruction, he was surprised that the aircraft had been able to ditch at sea relatively intact.

He checked his watch and saw that they had expended their bottom time. He motioned to the surface and Giordino nodded. They returned to the opening and exited the plane, swimming back to the opposite side. They followed their shot line to the surface, where an inflatable boat was moored a short distance from the *Macedonia*.

As they climbed into the boat and removed their gear, Giordino was the first to speak. "I thought she was a B-29 until I saw the red star. Looks like somebody took a can opener to her pretty recently."

"Yep," Pitt said. "And that was no ordinary bomb bay inside."

"You thinking what I'm thinking?"

Pitt gave a firm nod. "It would seem our buddies from Thracia Salvage have a sixty-five-year-old atomic bomb on their hands."

PART III

TWILIGHT'S LAST GLEAMING

The Lauren Belle approaching Baltimore

67

The abandoned farmhouse looked like any other in the rolling hills south of Kiev. Its white stucco walls had discolored to a dirty brown and were flaking in large chunks. The narrow windows had been boarded up, and the metal roof was streaked with rust. Its lone distinguishing characteristic, a crooked weather vane—the silhouette of a duck—swung loosely above the porch in the light breeze.

Vasko spotted the weather vane and turned his rental car into the weed-infested drive. He exited the car, stood, and listened. The faint sound of some cows in a nearby pasture wafted in the wind. He listened for other vehicles on the lonely farm road, but there were none.

He walked around the dilapidated house to the rear porch, which appeared to be an ongoing buffet line for a horde of termites. Vasko turned away from the house and paced in the direction of an adjacent potato field until he reached a small cellar door embedded in the ground. The door opened easily, and he stepped into the cramped room to find a large workman's toolbox. He carried the box into the daylight and opened it.

Inside were freshly pressed green camouflage fatigues and a matching ball cap. Vasko held them up. They were adorned with patches from the Ukrainian Air Force's 40th Tactical Brigade. He set aside the fatigues and pulled out a holstered Russian GSh-18 automatic pistol with a silencer and a pair of short-handled wire cutters. At the bottom of the box was a heavy rectangular packet wrapped in brown paper, along with an electronic detonator and a battery-operated timer.

Vasko carefully repackaged everything but the gun and carried the toolbox to the trunk of the car. He slipped the pistol under the seat and backed out of the farmhouse drive. Sticking to lightly traveled back roads, he drove west to the outskirts of Vasylkiv, a central Ukrainian city some thirty kilometers from Kiev. Finding a vacant field, he parked behind a high embankment and checked his watch. He had an hour until nightfall. With time to spare, he pulled out his phone and dialed Mankedo. The line was busy, as it had been the last few times he'd called. He tried a satellite number for the *Nevena* and got the same result. Finally, he dialed Hendriks, who was still in Bermuda.

"I prefer you don't call unless absolutely necessary," the Dutchman said.

"My boss has gone silent. I fear a problem."

"It shouldn't affect you. I can make some inquiries if you give me his whereabouts."

"I'll do so when I see you again. Did you make the transfer for our recovery?"

"Yes. Wired to the account in Cyprus."

"Have you received confirmation of its transfer?"

"Not from him, but I can assure you the funds were moved."

Vasko fell silent, wondering what had become of his partner of twenty years.

"Are you on schedule?" Hendriks asked.

"Yes. I found the materials and am arranging delivery."

"Very well. I hope you hurry back. Your next delivery will be waiting."

"Keep the rum chilled," Vasko said, but Hendriks had already hung up.

As the sky turned black, he retrieved the toolbox and slipped into the fatigues. He tucked the silencer into the box and returned to the road. A few miles north of Vasylkiv, he located a military air base. Avoiding the front gate, he drove to the opposite side of the tarmac and parked near some houses in clear view of the main runway.

Hendriks had informed him that an American transport plane was making twice-weekly deliveries of civilian aid to the Ukrainian government while en route to a NATO air base in Turkey. If the schedule hadn't changed, then a flight was due tonight.

Hendriks's information was soon proven accurate. The screaming whine from four turbofan jet engines fractured the night air as a massive gray aircraft descended to the runway. It was a C-5M Super Galaxy transport, operating from the 9th Airlift Squadron based in Dover, Delaware.

The big plane taxied to a stop near an open hangar and its rear loading ramp was lowered. Vasko grabbed the toolbox, crossed a ditch and short field, and approached a tall chain-link fence. He made quick order of snipping an opening and crawling onto the base. Walking quickly, he strode across an unlit section of the runway and approached the main hangar. A handful of Ukrainian MiG-29s were parked inside, next to a growing mountain of pallets being unloaded from the American plane.

Vasko pulled his cap low over his eyes and approached the C-5. He waited for a loaded forklift to slip by, then climbed up the loading ramp and entered the cavernous plane. A pair of Ukrainian airmen stood by the nearest pallets, checking an inventory list. Wearing the same green fatigues, they ignored Vasko as he moved forward with his toolbox.

He moved past the pallets to a pair of Humvees secured to the deck in the middle of the plane. His eyes grew big at the sight beyond. Several rows of antitank missiles were secured in low metal racks, bound for Turkey. Hendriks was a lucky man, Vasko thought.

He threaded his way to the last rack and knelt behind it. From the toolbox he removed the brown-wrapped package, which contained a block of PPV-5A plastic explosives favored by the Russian military. He taped the block to one of the missiles and began to insert the detonator.

"Can I help you, pardner?" said a voice with a thick Oklahoma accent.

Vasko looked up to see a hefty American gazing at him from across the bay. On his shoulder he wore a starred insignia surrounded by a thick band of chevrons.

"Hydraulic leak, Sergeant," Vasko said.

"Sorry, friend, but I'm the flight engineer on this bird and I didn't authorize any local repairs." He stepped closer, eyeing Vasko with suspicion.

Vasko set down the detonator and pulled the silencer from the toolbox. He casually raised the gun and pumped three shots into the airman. The sergeant gasped, then looked at his wounds in shock, before falling dead to the cargo floor. Inside the huge airplane, it all went unnoticed.

Ignoring the dead man, Vasko wired the detonator to the timer and powered it on. Setting the timer for ten minutes, he tucked the package under the missile rack, then dragged the sergeant's body alongside. He was making his way to the rear of the plane when a crash sounded ahead of him.

The forklift operator had knocked over a pallet, which had burst and spilled its contents of portable radios. A Ukrainian officer had appeared and was admonishing the forklift driver as Vasko tried to slip by.

"You there," the officer said, waving at Vasko. "Help clean up this mess. I'll go get a cart."

Vasko nodded and set down the toolbox, keeping his head low. As the officer set off down the ramp, he began gathering up the loose radios, waiting for the forklift to depart with another load. But the forklift driver dithered with caution, and by the time he started to remove the next pallet, the officer was returning with a cart.

Vasko quickly picked up the radios and threw them in the cart, his mind on the high explosives preparing to detonate. With the cart full, he began wheeling it down the ramp.

"Hey, wait a minute," the officer called.

"Yes, sir?" Vasko said. Despite the cool night air, sweat was beginning to drip down his temple.

"You forgot your toolbox."

Vasko nodded and scooped up the toolbox, avoiding eye contact with the officer. "Thank you, sir." He scurried down the ramp.

He ditched the cart inside the hangar and ducked outside, rushing down the flight line and away from the airplane. He reached the end of the hangar, cut around the corner, and checked his watch. It was too close now to be in the open, so he backed to the wall and waited.

As the antitank missiles erupted in succession, a ripple of concussions shook the ground. Vasko peeked around the corner as the entire midsection of the plane evaporated in a ball of black smoke. Debris rained down across the airfield, and he waited for the pelting to subside before stepping onto the tarmac.

As fire alarms rang through the night air, he crossed the runway, stopping only to pick up a charred gray fragment of aluminum from the C-5's fuselage. He ducked through the hole in the fence, threw the toolbox and aluminum shard into the rental car, and drove away, not bothering to look back at the billowing inferno he had just created.

68

The Sofia office of Europol occupied a corner section of the Bulgarian Criminal Police Directorate's headquarters, housed in a drab concrete building in the capital city's center. Wearing a patterned skirt and silk blouse that showed the wrinkles of too many hours at her desk, Ana was rifling through yet another stack of border patrol reports when something caught her eye. She glanced up to see Pitt and Giordino standing in the hallway, smiling at her through the window of her office door.

Ana rushed into the hall and gave each man a hug. "I didn't expect to see you two again before you left."

"We booked our flight to Washington from Sofia so we could see you," Pitt said.

Giordino shook his head. "Sorry to say, it's more than just a social call."

Ana led them into her office and pulled a pair of chairs close to her desk.

"How goes the hunt for Mankedo?" Pitt asked.

"We've had some interesting developments in the last few days but no luck in locating Mankedo, I'm afraid." She sorted through some papers and pulled out a photo of a workboat tied to a crowded dock. "Look familiar?"

"That looks like the workboat that was docked at Thracia when we raided the yard," Pitt said.

"It was found abandoned in Karaburun, a Turkish port near the Bosphorus."

"So he fled to Turkey," Giordino said. "Any chance of finding him there?"

She shook her head. "Istanbul is an easy place to disappear."

"It seems a lot of people are disappearing lately," Giordino said.

"Speaking of which, take a look at this."

She handed them a copy of a short news article. It told of the discovery of Bulgarian Ministry of Culture archeologist Georgi Dimitov, whose body was found washed ashore on a beach in Chios.

"Found dead in Greece?" Giordino said. "What do you make of that?"

"It's very odd. Some local fishermen reported an explosion at sea the night before his body was found. The Greeks are investigating."

"You may want to keep close tabs on that investigation," Pitt said. "Dimitov wandered off the *Macedonia* after we discovered the Russian airman on the wreck of the *Fethiye* and we never heard from him again."

"Do you think there's some sort of connection?"

Pitt and Giordino looked at each other.

"When we were tied up in Mankedo's warehouse," Pitt said, "do you recall seeing a piece of wreckage behind the truck?"

"I don't remember much."

"There was a weathered sheet of aluminum. It looked to be a cargo hatch, from an aircraft built fifty or sixty years ago."

"The plane that belonged to the Russian airman?"

"Yes. After our discovery of the deceased flier, not only did Dimitov vanish, but the *Macedonia* was hijacked. While it may be that Mankedo simply wished to use our ship to attack Sevastopol, he may also have wanted us away from the Ottoman wreck and the Russian bomber, which we now know is nearby."

"For what purpose?"

"To get at the bomber's cargo."

"Do you know what is was?"

"I have an idea." Pitt described the site of the wreck and its empty bomb bay.

"An atomic bomb," she whispered. "You think that's what was hidden on the back of Mankedo's truck?"

"It's a distinct possibility. We need to learn more about the aircraft to be sure."

"That certainly ups the stakes," Ana said, scribbling some notes.

"Any leads on the truck or our bald friend?" Giordino asked.

"Actually, yes." Ana slid her chair close to her computer. "We issued a regional alert to all seaports, border stations, airports, and rail stations. That's how we found the boat in Turkey."

She tapped at her keyboard and produced a grainy video feed of a gated roadway. "I just received this today. Take a look."

The video, a short clip from a security camera, showed a truck approach a gatehouse, stop briefly, then pass through. The video, taken at night, was short on clarity and detail. Ana played it again, this time stopping at individual frames.

"It's difficult to see the driver until the truck passes." She halted the video once more, catching the fuzzy image of a stocky driver with no hair.

"That's him," Giordino said.

"And that's our truck." Pitt pointed to the tarp-covered object on the flatbed. "Where was this taken?"

"The entrance to Stara Zagora Airport, a small facility about a hundred miles west of Burgas. It was taken the same day we were there. Or that night, I should say. The guard gate was unmanned at that time, but at least somebody reviewed the video later."

"So they've already flown it out of the country," Pitt said.

"Most likely."

The door to her office opened and Petar Ralin rolled in a wheelchair, a stack of files on his lap.

"We didn't expect to see you back to work so soon," Giordino said.

"Ana thought I'd get better care under her watch," he said, which caused her to blush. "And I thought I better keep an eye on her dangerous wanderings."

"Of which there have been a few," Pitt agreed with a laugh. "How's the leg coming along?"

"I should be out of the chair and on crutches in another day or two."

"I think he's secretly capable of walking now, but just likes me to push him around," Ana said.

Ralin smiled. "No argument there." He rolled forward and passed the files to Ana. "Stara Zagora Airport came through for us."

"I just showed Dirk and Al the video." Ana explained the discovery of the Russian bomber.

"This may be a key lead," Ralin said. "They sent a list of flight traffic for the evening, which is pretty light. The airport serves primarily commuter traffic and private planes, with little nighttime activity. There were four small plane landings and one large jet arrival before midnight. The jet arrived at eight-thirty and departed at five after nine. The airport provided its tail number, and we identified it as an Antonov An-124 transport plane, operated by a commercial charter company out of Ukraine."

"Little surprise that they would have transported the bomb to Ukraine," Ana said.

"Actually, they didn't," Ralin said. "I had to check a dozen airport databases, but I found that the plane next landed at Lisbon's Portela Airport around midnight. The aircraft then showed up at Bermuda's L.F. Wade International Airport, before returning to Kiev the following evening."

"You said the transport is owned by a charter company," Pitt said. "Do you know who chartered the plane?"

"Yes, although it took a number of threatening calls to Ukraine to find out. The company claimed they didn't have a flight plan for the charter but did finally identify the customer as one Peregrine Surveillance Corporation."

"A shell company?" Ana asked.

"No, a small holding company and subsidiary of a Dutch firm called Arnhem Flight Systems."

"Don't they make commercial aircraft instruments?" Pitt said.

"That's right," Ralin said. "They're a diversified aviation company known primarily for their avionics. Privately held by an industrialist named Martin Hendriks. Or they were. Hendriks recently cashed out, selling the company to Airbus."

"So someone at Airbus chartered the plane?" Ana asked.

"No, it was Hendriks. He still owns Peregrine. So he, or an employee of Peregrine, chartered the plane."

"He doesn't sound like the type who would be involved with Mankedo," Ana said.

Ralin shrugged. "Hard to say. He's an extremely private person. Public press about him is almost nonexistent. I did, however, find that his company has had numerous business dealings with Moscow over the years, so he would appear to be pro-Russian. His Peregrine company was in the news recently when one of his aviation drones helped rescue some shipwrecked sailors off of Ukraine."

"We need to know more about this Hendriks and if he has any facilities near Lisbon," Ana said. "I'll call the Europol office there and have them check the airport as well."

"A good idea," Ralin said, "but I don't suspect anything will pan out there."

"Why's that?"

"The Antonov transport was on the ground in Lisbon for less than an hour. They could have offloaded the weapon, but most likely stopped to refuel before heading across the Atlantic. At the end of the day, Bermuda's where you really want to be."

"But what's in Bermuda?"

Ralin smiled. "For starters, a multimillion-dollar oceanfront mansion owned by one Martin Hendriks."

69

The NUMA research ship *Iberia* wallowed in ten-foot seas as it battled a slow-moving summer storm that crept across the Mediterranean. Since leaving Sardinia, the ship had sailed into the teeth of it, sending her crew searching for their seasick pills.

Seated at the back of the bridge, Summer clutched a cup of coffee to keep it from sliding across the computer table. Dirk sat beside her, studying a blurry sonar image on a workstation monitor.

"It's a shipwreck, all right." He tapped a dark oblong object on the screen. "Whether it's our shipwreck, is difficult to say."

"The wave action is just too severe on the towfish," Summer said. "It's bouncing around like a rubber ball and scrambling the sonar images."

"The dimensions, fuzzy as they appear, look pretty close to the *Sentinel*."

"Should we check it out or keep surveying?"

Dirk turned to Myers, who stood near the helm. "Captain, how's the weather forecast looking?"

"The worst of the storm has passed. The seas should ease a bit over the next six hours and lie down within twenty-four. The extended forecast shows clear."

Dirk turned to his sister. "Sonar records will still be sloppy for a while. It's the best target we've had in three days of surveying. I say we prep for a dive and try to catch a soft spot in the surf to deploy."

Summer grabbed at her coffee cup, which was sliding across the table again. "It'll be calmer underwater. Let's do it."

An hour later, a yellow and turquoise submersible dangled over the stern, pitching with the movement of the ship. The seas had moderated slightly but were still risky for deployment. Dirk and Summer waited inside the vessel, eyeing the surrounding seas. After a sequence of heavy swells, the waves took a brief respite.

"Launch, launch, launch," Dirk radioed.

The submersible was lowered and quickly set free. Dirk flooded the ballast tanks and the submersible dropped beneath the turbulent surface. Twelve hundred feet later, a rocky gray seafloor loomed up through the viewport. Dirk engaged the thrusters and they propelled across the featureless landscape.

They found the wreck a few minutes later, a dark ship listing heavily on the seabed. As they approached from the stern, Dirk tapped his sister on the arm and pointed out the viewport. "I see a pair of guns above the stern deck."

The evidence greatly narrowed their prospects from the hundreds of merchant ships that littered the bottom of the Mediterranean.

Summer consulted a record of the ship in her lap. "The *Sentinel* carried nine four-inch guns: three forward, two aft, and two on each beam. Let's see what's forward."

Dirk elevated the submersible above the wreck and hovered over the aft guns before making his way forward. The corroded topside structure matched the layout in Summer's photo. Cruising past the wheelhouse, the submersible hovered over a trio of guns on the forward deck.

"There's your three forward guns," Dirk said. "I'd say we have a match."

Summer nodded. "It must be the *Sentinel*. The trick will be to investigate her interior at this depth. Dr. Trehorne sent plans for a similar ship of the class. He felt there were three likely places where a cargo of gold might be stored."

She pulled out the profile diagram of a British scout cruiser. "There's a forward hold just ahead of the guns, and two additional holds beneath the stern deck."

Dirk studied the diagram. "Access points will be the issue. Let's see what we can find forward."

He guided the submersible toward the bow, passing over the deck and a forward hatch cover that appeared corroded in place. He proceeded beyond the prow, swung around, and returned at deck level.

Summer pointed out the viewport. "Take us down along the starboard hull."

Dirk descended the submersible over the side rail. A dozen

yards back from the bow, a gaping oval hole presented itself just above the seafloor.

"The naval reports say she sank after striking a mine," she said.

"The reports didn't lie. Looks to be the open barn door to exactly where we want to go." He guided the submersible to the opening, then set the submersible onto the floor and powered off the thrusters.

Summer took over from there, activating a small cabled ROV affixed to a front rack. As she drove the vehicle into the hole, Summer focused on a video monitor that showed a live feed from the device.

The camera showed a jumbled mass of steel beams and plates that had collapsed in all directions, impeding any movement.

Dirk checked the diagram. "The hold looks to be another ten or fifteen feet aft."

"I'm not sure I can go another ten inches."

She reversed course and butted the ROV against an anchor chain. She followed the chain up until she found a gap beneath the overhead deck. She threaded the vehicle aft, past another maze of jagged metal.

She took a deep breath. "I'll get us aft, but I'm not sure about getting back out."

"I'm sure we've got a pair of scissors around here somewhere," Dirk said, knowing the ROV and its cable could be jettisoned if it became snagged inside the wreck.

Summer eased the ROV over a crumpled bulkhead and into a large open bay on the other side.

"That has to be the hold," Dirk said, straining to make out details on the monitor.

Summer smiled as she circled the ROV around the hold and descended to its base. The vehicle's lights revealed two large mounds on the deck, the remnants of once crated and stacked cargo. Summer brought the ROV alongside the first mound and let its thrusters blow away the silt. The water cleared to reveal an irregular mass of metal, with several tube-shaped pieces sticking out from the pile.

"They're rifles," Dirk said. "The wooden stocks have long since disintegrated, along with the crates they were stored in. Some of the barrels have rusted together, as has the congealed mass containing the bolt and trigger mechanisms."

Summer saw it now and nodded. She guided the ROV to the second mound and cleared away its silt, revealing a similar mass. She scoured the rest of the bay without results. "I think that's all that's here."

"I agree. Probably best to bring her home."

Summer retraced the ROV's path, extricating it from the wreck with considerable effort and returning it to the submersible's cradle.

"Nicely done," Dirk said. He checked the battery reserves. "I don't think we have the juice to get into the stern holds. I suggest we surface and swap batteries."

"Okay by me." Summer appeared visibly stressed from operating the ROV in such tight quarters. She remained silent as Dirk purged the ballast tanks and the submersible began a slow ascent.

"Given up hope?" he asked.

"I don't think the gold is here."

"We haven't checked the stern holds yet."

"I know. It's just a feeling. That, and the fact the ship is carrying a load of weapons. Doesn't really make sense if the *Sentinel* was on its way back to England with the gold."

"True, but the ship might have been diverted to meet the *Pelikan* with the weapons already aboard."

Summer stared into the darkness beyond the reach of the submersible's lights. "You're right. We'll reboot and take another dive. You don't suppose the Russians are collecting the gold off the *Pelikan* as we speak?"

"Not a chance."

Dirk's suspicion was borne out an hour later after they were hoisted aboard the *Iberia*. The seas had eased and the weather cleared, making visible on the horizon an approaching gray salvage ship that flew the flag of Greece.

70

Mansfield stared at the NUMA ship through a pair of binoculars, focusing on a work crew hovering about its submersible.

"Does it look like they are pulling up any cargo?" the captain asked.

"Difficult to say." Mansfield lowered the glasses. "A submersible wouldn't be the most efficient carrier."

"How long have they been working the site?"

"Not long," Mansfield said. "They left Sardinia four days ago. The last satellite image showed them surveying near here two days ago."

"There must be something of interest if they are still poking around. The sonar image looks good for the British warship."

"I'd like to see for myself. Please have the ship's submersible prepared. I will take her down after dark."

The captain stepped across the bridge and gazed at a ceiling-mounted fathometer. "Depth here is four hundred meters."

"Too deep for another ride on your underwater scooter," Mansfield said. "That's why I'll need your submersible."

"The depth is beyond the capability of our submersible. It is only rated to three hundred meters."

"What?" Mansfield stared at the captain. "You are a salvage ship. You carry a submersible that can't dive a thousand feet?"

"We are an eavesdropping ship," the captain said. "Our deployments are typically close to shore, in shallow water. We don't have the need, or expertise, for deepwater operations."

"What about an ROV?"

"Yes, I believe that is close to its depth limit. It can be deployed immediately."

Mansfield glared at the captain, then resumed his study of the NUMA ship. "It will have to wait. They're preparing their next dive."

He watched as Dirk and Summer climbed inside the submersible for a second dive. The seas were much calmer as they were lowered over the stern and submerged without incident. Mansfield remained on the Russian ship's bridge, studying his adversary and pacing. With some consternation, he watched some crewmen lower an object off the *Iberia*'s opposite deck, mistaking an oceanographic water sample for a recovery basket.

It was nearly dusk when the submersible reappeared and was brought aboard the research ship. Mansfield watched again as Dirk and Summer exited the sub, eyeing the Russian ship before climbing to the *Iberia*'s bridge.

"I need two of your best men," Mansfield said to the captain.

He sighed. "What for?"

"Transport and cover."

"After your fiasco in Greece?"

Mansfield shook his head. "I want to make a solo visit aboard their ship tonight. Since your underwater equipment is useless, I need to inspect their submersible and deck operations to find out exactly what they are up to."

"No. I won't have any more of my men killed."

"It is an oceanographic vessel. They would not be armed like those on the salvage ship."

"And exactly how do you know that?"

As the two men argued, a deck officer interrupted them. "Captain, I think you need to take a look off the port beam."

Midway between the two vessels, a pair of dark cylindrical spires rose from the sea. The objects grew in height, then showed themselves affixed to a wide black base that sprouted side fins as it continued rising. The men stared in shock as the object took the shape of a large submarine. The full profile of a Los Angeles–class attack sub showed itself and sat stationary between the two surface ships.

The radio aboard the ship blared a greeting. "Vessel bearing Greek colors, this is the USS *Newport News*. What can we do for you today?"

The Russian captain shook his head at Mansfield. "Care to ask *him* for a lift?"

71

Summer gazed out the bridge of the *Iberia* and smiled. "Rudi didn't mess around, did he?"

Dirk nodded. "After our ordeal in London, he promised us a shadow. Guess he's still got some pull in the Navy."

"Do you think Mansfield is on that ship?"

"It's possible. Captain Myers researched the vessel and found it's been seen all throughout the Mediterranean, flying flags of different countries. A home port in Russia is probably a good bet."

"Thank goodness for the *Newport News*. Of course, at this point, the Russians can have the wreck."

A crewman approached from belowdecks. "You have a call from a Mr. Perlmutter via satellite. There's a speakerphone in the conference room."

Summer looked at Dirk. "Julien's not one for high technology."

They followed the crewman to the main deck and into the conference room, which was little more than an empty cabin with a small table in the center. Dirk and Summer sat down and spoke into the speakerphone.

"Julien, are you there?" Summer asked.

"Yes, I'm calling from Charles's residence." Perlmutter's voice boomed. "How goes the search for the *Sentinel*?"

"Good and bad," Summer said. "We found the wreck last night. She's in good shape, lying intact in twelve hundred feet of water. We spent the day investigating her. We were able to access the forward hold and one of the stern holds, but we've seen no sign of the gold."

"It hasn't been salvaged, has it?"

"No, she doesn't appear to have been disturbed. Her cargo appears to be rifles, not gold."

"We thought as much," Perlmutter said.

"Do you know something we don't?" Dirk asked.

"Charles and I have spent the past few days digging through the Archives and we located an intriguing nugget today. Tell them, Charles."

Trehorne's voice joined the call. "We searched for everything related to the *Sentinel*, although a few of the ship's documents were missing. Fascinating vessel, actually, with an interesting wartime record. Did you locate any evidence of her sinking?"

"Yes," Dirk said. "She has a large breach near the waterline off the starboard bow. It would appear consistent with damage from striking a mine."

"Indeed. If you took any video recordings, I would love to see them. As I was saying, we examined the ship, crew, and squadron data—and finally stumbled upon something curious in the fleet records. During World War I, the Royal Navy regularly ran guns across the Mediterranean to General Allenby in Egypt in support of the Arab Revolt. We found note of a shipment of Lee–Enfield rifles delivered by steamer from England to Gibraltar, then sent on to Alexandria. Only the shipment never made it."

"Let me guess," Dirk said. "The guns were transported aboard the *Sentinel*."

"Precisely correct."

"So the *Sentinel* didn't rendezvous with the *Pelikan* and take on the Romanov gold?" Summer asked.

"That's the key question," Trehorne said. "The time line proved problematic at first glance, but Julian and I have a hypothesis. You see, the *Sentinel* was supposed to meet the *Pelikan* on February twenty-seventh near Chios. We found evidence which indicates the *Sentinel* was in Gibraltar on March second, taking on the shipment of rifles. The cruiser's top speed was twenty-five knots, so that would have been a challenging feat, given the distance between the two."

Summer rubbed her eyes. "So the gold remained on the *Pelikan*?"

"We don't think so. What we believe happened, my dear, is that the *Sentinel* and the *Pelikan* had their rendezvous a day or two earlier. If we go back to the original letter from Hunt to Admiral Ballard, he requested the *Sentinel* be at the meeting point *by* February twenty-seventh. It turns out the *Sentinel* was in Athens the week before. As she was already in the vicinity, we believe she arrived on-site ahead of that date, and the *Pelikan* was early as well. That would have allowed plenty of time for the *Sentinel* to take the gold on board and arrive in Gibraltar by March second."

"We found no orders rescinding the rendezvous instructions," Perlmutter said, "so there's no evidence that the *Sentinel* was pulled away before *Pelikan*'s arrival."

"If that was the case," Summer said, "what became of the gold?"

There was a long pause. "We don't know," Perlmutter said, "but the answer would seem to lie in Gibraltar. Charles has some contacts there, along with a strong suspicion. We intend to fly down and do some sniffing about. If you're finished with the *Sentinel*, why don't you forget about the *Pelikan* for the moment and meet us there?"

"Absolutely." Summer perked up. "I've had a bad feeling about the *Sentinel* since we got here."

The group made plans to meet and said their good-byes. After the call ended, Dirk shook his head with a grimace.

"What's wrong?" Summer said. "You don't think it's there?"

"I don't know if it is or it isn't. But I do know that Rudi's never going to trust us with a travel budget ever again."

Five hundred meters across the sea, a Russian communications specialist aboard the spy ship stopped recording the satellite call as the connection went dead.

Within the hour, Mansfield had listened to the conversation several times. He had to admit that the spy ship had finally proved its worth. Using a secure satellite line, he called Martina, who was still in Cagliari.

"Success?" she asked.

"No. We'll be back in port tomorrow. I need you to get us on a flight to Gibraltar as soon as possible."

"It will be done," she said in her usual efficient manner. "Is the gold there?"

"It can be nowhere else."

72

The raid on Hendriks's Bermuda estate went nothing like the assault on Mankedo's salvage yard. Ana made sure of it.

A dozen Bermuda police officers covered the main entrance while a second SWAT team of equal size approached from the beachfront. Though Ana initially had doubts about the Bermudans' experience and training, she was soon impressed by their zeal and planning. As a British Overseas Territory, Bermuda officially recognized Europol, and the local law enforcement authorities had provided all due cooperation.

Surveillance of the property during the prior twenty-four hours had revealed no activity other than the comings and goings of the gardeners. Hendriks's private jet had been seen at the airport recently but vanished about the time the surveillance began, which made Ana wonder if he had been tipped off by a local. No matter now, she thought. A 1950s-era atomic bomb wouldn't likely fit on a private jet.

At six a.m. sharp, she led a Bermuda police lieutenant to a

pedestrian door along the residence's closed gated drive. Ignoring the video cameras that sprouted from the top of the walls like kudzu, the lieutenant wedged a crowbar beneath the latch and pried open the door. He radioed the beach team, then signaled to his surrounding force to proceed.

Ana was already through the door when the lieutenant followed with his armed men. They fanned out along the drive and jogged to the imposing residence. Ana and the lieutenant approached the front door with half the men and tried the handle. It was unlocked. Ana and the men readied their weapons, then burst in.

From the kitchen, a dark-skinned woman in a tattered robe screamed at the sudden intrusion of armed men. She raised her arms to the sky and rocked back on her heels as Ana and the lieutenant approached.

"Where's Hendriks?" the policeman asked.

"Mr. Hendriks not here," she said. "He leave two days ago. No one here but me." Like many Bermudans, she spoke with a slight Caribbean accent.

"What's your name?" Ana asked.

"I am Rose, Mr. Hendriks's housekeeper. Mr. Hendriks not here."

Two armed policemen, who had approached from the beach, appeared from the rear of the house. "All clear in back," one said.

The lieutenant nodded. "All right. Help search the house."

As the men left, Ana pulled the housekeeper aside. "Rose, can you tell me who was here with Mr. Hendriks?"

"Some employees from his company. Two older men were here also. Doctors, I think. They all stayed in the guest quarters."

"Medical doctors?"

Rose shrugged. "I heard Mr. Hendriks address just one as 'Doctor.'"

"What were they doing here?"

"They worked in the garage laboratory. All secret. I'm not allowed to go in there."

"The building at the side of the residence?" Ana asked.

Rose nodded.

"How long where they there?"

"About two weeks. They all leave in a hurry a few days ago, including Mr. Hendriks."

"Where did he go?"

"I don't know. Probably to his home in Amsterdam. He doesn't come to Bermuda so much anymore without his family."

The police lieutenant reappeared with his men. "The house and grounds appear empty, Agent Belova. I'm afraid you might be chasing a false lead."

"The garage," she said. "I want to see the garage."

They made their way to the freestanding building. As they approached a side entry, they could see it was a large structure, its size concealed by thick foliage. A padlock secured the entrance, and the lieutenant called for a bolt cutter from a support vehicle. He snipped the padlock free, shoved open the door, and they stepped inside.

The research lab was still furnished, with computer terminals, test equipment, and lab benches filling the bay. While the lieutenant admired the test drone hanging from the ceiling, Ana focused on a more ordinary vehicle. Just inside the main door sat a weathered flatbed truck. She noted the black and white Bulgarian license plate affixed to the rear bumper.

"Lieutenant," she called. "They were here. This is the truck that was transported from Bulgaria."

The Bermudan stepped over and gazed at the empty truck.

"The weapon is gone now, if it was indeed here," Ana said. "Probably flown out with Hendriks and his crew."

"Maybe we can still confirm its presence." He waved over an officer carrying a wand that was wired to an electronic box. "Geiger counter," the lieutenant said. "If they swapped out any parts, there may be radioactive debris."

Ana nodded. "Check every square centimeter. Then I want passenger lists and details on every aircraft flown out of here in the past week."

"We'll get right on it."

As the lieutenant issued orders to his subordinates, Ana paced the lab, a thousand questions running through her mind. Could the Russian bomb still be functional? How big is it—and how powerful? And, most important, where did they take it?

She stepped past a lab table filled with old radio tubes and examined a large whiteboard. A series of mathematical formulas were visible where the dry marker hadn't been cleanly erased. But she ignored the writing and focused on a small map fastened to the corner. It showed a section of a large waterway that ran north and south, with several tributaries on either side. The labels were in English, but she didn't recognize the names. None, that is, except for a city on one of the western tributaries with a star next to it.

Washington, D.C.

73

Pitt was feeling a touch of jet lag when he stepped into his office at the NUMA headquarters, a towering glass structure on the banks of the Potomac. He'd been at his desk less than a minute when Rudi Gunn entered with two cups of coffee.

"Welcome back to the fray." He passed a cup to Pitt.

"Thanks, I could use a jump start."

"You've got about five minutes to enjoy it, then we need to head downtown."

Pitt glanced at his calendar. "I didn't think I had any meetings today."

"The Vice President tends to be in a hurry when he wants something," Gunn said. "His secretary just called. He wants to see us in his office in thirty minutes."

"Why the urgent social call?"

"He wants to know about the Russian bomber."

"Hallelujah," Pitt said. "I figured we'd have to kick and scream to get anyone's attention about it."

"Apparently, someone else has succeeded on that front."

They downed their coffee, and a waiting car drove them across the Arlington Memorial Bridge to 17th Street, then north to the Eisenhower Executive Office Building. The Vice President's expansive office was on the second level. While prior occupants had used it as a ceremonial office, Sandecker preferred its relative isolation, shunning his official office in the West Wing.

After clearing multiple layers of security, Pitt and Gunn entered the mahogany-floored office to find its owner pacing the floor like an angry bull.

A diminutive man with fiery red hair and a temper to match, Admiral James Sandecker was nobody's fool. His bearded face brightened at the arrival of Pitt and Gunn. Sandecker had been the founding father of NUMA and Pitt and Gunn had been among his first hires at the new federal agency. During their years working together, the men had formed a close bond that hadn't waned when Sandecker was drafted to the vice presidency after the incumbent died in office.

"Good to see you, Admiral," Pitt said, dispensing with his current official title.

"Come on in and grab a seat." Sandecker ushered them to a large conference table where several men in suits were already seated. Pitt recognized the director of Homeland Security, a man named Jimenez, at the head of the table, flanked by several other security officials. Sandecker made the introductions as Pitt and Gunn grabbed a pair of empty chairs.

Jimenez wasted no time getting to the point. "We understand

you have knowledge of a rogue weapon of mass destruction in the Black Sea region."

"We have circumstantial evidence," Pitt said, "that an early atomic bomb was recently salvaged from a Russian bomber that crashed in the sea off Bulgaria. Data from the plane's tail number seems to confirm its cargo."

He nodded at Gunn, who plugged a laptop computer into a tabletop video projector. A photo of a large silver plane appeared on a white wall at the end of the table.

"Dirk just retrieved the serial number from the sunken craft," Gunn said. "Aircraft number 223002 is a Tupolev Tu-4, like the one pictured here. It's a Russian heavy bomber built after World War II from the design of our own B-29 Superfortress. Our particular plane is a Tu-4A, which was a modified version capable of carrying a nuclear weapon. The plane was assigned to the Fifty-seventh Bomber Division and based near Odessa. It was on a routine training mission over the Black Sea on the night of April fourteenth, 1955, when it flew into a storm and was never seen again."

Gunn flashed up a contemporary Bulgarian newspaper clipping. "The Russians engaged in an extensive search for the plane in secret, but the efforts caught the attention of a few journalists along the Bulgarian coastline. The locals didn't know, of course, that the plane was carrying an atomic weapon. Based on the accounts we found, the Russians focused their search near the city of Varna, about thirty miles north of where Dirk found the wreckage."

"Its cargo bay was empty when you found it?" Jimenez asked.

"That's correct," Pitt said. "The bomb bay was configured to carry a single weapon, and the plane showed signs of recent salvage efforts."

Gunn presented another photo, this one a black and white image of a large bomb perched on a rack.

"Based on the plane, date, and the rack configuration, we believe this Tu-4 was carrying an RDS-5 atomic bomb," Gunn said. "This was an early Soviet nuclear weapon that yielded a destructive power of thirty kilotons of TNT. It predates the Russians' more deadly hydrogen bombs, and is peanuts by modern nuclear standards, but it still packs twice the power of the bomb dropped on Hiroshima."

One of the FBI agents cleared his throat. "You're telling me the Russians lost an atomic bomb sixty years ago and gave up trying to find it?"

Gunn nodded. "It was hardly the only one. There are in fact dozens of lost or unaccounted nuclear weapons from the Cold War era. Most, like the one carried on our Tu-4, were lost at sea."

"One of our own lost A-bombs was discovered just a couple of years ago by some sport divers," Pitt said. "A Mark 15 bomb that was jettisoned by a B-47 near Savannah in 1958."

"Would this Russian RDS-5 bomb still be functional?" Jimenez asked.

"Scientists I've spoken to believe so," Gunn said. "There's a good chance the bomb casing would remain watertight. If not, then only the electronic components would be damaged and they could be reconfigured with modern technology. There would be only a slight degradation in the radioactive components."

"The Savannah bomb was recovered intact and in good condition," Pitt said, "and that was resting in oxygenated, highly saline water. Our Russian bomb in the Black Sea was exposed to a much less corrosive environment."

"Any idea where the weapon is now?" Sandecker asked.

"We, and Europol, believe it was salvaged by Valentin Mankedo, a Bulgarian black market dealer," Pitt said. "There's reason to believe it was flown to either Lisbon or Bermuda on a chartered transport."

"I understand Europol believes this Mankedo has had dealings in the past with Ukrainian anti-government rebels, to acquire stolen nuclear materials," Jimenez said.

"I was a witness to his efforts to hijack a shipment of stolen highly enriched uranium that came out of Crimea." Pitt noticed an unease from the men around the table. "Is there an imminent threat?"

"Four days ago, an Air Force C-5 transport was blown up on the tarmac of a Ukrainian air base near Kiev," Sandecker said. "The plane was on a stopover delivering civilian aid that the administration recently authorized in support of the Ukrainian government. Three airmen were killed in the blast, but there were few leads to the responsible party. Then, yesterday, the U.S. Embassy in Kiev received a package addressed to the President." Sandecker opened a folder and held up a photo of a charred piece of gray metal.

"From the C-5?" Pitt asked.

"It's been sent to the FBI lab for analysis but is believed to be from the wreckage. Included with the souvenir was a letter written in Russian."

Sandecker shuffled through some additional papers and located a translated copy.

"'Dear Mr. President,' it begins. 'Take this as a first warning for your intrusion into our lands. Aid to the illicit government in Kiev must cease immediately. If there is not a public pronouncement that the U.S. will immediately halt all financial and political support to the administration in Kiev, then death will come to America and the Star-Spangled Banner will no longer wave over your historic capital.' It's signed by the United Armed Forces of Novorossiya."

"Which rebel group is that?" Gunn asked.

"It's something of a confederation of all the pro-Russian military groups operating in eastern Ukraine," Jimenez said. "Some in the region have come to calling the area Novorossiya, or New Russia. It's a rather clever way of making it difficult to pin responsibility on one group."

"That's a rather bold act, given their Russian sponsorship," Gunn said.

"The Russians themselves have issued a strong denial of involvement and have even taken the unusual step of absolving blame on any of the separatist groups. They're calling it a setup."

"Any possibility they are right?" Sandecker asked.

"We don't buy the motive, if that was the case," Jimenez said. "We suspect a marginalized separatist group acting out of hand with the Russians is the responsible party."

"And you think the same people have acquired the Russian A-bomb from Mankedo?" Pitt said.

"We don't have enough information to make a definitive link, but one could certainly connect the dots," Jimenez said. "The timing of this threat with your discovery of the bomber has more than a few people nervous."

"What's the President's reaction?" Gunn asked.

"He went through a lot of heartburn with Congress to obtain aid for the Ukrainian government," Sandecker said. "He's not prepared to walk away from the pledge of support he gave them to preserve their democracy." He stared at Jimenez. "At the same time, he expects Homeland Security to do its job here to neutralize any real or perceived threats."

"We've got resources on it," Jimenez said. "We'll get investigatory teams off to Lisbon, Bermuda, and Bulgaria right away."

As Jimenez spoke, Pitt received a text message from Ana. He held up his hand. "You can forget about Lisbon, Mr. Secretary. Europol just raided a residence in Bermuda, where evidence was found that the bomb was recently there. It's believed the weapon was subject to a possible refurbishment, as radioactive components were discovered."

"Where is it now?" Sandecker said. "What is their target?"

Pitt shook his head. "They don't know for sure," he said, gazing at Jimenez. "But they think it could be Washington."

74

Summer looked out the airplane window at the blue waters of the Mediterranean rushing close by as the Airbus A320 descended. She wondered if the pilot was ditching at sea, as the waves looked close enough to touch. A runway finally appeared and the airplane touched down an instant later, taking full advantage of Gibraltar International Airport's mile-long runway that began at the sea and ended at the sea.

As the plane taxied to the terminal, she caught a glimpse of the Rock of Gibraltar. The towering mountain represented the northern half of the Pillars of Hercules, the ancient entrance to the Mediterranean Sea.

Dirk leaned over from the seat next to her and pointed at the sheer face of the Rock. "I always assumed the Rock faced south, toward Africa. Its steep face actually looks east."

"Yes. Gibraltar's port and residential areas are concentrated to the west," Summer said. "The guidebook says the Spanish city of Tarifa, a few miles to the west, actually extends closer to Morocco."

They exited the plane and were surprised to find Perlmutter and Trehorne waiting for them in the terminal.

"You didn't need to meet us," Summer said, happy to see the two historians.

"The country's only three miles long," Perlmutter said. "We can practically walk to the hotel."

Dirk and Summer gathered their luggage, and the foursome squeezed into a cab for the ride into central Gibraltar. Perlmutter held the cab while they checked into a modest hotel. Returning to the cab a few minutes later, Dirk asked, "Where to now?"

"A friend of mine, an old schoolmate, is a major with the Royal Gibraltar Regiment," Trehorne said. "He's something of an expert on the wartime fortifications here and indicated he has full access to the World War I records. But I'm afraid we must backtrack to the airport to go see him."

Perlmutter grinned. "That should take all of five minutes."

It was closer to ten when they passed through the gates of Devil's Tower Camp, a small base southeast of the airport runway that housed Gibraltar's military forces. They found the base information center and were escorted to the office of Major Cecil Hawker. A droopy-eyed man with a light mustache, he warmly greeted Trehorne beneath a portrait of the Queen. He welcomed the others and offered them tea at a corner table that overlooked the parade field.

"I was delighted to hear from you, Charles," he said, "and quite intrigued by your treasure hunt."

"We're not sure where the trail will lead," Trehorne said,

"but, at the moment, it's making its way through Gibraltar. As you are the regiment historian, I know there is no one better qualified to examine the history here."

"That's just a side duty," Hawker said, "but it does afford me access to all of Gibraltar's state archives. I've spent some time examining the relevant time period, and also consulted with friends in the Royal Navy. Unfortunately, much of the naval records from that era, as well as a significant piece of the regiment's history, were lost or destroyed during the civilian evacuation of Gibraltar in World War II."

"Did you find any evidence of the *Sentinel*'s presence in Gibraltar in 1917?" Perlmutter asked.

"Not in the naval records. But I did find a curious document in the regiment's files." Hawker opened a desk drawer, pulled out a letter, and handed it to Trehorne.

He skimmed the document. "It's a note to the commandant of the regiment, a request for a security detail to transfer a ship's cargo to AEB Nelson for temporary storage. It's signed by a Captain L. Marsh, HMS *Sentinel*."

"What's the date, Charles?" Perlmutter asked.

Trehorne examined the header, then looked up with raised brows. "March second, 1917."

The room fell silent until Summer whispered, "That's after the scheduled rendezvous with the *Pelikan*."

"The same day they took on the shipment of Lee–Enfield rifles," Perlmutter said. "Unloaded one cargo and took on another, perhaps?"

"The letter indicated the storage was only temporary," Dirk said. "Was there any indication of its subsequent movement?"

"None that I could find," Hawker said.

"With chaos in St. Petersburg and the abdication of Nicholas in the works, the treaty may have been deemed void and the gold returned to the provisional government," Perlmutter said.

"Perhaps," Dirk said, "but Mansfield's actions suggest the Russians have no record of its return. Major Hawker, what do you make of this AEB Nelson storage reference?"

Hawker's eyes lit up. "I was quite excited by the reference. You see, the Rock of Gibraltar is a rather fascinating mount. Aside from dozens of natural caves, the Rock is riddled with over thirty miles of tunnels built over the centuries. Some date to the 1700s, but most were built in the last century to supplement the local fortifications. I must profess to being something of a tunnel rat myself, and the reference to Nelson scratched at my memory. I pulled some of the early tunnel plans and, sure enough, there was a tunnel line named Nelson built in the 1880s, when some of the first big artillery guns were hoisted up the Rock. But I couldn't find any references to a storage area or bunker named Nelson or the letters AEB, although they could indicate an auxiliary excavation boring."

"What's the status of the tunnel today?" Dirk asked.

"The Nelson tunnel and its surrounding arteries were closed off in 1920 due to a cave-in. It has been an abandoned area ever since, closed to access due to its perceived danger."

"Could we get in for a look?" Summer asked.

"The Gibraltar tunnels are administered by the Ministry of Defence." He gave Summer a wink. "Which means you came to the right place."

Summer noticed that Hawker had a large chart above his desk depicting the tunnels inside the Rock.

He pointed to an area on the north side of the mount. "I've studied the neighboring passages and believe the Nelson area can be reached, if there have been no additional cave-ins." He looked up and smiled. "But you will need a military guide."

"Can you take us in?" she asked.

"Meet me at Princess Anne's Battery at eight o'clock sharp tomorrow and we'll see what we can find." He looked at the sandals on Summer's feet. "I would strongly advise wearing sturdy footwear."

She smiled. "I'll wear snow boots, if I have to."

She had a spring in her step as they returned to their waiting cab. "Do you think there's a chance it's still there?" she asked the others.

"Only one way to find out," Perlmutter said. "You remember what we found in Cuba."

As they exited the base, their taxi drove past a sedan parked outside the entrance that immediately started its engine. In the passenger seat, Viktor Mansfield sat with a small parabolic listening device in his lap. He yanked off its earphones as Martina began following the cab.

"Anything?" she asked.

"No, not a thing." He tossed the gadget to the floorboard.

"This is not London, I'm afraid," she said. "We have few resources here."

He shook his head. "Then there's nothing to be done but follow them."

75

A half-moon cast a shimmering glow on the calm water, providing more than a mile of visibility. For secrecy's sake, Ilya Vasko would have much preferred a downpour, but the clear night would make his job easier.

From the aft deck of a blue tugboat named the *Lauren Belle*, he watched as an overloaded container ship passed on its way to Baltimore with a cargo of German autos. With the *Lauren Belle* anchored near the shoreline of Cape Charles, Virginia, Vasko took keen interest in the ships entering the nearby mouth of the Chesapeake Bay. Through binoculars, he studied each approaching vessel, gauging its size and, most important, if it was towing a barge.

It had been only a few hours since he had touched down in Hendriks's private jet at Newport News International Airport across the bay. The Dutchman had proved proficient once more, arranging a leased tug and barge that awaited him at the waterfront. Even the boat's four-man Ukrainian crew seemed a hardened mix of trustworthy mercenaries.

Three freighters and thirty minutes later, Vasko saw what he was waiting for. A large oceangoing tug with an extended stern deck rounded the cape from the Atlantic. Under the moonlight and the vessel's running lights, he could see she had an orange hull and a white superstructure. She was also pulling a small barge. The icing on the cake was a powerful blue light that shone above the wheelhouse.

Vasko lowered his glasses and turned to a crewman pacing the deck. "That's our boat. Give her a signal."

The crewman activated a spotlight on the rail and aimed it toward the incoming ship, flashing its beam several times. The blue light on the approaching vessel blinked in acknowledgment and the big tug slowed and eased alongside the *Lauren Belle*. The ocean tug passed down a leader line to Vasko's crew, who looped it around a hydraulic capstan.

Given an *All clear* sign a few minutes later, Vasko's men activated the capstan, reeling in the leader line and the orange tug's tow cable to its trailing barge. As they transferred the line, a heavy wooden crate was also passed down and placed behind the *Lauren Belle*'s wheelhouse.

The barge had been nearly a hundred meters behind the ocean tug, but Vasko drew it within twenty meters of the *Lauren Belle*. He then called up for the boat to proceed with the transfer. The orange tug pulled ahead to a second barge just upstream that Vasko had affixed to an anchored float. The ocean tug completed the swap, retrieving the tow line from the float and securing the barge to its stern.

With no fanfare, the orange vessel pulled ahead, towing the replacement barge. Under the night sky, the two barges appeared identical. Vasko watched the tug and its new cargo move up the bay and disappear into the distance, then turned to his crewmen. "Pull the barge up to the stern."

They activated the capstan, pulling up the barge like a toy on a string. When the bow of the barge kissed the *Lauren Belle*'s stern, Vasko slipped over the rail and jumped aboard. Like the barge he had just traded, the blunt vessel held four covered holds. Vasko skipped the first three and moved to the one at the stern and unclasped its cover. He raised the lid and shined an LED flashlight inside. The interior was empty.

He climbed down a rusty steel ladder into the hold and searched more carefully. In the two stern corners he found what he was seeking: a pair of small packages in brown paper like the one from the farmhouse in Ukraine. He left them in place and located a small satchel beneath the ladder that held a simple radio transmitter.

Vasko took the satchel, climbed out, and resealed the hold cover, then moved to the first hold. He checked that no ships were approaching, raised the lid, and climbed inside. At the bottom of its ladder, he turned and faced the RDS-5 bomb.

The atomic weapon rested on a heavy wooden pallet, secured to the deck by canvas straps. During its refurbishment, the bomb had been painted a nonreflective black, which lent it a more ominous appearance. Vasko scanned the weapon with his light until he found the control box, which rose from the curved skin ahead of the tail assembly. He unscrewed its top-sealing glass panel, which gave access to a small bank of dials and LED displays. The readouts were all dark. He found a small, nondescript toggle positioned at the bottom. Holding his breath, he reached in and flicked the switch.

The panel came alive with flashing lights and digital readouts. He waited a moment for the electronics to settle, then checked one of the displays. Confirming it showed the number 25, he sealed the glass plate. Just like that, the bomb was activated. Now all he had to do was complete the delivery.

He sealed the hold cover, returned to the tug, and ordered the crew to get under way. As smoke billowed from the funnel and the *Lauren Belle* pulled ahead, Vasko stared at the lethal black barge, contemplating the many ways to spend ten million dollars.

76

The morning sun was already heating the stone pavers around Princess Anne's Battery when Summer, Dirk, Perlmutter, and Trehorne piled out of a cab. A winding road had taken them high up on the north side of the Rock. An open emplacement of guns stood on a bluff, overlooking the airport and the coast of Spain.

Hawker waited for them with a duffel bag strapped over his shoulder. "Good morning," he said. "Glad to see you found the place without any trouble."

Summer scanned the coastline. "It's a beautiful vantage point."

"Yes, and an important location in the historical defense of Gibraltar. Cannon were first brought up here in 1732 during the Great Siege of Gibraltar, when Spain and France tried to kick us out. British forces held out for over three years before the siege was eventually lifted."

"Crossing the flats over that isthmus with Spain would have been suicidal under aim of a sharp gunnery crew," Trehorne said.

"Most certainly. The site here was manned all the way up to the 1980s." Hawker pointed to one of four World War II–era five-inch guns emplaced around them. "The batteries were linked by tunnels, dating back decades. We can gain entry behind that Mark I gun over there."

He led them across a parking lot, where a handful of tourists were eyeing the view near a gray sedan that had just entered. Hawker stepped past the gun emplacement to a steel door embedded in the rock. He produced a brass ring of skeleton keys and shoved one into the ancient lock. The mechanism turned freely and he pulled open the thick door, revealing an unlit tunnel that spewed cool air.

"A back door entrance, if you will." He opened his duffel bag and distributed a supply of flashlights and hard hats. "I can state with authority that it's no fun scraping your head on a limestone chandelier." He donned the last helmet.

The dark tunnel was wide and high enough for them to walk through upright, except for Dirk and Summer. They passed an empty side room, which Hawker explained was once used as an ammunition magazine for the battery. From there, the tunnel narrowed, brushing the sides of Perlmutter's wide frame.

As they descended farther into the Rock, the interior became cool and damp. Summer felt the clammy air and inhaled the musty smell, and she could almost hear the echoes from the past.

"Please stay close," Hawker said, "I don't want to lose anybody."

The passage grew tighter, and Hawker hesitated when they reached a cross tunnel. The one to their right had a chain barrier with a small placard that said NO ENTRY.

Hawker stepped over the barrier. "This should take us to Nelson."

As the others followed, their hard hats often scraped against the low ceiling. Hawker pointed to some cut marks above them. "These were all hand-excavated with hammer and chisel, and just a small amount of explosives, in the eighteenth and nineteenth centuries. They're an offshoot of the Great Siege tunnels. The Nelson branch should be just ahead."

Dirk turned to his sister. "A long way to be carting some gold."

"Made all the safer on account of it," she said.

They threaded their way through a serpentine section of tunnel and reached a small clearing. Hawker stopped in front of a rusty iron gate embedded into the rock and shined his light through the bars. Just beyond, a nearly vertical shaft descended into blackness.

Hawker faced the others with a wary grin. "This is it. The records indicate there was a cave-in during the original excavations. The shaft was cleared away in the 1880s to create a storage bay, possibly for powder reserves. Apparently, there was another collapse years later, then it was sealed off."

"Was it named for Admiral Nelson?" Dirk asked.

"The Battle of Trafalgar was fought nearby in 1805. Lord Nelson was killed during the engagement and his ship, HMS *Victory*, towed to Gibraltar for repairs. Several of the *Victory*'s crew are buried in Trafalgar Cemetery back in town. The tunnel was, no doubt, named in his honor."

Hawker tried his supply of skeleton keys, but none turned the mechanism. After several failed attempts to open the lock, Perlmutter asked him to step aside. Using his mass, the historian raised a foot and stomped against the latch with the weight of his heel. The gate flung open with barely a protest.

The big man peered over the precipice and shook his head. "I'm afraid you'll have to take it from here."

Hawker crawled to the edge and shined his light into the depths.

"Looks to be about twenty feet to the bottom." He opened his duffel and retrieved a static nylon climbing rope. "If fifty feet doesn't do the trick, then we've got bigger problems." He tied one end around the gate's stanchion. "Anyone care to join me in the descent?"

Dirk and Summer stepped forward, but Perlmutter and Trehorne shook their heads.

"You may need a couple of old mules up here to pull you out," Trehorne said. "Julien and I will stand by at the ready."

Hawker slipped the rope between his legs and pulled the loose end from his right hip, then crossed it over his left shoulder, gripping it behind his back. Secured by the Dulfersitz rappelling technique, he stepped over the edge and lowered himself down the shaft, using the friction from the rope as a brake. He was gone from view less than a minute before he shouted up, "All clear."

Summer descended next, clipping her flashlight to her belt

and duplicating the rope configuration. She let herself down slowly, pushing off on the shaft's smooth limestone walls. After ten feet, the narrow enclosure expanded into an open cavern where the ceiling had given way during excavations below. Hawker's light guided her to the floor and she slid down the remaining distance, landing on her feet.

"Well done," he said. "I think it's closer to a twenty-five-foot drop, actually."

He helped her release the rope and called up to Dirk.

"It would be a lot less nerve-racking if someone had left the lights on," she said.

A few seconds later, Dirk dropped to her side. They swung their flashlights around the cavern, highlighting piles of crumbled rock and a small passageway to their right.

Dirk aimed his light at the opening. "Your honors, Major."

"My pleasure." Hawker hunched down and scurried through the tunnel, Summer fast on his heels. After a short distance, the trio entered a square room about twenty feet across. But the room was completely empty, save for an upright wooden rack in the corner. Summer walked the perimeter and examined the floor and walls for any indication a Russian treasure had once been stored there but found nothing.

As Hawker examined the rack, he noticed a faint smell of gunpowder. "Looks like a musket rack. I'll bet the room was used to store small arms and perhaps some gunpowder."

"But not gold," Summer said.

"It would seem not."

She heard an echo of Perlmutter's voice and ducked back to the entry cavern. "Julien?" she called.

"Summer, what have you found?" his voice bellowed in a curt tone.

"Nothing, I'm afraid."

"The gold. It wasn't there?"

"No, it doesn't appear as if it ever was. We'll be up shortly."

She turned to rejoin Dirk and Hawker, then hesitated. Something wasn't quite right. She swung her flashlight around the cavern, then realized what it was.

The rope was missing.

"Julien!" she shouted. "Where's our rope?"

Her question was met by silence.

77

As Perlmutter and Trehorne waited for the team below, a crisp voice from behind them nearly startled them over the shaft's edge.

"Please raise your hands and step back to the wall," Mansfield said in a firm but polite way.

The two historians turned to find Mansfield and Martina standing a few feet away, pistols leveled at their chests. The men backed away from the shaft and stood against the rock wall.

Mansfield clicked on a penlight, stepped to the edge, and peered down. The distant voices of Dirk, Summer, and Hawker echoed from below. He knelt, pulled up the rope, and tossed it to Martina. Without a word, she pulled out a folding knife and began cutting it into shorter lengths.

"A nice hiding spot," Mansfield said, turning from the shaft to the men. "Did you meet with success?"

When neither spoke, Mansfield pointed his weapon at Perlmutter. "You, come to the ledge. Please ask your friends what they have found."

"Listen here—"

Mansfield jammed the pistol into the side of Perlmutter's neck. "Save it for your friends," he whispered.

Perlmutter did as he was told, obtaining Summer's report. Then Mansfield forced him onto his knees beside Trehorne while Martina tied their wrists and elbows behind their backs with sections of the climbing rope.

"Tie the big one's feet, then take the other one away," Mansfield said.

Martina bound Perlmutter's ankles, retrieved her gun, and pulled Trehorne to his feet. Taking his flashlight, she marched him into the tunnel and around the first bend.

As Summer shouted from below, Mansfield stepped over to Perlmutter, stuck a foot on his shoulder, and shoved him onto his back. "You're a historian, aren't you? Why don't you tell me about the Romanov shipment?"

Perlmutter shook his head. "I don't succumb to criminal extortion."

Mansfield nodded, then picked up a length of rope and tied it around Perlmutter's head and over his mouth.

The Russian rose to his feet, clutching another piece of rope. "I'm going to visit your friend. Don't go anywhere."

He walked a short distance around the bend to where Martina waited with Trehorne. She held a guidebook and a folded sheet of paper in one hand and her pistol in the other.

"I searched him and found these." She passed the items to Mansfield.

He scanned the book's title. "*A Pocket Guide to the Caves and Tunnels of Gibraltar.* Very handy." He tossed it to the ground.

He unfolded the paper and studied it under his penlight. It was a copy of the letter from the *Sentinel*'s captain requesting security for its cargo. "A bit more interesting. So, the *Sentinel* did in fact obtain the *Pelikan*'s cargo and brought it to Gibraltar. But it was never shipped on to England, was it?" He waved his gun under Trehorne's chin.

"No evidence that we could find," Trehorne said.

"And this tunnel. This is AEB Nelson?"

Trehorne nodded.

"Who's your Army friend?"

"Major Cecil Hawker of the Royal Gibraltar Regiment. An expert on Gibraltar's tunnels."

"But not on Gibraltar's gold," Mansfield said. "So if not here, then where?"

Trehorne shook his head.

From the frustrated look in Trehorne's eyes, Mansfield believed he was telling the truth. The Russian passed a length of rope to Martina. "Tie his feet, please."

He then raised his pistol and pointed it toward Trehorne's left eye. "Thank you for your cooperation."

The gunshot echoed through the tunnel like a cannon blast. Perlmutter flinched at the sound and opened his eyes a few seconds later to see Mansfield standing before him.

The Russian removed Perlmutter's gag, then raised his pistol. "Your friend wasn't very talkative. Now, tell me what you are doing here."

Perlmutter swallowed hard. "This is Nelson's tunnel." He tilted his head toward the open shaft, then summarized the research that had led them there.

"Where would the gold be, if not here?" Mansfield asked.

Perlmutter shook his head. "I haven't a clue. Perhaps it was returned to Russia."

Mansfield retied the rope gag. "You and your friend are smart fellows. Good-bye." He strode off through the tunnel, his small light beam quickly fading to black.

From the depths of the shaft, Summer called up in alarm. Perlmutter inched his way in the darkness, carefully approaching the edge and peering over. Flashlights illumined the steep walls below. He could see his friends were duly trapped.

While edging across the ground, Perlmutter had felt the sensation of dragging a tail. After tying him up, Martina had left some excess rope attached to his feet. He tucked in his knees, rolled to one side, and felt a length of rope about six feet long extending from his ankles. She had tied them with a secure knot, then added several loops that were bound more casually. If he could work loose the outer bindings, there might be enough rope to do some good.

Perlmutter crawled away from the opening and felt around for a small rock. Instead, he found the edge of the gate. Jamming his feet against the edge, he pulled up on his legs, trying to catch the rope and its outer knot. He did it all by feel, as visibility in the tunnel was like working with a bag over his head. Over the next uncounted minutes, he repeated the move a dozen, maybe a hundred times, until his legs ached and his breath came in gasps. He finally felt a loose coil on top of his feet—and realized he'd done it. Kicking the rope away, he slithered back to the edge of the shaft. The big man pivoted his body and extended his legs—and the loose rope—over the edge, while anchored on firm ground by his immense mass.

In the cavern below, Summer felt a shower of grit from above. She shined her light upward and saw Perlmutter's portly calves and feet dangling over the side with a ten-foot length of rope swaying from his ankles.

"Julien!" she shouted.

He kicked his legs, which made the rope sway.

Hawker came over and looked up the shaft. "It's too far out of reach, I'm afraid."

"We might get to it if we can step up from our end," Dirk said. "Major, can you give me a hand with that gun rack?"

He led Hawker into the store room. They pulled the musket rack from the wall and carried it to the base of the shaft.

Dirk shined his light at the dangling rope, trying to gauge its distance. "I might be able to reach it from the top of this thing."

"If you don't break your neck in the process," Hawker said, testing the fragile rack.

They centered the rack under the rope, and Dirk climbed atop its narrow crown as Hawker held it secure. Summer reached up and held Dirk's legs as he stood atop it, fighting for balance. He reached up, but the rope was still a foot or two out of reach.

"Hold that rack tight, Major," he said, then shouted upward. "Brace yourself, Julien. I'm coming your way."

He bent his knees and sprang off the rack, leaping for the end of the rope. Clasping it with an outstretched hand, he swung forward, then grabbed hold with his other hand.

The sudden tug pulled Perlmutter toward the edge and the big man struggled to hold position. He grunted in pain as Dirk pulled himself hand over hand until getting his legs around the rope, then shinnied to the top.

Dirk nearly slipped as he got himself over the edge. He rolled onto his back to catch his breath. "Maybe you and I should join the circus?" he said to Perlmutter between breaths.

Hearing a muffled reply, Dirk pulled his flashlight from a back pocket and played its beam over the bound man. Starting with the gag, he quickly untied the assorted bindings.

Perlmutter rubbed his ankles. "You about snapped my legs off."

"Sorry, I had to jump for it. Where's Trehorne?" Dirk shined his light about the area.

Perlmutter shook his head. "You heard the gunshot?"

"Yes," Dirk whispered. "Let's get the others up."

He quickly spliced the ropes together and retied one end to the gate, then tossed it over the side. When Summer confirmed she had looped it around herself, the two men helped pull her up.

Hawker was hoisted up a minute later. "What the devil went on up here?" he asked.

"Our Russian friends paid us a visit," Perlmutter said. "Afraid they got the jump on Charles and me."

"Mansfield? Here in Gibraltar?" Summer asked.

"Yes, and the woman, too. They took Charles away . . ." He waved an arm at the tunnel passage and stepped in that direction. Moving warily, he led the trio around the bend, then hesitated at a snorting noise. "Quick, the light!"

Summer passed him her flashlight and he shined it ahead.

There was Trehorne, hog-tied on the ground but with no sign of blood.

"Charles?" Perlmutter said.

Trehorne's eyes popped open and he blinked rapidly. "I must have slumbered off. Can you please take that blasted light out of my eyes?"

Perlmutter and Summer ran over and untied him.

"We thought they shot you," Hawker said, helping him to his feet.

"I feared as much, for a moment." Trehorne rubbed his head. "The fool fired his gun right next to my ear. I can't believe they tracked us in here." He gave the others an apologetic look. "I'm afraid they took the *Sentinel*'s cargo letter. I had a copy in my pocket."

"They won't get out of the country with it," Hawker promised.

"The letter doesn't matter. They know everything we do now."

"And, so far, that hasn't earned us any great benefit," Perlmutter said, rubbing his wrists.

"True," Trehorne said, gazing down the dark tunnel. "What bothers me is what they know about the gold—that we don't."

78

Hawker found them at an outdoor Spanish café next to their hotel, licking their wounds with afternoon tapas and drinks. Perlmutter and Trehorne were on their third Scotch, while Dirk and Summer felt too defeated to move past a single sangria. Summer tried to lose herself in Trehorne's Gibraltar guidebook, which she had picked up in the tunnel.

"Some encouraging news," Hawker said, pulling up a chair. "The Royal Gibraltar Police are now on the hunt for the two Russians. The airport and the commercial ship docks are on alert and every major hotel will be canvassed by evening. Gibraltar is not an easy place to hide. We'll find them."

"Good of you to help, Major," Perlmutter said, "but there's little point in apprehending them now."

"After they assaulted you and Charles and tried to leave us all for dead?"

"Julien's right," Trehorne said. "It was an unpleasant tussle, but, at the end of the day, no harm was done." He stared at his half-empty glass, disillusionment in his eyes. "We came to Gibraltar to find the gold and beat them to it. It would seem there is no gold to be found."

"Still, it doesn't make sense," Dirk said. "There's no evidence it was shipped to England or returned to the Russians."

"All we have to go on is Captain Marsh's letter from the *Sentinel*." Perlmutter looked at his Scotch. "We followed its lead, and there was nothing to show for it."

"But what if we looked in the wrong place?" Summer lowered the guidebook to reveal a hopeful smile.

"What are you getting at?" Trehorne asked.

"There's a chapter in your book about historic caves of Gibraltar. It mentions one called La Bóveda—which was also known as Nelson's Cave, for a time, in the nineteenth century."

"Nelson's Cave, you say?" Perlmutter regained his booming voice.

"Yes. The only problem is, the book says the cave was sealed up in 1888."

Hawker stared at the ground, searching his memory. "*La Bóveda*. That's Spanish for *The Vault*. There must have been a church on the site, at one point. I've heard the name, but I can't recall the location."

"The book says it was formerly accessed at Number 12, Lime Kiln Steps."

"That's just a few blocks from here." Hawker turned pale. "Oh, my. Number 12, Lime Kiln Steps. Oh, my." He reached over and took a healthy slug of Trehorne's Scotch.

"What's come over you, Cecil?" Trehorne asked.

"It all makes perfect sense. It's my blunder, I'm afraid. My blunder." He set down the glass with a quivering hand and stared, wide-eyed, at the group. Shaking his head, he muttered, "Where else would they have put it?"

MARTINA SAT on the second-story balcony of their rental flat, seeming to sun herself but in fact scrutinizing the pedestrian traffic on the street below. When she heard Mansfield complete a telephone conversation in the adjacent living room, she stepped inside and closed the balcony door. "Did you arrange for a boat to get us out of Gibraltar?"

"Why, no." He gave her a bemused look.

"It is not safe. We should leave tonight."

"Leave?" He laughed. "Just as we struck gold?"

"What are you saying?"

"The letter you took from the British historian." He waved Trehorne's copy. "It has the answer after all."

"But we were at the Nelson Tunnel. They said it was empty. Did they lie to us?"

"No. The fools were pursuing the wrong clue. On a lark, I phoned your London banking friend to see if he had any contacts in Gibraltar. I read Bainbridge the letter and he said the answer was obvious."

"What was obvious?"

"The storage. It was made at AEB Nelson. He didn't know the Nelson reference but said the AEB could only be one place. The Anglo-Egyptian Bank."

"Only a banker would know that. What is this bank?"

"It was a private British bank established in 1864 in Alexandria to fund trade with Egypt. It acted as the primary bank to the British authorities throughout the Mediterranean. A branch office was opened in Gibraltar in 1888."

"It must be long gone by now."

"Actually, no. The bank was acquired by Barclays in the 1920s and is still operating. The Gibraltar branch is even in the same location."

"You think the gold is still sitting in this bank?"

"It's possible. Bainbridge says there is some logic in the British having placed it in a private institution rather than the Bank of England. He called it 'plausible deniability.'"

"How do we find out?"

"I just called our embassy in Madrid. They'll have a diplomat here in the morning with a formal requisition."

"It might be a bit embarrassing for you if it isn't there."

"Agreed. That's why we're going to pay them a visit now and find out."

"Now?"

"There's no time like the present."

"We better not take a cab. How far is it?"

"Less than a kilometer. The bank is located on an oddly named street. Lime Kiln Steps."

The former Anglo-Egyptian Bank Building was a neoclassic structure with a façade of tall doric columns and a high-pitched roof, which disguised its modest interior size. Located near the site of an eighteenth-century kiln that produced quicklime for mortar, the rear of the structure backed against a rising incline of the Rock.

Mansfield stopped in front of the building, noting the year 1888 engraved on the cornerstone. A plastic BARCLAYS sign hung over the front pediment, covering the stone-carved letters AEB.

Mansfield wore dark glasses and Martina was concealed under a hat and scarf when they stepped into the marble-floored lobby and approached an information desk. Mansfield looked past a row of cashiers' stalls to a large stainless steel vault door. It was built right into the limestone rock.

A woman at the information desk greeted them warmly, but, before they could respond, a man in a dark suit emerged from a side office and rushed over to them. "I'm terribly sorry," he said in a flustered voice, "but the bank is now closed."

Mansfield motioned toward some people in line at the cashiers' windows. "They are being helped."

"Yes, but they entered before we closed. The door should have been locked a few minutes ago."

Mansfield glanced at a wall clock, which read four-fifteen.

The man caught his glance. "We close early on Fridays."

"Are you the bank manager?" Mansfield asked.

"Yes. My name is Finlay. I would be happy to help you to-morrow."

"That would be fine. For the moment, we would just like to inquire about a gold deposit made with your bank some years ago."

Finlay gave him a blank look.

"It was a rather large deposit, made in 1917."

Finlay blinked rapidly, then cleared his throat. "I would be happy to look into it tomorrow. However, I will require documentation regarding the deposit."

Mansfield had his answer and smiled graciously at the banker. "That will be fine. Shall we say noon?"

"Yes, noon or anytime after will be perfect," Finlay said. "May I have the name?"

"Romanov."

The banker turned ghost white but retained enough composure to escort the smiling Russian couple to the door. After watching them walk down the street, he rushed back to his office and closed the door. Circled around his desk were Hawker, Perlmutter, Trehorne, Dirk, and Summer, who had watched the encounter through the office's smoked-glass window. Finlay nearly collapsed into his desk chair.

"What extraordinary timing." He tapped his desk calendar, which read July 21. "Entering the bank just on the heels of your arrival."

"I still say we should have had them arrested on the spot," Hawker said.

Dirk looked at Finlay. "I think it's safe to say that they'll be back tomorrow."

"It will make for an interesting visit, I should think." Perlmutter's eyes sparkled with mirth.

"There will be plenty of security on hand, I can assure you," Finlay said. "You'll be back tomorrow as well?"

"Absolutely," Trehorne said.

Summer smiled. "You did promise us a tour of the Nelson Cave."

"Yes, I did; didn't I? Well, I thank you again for your timely visit, and I'll look forward to seeing you tomorrow."

The banker escorted the visitors out of the building, then

paced the lobby until the last customer had left. He locked the door with a sense of relief, shut himself in his office, and retrieved a dusty bottle of brandy from the back of a cabinet. He poured himself a stiff shot.

A few minutes later, the head teller entered with a computer printout. "Here are the daily transactions, Mr. Finlay. Is there anything else?"

"No. You and the staff may close up and leave."

As the woman turned to leave, Finlay stopped her. "Miss Oswald? There is one thing. Would you please inform the night watchman that I intend to remain on the premises all night."

"You're staying here? In the building?"

"Yes." He gazed toward the vault. "I don't believe I would obtain any sleep at home tonight, so my insomnia shall be satisfied here."

79

As an army of FBI agents descended on Bermuda to join Ana's Europol investigation, Homeland Security officials increased safety measures around the District of Columbia. Access to federal buildings was carefully scrutinized, while security was elevated at all nearby airports. Spot roadblocks were set up around the District and small boats patrolled the Potomac. At the National Underwater and Marine Agency headquarters, the staff assisted in the search for the atomic bomb using their marine resources database.

Pitt stepped into the fifth-floor computer center, where he found Rudi Gunn, Hiram Yaeger, and Al Giordino seated next to a half-eaten box of donuts that had fueled them since sunrise. He joined them at a curved table that faced a floor to ceiling video screen. The screen was split between a global map showing the location of NUMA research vessels and marine resources and a satellite image of an island chain that Pitt recognized as Bermuda.

Giordino slid the donut box Pitt's way. "You're lucky Hiram's gone gluten-free or they'd be decimated by now."

Pitt reached into the box. "What do you hear from Homeland Security?"

"Nothing concrete," Gunn said. "They're scrambling to investigate every cargo flight from Bermuda to the U.S. in the past week. They've reported nothing promising, but they have a lot of catching up to do."

"What about sea transit?"

"They've issued alerts to the commercial port authorities and have tagged a pair of inbound container ships for inspection in New York. The Coast Guard is also initiating random searches of vessels bound for Boston, New York, Philadelphia, and the Chesapeake. Locally, the Coast Guard has established a security zone around Washington in the Potomac and Anacostia Rivers. But Homeland Security analysts seem to believe the bomb was flown out of Bermuda and may in fact have been taken back to Ukraine."

"That may be a false hope," Pitt said. "I spoke to Ana earlier. She and her team have grilled as many cargo workers as she could round up at the Bermuda airport. Several were witness to a truck being offloaded a week or two ago with a large covered object on its bed. No one has reported seeing a similar object being shipped out."

"A bomb of that size would be easier to load onto a ship than a plane," Giordino said.

"That's what Ana believes."

"Does she have any other leads?" Gunn asked.

"She's trying to track down the Dutch industrialist Martin

Hendriks. As soon as she briefs the FBI team that just arrived, she's headed to Amsterdam."

"Hendriks would seem to have the funds to support the United Armed Forces of Novorossiya—or whoever is toting the bomb around," Gunn said.

"Agreed," Pitt said. "I think we need to take seriously the threat by sea."

"We've been working it, chief," Yaeger said. He typed into a keyboard, which brought up a data table next to the satellite image of Bermuda. "The commercial port authorities in Bermuda have shared reports of all seagoing traffic in and out of the country the past week. This list shows ship name, registered owner, and reported destination."

Pitt scanned the list. "I count six U.S.-bound ships."

"We're tracking them all." Yaeger pulled up a map of the Eastern seaboard, with four red lights blinking at points in the Atlantic and two lights on the coastline. "One of the ships, a container vessel, has already docked in New York, and the second is due in today. Both will be searched by Homeland Security. A third ship has docked as well, an oil tanker that reached Charleston two days ago."

"Probably not a prime suspect," Pitt said.

"We checked some satellite photos of her and there was nothing suspicious on her decks, so we feel the same."

"That leaves three ships in transit."

"One is a cruise ship headed to Miami and the other two are freighters due to dock in the next two days. One is bound for Houston, the other Newark. We've passed the data to Homeland Security and inspectors will be waiting for all three."

"Those are all manageable," Pitt said. "The larger worry is an unregistered ship running silent or a smaller private vessel."

"That's what we've been focusing on," Gunn said. "We're limited to just satellite imagery on that front. Hiram has been busy collecting photos since last night."

"The satellite coverage over Bermuda is worse than Bulgaria," Yaeger said, "but I've pulled what I could. Unfortunately, there's quite a few yachts and pleasure crafts visiting Bermuda this time of year. To make it manageable, I've dispensed with any craft under thirty feet."

Yaeger instructed the computer to sort and scan the downloaded images, restricted to those taken of vessels in the waters west of Bermuda. The supercomputer quickly reviewed, matched, and collated the images, presenting Yaeger with a long list.

"There's about forty," he said. "No easy way around it, we need to take a look at them one by one."

The group began poring over the images, noting size, type, and apparent destination of each craft. Many vessels were eliminated as pleasure boats incapable of transporting the bomb.

Gunn kept a running tally. "We're down to a very large sailing boat that's close to Boston and two luxury yachts aimed for Miami. Are there any other possibilities?"

"There's one more on the list," Yaeger said. "Visible westbound from Bermuda three days ago."

He pulled up a satellite photo of a white speck off the Bermuda coastline. He zoomed in until it filled the screen. It was actually two vessels: an orange and white tug pulling a barge. Pitt noticed the tug was distinguished by an extended open rear deck. The picture was crisp enough to show its long hawser, secured to a trio of bollards on the enclosed barge, which was small and painted black.

Giordino stared at it and whistled. "That certainly has potential."

As he had with the photos of the other vessels, Yaeger scanned the image and instructed the computer to search for additional matches near the U.S. A minute later, two more images popped onto the screen.

"The first was taken early yesterday morning—at six, local time," Yaeger said. The tug and barge were visible somewhere in the middle of the ocean. Yaeger adjusted the scale to see their position relative to the East Coast. "She looks to be traveling northwest about a hundred miles off the coast of North Carolina."

"Likely heading for Chesapeake Bay." Pitt leaned forward in his chair. "Where does the most recent image place her?"

Yaeger enlarged the second photo. "Just snagged this one." He noted the time marker. "Five-thirty this morning."

The two vessels appeared in an inland waterway. Yaeger zoomed out, revealing a western tributary of the Chesapeake, the vessels sailing north. At the top of the image, they saw an all too familiar bend in the river.

"They're in the Potomac," Giordino said.

"The Coast Guard has a patrol boat on watch north of Quantico," Gunn said. "They should pick it up as it comes closer to D.C."

"Let them know to target it," Pitt said. "Then alert Homeland Security to throw everything they have at it." He studied the image. "They're only twenty or thirty miles out by now. What do we have available at Reagan National?"

"There's a Robinson R44 in the NUMA hangar," Gunn said.

"Get it fueled and ready."

"I'm not sure we have any pilots on standby."

Pitt nodded at Giordino before replying to Gunn.

"You're looking at 'em."

80

Pitt and Giordino were out the door before Gunn could start punching numbers on the telephone. They raced through post-morning rush hour traffic and reached Ronald Reagan Washington National Airport, just south of the NUMA building, within minutes. Pitt sped past his home, a converted hangar on a remote section of the grounds, and headed to the private aviation terminal. A bright turquoise helicopter was already idling in front of the NUMA hangar. A waiting flight crew passed off the chopper and they were in the air minutes later, with Pitt at the controls.

He guided the Robinson R44 over the Potomac and followed the river south, scanning ahead for the tug and barge. Near Mount Vernon, they passed a pair of Coast Guard fast-response boats speeding downriver. The helicopter flew over the Mason Neck peninsula a few miles later and Pitt spotted an orange vessel. "That's our target."

As they approached the town of Quantico and its neighboring Marine base, they clearly saw the tug and its trailing barge. A Coast Guard patrol boat was already alongside, guiding the tug toward shore.

"Looks like they're herding her to the Quantico public marina," Giordino said.

Pitt circled over the vessels, then backtracked to Quantico. An empty parking lot sided the marina, and Pitt set the helicopter down. He and Giordino were standing at the dock when the tug pulled alongside. The two Coast Guard fast boats arrived seconds later, and the dock was soon teeming with armed men.

"What's this all about?" cried the tug's captain, who spoke with a faint British accent. A sweaty man in shorts and a T-shirt, he was marched off the vessel at gunpoint.

Pitt and Giordino climbed aboard the barge as it drifted against the dock and began hoisting open the covered holds. A Coast Guard lieutenant joined them as the first cover was removed and they peered inside.

"Sand," Giordino said.

The remaining three holds were equally full of fine-grained sand. Pitt jumped into the first hold and probed a few feet down with the handle of a fire ax, but found nothing. He repeated the exercise in the other three holds.

"Anything?" Giordino asked.

Pitt shook his head. He climbed back onto the deck as the lieutenant pointed to the tug.

"The captain claims they're on a government job to dump sand along the Anacostia River for shoreline refurbishment. We have orders to impound both vessels for a full inspection. We'll pull out every last grain of sand to make sure there's nothing hidden below."

"Thanks, Lieutenant," Pitt said. "I suspect that's all you will find."

He and Giordino stepped to the front of the barge and gazed at the tug docked ahead of them.

"Guess we can call this baby the *Wild Goose*," Giordino said, leaning against one of the barge's twin hawser bitts. "I'm thinking the bomb must have gone east from Bermuda, not west."

"Maybe," Pitt said, "but why would somebody haul a barge of sand halfway across the Atlantic?"

"It might have come over empty and they took the sand on somewhere in Virginia."

Pitt gazed at Giordino, considering the idea, when the answer came to him. "No, Al. This is a different barge. They've been switched."

"How do you know?"

Pitt pointed to the two bollards securing the tow line. "Because you're sitting on the proof."

81

Hiram Yaeger confirmed the satellite image of the tug taken the day before showed it pulling a barge with three forward hawser bitts. Detailed analysis also revealed differences in the paint and rust markings between the two barges.

The news set off a full-blown dragnet along the Potomac, with every available Coast Guard and local law enforcement boat and helicopter deployed in the search. Pitt and Giordino aided the cause, flying the Robinson as far south as the Chesapeake before backtracking up the river.

Obtaining permission to land at the Marine Corps Air Facility along the river at Quantico, Pitt brought the chopper down for refueling. As they waited for a fuel truck, they heard a loud underwater explosion from an inlet beyond the airfield. A Marine ground crewman noticed their interest.

"Just some Force Recon boys practicing underwater demolitions," he said. "The runway's going to smell like dead fish for the next week now."

"We'll make sure not to go for a dip," Giordino said.

Pitt paced around the helicopter until the fuel truck finally arrived. "We need to expand the search area," he said. "They could have gone to Norfolk, up the Chesapeake, or maybe even stayed in the Atlantic to hit Philadelphia or New York."

"That's a lot of real estate to cover—" Giordino paused to take a call from Gunn at NUMA headquarters.

Pitt oversaw the refueling as another explosion sounded from the inlet. He stepped away from the helicopter and watched a small fountain of water erupt on the far side. The upheaval reminded him of the sinking barge in the Black Sea. Suddenly, it all came together: the connection between the Bosphorus, Sevastopol, and Washington.

"Al, do you still have Rudi on the line?"

Giordino nodded and handed him the phone.

"Rudi, I need you to find out where there are anoxic zones in the waters around here, be it the Potomac, the Chesapeake, or Delaware Bay. A dead zone near a highly populated area might be the actual target."

"I'll get Hiram right on it. What's the draw of a dead zone?"

"Hydrogen sulfide gas."

"Sure, anoxic waters are loaded with hydrogen sulfide. We've surveyed subsurface concentrations of the stuff off the Mississippi River delta and the Oregon coast . . . and in the Chesapeake."

"That's the key, Rudi. The crew of the *Crimean Star* were

killed by hydrogen sulfide gas and Mankedo was attempting to release a cloud of it outside Sevastopol."

"Create a cloud of hydrogen sulfide? Yes, it could kill thousands."

"Think what an atomic bomb set off in a concentrated dead zone could do."

Gunn fell silent at the thought.

"Find us the anoxic zones, Rudi," Pitt said, "and I'll find us that barge."

Pitt and Giordino were back in the air when Gunn responded minutes later, with a call patched through to the helicopter's radio.

"Hiram just laid in a regional map of known dead zones, based on past water samplings combined with current data points. As you know, large portions of the Chesapeake Bay become oxygen-deprived in the summer months when nitrogen and phosphorous pollutants combine with warm water temperatures to create algae blooms. Unfortunately, the timing is perfect, as we are approaching the peak season."

"Where are the key hot spots?" Pitt asked.

"It might be easier to define what's not," Gunn said. "A major seam runs nearly the length of the Chesapeake, beginning near the mouth of the Potomac and stretching up to Annapolis. It's centered on the western side of the bay. There are some additional pockets farther north we'll identify once Hiram finishes loading the data."

Pitt was already banking the helicopter to the east, crossing over Waldorf, Maryland, on a path to the Chesapeake Bay.

"Washington doesn't rate?" Giordino asked.

"While I would think twice about swimming in the Anacostia River," Gunn said, "both it and the Potomac have historically shown minimally active dead zones."

"We'll shoot for Annapolis," Pitt said.

They soon reached the Chesapeake and Pitt banked the Robinson to the north. They cruised above the western side of the ten-mile-wide bay, performing flybys over several commercial vessels and a large sailboat Pitt recognized as a skipjack. The Severn River inlet loomed to their left and Pitt followed the waterway west, curling around Annapolis and its surrounding creeks. Aside from a few rusty dredge barges filled with mud, nothing resembled the black tow barge.

As Pitt looped back to the Chesapeake, Gunn called again. "We found several more anoxic zones farther north."

"Any near population centers?" Pitt asked.

"The Patapsco River is loaded with them."

"Baltimore?"

"Yes, just outside the Inner Harbor." Gunn paused for a moment. "Winds in Baltimore are currently out of the southeast at around ten knots. If your theory is right and they set it off in the Patapsco, they could kick up a cloud of hydrogen sulfide that would drift right over the city."

"There's three million people there," Giordino said.

"The gas would be exponentially more lethal than the bomb itself," Gunn said.

"It fits the threat," Pitt said. "Rudi, do you remember the letter to the President from the Ukrainian rebel group?"

"Yes. Didn't it say they were going to hit Washington?"

"No. They said they would strike our historic capital. And

they said the Star-Spangled Banner will no longer wave. Direct lyrics from our national anthem."

"Of course," Gunn said. "Fort McHenry. Francis Scott Key. He wrote the original poem from Baltimore."

"Not only that, but if I'm not mistaken, Baltimore was an early, temporary capital for the Continental Congress before New York and Washington, D.C."

"I'll alert the Baltimore Coast Guard station at once."

"We'll be there in a flash. Pitt out."

Pitt nudged the cyclic control forward to squeeze more speed out of the Robinson as he angled back north up the Chesapeake. The entrance to the Patapsco River appeared on the horizon less than ten miles away.

"I sure hope you're wrong about all that," Giordino said.

"So do I," Pitt said. "So do I."

But five minutes later, upon reaching the approach to the Patapsco River, they spotted a small black barge under tow to Baltimore.

82

"Wagner's Point is three miles ahead." The *Lauren Belle*'s helmsman pointed out the pilothouse window to a landmass just beyond the Francis Scott Key Bridge.

Vasko glanced at the approaching highway bridge, then turned his attention to a nautical chart of Chesapeake Bay. Provided by Hendriks, it marked in purple highlights the bay's low-oxygen zones. They were already sailing over such a zone, but their target was a southern tributary of the Patapsco River past the Key Bridge. It not only had a history of high anoxic rates during the summer but the site had the added advantage of being within sight of Baltimore's Inner Harbor.

He stepped across the small pilothouse and showed the chart to the helmsman. "Take us just off the tip of the Point. We'll cut and sink the barge there. What's our top speed without a tow?"

"She'll do close to fifteen knots."

"There's a charter plane waiting for us across the bay at a place called Smith's Field. Get us there as fast as possible, once we cut the barge loose."

"Will do." A thumping noise vibrated through the bridge, and he pointed out an open rear door. "Looks like you've got a visitor."

Vasko turned to see a turquoise helicopter hovering over the barge.

"Where's the crate that was passed aboard?" he asked.

"Right behind you."

Vasko kicked away some jackets to find the crate at the rear of the bridge. He unlatched the container to reveal four AK-47 rifles and some gas masks on a top shelf. He moved those aside in favor of a rocket-propelled grenade launcher that was fastened above a row of projectiles. He removed the launcher and loaded one of the rounds.

Five hundred feet above the barge, the NUMA helicopter accelerated forward.

"We better alert Rudi to get Homeland Security on them now." Pitt was satisfied they had the right barge, affirmed by its three forward bollards. As they skimmed above the tow line, Giordino gave him a warning.

"Man on the deck with a weapon."

Pitt had seen him as well. It was Vasko, raising a heavy weapon to his shoulder. Pitt pitched the Robinson's nose down, to force more speed, while rolling sharply to the right.

Vasko had little time to aim at the fast-moving chopper, so he simply pointed and shot. The RPG burst from the launcher just as Pitt flung the helicopter nearly onto its side.

The projectile whistled past the Robinson's fuselage, coming within a whisker of missing the helicopter altogether. But by the thinnest of margins, the RPG tagged the spinning tail rotor— and detonated.

The blast demolished the tail assembly and sent a shower of shrapnel into the underside fuselage and engine compartment. The wounded helicopter shot past the tug before the mortal blow began to take effect. Inside the cockpit, smoke from the damaged engine filled the air. Pitt could feel the Robinson begin to spin from the loss of the tail rotor. He reached for the collective stick and cut the throttle.

The seemingly counterintuitive move disengaged the engine from the main rotor, eliminating the torque-producing spin. It also created a state of autorotation, where the freewheeling main rotor slowed the helicopter's descent. With some forward momentum, Pitt could descend in a semicontrolled glide. But he had only a few seconds before they touched down.

"Wet landing," he called out, knowing the shoreline was more than a half mile away.

"Watch out for a large vessel ahead." Giordino choked out the words.

The cockpit was filled with a thick blue haze. The two men could barely see each other, let alone anything in their path. Pitt had his face pressed to the side window, watching the water draw near, then glanced forward. The image of a large black mass was faintly visible, but they wouldn't make it far enough to fear a collision.

Out the side window, Pitt watched the helicopter drop altitude until they were fifty feet off the water. Then he pulled back on the cyclic control to raise the nose, flaring their speed. At just ten feet, he goosed the throttle for a burst of lift, then killed the power.

The Robinson struck the bay with a hard jolt. Landing flat, the helicopter held afloat for just a second as smoke poured from the engine. The chopper then plunged beneath the surface, its main rotor slapping the bay. Two of the blades splintered on impact, spinning across the water.

Amid a thrashing of white water and air bubbles, the Robinson sank to the bottom of the bay, disclosing no sign of its occupants.

83

"I guess there's no avoiding a swim," Giordino said as water swirled up to his knees.

Pitt unbuckled his seat belt. "We'll have to wait till she floods to get the doors open."

Though they had descended without power, Pitt had made a textbook emergency landing, without injury. Their only problem was they had landed in water.

While the Robinson was completely submerged, the cockpit was only partially flooded. The two men calmly waited for the water inside to rise above the doorframes. The helicopter was twenty feet deep and sinking fast. They took a last breath from the remaining air pocket, shoved open their side doors, and stroked toward daylight.

They broke the surface, gulping for air, and were orienting themselves for a swim to shore when a pair of ropes splashed into the water beside them.

"Grab hold and we'll pull you aboard," a man yelled.

Pitt turned and saw a massive black-hulled sailing ship moving down the bay. He reached for the nearest rope and was yanked to the vessel's curved wooden hull. Cannon protruded from a white ribbon of gun ports a level beneath its main deck. Pitt recognized the ship with surprise. She was the USS *Constellation*, a pre–Civil War sloop and long-standing museum ship based in Baltimore Harbor.

Hauling himself up the rope, Pitt reached the side rail and hopped onto her deck. A small group of middle-aged men gripped the other end of the rope while another team pulled Giordino aboard.

"Thanks for the line." Pitt shook off the water. "I didn't expect to see the *Connie* out, stretching her legs."

A keen-eyed man in a yellow Hawaiian shirt approached. "She just came out of dry dock. We're making a test run to prove she's seaworthy. We hope to sail her to New York and Boston later this summer." He reached out a hand. "My name's Wayne Valero. I head up the *Constellation*'s volunteer sailing crew."

Pitt introduced himself as Giordino climbed aboard and joined them.

"You boys were pretty lucky," Valero said, eyeing them inquisitively. "One of my men said you were shot down."

Pitt pointed over the rail at the tug and barge passing in the opposite direction. "Would you believe that barge is headed to Baltimore with a bomb aboard?"

"I'd believe it from two men who just swam out of a burning NUMA helicopter," Valero said.

"We could use your help to stop them."

Valero puffed out his chest. "That's what the *Constellation* was built for. Tell us what we can do."

Under Pitt's direction, the old warship made a sweeping turn to port. The veteran crew of sailors expertly worked the sails and rigging, turning the ship around and onto a northwesterly heading up the Patapsco River. With the sails on all three masts billowing, the ship moved briskly. Pitt could see they would soon overtake the tug and barge.

As the city of Baltimore appeared off the ship's prow, he approached Valero. "The *Connie*'s guns—are they operational?"

Valero pointed to the stern. "There's a twenty-pound Parrott gun on the aft spar deck that's fired in demonstration all the time. We've got quite a bit of powder stored below, leftover from the Fourth of July celebrations."

"How about shot?"

Valero thought a moment. "The Parrott's a rifled gun, so it fires a shell. There's a display case on the gun deck with a couple of samples for a twenty-pounder."

He led Pitt and Giordino down a level to the gun deck, where rows of eight-inch cannon lined the gun ports. They approached a wall display covered in an acrylic sheet that contained weapons and shot that would have been used aboard the *Constellation* after her launch in 1854.

Giordino grabbed the acrylic covering and, with a heave, tore it from the wall. "My apologies to the museum," he said to Valero, "but if we don't stop these guys, there may not be any future visitors to the ship."

"I'll take the heat," Valero said. "You'll want to grab the two shells on the lower left. The ten-pound round shot can also be used in a pinch. I'll get the powder and primer and meet you topsides."

Giordino nodded toward Valero as he disappeared across the deck. "Lucky we found a guy who's with us."

"Does seem like a kindred spirit," Pitt said, prying a pair of cutlasses from the display.

They hauled the swords and ammunition up to the spar deck and the Parrott gun at the aft rail. In 1860, Captain Robert Parker Parrott had designed his first rifled cannon, and copies in multiple calibers were used extensively by both armies during the Civil War. Known more for their accuracy than their durability, Parrott guns like that aboard the *Constellation* could fire a nineteen-pound shell over two miles.

Valero arrived at the gun with a limber chest full of black powder bags, then called to some of the volunteers. "Vinson, Gwinn, Campbell, Yates—come over and help man this gun. I'll take the helm."

"We'll fire from the port rail," Pitt said. "Have your men keep their heads down. They have weapons."

"No worries. I'll bring her right alongside." Valero stepped to the helm, ahead of the mizzenmast.

Pitt and Giordino, with the help of the volunteers, rolled the Parrott gun to an opening along the port rail. Pitt placed a two-pound aluminum cartridge of powder into the muzzle, and one of the men shoved it to the breech with a ramrod.

Giordino pointed to the armament lying on the deck. "What's your choice?"

"Let's start with a solid shell."

Giordino placed a ten-inch-long solid shell in the muzzle, and it was rammed down to the powder. The crew shoved the gun's carriage to the rail and secured it with ropes. Pitt jammed a friction primer into a vent on the cannon's breech, puncturing the powder bag. He tied off the end of the primer to a thin lanyard and stepped away from the carriage with the other men.

The tug was barely a hundred yards ahead, with Valero making straight for her. The tug seemed to notice the *Constellation*'s approach and veered to port.

"They're trying to elude us in the shallows," Giordino said.

The *Constellation* heeled to port in pursuit.

"Apparently, we have a captain lacking in fear," Pitt said.

The *Constellation* closed on the tug. When it was less than twenty yards off, the ship swung slightly to starboard to bring the loaded cannon to bear. Pitt stood behind the gun and waited until the tug's pilothouse came into view, then pulled the lanyard.

The Parrott gun erupted with a boom and a belch of smoke, launching its projectile at point-blank range. The blunt-nosed shell blew through the tug's wheelhouse, shattering the helm in a shower of wood splinters and severing the pilot's left arm.

Standing behind the carnage just outside the bridge, Vasko responded in kind. He reloaded the RPG launcher and fired a grenade into the ship. The armor-piercing round penetrated the orlop deck before detonating low in the ship, rupturing its hull planking and flooding the bilge. The tug's three uninjured crewmen retrieved the AK-47s and began spraying the *Constellation* with fire.

"Keep low and reload," Pitt shouted. The volunteers pulled the Parrott gun back and swabbed its barrel with water.

The wooden warship had pulled ahead of the tug, exposing the men on the aft deck to the opposing fire. Bullets chewed up the side rail and deck as the gun crew hurried to reload the cannon.

"This one's a canister round," Giordino said as the next shell was rammed down.

As the cannon was shoved forward, one of the gun crew fell to the deck, exclaiming, "I'm hit." Pitt angled the weapon toward the tug's aft deck and fired again. The canister shell was packed with lead balls that dispersed at firing like a giant shotgun. The *Constellation* was too close to the tug for the blast to cover a wide area, but the concentrated fire struck one of the gunmen, killing him instantly.

Aboard the tug, Vasko reloaded and fired another RPG, this one better aimed. The projectile whizzed just over Pitt's head and struck the mizzenmast a dozen yards away. The entire vessel shook, and splinters and shrapnel peppered the gun crew. The blast ignited the mizzen, sending flames skyward as canvas and rigging began to burn.

Pitt tried to rally the gun crew for another shot as cries from the wounded mingled with the yells of men trying to put out the fires.

"Last of the ammo," Giordino said. He held up a twelve-pound solid shot that was made for a smaller, smoothbore gun.

Pitt glared at the tug. "Let 'em have it."

The cannon was pushed out and aimed astern, as the *Constellation* had moved well past the tug. Pitt aimed for a man firing an assault weapon on the tug's aft deck. As he pulled the lanyard, the ship jarred to a halt with a grinding sound from below. The gun fired astray and the men around it were knocked off their feet.

"We've run aground!" a crewman shouted. "Watch out for the mizzenmast!"

The jolt from the sudden stop sent a crack through the damaged mast. The massive timber splintered a few feet above the deck and careened over to port. Rigging snapped and the burning sail collapsed as the mast sank to the side until kissing the port rail. Canvas and rope dangled into the water as the yardarms poked beneath the surface. Flames coursed in a new, upward direction.

Amid the chaos, Pitt heard a cry that the captain was down. At the base of the mizzenmast he found an injured Valero sprawled on the deck, a pair of volunteers tending to him. He had taken a near hit from the RPG, and Pitt could see it didn't look good.

The ship's leader gazed up at Pitt through glassy eyes. "How did the *Connie* do?"

"She was splendid."

"Stop them," he said, then his eyes fluttered closed.

"I will," Pitt said. "And I'll never forget what you've done."

He turned to the rail and was surprised to see the tug approaching. The first shot from the Parrott gun had wrecked the tug's steering gear and hydraulics. The uncontrolled rudder had shifted back to center, and the vessel eased to its former heading.

Pitt caught a glimpse of Vasko in the shattered pilothouse, spinning the broken ship's wheel to no avail. Advancing parallel to the *Constellation*, the tug sailed beneath the fallen mizzenmast—and directly into the lower yardarm. The yardarm snapped at the waterline, but as the tug drove forward, the remaining timber burrowed into its deck and wedged against the wheelhouse. The tug shoved against the yardarm but fought the full weight of the grounded ship. With the barge dragging from behind, the tug churned to a halt.

Pitt saw a pair of ropes dangling from the upper yardarm by the rail—and recognized an opportunity. He sprinted back to the gun crew. "Quick, load and fire a double shot of powder."

He scooped up the two cutlasses he had brought from below and handed one to Giordino.

"What's the plan?" Giordino asked.

"Follow me," Pitt said. "We're going to board her."

84

Vasko looked out the shattered bridge window and cursed.

The tug had turned away from the shallows and was headed upriver toward Wagner's Point—just where he wanted to go. He'd get one of his crewmen to manually manipulate the rudder controls below until they reached the target site, then release the barge and escape. The only problem was, the ancient ship that was sailing ahead of them.

The *Constellation*'s cannon had at least fallen silent, quieted by his last grenade or the multiple fires that burned aboard the wooden vessel. To make sure, Vasko stepped to the back of the wheelhouse and reloaded the RPG launcher. Rising to take aim, he was shocked to see the *Constellation* had run aground and was right off the tug's bow. He lunged at the *Lauren Belle*'s wheel to avoid the fallen mizzenmast, but it spun freely in his hands.

The tug barreled into the yardarm and ground to a halt as sheets of burning sail draped from above.

Vasko stepped out the rear of the bridge only to be met by the point-blank roar of the Parrott gun. No damage ensued this time, but a cloud of thick white smoke enveloped the tug. Then Vasko saw two apparitions emerge from the haze, a pair of men swinging onto the tug with swords clamped in their teeth.

Pitt landed first, his rope carrying him near the *Lauren Belle*'s stern. He dropped, took a step, and ran headlong into Vasko's two remaining crewmen. One was kneeling to reload his rifle while the other stood, aiming at the Parrott gun crew. The standing gunman turned and swung his rifle stock, but Pitt was quicker. He ducked the blow, spun, and rammed the blade of the cutlass through the man's torso.

The gunman staggered against him and Pitt released his grip on the hilt and pushed the dying man aside. He turned and dove onto the second gunman, attacking before he could reload his weapon.

The second gunman was bigger than Pitt and sprang up on powerful legs. He shoved his rifle into Pitt's midsection and used it as leverage to throw him over his shoulder. Pitt tumbled to the corner of the deck, rising in time to catch a blow from the rifle's stock to his left shoulder. Pitt countered with his right fist, catching the gunman's cheek and dazing him. Pitt then reached down and wrestled for control of the gun.

Just behind the bridge, a similar battle took place. Giordino had landed near the wheelhouse and emerged from the smoke to find Vasko aiming another RPG at the *Constellation*.

He lunged forward and swung his cutlass in a powerful arc.

Vasko caught sight of him at the last second and raised the launcher in defense. The antique sword struck the steel frame of the launcher and the blade snapped at the hilt.

Vasko looked his attacker in the face, shocked to see it was Giordino.

"You again!" he swore.

"You were expecting Mary Poppins?" Giordino swung the sword's hilt up and punched Vasko in the stomach.

Vasko grunted and swung the launcher in return, striking Giordino in the head.

Giordino dropped the hilt and grabbed hold of the launcher, turning the business end away from the *Constellation* and toward the rear of the tug.

The two men applied brute force against each other for control of the weapon.

"It's no use, shorty," Vasko taunted, holding firm on the launcher.

Giordino said nothing. He applied his strength against the bigger man until Vasko gritted his teeth and contorted his face. Giordino held like a rock, showing no sign of strain.

Realizing he was losing the battle, Vasko leaned away, dropped a hand to the pistol grip, and squeezed the trigger.

The mini rocket blasted out of the launch tube. The projectile skittered across the deck, struck the stern tow cable bitts at the center transom, and exploded with a deafening roar.

The burning exhaust had blown into Giordino's face, temporarily blinding him.

Vasko took advantage. He kicked Giordino in the groin, then ~ped the launcher away and pummeled his head.

With a vicious roundhouse blow, Giordino was knocked backward and bounced off the side rail. As he fell to the deck, he regained a fraction of his vision. He squinted aft across the deck but found it empty.

Pitt and the other gunman had vanished.

85

Pitt heard the rush of the RPG launch and squared his back to the stern. The grenade detonated barely twenty feet away. The explosive force blew him over the rail and could have killed him if not for his human shield. Still clinched with the gunman, the bigger man absorbed the shrapnel and the blast's main concussion.

They hit the water together, and the other man's grip went limp. Pitt let go of him, fighting a wave of pain and disorientation. His ears rang and his lungs felt purged of all air. He sensed he was drowning. He stretched his limbs and tried stroking, hoping to find the surface. A long object slid across his body and he reached for it and hung on. It was the hawser and it carried him to the surface for an instant. He barely had time to fill his lungs when the heavy cable began to descend, yanking him back under.

His senses returning, Pitt began pulling himself up the cable, slowly at first, then with more urgency. Straining hand over hand, he reached the surface once more, just a short distance from the black barge. He glanced over his shoulder. The *Constellation* and tug lay a hundred yards upriver. The barge was drifting free, and he was floating with it.

Outside the tug's wheelhouse, Vasko tossed aside the grenade launcher and looked to the damaged stern. As the smoke cleared, he saw the end of the tow cable unravel from the mangled bollards and slip over the transom. The barge was free and there was nothing he could do. He watched for a moment as the barge floated toward the center of the Patapsco. It was still within the dead zone, and the water was plenty deep for his needs.

He stepped onto the bridge and felt the *Lauren Belle* start to move. Free of the barge, the vessel had regained enough power to battle past the *Constellation*'s mast and yardarm. Vasko looked past the ship, eyeing the tall buildings of Baltimore, then stepped to his weapons crate. He retrieved the satchel with the radio transmitter keyed to the barge's explosives.

On the deck, Giordino opened his eyes to see a wall of flames. It was a burning sail, ripped away by the roof of the tug's pilothouse as it churned past the fallen mast. An antenna above the bridge caught a section of the flaming sail and dropped a curtain of canvas over the side of the wheelhouse.

Giordino sat up and saw the *Constellation* slipping behind. Two of the Parrott gunners leaned over the rail, staring at the tug.

Giordino called up to the men. "Powder. Toss me some bags."

The gunner named Yates disappeared for a moment, then returned to the rail with three of the black powder bags. He expertly tossed them across the water, the aluminum foil cylinders landing at Giordino's side. Giordino snatched two of the bags and threw them to the base of the wheelhouse doorway. Vasko stepped through it a minute later.

In his hands, he held the radio transmitter. Aiming it toward the drifting barge, he pressed the transmit button. A second later, two muffled blasts erupted from the rear of the barge, accompanied by small puffs of gray smoke. Vasko smiled, paying no regard to a man in the water clinging to the barge's hawser.

He turned and noticed Giordino sitting near the rail, leering at him with a sardonic grin.

"Still with us, my short friend?" Vasko said.

"Here to say good-bye."

"It will be my pleasure." Vasko leaned inside the bridge and dropped the transmitter into the crate, exchanging it for a loaded rifle.

As Vasko turned in the doorway, Giordino used his teeth to rip open the third bag of powder and tossed it at Vasko's feet.

Vasko looked down in confusion as a trail of spilt powder ignited from the burning sail and sizzled toward the bundles at his feet. He didn't have long to look.

The explosion echoed off the hull of the *Constellation* and covered the tug once more in a white haze.

When the smoke cleared, Giordino approached the shattered wheelhouse.

Vasko lay on the deck, his legs blown off and a look of shock in his fading eyes.

Giordino gave him an unsympathetic gaze, then uttered the last word.

"You can call me Al."

After watching him die, Giordino stepped to the tug's stern. He looked downriver and spotted the drifting barge, receding in the distance. A lean, dark-haired man climbed out of the water, then stood and gave him a wave from the prow of his atomic chariot.

86

Pitt was still in the water when he heard the muffled explosions from the far end of the barge. He pulled himself up the cable, rolled onto the deck, and caught his breath. As he labored to his feet, he could sense a slight list to the stern.

He made his way to the cargo holds. Each of the four compartments was covered by a light fiberglass cover. He uncoupled the first cover and found the Russian RDS-5 bomb secured to a large pallet. He regarded it for a moment, then checked the other three holds. They were all empty, save for a rusty drum and some chains in the second hold and a rising swirl of water in the fourth. Pitt guessed the barge had less than fifteen minutes afloat.

He returned to the first hold and climbed inside to examine the weapon. The RDS-5 was slightly bulbous, five feet wide and twelve feet long, tapering to a circular fin assembly. Its smooth black skin was broken by a raised panel near the tail. Pitt peered into the glass-topped panel and saw the bomb was very much alive. A myriad of LED displays glowed with numbers. Next to the panel box, a small dial protruded from the bomb's surface—a simple depth gauge. He looked back at the panel. Two of the LED displays were marked with labels. One read CURRENT DEPTH and showed zero. The other read CHARGED DEPTH and was fixed at twenty-five feet.

A feeling of dread came over Pitt. While Giordino may have dispatched Vasko, it no longer mattered. The bomb was set to detonate at a water pressure depth of twenty-five feet. When the barge sank, the bomb would go off—simple as that. Pitt considered smashing the displays or shattering the depth gauge but feared the weapon was programmed to detonate with any outside interference.

He scrambled out of the hold and looked around. The barge was a half mile from land. With the barge having no means of propulsion, it would be impossible to get it across the current to the shallows before it sank. He scanned the river. There were numerous small pleasure boats nearby, most flocking to the burning *Constellation*. But they were all too small to move the heavy barge. Peering toward the bay, he spotted the skipjack he'd seen from the helicopter, tacking downwind.

The barge was listing heavily now, with water beginning to lap at the deck. Pitt gazed back at the skipjack. It was his only option.

The oyster boat had just entered the Patapsco and was sailing near the center of the river, far off the barge's line. Pitt had to close the gap—and quickly. He ran to the second hold and muscled the empty drum up to the deck. Retrieving bits of rope and chain from below, he fashioned a harness around the drum and attached a twenty-foot leader of rope. He dragged the assembly to the upriver end of the barge and tied the leader to a starboard corner bitt. Then he lowered the drum over the side, letting it fill with water and drag horizontally behind the barge.

The makeshift drogue tugged on the inshore stern, nudging the downriver bow slightly to port. It wasn't much, but it was enough to put the sinking barge on a more direct path with the skipjack.

Sailing up the river, a grizzled oysterman named Brian Kennedy eyed the barge, noting it was drifting free of a tug. It was clearly sinking, and he turned to take a closer look. His boat, the *Lorraine*, was a large skipjack, a wide-beamed and highly maneuverable class of sailboat. Designed for oyster dredging on the Chesapeake, skipjacks once sailed in abundance on the waterway. Overfishing saw their decline, and the *Lorraine* was one of a just handful still in use.

Oystering was out of season, but Kennedy was testing a new sail on his prized vessel. When he saw a tall man wave at him from the barge, he tacked across the river and pulled alongside. Its head end was already submerged, and waves were splashing over its low deck from all sides.

"You better jump aboard, mister, she's about to go under."

"I've got a live cargo in the first hold I need to pull out," Pitt said. "Do you have a power dredge?"

The oysterman stared at Pitt. He was dripping wet, yet his

clothes were singed and marred with blood. Water splashed around his ankles, and there was urgency in his eyes, yet he stood with a remote coolness.

"Yep, I do," Kennedy said. "With a freshly rebuilt motor. You'd best be quick about it."

He swung a boom across that held a large dredge basket from a cable. Pitt grabbed the dredge and hauled it into the hold as the oysterman let out cable from a power winch.

The hold already had two feet of water sloshing around its bottom, with more spilling in from the wave action. Pitt heaved the dredge into a corner and uncoupled the cable from its mount. He groped in the water at the base of the bomb and located a lift chain he'd seen earlier.

"You better get out of there now, mister!" Kennedy yelled.

The water was pouring in faster as Pitt gathered the four end pieces. Holding them above the bomb, he locked them onto the cable. "Okay, lift her!" Pitt shouted.

He barely got the words out when a cascade of water poured in from all sides of the hold. Pitt grabbed the cable and pulled himself on top of the bomb as the compartment flooded. The cable drew taut and the bomb rose off the pallet, banging against the sides of the hold as the barge began to slip away. Pitt held his breath as a torrent of water flooded over him. He felt several more vibrations from the swaying bomb smacking the metal bulkheads. Then the noise stopped and the water around him calmed.

On board the *Lorraine*, Kennedy watched in shock as the barge sank, taking the tall man with it. The winch motor strained and the taut cable drew the skipjack onto its side, the boom nearly touching the water. The oysterman thought the dredge had snagged on the barge and he was about to release the cable when Pitt's head popped above the surface.

He shook the water from his eyes and looked up at Kennedy. "We got her. Bring her home."

Kennedy held steady on the winch as the mechanism strained to lift the heavy weight. As the boat slowly righted itself, he stared agog as Pitt emerged from the water riding atop the massive black bomb.

"You're . . . you're sitting on a bomb," he stammered. "Is it a dud?"

"No," Pitt said with a crooked smile. "It's atomic."

87

The Army helicopter swooped low over Maryland's Eastern Shore, hovered over an empty vacation cottage, and landed on its driveway. A team of military bomb disposal and nuclear weapons specialists climbed out and rushed to the backyard. The cottage overlooked a scenic cove off the Chesapeake called Huntingfield Creek, where a small dock stretched over the water. Sitting abandoned at the end of the dock was the Russian atomic bomb.

A high-power radio frequency jammer was activated next to the bomb to prevent detonation by a remotely transmitted signal. The ordnance crew then carefully examined the bomb, confirming it was activated by a depth gauge. They overrode the pressure sensor, disassembled some outer components to remove the triggering mechanism, then finally disarmed the thirty-kiloton weapon.

Halfway across the Chesapeake, Pitt stood in the bow of the *Lorraine* and watched in amusement as a Coast Guard boat shooed them toward Baltimore. A flurry of law enforcement boats raced around in a panic, attempting to establish a five-mile safety zone around the remote dock where Pitt had deposited the bomb.

The skipjack sailed back to the Patapsco River, where they came upon the grounded *Constellation* just shy of Baltimore Harbor. The old sloop of war was surrounded by a half dozen police and fireboats. Her dead and wounded had been removed, the fires extinguished, and pumps activated to relieve her flooded decks. Pitt noticed the tug, the *Lauren Belle*, was still alongside the ship's port beam, a handful of police officers inspecting her every inch.

"Going my way, sailor?" came a shout from the *Constellation*'s spar deck.

Pitt looked up to see Giordino, waving from the ship, and had Kennedy pull the skipjack alongside. Giordino said good-bye to his gun crew friends, climbed down a police boat's mooring line, then hopped aboard the *Lorraine*.

He was a mass of powder burns and bruises yet offered a wide grin. "I should have known you'd be out taking a leisurely cruise while the rest of us were getting our hands dirty."

"You know I abhor manual labor," Pitt said. "Is the *Connie* going to make it?"

"She's got a one-way ticket to dry dock for a while, but she'll be fine."

"Her crew helped save a lot of lives today."

"Where did you deposit the bomb?" Giordino asked. "I tried to go after you, but the tug's helm was disabled by our final blast."

"Along with our bald friend, I presume?"

Giordino smiled.

"We found a quiet cove across the bay," Pitt said, "as remote as possible."

Giordino looked to Kennedy at the helm and shook his head. "That was quite an oyster you boys hauled aboard."

The oysterman nodded as if it was all in a day's work.

The skipjack sailed into Baltimore Harbor, whose waterfront was a blaze of flashing police lights. The *Lorraine* maneuvered into the empty Coast Guard dock, which was surrounded by law enforcement officials. As Pitt and Giordino climbed out of the boat and helped tie it up, a pair of black limousines rolled onto the dock. A Secret Service detail sprang from the first while Vice President Sandecker and Rudi Gunn emerged from the second. The two men made their way to Pitt and Giordino.

"Fine work, boys," Sandecker said through teeth clenched on a cigar. "We just got word that the Army bomb squad safely defused the weapon."

"At thirty kilotons," Gunn said, "that would have been quite a bang."

Sandecker looked at Pitt. "How did you figure out Baltimore was the target and not D.C.?"

"It was the Black Sea," Pitt said. "The same folks used explosives to release hydrogen sulfide gas trapped in the sea's anoxic waters. Similar conditions exist in the Chesapeake during the summer right outside the harbor." He pointed past Fort McHenry to the Patapsco River.

"We still don't know exactly who was behind it," Gunn said. He looked at Giordino.

"There were no survivors on the tug, I'm told."

"No survivors," Giordino affirmed.

"It was the same crew from Bulgaria, part of Mankedo's crowd," Pitt said. "Ana Belova of Europol is running down their financial backer. We'll know more shortly."

"If they're Ukrainian rebels, I can tell you they just barked up the wrong tree," Sandecker said. "The President is furious—and prepared to ask Congress to release more aid and arms to the Ukrainian government."

"Maybe that was their goal," Pitt said.

"What do you mean?" Gunn asked.

"First, there's an attempted attack on Sevastopol using an American ship. Next, a U.S. airplane gets blown up after bringing aid to Ukraine. Finally, there's an attack on the U.S. under the guise of the pro-Russian Ukrainian rebels. Sounds to me like someone's trying to start a war."

"Or maybe just kick the Russians out of Ukraine," Gunn said.

"Perhaps they're smarter than us all." Sandecker examined his cigar. "At any rate, the President wishes to extend his personal gratitude for what you did in saving the country." He motioned toward the limos. "He's at Camp David right now waiting to see you."

"Please thank the President for me," Pitt said, "but I can't see him right now."

"You're turning down the President? But why? What do I tell him?"

Pitt nodded toward the *Lorraine*. "Tell the President I couldn't make it because I owe a Chesapeake Bay oysterman a very large and very cold beer."

EPILOGUE

MORNING'S FIRST BEAM

The Vault at Nelson's Cave

T he morning of Saturday, July 22, broke clear and sunny in Gibraltar. The summer tourists crowding the sidewalks were already searching for shade when a cab pulled up to the former Anglo-Egyptian Bank Building just after noon. Mansfield held the car door open for Martina and a stout man from the Russian Embassy in Madrid, making mental note of a pair of Army trucks parked down the street. Following the others inside the bank, he froze amidst a throng of British soldiers milling about the lobby.

It wasn't the soldiers that prompted him to check the holstered gun he wore beneath his jacket. It was the presence of a few too many familiar faces standing by the bank manager. Dirk, Summer, Perlmutter, Trehorne, and Hawker all stared at Mansfield as if he had just arrived late to a birthday party. Still, no words were spoken, nor were any bank guards called.

Finlay stepped across the lobby and shook hands. "Mr. Romanov, nice to see you again."

The bank manager sported dark circles under his eyes and wore the same suit he had the day before, with some added wrinkles. But Mansfield noted that Finlay's prior nervous disposition was notably absent.

"Good morning, Mr. Finlay. May I introduce Alexander Vodokov, with the Russian Ministry of Foreign Affairs."

The pudgy lawyer stepped forward and shook Finlay's hand. "I represent the Russian Federation and wish to make a formal claim on a deposit held in this institution." He presented a requisition signed by the Ambassador.

"Do you have an account number?"

"No. But I think you know of the deposit. It was a large sum of gold bullion placed with the Anglo-Egyptian Bank in March 1917, on behalf of Tsar Nicholas II."

"Protocol would dictate some proof of deposit," Finlay said without batting an eye.

"The funds were deposited by the Royal Navy, from the HMS *Sentinel*, on behalf of the Russian Imperial State, as a by-product of the Treaty of Petrograd."

"Do you have a copy of the treaty?" Finlay asked.

Vodokov rifled through an attaché case and retrieved a stapled document. "This is a signed copy."

Finlay took the document. "If you'll excuse me." He stepped behind the cashier's window to a copy machine and made two duplicate sets. He locked one in a cashier's drawer, handed the other to an assistant, then returned to Vodokov.

"As a representative of Barclays Bank and holder of the deposit in question, I regret to inform you that the Russian Federation's claim for ownership has terminated." He passed the treaty back to the diplomat.

Mansfield stepped forward. "What are you saying?"

"The document is quite clear, even if my Russian is not," Finlay said. "The treaty calls for the British holding of the assets until the restoration of the Imperial Crown—or a subsequent century from the anniversary of the first Romanov's ascension to the Crown—whichever comes first."

"Let me see that." Mansfield ripped the treaty from Vodokov's hands and skimmed through the terms.

"You know your Russian history better than I," Finlay said, "but Michael I was the first Russian Tsar from the House of Romanov. History shows that he was crowned to the throne on July twenty-second, 1613. I'm afraid the hundred-year mark from the treaty's signing in 1917 has just legally passed today at noon, per the language in the document." He eyed a wall clock. "The assets have now reverted to the British government, which has made arrangements to take possession."

He motioned toward the soldiers across the lobby. The men took position, forming an armed cordon leading out the front door, save for two husky men who followed Finlay into the open vault. The soldiers emerged a minute later, carrying a small but heavy wooden case they hauled out the front door. They deposited it in one of the Army trucks now parked at the curb, then returned for the next case.

After watching the scene, the diplomat blew up. "This is an

outrage!" he screamed at Finlay. "My government will be filing a formal protest." He turned to Mansfield. "Why didn't you make this known sooner?"

"We just made the discovery late yesterday."

"There will be unpleasant reprisals." He stormed out of the bank, hailed a cab, and vanished down the road.

Mansfield smirked as he watched the diplomat depart, then approached Summer and the others.

"Congratulations, and well done," he said. "What is your American saying, a day late and a dollar short?"

"About two billion dollars short, in this instance," Summer said.

"Apparently, we shall all go on our way empty-handed."

"You should go and be placed behind bars," Hawker said.

"Now, Major, that is not the manner of the Western victor." He gave a slight bow. "Farewell." He turned and sauntered out of the bank without looking back.

Martina accompanied him out the door, shaking her head at his blasé attitude.

"We have failed miserably," she said. "Are you not concerned about the wrath of Moscow? Vodokov is right. There will be reprisals."

Mansfield shrugged as they walked past the Army trucks. "My dear comrade, you are looking at a survivor. I will simply avoid Moscow until the next intelligence crisis erupts, at which time this incident will be brushed aside."

"But what about the chief directorate?"

"Kings, presidents, and chief directorates may come and go, but Viktor Mansfield shall always be on the decadent steps of the Wild West, fighting for Mother Russia." He slipped his arm around hers. "What do you say we go have a drink somewhere?"

The stern agent regarded him with bewilderment, then finally succumbed. "Very well."

Perlmutter watched the couple stroll away. "He certainly understands our mind-set. There's little point in arresting him now."

"His undercover days around here will be over," Hawker said. "I suppose that's the important thing."

Dirk shook his head. "I'd still like to send him a bill for our damaged submersible."

Finlay approached the group with an energetic buzz. "May I show you Nelson's Cave now?"

Summer smiled. "Please do."

He led them through the huge steel door into the vault. It had been built into a natural cave, adding only a concrete floor and the frame for the vault door. The arched limestone ceiling and walls extended nearly fifty feet into the hillside.

"This was originally called La Bóveda Cave by the Spanish," Finlay said. "It was renamed Nelson's Cave in 1805, when a number of dead sailors from the Battle of Trafalgar were brought here before burial. By the time the Anglo-Egyptian Bank acquired the property in 1887 and constructed the building to incorporate the cave, the Nelson name was mostly forgotten."

"A clever way to build a vault," Perlmutter said.

"They were probably saving construction costs," Trehorne said.

"You may be right." Finlay rapped a knuckle against the side wall. "The limestone is at least thirty feet thick throughout, so it's certainly a secure spot to store money."

"Or Russian gold?" Summer said.

Finlay led them past several rows of safe-deposit boxes and a large cash safe to a caged area at the back. An aged iron gate had been opened, exposing a large stack of wooden crates. The two soldiers were inside retrieving another crate and squeezed past the group.

"Romanov gold, to be precise," Finlay said, answering Summer's question.

"Brought here so the Bank of England could deny possession?" Trehorne asked.

"That's my understanding. The gold was shipped out of Russia and transferred to the HMS *Sentinel* under great secrecy. The *Sentinel* brought it here for temporary safekeeping, pending transfer to England. But two things happened. Public protests in St. Petersburg increased, leading to the Tsar's abdication. And the *Sentinel* was sunk, just days after delivering the gold. Those in the know in England generally believed the *Sentinel* was lost with the gold aboard. The Anglo-Egyptian Bank manager in Gibraltar and a Bank of England regional representative cut a deal to hold the gold here, pending clarification of the political situation in Russia." He shook his head. "I've been told that the Bank of England representative was killed when his ship was torpedoed on the return to England."

Trehorne rubbed his chin. "So even the Bank of England was in the dark?"

"Until about two weeks ago, when we notified the governor of the bank and requested they provide transfer and security."

"Who else knew?" Summer asked.

"Virtually no one outside of Gibraltar. The Queen and the Prime Minister were reportedly shocked at the news. They hope, of course, to keep the gold's existence a secret."

"Fat chance, in this day and age," Dirk said. "Where's it headed?"

"The Army is moving it to the airport for a military flight to London. It will be stored in the government's gold repository in downtown London, under Threadneedle Street."

Summer looked to Finlay. "How did you know today was the day?"

"We had a draft copy of the treaty in our files, so we're well aware of the termination date. You can imagine my shock when you entered the bank yesterday, followed by the Russians."

"A very close shave," Trehorne said.

"You don't know the half of it."

"Because you didn't have a signed copy of the treaty?" Perlmutter asked.

"Exactly," Finlay said. "We had no legal standing until today, when the Russians brought us the signed copy. Now we have proof of the treaty's ratification. The British government can thank you for that."

"What of the other elements of the treaty?" Dirk said. "Will the government make a claim for the lost mineral rights?"

"Who's to say? It would make Great Britain the richest nation in the world if those rights were ever acknowledged. But the Russians would sooner declare war, I suppose. It will probably be swept aside in the name of diplomatic secrecy. A pity for you, actually."

"Why's that?" Summer asked.

"Otherwise, I suspect honorary knighthood from the Queen would have been in order for you all."

"Knighthood?" Trehorne said. "My, now, that would have been something."

Summer shook her head at the thought. "May we see the gold?"

"Certainly." Finlay led them into the cage and to one of the crates. He pried off the lid and exposed a solid bank of shiny gold bars, identical to the one Summer had found on the *Canterbury*. Finlay passed one around, letting each person admire it.

"There's also a crate or two of uncut gemstones in the mix," Finlay said.

Summer was the last to examine the gold and lost her grip as she handed it back to the banker. The heavy bar clinked as it struck the floor.

"I'm sorry, Mr. Finlay. It's not every day I let a billion dollars slip through my fingers."

"Quite all right." He retrieved the bar. "I can imagine your disappointment after a long and difficult hunt to locate the gold."

"It made for a few sleepless nights," she said.

As they made their way back to the lobby, she noticed Dirk was smiling. "You seem a bit happy, given the circumstances."

"I'm just thinking how lucky I am."

"Lucky? We busted our tails to find the gold—and it was sitting in a bank all along. It was, and will remain, one big fat secret. What's so lucky about that?"

"Because of that secret," Dirk said with a grin, "I won't be forced to call you Dame Summer for the rest of my life."

89

Martin Hendriks watched from the window of a rented apartment as Dutch police stormed his gated residence just down the street. Had he looked carefully, he would have seen a black-haired Bulgarian woman leading the charge.

After the failure of Vasko, he knew it would be only a matter of time before the trail led to him. But, so far, his name had been left out of the publicity surrounding the investigation. That was key.

He left the apartment by the back door and stepped into a limo waiting in the alley. "One stop along the way," he told his driver of many years.

He stared out the window, ignoring the passing canals of Amsterdam and the mass of bicyclists alongside. The limo traveled east to the town of Zwolle and entered a large cemetery called Kranenburg. The driver knew exactly where to go. He circled a small pond and pulled to a stop beneath some towering red oaks.

The change in motion jarred Hendriks to his senses. He climbed out and strode to a modest tombstone with three names carved in the marble. He sank to his knees in front of it, but for once the tears didn't come. The pain, however, was still there, strong as ever and still refusing to ease with the passage of time.

"It won't be long now," he whispered. He reached into his pocket and touched his metallic keepsake.

After a long contemplation, he kissed the headstone and rose uneasily to his feet. He shuffled back to the car in a trance and slumped into the backseat. Not until nearly an hour later, when the limo crossed into Germany, did the grief retreat and the determination for his next action come into full focus.

The limo drove to a little-used airfield near the town of Wesel, where his private jet waited. Hendriks shook hands with his driver and boarded the plane, which promptly took to the skies.

The jet flew east, crossing Poland and Belarus before entering Russian airspace under prior approval. Less than an hour later, the plane touched down at Chkalovsky Airport, a military airfield northeast of Moscow. Hendriks looked out the window at an orderly row of new helicopters parked on the tarmac, fronted by a crisp regiment of Russian soldiers standing at attention.

The jet parked by a hangar, and Hendriks was escorted to a group of officers standing on a red carpet near a dais. General Zakharin turned to welcome the Dutchman.

"Mr. Hendriks, it's good to see you again. You have arrived just in time."

"Thank you for inviting me, General."

"We're celebrating the deployment of our new class of attack helicopter, the Mi-28NM," Zakharin said. "President Vashenko will be making an inspection, so I thought it a good opportunity to show him the Peregrine. Perhaps you can arrange a demonstration, like the one you gave me a few weeks ago?"

"I would be delighted," Hendriks said. "If you'll excuse me, General, I better check on the status of our drone."

He walked to his green tractor-trailer that was parked at the edge of the tarmac. His assistant, Gerard, met him at the Peregrine's control panel positioned nearby.

"Any troubles at the border?" Hendriks asked.

Gerard shook his head. "No issue at the border crossing or entering the air base."

"What's the Peregrine's status?"

"I launched her as you instructed before dawn. She's currently ten miles north of us." He rapped a knuckle on the control console. "After you take it on manual for the demonstration, she's programmed to revert to a low-altitude flight from here to the Baltic Sea."

"Thank you, Gerard. I'll take it from here." He pointed toward his jet. "I would like you and the driver to board my plane at once. It will take you to Stockholm. Remain there until you hear from my attorney."

The technician looked at his boss and nodded. "I understand. Good-bye, Mr. Hendriks."

The jet took off moments before President Vashenko's motorcade entered the airport and rolled to a stop next to the dais. The Russian president inspected the troops, gave a short speech, and was taken for a ride in one of the attack helicopters. After discussing the flight with his aides, the president was steered to the dais by General Zakharin, where Hendriks had repositioned the Peregrine's console.

"Mr. President," Zakharin said, "may I present Martin Hendriks, the developer of the Peregrine drone."

"I have heard good things about your drone," Vashenko said. "I understand it even saved some Russian sailors in the Black Sea. Where is your invention?"

"It is in the skies above us, Mr. President. As I demonstrated to General Zakharin, its long-range capabilities make it difficult to detect. I invite you to try to identify its location, if you can."

Vashenko scanned the skies while listening for a motor but saw and heard nothing. Hendriks, meanwhile, used the Peregrine's high-power camera to target the dais a few feet away. He turned the video screen to show Vashenko.

"We are standing right here." He pointed to the screen. "If I activate the laser targeting system, which happens to work with your Vikhr antitank missiles, you can see it lock onto our position."

He typed into a keypad and a flashing red ring appeared on the screen, encircling the image of the men.

"Very impressive," the president said. "Tell me, from which direction is the drone flying?"

Hendriks ignored the question.

"The Peregrine is armed and ready now," Hendriks said. "If I wanted to kill you, I would simply press these two red buttons to launch the drone's missiles."

As he reached down and pushed the buttons, Vashenko gave a nervous laugh. "Now, why would you want to do that?"

Zakharin pointed to the northern sky. "Is that it? What are those two puffs of smoke?"

As Vashenko turned to look, Hendriks whispered in his ear.

"Mr. President, I am about to kill you in the same manner you killed my family in the skies over Ukraine."

Hendriks reached into his pocket and retrieved the metal object that never left his side. It was a scarred and melted cross that had once been worn around his wife's neck. He held the cross in both hands in front of him and squeezed it tightly, then looked up and watched the twin missiles arrive.

90

A cool breeze drifted across the knoll, refreshing the wedding guests gathered around a small gazebo. Fresh flowers and streamers decorated the structure in the traditional Bulgarian wedding colors of red and white. Just beyond, the sparkling Black Sea provided an azure backdrop under a bright September sun.

The bride wore a simple white dress, which ruffled in the sea breeze. The groom was attired in a dark suit with red tie and carried a black cane. After completing their wedding vows, Ana and Petar Ralin turned and kissed in front of the gathered guests, prompting a roar of approval.

The newlyweds mingled with their families as champagne was poured and the younger members of the wedding party began dancing. As they worked their way through the crowd, Ana and Petar reached a tall couple standing near the side.

Ralin shook Pitt's hand. "We are so happy you could join us today."

"Wouldn't have missed it." He introduced his wife, Loren. A congresswoman from Colorado, she wore a violet dress that matched her eyes.

Ana gave Pitt a hug, then turned to Loren. "Petar and I wouldn't be here today if it wasn't for your husband."

"You've all had quite an ordeal," she said. "I'm just happy it's led to this special day."

"Do you have a honeymoon planned?" Pitt asked.

Ana smiled. "We're going to Chios, in Greece, for a week."

Ralin shook his head. "She insists on working, even on our honeymoon."

"We're going to try and confirm it was the *Besso* that sank there," Ana said. "I've been in touch with your children about a Russian World War I submarine that was lost in the area and may have drawn the *Besso* to salvage her."

"I've heard a bit about that," Pitt said. "Mankedo may have thought he had a hoard of gold there and got tangled up with some Russian agents in the process."

"He should have quit while he was ahead," Ana said. "In our investigation of Martin Hendriks, we found a twenty-million-dollar transfer was made to Mankedo at a Cyprus bank, and another five million dollars to his late associate, Ilya Vasko. No one ever collected it."

"I guess it's now clear that Hendriks wasn't supporting the pro-Russian rebels in Ukraine after all."

"Just the opposite. We were slow to discover that his wife and two children had been killed on Malaysian Airlines Flight 17 when it was shot down near Donetsk in 2014. His actions were all in the name of vengeance against Russia and the rebels."

"The man nearly started World War III," Loren said.

"Yes, but, in a sense, he succeeded," Ana said. "The U.S. is now providing greater support to Ukraine, and the new Russian president has withdrawn all military forces from the region. Violence is waning, and Ukraine might even regain its lost lands."

"Ana, enough shop talk," Ralin said. "We are here to celebrate."

"I'm sorry, Petar, you are right. Loren and Dirk, what are your plans while here in Bulgaria?"

"We're hoping to visit the Rila Monastery and drive the coastal road to Varna," Loren said.

"Along the way," Pitt added, "I plan on exploring that Ottoman shipwreck we found. After that, there's a rusty old Italian car I'd like to see about acquiring."

"Ana," Loren said, "you better fill me in on where to go shopping while he's underwater."

Pitt took Ralin by the arm. "Come along, Petar. I'll buy you a drink while I can still afford it," he said with a wink. "We can toast to rich shipwrecks, vintage cars, and strong women."

As the two men moved off toward the bar, Ana turned to Loren. "He's a man of a different age, isn't he?"

Loren looked over at Pitt with pride and smiled.

"Yes. But I'm glad he's living in this one."